Without Him

Praise for Fiona O'Brien

'Fiona O'Brien serves up a full helping of wisdom, fun and pure unadulterated escapism' Cathy Kelly

'Throws open the door on Dublin's super-rich . . . a great read' *The Irish Times*

'O'Brien proves herself to be an Irish Jilly Cooper . . .' *RTÉ Guide*

'A polished read with a lot of perceptive insight . . . a sophisticated balance between glamour and depth' *Irish Independent*

'The right mix of heartfelt emotion and upbeat humour' *Image*

'If you like Jackie Collins . . . then you won't be disappointed' *Daily Mail* UK

'A glorious saga from one of Ireland's real stars . . .' *The Bookseller*

'Written with such style you could not help but love every minute of it. A fabulous read' *Woman's Way*

Without Him

Fiona O'Brien

HACHETTE
BOOKS
IRELAND

First published in Ireland in 2010 by Hachette Books Ireland

A Hachette UK company

I

Copyright © Fiona O'Brien 2010

The right of Fiona O'Brien to be identified as the Author of the Work
has been asserted by her in accordance with the Copyright, Designs
and Patents Act 1988.

A CIP catalogue record for this title is available from the British Library.

ISBN 978 0 340 99489 4
UK Hardback ISBN 978 0 340 99483 2

Typeset in Plantin Light by Palimpsest Book Production Limited,
Falkirk, Stirlingshire

Printed and bound by Clays Ltd, St Ives plc

Hachette Books Ireland policy is to use papers that are natural,
renewable and recyclable products and made from wood grown in
sustainable forests. The logging and manufacturing processes are
expected to conform to the environmental regulations of
the country of origin.

Hachette Books Ireland
8 Castlecourt Centre
Castleknock
Dublin 15

www.hachette.ie

A division of
Hachette UK
338 Euston Road
London NW1 3BH

For Cathy,
cherished friend, mentor, inspiration.

'Never judge a man until you've walked two moons in his moccasins.' Native American proverb.

Prologue

The Scene with Harry Fegan

Dublin's social scene has been dealt yet another dastardly blow by the departure of high-flying businessman Charlie Fitzgibbon to far-flung shores.

Cheeky Charlie, as he is known to friends and, indeed, foes alike, has been keeping a remarkably low profile since the sudden and rather public demise of his property and investment empire just last month. Repeated attempts to contact Charlie for interview have been refused by his solicitor and company phones play a recorded message.

His lovely wife Shelley, who featured regularly in the social pages along with her husband, has been unavailable for comment.

Friends of the convivial couple remain tight-lipped but concerned. 'Times are tough for all of us,' said a neighbour on the exclusive Glenhill Road in south Dublin where the imposing Fitzgibbon family residence appears to be spookily uninhabited, 'but we all wish Charlie and his family well.'

Reported sightings of maverick man-about-town Charlie with a beautiful blonde in both Portugal and South Africa remain unconfirmed.

The Scene says come back Charlie, all is forgiven. Dublin's lamentably dull without you.

Shelley

Don't ask me how we got through Christmas – I really don't know how, but we must have done, because it's been and gone. And unbelievable though it still seems, so has he.

It's funny, actually saying that – in a way it's sort of a huge relief. *The worst has happened,* I thought. Things can't get any worse.

But then, of course, they did.

'*I'm* not answering it,' Emma, my fifteen-year-old, said, shooting me a look that managed to combine both utter disdain and terror. I couldn't say I blamed her.

Returning her attention to *Coronation Street,* which was the only thing that allowed us to sit together amicably (or perhaps, rather, in grim silence) in the same room these days, she studied the television mutely as the doorbell rang for the third time.

'Mum!' Mac yelled from the kitchen. 'Could somebody actually, like, *get* that? I'm trying to do my homework here.' The plaintive tones of my eleven-year-old 'beautiful boy', as I privately called him, roused me to action. Mac could get to me when no one else could, with a mere tilt of his head or a bat of his eyes, or in this case, an inflection in his adoringly pre-adolescent voice, even from another room – make that another continent. Shameful admission, I know, but I'm nothing if not honest. It's not that I don't love my daughters – I'm mad about them, they're beautiful and talented – but Emma can be unbearably moody, and Olivia . . . well, let's just say that these days Mac is so much *easier* to love.

'*Mum!*'

'Okay!' I yelled back, struggling to my feet. 'I'm getting it.'

I'm not old – only forty-five – but, God, I feel old, and tired, very tired. The past few weeks had been, well, challenging.

'Yes?' I said tersely to the well-built man standing on my doorstep.

He stood proudly, the ringleader, hands on hips, a slight swagger, well-dressed too, I noted, casual but thought out. He was accompanied by two others behind him, shuffling and studying their feet with great interest, one of them mindlessly kicking my meticulously groomed gravel.

'Do you mind?' I said, glaring at the offender pointedly.

'Sorry, ma'am.' He stopped, shamefaced.

I returned my enquiring gaze to the leader, who was now eyeballing me and clearing his throat. He seemed vaguely familiar, with those piercing blue eyes. A woman remembers these kinds of things, even during times of great stress.

'I've come about the kitchen,' he said, matter of factly.

Of course! The penny dropped. That's where I remembered him from. This rather attractive man and his team had installed our state-of-the-art designer kitchen, oh, about what? Eight months ago, now. How could I ever forget? The upheaval, the dirt, the hell that was workmen – even very good-looking workmen.

'That's very kind of you,' I replied, smiling. 'If it wasn't such a bad time, I'd invite you in,' I said, thinking absurdly of *Corrie* and the plot I was missing that would be unravelling in my absence – not unlike my life. 'Everything is working perfectly, thank you, couldn't be better. In fact, I recommended you to all my friends – every one of them.' Which wasn't many, I reflected grimly. Not since . . .

'I don't think you understand, Mrs Fitzgibbon,' he said, firmly planting another foot forward on the upper doorstep. 'I realise this may be difficult for you, but I've been as patient as I can. Seeing as how your husband has blatantly ignored our claims and clearly those of a lot of other people,' at this he raised his eyebrows, looking very grim and meaningful, 'I'm left with no choice but to remove my kitchen.'

My kitchen, he called it – *my* kitchen. I stood there, transfixed.

'I take it,' he ventured with a little less severity, 'that Mr Fitzgibbon is not at home?'

I blinked rapidly in response.

'Because I'll gladly take the matter up with him,' he continued in the absence of any sensible contribution to the surreal conversation from myself.

'I don't relish this, you know.' He was looking uncomfortable now, his deep baritone rising a notch. 'I really do *not* like having to have these kinds of exchanges with a woman – no offence, of course.' He rubbed his nose.

I circumnavigated the crucial question, focusing on the imminent, more pertinent matter. 'I'm afraid, Mr, er, Mr . . . ?'

'O'Callaghan. Alan.' He held out his hand, which I shook.

'Yes, of course, Mr O'Callaghan—'

'Alan, please,' he insisted.

'Yes, er, thank you, Alan. You see, it's a very bad time . . .'

'I don't doubt it, Mrs Fitzgibbon.'

'And if you could just give me a few weeks . . .'

'It's been six months now, Mrs Fitzgibbon.'

'Shelley, please,' I smiled weakly.

'Er, Shelley. Even the deposit cheque bounced. We usually don't install anything without a deposit, but given the circumstances and the long-standing working relationship we had with your husband, we thought, well . . .'

I winced.

'But at the end of the day,' Alan continued, 'still no payment. So, much as it pains me to, I'm taking my kitchen back. And I'm very sorry about the inconvenience, Shelley, but business is business, whatever time of day it is, so if you don't mind . . .'

'No, of course not,' I said politely, ushering him in, years of conditioning coming into play. 'You must do whatever you have to, but if you wouldn't mind giving me just a moment,' I was babbling. I could hear the fear bubbling in my own voice like a runaway brook. 'It's my son, you see, he likes to do his homework there. I'll just get him settled somewhere else.'

'We'll make this as painless as possible,' said Alan, looking genuinely upset as he stood uncertainly in the hall. 'I give you my word.'

I ran to the kitchen then, down those three familiar steps, coldly oblivious to the gleaming expanse of glass walls, the seamless sheets of stainless steel, the Viking Range oven and Subzero fridge, the shining white presses and cool terrazzo worktops that had given me such undiluted pleasure, and noticed only Mac's hunched, skinny form crouched over the table, head bobbing in rhythm to his headphones. But it was his finger, trailing conscientiously along under every line in the book he sought to understand, to memorise, that made me stop short and gasp for breath, for words. That, and the habit he had acquired lately of brushing back a forelock of hair repetitively, nervously, even, from his forehead that made what I had to do so painfully hard.

'Mac,' I said, gently putting a hand on his shoulder.

'What?' he started, regarding me accusingly. When I just shrugged, the helplessness of the gesture frustrated him further. 'What?' he demanded, pulling his earplugs out and glaring up at me. 'What is it now?'

'I need you to go to your room, Mac, and finish your homework there. Now, please.'

It must have been the 'please' that did it, or maybe it was my face – who knows? But suddenly Emma was standing there beside me, her face flushed, tossing her ringlets over her shoulders. 'C'mon, Mac,' she said. That got his attention. His über-cool fifteen-year-old sister commanded poorly feigned derision at the very least and open adulation at most. 'Let's go upstairs. I'll help you with your homework, then we can play *Mario Kart.*'

He went then without further protest, soundlessly gathering up his books and iPod, following his sister, grateful and unquestioning of her sudden, unsolicited interest.

As they disappeared from view, her arm slung carelessly over his shoulders, I watched wordlessly as she first prodded, then chased him up the stairs, their pounding feet receding with each flight. And suddenly I felt more alone than I could ever remember.

'Ahem.' It was Alan and his helpers interrupting my thoughts. 'Is it all right if we . . .' he gestured, a sort of sweeping wave that said more than he could ever know.

'Fire ahead,' I said breezily, leaning back against a pristine countertop while I could. The two helpers followed him, avoiding my eyes, setting down their tools of the trade and donning their overalls. I watched them all, deliberately. I wasn't going to make this easy.

'Can I offer you some tea? Coffee, perhaps?' I asked archly. The Polish guys had the grace to look uncomfortable and muttered something hopeful but unintelligible. Their boss Alan, on the other hand, perked up greatly. This was Ireland, after all.

'That's very decent of you, Shelley.' He gave me a man-to-man smile, relieved that I was being sensible about the matter after all. 'Tea with two sugars if you don't mind, and the lads like a cup of coffee, isn't that right, lads?' he looked at them expectantly.

'Right,' I said briskly. 'One tea, two coffees, coming up.' I pulled out the jar of instant coffee I kept for unwanted callers, studiously ignoring the Nespresso machine the Poles looked at longingly. Banging the kettle on, I flung a tea bag into the first mug I could find from the back of the cupboard, which turned out to be an effort from one of Mac's early school art classes that he had made for his dad. It was bright blue, chunky, uneven and had the face of a weirdly grinning fox on it. Inexplicably, the sight of it suddenly made me burst into tears, which, despite Alan and his Polish helpers' mortification, became loud, unrestrained sobs that I seemed quite unable to control.

'Ah, here. Ah, now. Ah, *Jaysus*,' said Alan despairingly.

'Please, madam,' murmured a Polish voice, and I felt a consoling hand on my shoulder. Of course, that only made me worse.

In the event, Alan made the tea while Marcus and Marik (I learned their names later) helped me sit down at the kitchen table and stood looking awkward until I had composed myself, which wasn't easy, considering I had been doing some seriously ugly crying, the kind that leaves your face red and swollen, eyes like slits. Not attractive. I wiped a hand under my streaming nose. Marik handed me a tissue. Alan set a mug of tea in front of me that you could trot a mouse on, as my late mother would have said. 'Good and strong with two sugars, for the shock,' he explained. They seemed to have all the answers.

Then I left them to it. With as much dignity as I could muster, I went back to the empty study. The news was on, more earnest reporters telling me things I already knew. I changed channels and poured myself a brandy. I never drank brandy, ever, but then, I had never drunk tea the colour of tar with two sugars in it before tonight, which had, as Alan pronounced, proved strangely comforting. Or maybe it had been the company of three strong men sitting beside me, even if all they were feeling for me was pity. I didn't care. It was better than nothing.

It didn't take long, just a few mindless programmes –
America's Next Top Model, *A Place in the Sun* and an amazing
episode of *Planet Earth*, which, along with the brandy, had
tears coursing down my face again as I watched brave little
seals hurling themselves into shark-infested waters, blindly
following a time-honoured tradition in which instinct would
force them to dice with death as their predators lurked before
them, pouncing menacingly. And all their poor mothers could
do was watch and hope and try to protect them, pulling them
out of the sea, some already savaged, and bleat pathetically
as they tried to nudge their babies back to life. It was all so
bloody cruel. Three programmes was all it took for a kitchen
that had taken weeks and *weeks* to be installed to be very efficiently taken out. It struck me, even then, as rather ironic.

'That's it, Shelley.' Alan knocked discreetly on the open
door. 'We're all done.'

I got up to see him out. 'Well, that's it then,' I repeated.

'We'll be off now, leave you in peace,' he nodded.

'Yes, well, goodnight.'

Marik muttered something in Polish to Marcus, who shook
his head. It sounded ominous.

'You're all right, here, Shelley?' Alan enquired. 'On your
own, I mean?' Concern flickered.

'I'm not on my own,' I said firmly. 'I have my children.' I
raised my chin fractionally, reminding him we were still a
family, still a unit. Even if our surroundings were being
dismantled, our spirit would remain intact. I was channelling
Anne Boleyn prior to her execution in the current series of
The Tudors.

'Well . . .' He looked uncertain, and again there was a
murmured exchange between the Poles. 'Just you mind
yourself.'

'Thank you,' I said. And I meant it. He had been nice,
under the circumstances.

I said goodbye to them all, and just as I was about to close the door, Alan looked back. 'I know it's not my place to say this, and maybe it's not what you want to hear, but I think he's an absolute *louser*, that husband of yours, leaving you here to face all this. A bloody little *louser*. A lovely woman like yourself deserves a lot better.' And with that, Alan got into his Jeep and drove off, followed by Marik and Marcus in the lorry.

I closed the door and wandered down to the bleak landscape that used to be my kitchen. All that was left was the kettle and the microwave, not even the table to sit at. I briefly remembered another time, another kettle, another microwave and a lot less space, and it had been pure, unadulterated bliss. Not like this. A million light years from this.

'It looks a bit like an aircraft hanger, doesn't it?' It was Emma, standing at the doorway, head tilted as she surveyed the expanse of carcasses and tiles. She walked towards me and stopped. I tried to meet her eyes and failed. I was afraid of what I would see. It might have been compassion, or fear, or both, and that would have destroyed me. I had to hold it together – for the children, of course.

'Are you okay?' It should have been me asking the question, but she got there first.

I nodded and smiled a tight little smile. 'Where's Mac?'

'In his room, downloading porn.'

'What?'

She grinned. 'Music. He's done his homework and he's downloading Dizzee Rascal.'

I tried to smile but covered my face with my hands instead and took a deep breath.

'Mum?'

'Yes.'

'What's going to happen now?'

'I don't know, Emma,' I said. 'I don't fucking know.' That's when it really hit me how bad things were. I never used language in front of my children. Not knowingly, anyway.

'It's only a kitchen, Mum,' she said. 'I'm going to bed. You should too.'

She was right, of course. That's what was so wonderfully annoying about Emma. She was almost always right.

Emma

'We're screwed,' I said nonchalantly before taking a sip of my cappuccino. Better to bite the bullet, I figured.

Across the table, Sophie chewed her lip and looked worried.

'How d'you know? For sure, I mean,' she added hastily, looking around as if she was scared someone would overhear us.

'Three men came in and took out our kitchen last night.'

Her face expressed the words she couldn't. 'You're telling me . . . ?'

'Exactly.' I shrugged.

Sophie wasn't usually lost for words, but this stumped her. 'Well,' she said, searching, 'it's only a kitchen, I guess.'

'That's what I said.'

'So how are you managing?'

'Without a kitchen, or in general?'

'Jeez,' she said, pausing to consider. 'This sucks.'

We were in Dundrum, the mall where we hung out after school when we could. Sophie's mum was picking us up at five p.m. sharp. 'I'll get this,' she insisted as we went to pay.

'It's okay,' I said. 'I'm still good for a coffee – might as well enjoy it while you can.'

We wandered aimlessly for the half an hour or so that remained, checking out the usual stores, smearing on lipstick and anti-ageing creams. I bought a purple-red nail polish with the pleasing name of Scab. 'That'll come in handy,' I quipped, 'when I'm picking it off.'

We were passing a major low-priced chain store that previously we wouldn't have been seen dead in. I marched through the entrance.

'What're you doing?' Sophie hissed.

'Embracing reality,' I said. 'You don't have to come in if you don't want to.'

'You're being ridiculous,' she said, reluctantly following me. I knew her purchasing curiosity would get the better of her, however offputting the venue. I soon found what I was looking for.

'Oh, God, Em, not shoes, *please* not shoes. I mean accessories or tees, maybe, but not shoes.' She turned her back and pretended to examine some allergy-inducing jewellery while I rummaged through the already dishevelled shelves.

'Result!' I said, pulling on the suede, flat-heeled, over-the-knee boots that folded down in a cuff. I had seen them featured on a slot on *Morning TV* – fashion on a budget. They were twenty euro. I found my size in every colour – brown, green, black and deep purple. Smoothing them over my skinny jeans, I fought to look at them in the knee-high mirror provided, where three other girls jostled to view shiny, platformed and ankle-strapped footwear, respectively.

'Actually,' Sophie conceded from a discreet distance, 'they're not bad.'

'Why don't you try a pair?' I met her eyes; it was an unspoken challenge.

She hesitated for about thirty seconds, then pulled a pair on. 'They're as soft as gloves,' she said wonderingly, 'but . . .'

I could tell she was wrestling. Sophie never bought anything that wasn't designer labelled. It was just the way things were, but the boots looked good on her.

'Sophie,' I said, gathering mine up and heading for the checkout, 'get with the shift – labels are really over.'

Her eyes darted uncertainly, then she caved. It might have

been a gesture of solidarity, or pure common sense – who knows? 'I'll get the black. You can't have too many pairs of black suede, right?'

'Right,' I said. I paid cash and waited while she used her card.

'I don't need a bag,' she said to the cashier. 'I can put mine in with yours, can't I?'

'Sure,' I said, smiling inwardly. This was a first. I couldn't expect Sophie to go all the way and sport a Pricerite bag – she was still in shock.

'I'm going to wear mine now.' I pulled off my Uggs and put them in the bag with the other boots. The soft black suede moulded perfectly to my black skinny jeans.

'You're so lucky, you have such long legs,' Sophie grumbled. Hers were just an inch shorter, but it was a fairly constant, good-humoured refrain. 'Let's go,' she urged. 'Mum will go mental if we're not outside on the dot.'

She was afraid someone might see us, of course. 'C'mon, then,' I said, linking her arm as we left the store.

I had known Sophie since we were five years old. This was hard for her. She was doing her best, I knew, and it was a pretty good best, all things considered. I mean, it's not easy, is it, to have a best friend whose father has vanished into thin air, leaving behind a lot of what was beginning to look like serious trouble – but I wouldn't think about that now.

'Are you okay?' she ventured as we waited for the lift.

'Sure, I'm fine.'

'Really? I mean, you're being so, like, *strong* about all this.'

'I have to be.'

'How's your mum coping?'

'She's doing okay,' I lied. 'It's Mac I'm worried about.'

'What about Olivia? She must be a support,' she said, referring to my twenty-four-year-old narcissistic, publicity-craving older sister.

'Are you crazy?' There was only so much pretending I could do. 'All she cares about is the press coverage and how this is going to affect her non-existent career prospects and her relationship with Bob the Builder.' Olivia's body-building, sunbed-worshipping boyfriend, Robert, was a regular topic of derision for us both.

'So how is Mac?'

'Crushed,' I said as we got the lift.

She digested the information as we descended three floors and got out, heading for the car park. 'Has he said anything?'

'No. He doesn't have to.'

Sophie shook her head. 'That sucks.'

'You could say that.' I could see her mother's black Porsche Cayenne pulling up.

'He'll talk when he's ready,' I said knowledgeably, hoping I was right.

'You're scaring me.' Sophie looked at me, shaking her head and grinning, trying to lighten the mood. 'You're getting so, like, what's that word?' She scrunched up her forehead in concentration. 'Wise,' she said. 'That's it – wise.'

I looked at her and smiled. 'Sophie,' I said, feeling the familiar weight settle on my shoulders, 'I was born wise.'

'Hi girls!' Sophie's mother, Jackie, said brightly as we got in, Sophie in the front, me in the back. 'You've been shopping, Emma. What did you get?' Her eagle eyes took in the Pricerite bag.

'Just boots.'

'Boots?' I could tell she was thrown, but she recovered quickly. 'Good for you. I'm always telling Sophie she should shop around, look for good value, but Sophie loves her labels, don't you, hon?' She glanced fondly at her daughter. 'Wonder who you got that from, hmm?' she laughed. It was a light, tinkling sound. 'You're so sensible, Emma.'

'I have my share of labels too, Jackie,' I reminded her.

'Of course you do, but you know,' she said, allowing her voice to drop as if she was sharing a conspiratorial truth which had just dawned on her, 'everything's different now with this horrid credit crunch business. We're *all* going to have to tighten our belts.' She made it sound like an unwelcome fashion statement, sort of like eighties shoulderpads and power suits making a come back.

You don't know the half of it, I felt like saying, but didn't. I could already feel embarrassment seeping from Sophie's every pore. You couldn't hold anyone responsible for their parents – after all, we all had them. And most of the time I liked Jackie.

'Sophie got a pair too,' I said.

'A pair of what?'

'Boots, like the ones I got. In black.'

'That's nice.' She smiled at me in the rearview mirror, but I knew she thought it wasn't nice at all. 'You'll have to show them to me when we get home, Soph. So what do you think of my hair, girls?' She gave her blow-dried curls a little shake. 'I had quite a lot off.'

'It's really nice, Jackie,' I said. 'You always look great anyway.' This brought the conversation back to safer ground, but it was true. Jackie was tall, blonde and thinner than anyone in our year. The other mothers always compared themselves to her, accompanied with a lot of *if onlys*. If only I looked like Jackie, if only I had Jackie's hair/legs/figure/husband. Jackie was the benchmark. Sophie pretended not to like it, but I knew she loved it.

Her dad was nice too – a bit scary, but nice. He was something to do with mobile phones and media stuff and they were loaded. He travelled a lot and was always in the papers, buying and selling companies and giving his view on the 'current situation'. People seemed to listen to him, even politicians –

especially now. But as far as I could tell, nobody knew what to do – not now. Anyone could see they hadn't a clue. All those parents and friends of parents who had got us all into this mess – they kept talking, but no one knew what to do.

Me? I was happy with my own mum, which was just as well, as she kept reminding me she was the only one I had. She was pretty, the kind of mum you often saw in American sitcoms. Not scary pretty, but cute. She had a good figure, although she was always giving out about her too-tight size twelve jeans, but she said buying a pair of size fourteens would be giving in. She had nice skin that always tanned really easily, and she got these freckles on the bridge of her nose when she had been out in the sun without her sunblock. Her hair was light brown and shiny and sometimes she got highlights in it. Her eyes were what I liked best about her, though. They were green with hazel flecks and crinkled up when she smiled, and she had really long thick eyelashes I'd have killed for, even without mascara. Most of all, she was fun. She really made us laugh, even when we were sick or miserable. Except now, even she couldn't laugh . . .

'Here we are, Emma.' We had pulled up outside my house and I barely noticed.

'Here,' I said to Sophie, taking out her boots from the bag. 'Don't forget your boots.'

'Oh, wow, yeah, thanks, Em. See you tomorrow.'

'See ya,' I said, getting out of the car. 'Thanks very much for the lift, Jackie.'

'You're welcome, Emma.' She smiled at me. 'Tell your mum I'll give her a ring next week – we'll have a bite of lunch maybe.'

'Sure. I'll tell her.' I closed the door and waved them off. I knew she probably wouldn't. Jackie had already had one of her lunch parties and hadn't invited Mum. Another friend of hers had let it slip and Mum had been really upset. She hadn't said anything, but I could tell. She wasn't especially close to Jackie, not like me and Soph were, but she had always been invited to stuff Jackie gave – they 'mixed in the same circles', as the gossip columns put it. Or they had up until recently.

I let myself in the front door and imagined the conversation Sophie would be having with her mum in the car on the way home without me. And I wished I could have seen Jackie's face when Sophie told her about our kitchen incident. It almost would have made it worthwhile.

Our house was really nice; everybody said so. My parents had done a lot of work to it since they had bought it twelve years ago – in 1997, I think it was, before property prices had gone mad. I don't remember, of course, I was only three years old. But I remember running around the huge garden and Olivia chasing me with a dead jellyfish on a stick that the boy next door had given her. She got into trouble for that.

I looked into the empty aircraft hanger kitchen and saw that Mum – or someone – had moved the table from the formal dining room into it, and some chairs. It looked weird. I was just about to head up to my room when I heard her voice calling me from the study.

'Emma, is that you? Come in here, would you?'

I walked slowly back, and as I got closer to the room, I heard muffled sobs and a few half-hearted wails. I recognised Olivia's voice immediately.

'Hi,' I said, taking in the scene. 'What's up?' At a quick glance, things didn't look good. Olivia was crying and hiccupping and Mum had her arm around her, trying to console her. Mac was sitting on the sofa opposite them, staring over their heads at a spot on the wall. He looked as if he wished he could be anywhere else. I braced myself.

'Sit down, Em,' Mum said gently.

I sank onto the sofa beside Mac and looked enquiringly at

her. She had been crying and her face was sort of tense looking, as if her skin was stretched too tightly across her cheekbones. For a second, I was scared rigid. *Please God, oh please God, let no one be dead, especially not Dad.* In that moment, I hated him more than at any other time in this whole mental scenario.

'There's something I have to tell you,' said Mum. Judging from the lack of general enthusiasm in the room, I thought the others were already in on the act. I was wrong.

'What's happened?' My voice sounded strangely high.

'What's happened?' shrieked Olivia. 'What's happened is everything's gone! Everything! And I've been manhandled out of my apartment. That's what's happened.' She relapsed into sobbing. I looked at Mum.

'Olivia's had a bit of a shock.' She stroked her hair and held her to her, rocking her gently.

'A shock?' I was still in the dark.

'Three men,' my sister hiccupped, 'three – this morning. And Robert's left me. I've lost everything. Everything.' She wasn't making a lot of sense.

'Hush, sweetheart.' Mum looked helplessly at her. 'It'll be all right, I promise. I know this is all horrible, but—'

'Horrible?' Olivia looked up at her, aghast, her sobbing momentarily abandoned. 'Horrible? Is that what you call it?' She looked at Mum as if she was mad. 'We're ruined! Don't you get it? We're all ruined! I hate him, I hate him, I hate him, I *hate* him!'

'Well I must say,' I interjected, 'I was never a big fan, as you know.'

If looks could kill, I would have been flat out on the floor. 'Not Robert,' she hissed at me. 'Dad! I wish he was dead! I wish—'

'Shut up!' I said, springing up, my fists clenched. 'Don't you dare say that, you selfish little cow!'

'Stop it, girls! That's enough.' Mum's voice was a whip crack. I followed her gaze to Mac, who was sitting immobile. His face had gone very white, with two red spots flaming on his cheeks.

'Sorry,' I mumbled, sitting down again. I looked at Mac, but he kept staring straight ahead.

'I need you to listen very carefully to what I have to say,' Mum said. Even Olivia straightened up.

'Whatever has happened – or might happen – the important thing I want you to remember is that we are still a family, right? Whatever happens, wherever Dad is, whatever anyone might say to you, or infer, the only thing that matters is that we are still the same and we'll make it through this together. Do you understand?'

We didn't, but we nodded anyway – you couldn't not have. It was something in her face, her tone of voice.

'What Olivia has said is partly true.' She paused. 'We *have* lost everything – financially, that is.'

I studied the floor. It wasn't exactly a surprise, but it was weird, hearing Mum talking in this voice, as if she was an air hostess giving us all instructions to evacuate the emergency exit, without panic. *Proceed as normal, in an orderly fashion.*

'Dad is in trouble. A lot of trouble – I know that now. That's why he had to go . . . away like this.' Her voice almost broke, but she kept it together. 'And it's up to us to do the best we can in his absence.' She took a deep breath.

Here it is, I thought, here comes the proverbial. But even I wasn't prepared for what came next.

She swallowed. 'The house is gone. Our home, here, it's been sold. It belongs to – to someone else now.' She took another breath and gave Olivia another reassuring squeeze, and smiled. 'That's why Olivia had to, er, leave the apartment at such short notice – *all* of Dad's properties have gone.'

Olivia sniffed reproachfully, but she was listening, acutely.

'So . . .' I tried to formulate the question that was hammering in the front of my brain. 'Where are we going to go? What's going to become of us?' I willed her not to bull-shit us.

Mum smiled bravely at me – at all of us. That's when I knew it was going to be bad. But nothing could have prepared me for what was coming – *nothing*.

'We're going to live with Granny,' she said quietly. 'For the immediate future, at any rate.' She said it as if it was the most natural thing in the world, but even she couldn't disguise the horror of the words that escaped her.

Let me just explain something here. In our house, the word 'Granny' probably doesn't have the same meaning it would in, say, everybody else's. First of all, us kids had met her on barely a handful of occasions, mostly involving churches – you know, baptisms, first holy communions, confirmations, that sort of thing. Second of all, my dad had cut off any normal contact with her years ago – or she had with him – probably over something totally insignificant, who knows, but the subject was never broached – not by us, anyway. And thirdly, from the little I knew of her, she lived alone in a really, really small house. I had never been in it, of course, but Dad used to laugh about it and tease us when we didn't know what words like 'larder' and 'pantry' and 'scullery' meant. He used to say things like, 'When I was young we only had one bathroom in the house – and even that had a separate toilet.' We didn't believe him, of course, until Mum said it was true, and that that was what a lot of houses had been like until they had had work done on them – sort of like those makeover programmes, I suppose – and that before we had gotten rich in this country and the standard of living had improved, a lot of people had only ever had one bath-room. Apparently Granny was one of them. That was the bit I was having trouble getting my head around.

Vera

How did it happen? *How in the name of God did it happen?* That was the question that reverberated in my mind as I tried to go about my duties in any kind of normal manner. The shop was busy today, more so than usual, and that helped. I worked there three days a week and loved it. At my age it's important to keep occupied. I'm a firm believer in hard work, not that you could call working in a charity shop hard, as such, but these days we were busier than ever – a sign of the times.

I had started here ten years ago now, after Arthur had died, and it had got me through those awful bleak beginnings of sudden widowhood that nothing or nobody can prepare you for, long after the wake and funeral, and long after the kind and thoughtful words and deeds of friends and neighbours have passed. Those terribly strange moments when you feel as if your world has utterly diminished, becoming grey and lifeless, and uncommon sounds that you never noticed before, like the ticking of the kitchen clock, or the slight crackle of the television when you switch it off, suddenly beat long and loudly in your ears. For a while I almost thought I was going mad until I was told by countless women in the same situation that it was entirely normal – to be expected. Keep busy, everybody said, that's the trick. *But I have kept busy all my life*, I thought. I was a keen gardener, I knitted and I did the flowers at the church on a regular rota. Ah, but those are solitary occupations, a wise soul pointed out to me. You need to get out, be around other people, *engage*. She was right, of course; I had no idea how right. And so I walked in off the street to the charity shop, filled out a form the rather brusque young woman gave me (I later understood she had been particularly stressed that day; once I got to know her, Joan was a sweetie), waited rather anxiously at home while they checked my references and breathed a sigh of relief when she phoned me a few days later to ask when I could start and how many hours I would be prepared to put in. I started off doing three mornings, Monday, Wednesday and Friday, which quickly turned into full days – well, until four o'clock, at any rate, when we older people left it to the youngsters, who closed up shop at six. They were a dear bunch I worked with. Joan was the boss, really, a wonderful girl who had left her very high-powered career suffering from stress. From what I understood, I think she and her husband had been trying to start a family without success, and she had been advised to give up her position in a big law firm and pursue something less cut throat. So far, sadly, there was no sign of the much longed-for baby. I had to keep myself once or twice from telling her that this might have been a blessing in disguise. Children, even the most longed for ones, can sometimes be a source of great misery. I should know. But nobody ever tells you that, and of course, it wouldn't do say such a thing, but all the same, I often think . . .

Then there were the oldies: myself, a sprightly seventy-nine; Maura, seventy-seven, a retired nurse, also a widow who lived with her increasingly demented younger brother; and Tom, a confirmed bachelor, very dapper dresser and the youngest of our lot at seventy-five.

The youngsters came on sometimes later in the day but mostly worked weekends: a rather overweight and bossy girl, Barbara, who dressed in ridiculously inappropriate clothes for her shape; and Zoe, a dear slip of a thing, studying social science, who sported a terrifying amount of piercings in her ears, her lip and even, I shuddered at the thought, one on her tongue. Roger, an environmentalist, who looked and dressed like a twig, in varying degrees of shabby greens and browns, completed our happy band.

I sat now in the tiny back room where we made tea and kept the huge mountains of black bags containing donated clothes and bric-a-brac that would have to be sorted through, deemed saleable or not and eventually priced and displayed. It was eleven o'clock and Maura and I were having our tea break. She helped herself to a chocolate digestive and gestured for me to do the same before sitting down and letting out a long breath. I wondered how much to tell her and then decided to come clean. The older I become, the less inclined I am to bother with pretence of any kind.

'What is it?' she asked, looking at me shrewdly. 'You haven't been yourself for days, Vera.' Her plump face radiated concern.

'It's Charlie,' I began, and then stopped, struck yet again by the sudden, tragic absurdity of the situation. How could I possibly explain? And how much of this sorry saga had they all already worked out?

Sooner or later, most people always asked me the inevitable question. 'Is Charlie Fitzgibbon a relative of yours?' they would enquire eagerly. And I would tell them yes, that in fact he was my son, the younger of my two boys. They would make nice comments along the lines of how lovely it must be to have such a success story in the family, how proud I must be of him and so on. I would smile and nod and make some sort of agreeable reply, something they would expect to hear, and they would go away pleased that they had made and commented on the connection, sometimes even noting the physical resemblance between us. If they had known, really known, about my relationship with my son, they would have never mentioned him to me. But there was no point going into that. People wouldn't understand. They would feel awkward, embarrassed, even, for me. It was easier to let them think what they wanted to – that I was the proud and happy mother of a successful and indulgent son who cared for me and no doubt kept me in a manner to which I had, during the course of his meteoric success, become accustomed. The truth, or the bits of it I felt able to reveal, was known to very few people. Maura and Tom, whom I worked with, were among those few. There are some things that only people of your own vintage are really, truly able to grasp. Younger, more inexperienced types meant well, of course they did, but it took the accumulation of years to acquire the realisation and eventual acceptance that some events and situations in life were just plain sad, and there was no fairness or accountability in the matter.

'It did occur to me,' Maura said kindly, 'that all this must be dreadfully difficult for you, but I didn't like to, you know . . .' She stopped, unsure of how to proceed. She was referring, of course, to the spectacular and very public collapse of Charlie's investment empire, which had been covered by every newspaper in the country, not to mention national television. In the light of the ever-increasing horror stories about the economy in general that followed, Charlie's debacle almost seemed inconsequential. But it was the insidious, invisible threads linking it, and indeed *him,* to the frenzy of greed that had brought our country to its knees and wiped out diligent and innocent people's savings and pensions that filled me with skin-crawling horror whenever I thought of it – which was constantly.

'Everyone thinks the world of you, Vera,' Maura was saying now. 'You mustn't upset yourself about what's happened. Even if you had known anything about it, what could you possibly have done? You're a victim of these horrible events as much as anyone is.'

'He's my son,' I said quietly, silently acknowledging the conflicting emotions of guilt, loss, love and acute sorrow that fact brought me.

'How are they coping, his wife and the children, without him?' She went on. 'Have you heard anything from them?' Maura knew how delicate the situation was, not to mention unconventional, and not in a good way.

'I have, yes, and that's what's been on my mind.' I took a deep breath and told her. 'It's worse than they thought. Much worse. The house is gone and they have to be out within two weeks.'

'Two weeks?' She looked appalled. 'But it's the family home – can't she apply to the courts? They can't just put you out.' Maura was nothing if not practical.

'It's not that straightforward,' I said. 'Nothing ever is with Charlie. He sold the house from under her, without her knowledge – forged Shelley's signature, apparently.' I let that sink in and watched her face redden.

'But all the more reason to get legal help, surely. I mean, that's illegal, isn't it? Oh, I'm sorry, Vera, I didn't mean to imply . . .'

'It's all right, Maura,' I reassured her. 'But to answer your question, yes, of course it's illegal, but the people he signed it over to apparently are some Russian crowd, people he owed money to – a great deal of money – and her solicitor advised Shelley that they are not the kind of people you want to tangle with, if you get my drift.'

It was clear that she did as Maura shook her head wordlessly at me, well-meaning advice momentarily abandoned. 'Dear God.'

'Precisely.'

'What are they going to do?'

'The only thing they can do, under the circumstances. Move in with me. Come and live in my house.' I had hoped saying it like this, matter of factly, would make it feel like the plausible resolution it should be – but it didn't. Not since the moment I had picked up the phone and listened incredulously to Shelley's stilted, tremulous and heartachingly apologetic account of what had happened had any of this unfolding saga seemed a part of anything that remotely approached reality.

'But – but,' Maura was doing the maths, 'will you have room? I mean, there are what, three children? And you have how many rooms?'

'Three – and one bathroom,' I confirmed as Maura chewed her lip. 'Shelley will have Charlie's old room, the girls will have to share the spare bedroom and Mac, the youngest, will have to have the box room, the attic. I'll get someone to fix up a bed in there.'

Maura rallied bravely. 'Well I think that's terrific, I really do. And I'm sure it will work out wonderfully. You won't know yourself with all the company – it will be good for you.'

I allowed myself a smile. 'We'll just have to make the best of it. One day at a time and all that.'

'If there's anything I can do, you just holler, you know that, don't you?'

'Of course,' I said. 'You can count on it.'

'Now that I think of it,' she said as she finished her tea and got up, 'I'm sure a lovely set of unopened bed linen came in last week. I remember distinctly thinking it would come in useful for someone – let me just have a rummage.'

I brought the mugs to the sink and began to rinse them under the taps, listening to Maura prattling on determinedly, happier now that she had a practical task to apply herself to. Extra bed linen, I thought to myself, was the least of my worries. It was the many other, terrifyingly unfamiliar emotional resources we would all have to call on that would test us.

But then I remembered what my dear late Arthur would have said. 'One hurdle at a time, Vera. One hurdle at a time, old girl.'

I went back into the shop and relieved Joan from her position behind the till.

'That'll be four euro,' I said briskly to the man buying the bunch of five CDs.

'Recession, how are you?' he said derisively, attempting to haggle. 'You can do better than that, surely? This place is daylight robbery.' He grinned in what he probably thought was an engaging manner. I knew his type. He was well dressed, clearly not in any need. They were always the worst, always the ones looking for something for nothing.

'This is a charity shop,' I said, 'not a chain store. It says so right above the door as you come in.' I gave him a look that brooked no nonsense. 'It's all in a good cause.'

'Humph.' He handed over his four euro grudgingly. 'That's what they all say.'

Later, when I had got the Dart home and done a bit of dusting, I thought about things as I made my dinner – a reheated chicken breast, steamed spinach and some nice pan-fried potatoes. I set my tray as I always did, right down to the linen napkin I rolled in its sliver ring, and sat down in the living room to watch the six o'clock news. If Arthur could see me he'd be spinning in his grave, and I can't say I'd blame him. He was a stickler for discipline and good manners, and having your dinner on a tray in front of the television would have been his idea of complete debauchery. It wasn't that he was difficult, not at all, he just believed in doing things the *right* way, and the more I see of life, he had a point. I crossed myself, said the few words of grace I still remembered and then said aloud to him as I took up my cutlery: 'Arthur, I know you can hear me, and I know you don't approve of my eating in front of the television like this, but it's lonely here without you. And it's practical, this tray. Why would I want to be setting a table for just one? And I get to see the news as well and keep up to date,' I said with a touch of defiance. 'But I won't be on my own for much longer, Charlie's family are coming to stay, Shelley, Olivia, Emma and Mac, and I'm looking forward to it.' That's when I cracked (I could never hide anything from Arthur). 'Oh God,' I said, flinging down my knife and fork and covering my face, 'Oh Arthur, it's awful, it's dreadful, worse than you could ever imagine. They've lost the house. He sold it from under them, and you know Shelley's parents are gone, she has no one else, and of course I said they must come and live here. But Arthur, they'll hate it – and they'll hate me. We don't even know each other. I've barely met the children on more than three occasions – and you were with me then. I don't know how I'm going to manage, I really don't.' And, I'm ashamed to say, I began to cry. When I looked up through the blur of self-pity, Arthur's straight, handsome features looked right back at me from the mantelpiece. I loved that photo, I really did. It was one of the few I had where you got to see the real man. Integrity radiated from his face, and although his expression to a stranger might have seemed stern, to me, or anyone who knew him, the kindness shone from his beautiful brown eyes. Of course, he was wearing his regalia, the wig and gown he'd donned as a barrister before he became a judge, but even then he could never fool me. Underneath the steely exterior that was Arthur Fitzgibbon to the rest of the world was a man as soft as butter to those he loved, which, I never ceased to thank the good Lord, included me.

We met at a dance in the Gresham Hotel. I can still see it now, the huge, glittering ballroom, the band and everyone dressed to the nines, the women in wonderful evening dresses and the men in black tie. It was my first time there and I felt awfully immature, although my mother had made me a beautiful coral silk dress for the occasion modelled on one we had seen in a Doris Day movie. I was just twenty-three and had started work as a radiographer in a local hospital. The evening was proving tedious, so I decided to make my way to the powder room to escape our rather boring table (I had been asked to make up a party) and, more to the point, my extremely dull date for the night, when I heard a deep voice behind me say, 'I've been watching you all evening and you simply must have this dance with me.' I wheeled around to see a tall, very attractive man smiling confidently at me. He had dark brown hair, nice teeth and the most gorgeous dark brown eyes. He reminded me immediately of Cary Grant – all that was missing was the cleft in the chin.

'I'm afraid I have a date for the evening, Mr . . . ?' I said primly. It wasn't done to just swan off and leave your party with someone you hadn't even been introduced to – this was 1954, remember.

'Well, that's his problem, isn't it?' He grinned rather infuriatingly and held out his hand. 'And the name's Arthur, Arthur Fitzgibbon.'

I shook it, smiling despite myself. 'I'm Vera. Vera Callaghan.'

'Oh, I know who you are, Miss Callaghan. I've made it my business to find out your name. Dublin is a very small town, I'm sure you'll agree. Now come and have that dance with me.'

'Quite apart from anything else, Mr Fitzgibbon—'

'Arthur,' he insisted.

'Arthur, then, I'm on my way to the powder room.'

'Then I shall wait outside for you.'

And he did. He was there hovering discreetly to the left of the door when I came out, attracting, I noticed, many appreciative glances from the girls who passed him by.

Of course I danced with him, I was in his thrall by then. And he was a superb dancer – he jitterbugged, jived and waltzed divinely. Then, breathless after three twirls around the floor in succession, I allowed him escort me back to my table after taking my phone number and promising to call.

I was greeted with tightly disapproving smiles and my date for the night was scowling into his coffee, but I didn't care.

'That was Arthur Fitzgibbon you were dancing with, wasn't it?' said a girl to the right of me, inhaling deeply on her cigarette as she leaned over, throwing her arm across the empty chair between us.

'Yes,' I replied brightly, 'do you know him?'

She smiled condescendingly at me. 'We all know him. Arthur Fitzgibbon leads every girl in Dublin to the altar and then drops her. I wouldn't get your hopes up, dearie, you're just a new face – that's all.' She leaned back as her boyfriend reclaimed his seat. The flurry of excitement and flattery I had felt was crushed instantly.

But she was wrong. Arthur called me just as he said he would, and six months later we were married. And no girl on earth could have asked for a better husband. So it just goes to show: *Believe none of what you hear and half of what you see,* as my dear mother used to tell me.

I roused myself back to the present and tried to watch the news, but I was fed up with all the economic doom and gloom. It was really hard to take it all in without becoming quite extraordinarily angry. To see all the things my generation had worked so hard for, all the privileges young people today took so much for granted, be squandered and then to watch that crowd of nincompoops in government sit back and let the country be brought to its knees – it was thoroughly scandalous. I finished my dinner quickly and turned off the television, making a mental note to telephone my accountant tomorrow. Thank God I wasn't in bank shares, but pretty much everything else was in a slump too. Still, I was more fortunate than many, and luckily I didn't have a mortgage. In my day, debt really *was* considered to be a four letter word – now I understood why. Arthur had worked hard, back-breakingly hard, to pay off all our borrowings and leave me, as he used to say, nicely off. His judge's pension also meant I was quite comfortable, and I had always been careful with money.

I took my tray into the kitchen, loaded the dishwasher and then stood back, looking at the room critically, the way a stranger might. I suppose it would be considered old-fashioned now, but when we bought the house in 1965 we had done what we thought to be the necessary amount of work needed to it. We had redone the bathroom with a nice rose-coloured suite and separate loo, painted the house inside and out and brought in what little furniture we had and added to it gradually over the years. The kitchen, which had really been in need of the most work, ironically was kept to a minimum. That was because Arthur liked things the old-fashioned way. He allowed me my new navy and white Formica presses as long as we left in the larder and the scullery, so we didn't knock the whole area into one as everyone else seemed to be doing. But I got my electric oven and gas hob, so we were never caught out with a strike or a power cut. By modern standards it was still a small kitchen, still a series of little rooms, really, but there was never more than one person cooking, and we had always eaten in the dining room anyway.

Now, though, I dubiously regarded the place with new eyes. How would we manage, Shelley, the children and I? Meals, for example, shopping and cooking and so on? I suppose we would have to work out some sort of rota, establish some sort of ground rules that would be acceptable to us all. I wouldn't think about that just now.

I left the kitchen and walked upstairs, passing the loo and

the bathroom on the return, then on up three further steps to where the three bedrooms branched off the landing. There was the master bedroom that had been mine and Arthur's, still with the double bed I couldn't bear to part with. And why should I? In there, I could feel him with me, not physically, of course, but close, especially when I went to sleep. I had had it done in nice pale pink wallpaper and pale green silk curtains with a pink floral pattern, and his silver brushes still sat on the mahogany dresser. Then there was my dressing table, with the small mahogany mirror on top that you could manoeuvre at a suitable angle, with two small drawers underneath. It was all really much the same as it always had been. The only addition was the electric blanket I had succumbed to – and it was bliss. Maura had quite rightly pointed out that it was a necessity and not a luxury, that it would keep my limbs warm and therefore more limber as age and all its trials encroached. That was the easy bit. I took a deep breath and walked into Charlie's old bedroom. There was still the four-foot bed – not quite single, not quite double – and the row of built-in wardrobes along the facing wall. This was where I would put Shelley. It was neat and tidy and there was room for a few of her belongings. Then I went across the landing to Patrick's old room, my elder son, who had emigrated and made his life in Canada. Patrick had been killed tragically in a car accident almost ten years ago now. I still found it hard to believe he was gone, even after the devastation. No parent should have to bury their child, and although he would be fifty now, he had never married, never settled. I used to worry about that when he was alive, but now, well, perhaps it was just as well. It was smaller, this room, but there was plenty of space for the twin beds I had installed for visiting guests. The girls, Olivia and Emma, would live here and they would somehow have to manage with the small freestanding wardrobe – I wouldn't think about that

now, either. Tomorrow, my odd job man, Billy, was coming
to have a look at the box room in the attic. There was a trapdoor gizmo in operation at the moment, which I wouldn't
dream of attempting, but Cormac, or Mac, as they called
him (I did hate abbreviated names), was eleven, he would
probably enjoy it. Luckily the room had been wired, so there
were a couple of sockets, but the thought of trying to get a
bed up there seemed impossible. Still, it was the only way.
We would have to make do as best we could.

I went back downstairs and made a cup of hot chocolate
before turning in and tried desperately to quell the rising panic
that was coursing through me. It would be all right, I told
myself firmly for the umpteenth time – everything would be
fine. For heaven's sake, this was my own flesh and blood I
was talking about. But that was the very problem. If I had got
it so badly wrong before, who was to say I wouldn't fare even
worse this time? There was no telling with families, none at
all. Just because you all came from the same gene pool didn't
mean a thing. Why, on paper, Arthur, me and the boys were
a family made in heaven, and instead . . . well, things had
turned out very differently, and who, if anyone, was to blame?

With a weary heart I locked up the house, turned on the
alarm and went upstairs. In two weeks' time, there would be
a family in this house again. A real, live family. A family who,
without doubt, would not want to be here. A family who
would have lost a veritable mansion with their own rooms
and rules and memories that lined the walls. No, they would
not want to be here – I could understand that. But they were
my family, even if we were all virtual strangers, and that was
what I had to hold on to. Maybe, just maybe, this was my
second chance. After all, hadn't I prayed for one often enough?

Caroline

He can't do this to me, he cannot do this to me, I won't bloody let him! That was the loop that was playing in my head once it had really sunk in and the shock had begun to abate intermittantly. It was ridiculous, of course, because he had already done it, but it made me feel better to try to pretend there was something I could do about it. I had never experienced such all-consuming anger. I didn't know it was possible to feel murdurous rage towards another human being, never mind the man who claimed to love me and who had been my lover, my soul mate. My job was gone, my investments wiped out and I'd had to get out of the penthouse appartment because he'd signed it over to some investors. If it wasn't so bloody tragic, it would be farcical. Which meant, apart from anything else, that since I had let my mother move into *my* house that I had bought five years ago, I had to move back in with *her*. And she was acting all miffed and put out – as if it was *my* fault.

'But surely you must have known something?' she said, over and over again.

'How many times do I have to tell you? I knew nothing, *nothing*, until the fraud squad came in with a search warrant for the office!' I yelled.

'But you were sleeping with him, Caroline,' she pointed out obtusely, with that stubborn look on her face. 'You said you were. And working with him – how could you *not* have known something?'

That was when I had slammed down my drink and stormed out the door. 'There's no need to take it out on me,' she called after me, wounded. 'This isn't easy for *me*, you know.'

If I'd stayed a minute longer, I'd have slapped her. That woman had never done a day's work in her life, she had probably put my father in an early grave with her nagging and I had looked after her royally ever since then. My two brothers, who were married, barely showed up except to be waited on hand and foot – they did absolutely nothing for her and she still worshipped them. Mistake number one had been letting her move into my newly built townhouse because she found the small house where she and my father had lived depressing. Then she promptly turned around and sold her own house, at the height of the market. I hadn't seen that one coming either. Quite an operator, my mother, and at the rate she'd been spending on herself – *'It's about time I did something for me; after all, your father wasn't exactly generous'* – I'd say she was getting through a fair whack of her capital.

Of course, I had the penthouse then that Charlie had given me – only he never got around to putting it in my name as he'd continually promised. I didn't want to risk pushing him about it – being the other woman is about making things fun and uncomplicated for a married man, they get enough of the other stuff at home. He always said we were alike, Charlie and I – cut from the same cloth. *You understand me, Caroline, you're the only person I can really be myself with.* Now I wondered what that said about me – apart from what a complete fool I was. I gave up everything for that man. Everything. I even believed him when he said we'd be together, properly, just as soon as the kids were grown up, only a few more years. *Mac's only eleven, baby, I couldn't do it. I couldn't leave them now, I couldn't live with myself. It would destroy us, you know that.* Seems he was able to live with quite a lot, as it turned out, mostly lies.

I thought I knew that man. All I knew now was what a

complete and utter idiot I had been. Everyone knew about our affair – it was common knowledge in the office and Charlie was quite brazen about being seen in public with me; it was one of things I loved about him. I couldn't stand those men who hid their mistresses away. Of course it helped that we worked together a lot. I was a tax consultant and worked out the roundabouts and loopholes of his clients' deals and investments to make them even richer. Sure, I was well paid, but I'd been sensible, or so I thought, investing heavily in Charlie's development schemes. Now I – and a lot of other people – had been simply wiped out. And I still had a mortgage to pay, to keep my mother living in the style she had so effortlessly become accustomed to. I couldn't even live in my own house to lick my wounds in peace. More to the point, I could forget about getting another position even remotely resembling anything I was so highly qualified for. Quite apart from the financial sector debacle, my associations with Charlie would see to that. So you could understand why I was feeling bitter.

The only thing that made me feel even marginally better was that he had done the dirty on his own family too, his own flesh and blood, just upped and left and fled the country. And even that hadn't been the worst of it – not as far as I was concerned. No, the very, very worst thing about it all – I still had to take deep breaths when I even began to contemplate it – was that I had discovered I wasn't the only other woman in his life. He'd been involved with some South African woman for the past few months, the emails were there to prove it. He hadn't even bothered to hide them that well – maybe he didn't have time or maybe he wanted me to find them, who knows? And if he had been seeing her, then who else had he been seeing? The questions, all hideous to me, kept on coming. So you could understand how I now hated Charlie Fitzgibbon, couldn't you? In fact, hate was much too small a word for what I was feeling. I wanted to kill the bastard.

Elsie

I knew him better than anyone.

It wasn't just that I had worked for him for twenty years. You can work side by side with someone and know absolutely nothing about them. You can even be married to someone and know pretty much nothing about them. I imagine that's what Shelley must be feeling now, poor thing. I could hardly bear to think of what she and the children must be going through. I had retired ten years ago, long before any of this madness had started. Thank God for that. At the time he had begged me to reconsider, but Larry, my husband, had come into a bit of money and, as he pointed out, we didn't need the extra income any more. I was fifty-five by then, and the idea of seeing a bit of the world and maybe spending more time in the timeshare we had bought in Gran Canaria was becoming more and more appealing.

Although I did love my job as Charlie's PA. He was a wonderful boss. I remembered the day he joined our firm, way back, as a keen young trainee accountant. Even then he had a way with people. I could have told anyone he would go far. It wasn't long before he was given his own clients and of course needed his own secretary, and as old Mr Granger was retiring, they asked me I if I would like the job. It was much easier than getting in someone new, seeing as I knew the ropes. I worried that Charlie wouldn't want someone older working for him, that he'd have preferred someone his own age, maybe younger even, but he had been delighted with the idea. And we worked well together. He was a quick study, never needed to be told anything more than once. A whizz kid, that's what the directors called him, pleased at how successful their young turk was turning out. And he was such fun. The whole office used to perk up, especially the girls, when he was about. And the number of phonecalls and messages I had to take from them, all lovestruck young things! He had a real way with the ladies – that was clear straight away. He didn't even have to try, it was just his manner, I suppose, it was natural to him, that's why he was so attractive. He had sex appeal, I suppose that's what you call it – even I could see that, and I was, what? Eighteen years his senior, Moneypenny to his James Bond – that's what he used to joke as he rose through the ranks, going from bigger and bigger offices and then bigger, more prestigious firms until inevitably, of course, he went out on his own. And he always insisted on taking me with him. It was very flattering, really, and he always insisted I got a good raise and a generous bonus every year.

'Don't be silly, Moneypenny,' he'd say when I tried to protest, to say that I couldn't face yet another move. 'I couldn't do any of this without you, you know that. Who would I tell all my deepest, darkest secrets to?'

He could always make me laugh, that Charlie. And I don't mind telling you I was highly relieved when he married Shelley. A beautiful young girl she was, not just pretty, but kind and thoughtful, too. Not like some of the ones he went about with, glamour girls, to be sure, but hard nuts, some of them, cold as ice underneath all the cooing and hanging on they did to him. Yes, Charlie could have gone very wrong marrying a few I remembered. But he didn't, he married absolutely the right girl for him. Shelley adored him, there was no hiding that. But she was genuine and sensible, and I knew she would make him a wonderful wife.

'You like her, don't you, MP?' he said to me one day after he'd come back from lunch with her.

'It's not my business to comment on your girlfriends, Charlie,' I said curtly.

'But you do, MP. You have no idea how much you comment without saying a word.' He grinned at me. 'Your face says it all – I can read you like a book.'

'Then why ask me?' I said, rather miffed, although it was probably true. Not much got past that boy. 'But yes, since you ask, I think Shelley's a lovely girl, the kind a man should consider himself very fortunate to get – if he got her, that is.' Of course there was no doubt that Shelley was madly in love with him at this stage, but it didn't do to let any man think a girl was a sure bet.

'Well I agree with you, MP,' he said. 'I think she is particularly lovely.' And he got a tender, faraway look in his eyes that warmed the cockles of my heart.

'More to the point,' I said, 'what does your mother think of her?' Personally I thought Shelley would be every prospective mother-in-law's dream, which was why what he said next threw me somewhat.

'I couldn't care less what she thinks of her. Doesn't matter to me in the slightest.' He scowled, his face darkening in a most unusual manner. 'In fact, I don't think I'll even bother to introduce her.'

'You mean she hasn't met her?' I was incredulous. 'You haven't brought her home yet? But you've been dating for, what, over six months now.' I knew I had said too much, put aside my natural reserve, but really, I could hardly believe it.

'No,' he replied, his mouth settling in a thin line, 'no I haven't, and I don't intend to either.' At this I was stumped for words, so I wisely held my tongue. That was when I first realised that Charlie was very odd about his mother. In fact, when I thought about it, he never mentioned her and only rarely referred to his father, who I knew was a successful barrister, then later a judge. It was all rather peculiar. I found out more later, of course, much later, which was when I discovered it was better never to refer to Charlie's family. Not unless he brought them up, which was almost never, unless he felt it necessary to drop them into conversation with one of his bosses or a client who he knew would be impressed.

From then on I never enquired, and in some way I began to take on a more motherly role in his life. Charlie needed mothering. Oh, he was perfectly capable and smart as paint, but there was something vulnerable about Charlie, something only a more mature woman would spot. Which was why, as I said, I was so glad when he married Shelley. She was just the right girl for him. And of course he introduced her to his mother, sure she was there at the wedding, looking very elegant, I remember, in a pale yellow silk dress and coat. And he was the spitting image of her. That was the only time I had ever seen Charlie nervous, on edge, but it was to be expected, I suppose, grooms usually were.

And the children! Charlie adored his family when they came along one by one. Olivia was a honeymoon baby, and then they had quite a wait for Emma. I know (Charlie told me) they'd had to seek medical intervention, so to speak, which was why there was the ten-year age gap between the girls. And then finally little Mac came along four years later. Charlie was overjoyed to have a son, but it was Emma he loved best. He never said it, but you could tell, and she adored him too. That pair had a very special bond. Even Shelley said so. That's what made this so terribly, terribly sad. Beyond sad – tragic. That Charlie would abscond like this, leave every-thing, even his own beloved family, and run away, abandoning them like this. It was simply unthinkable. I had gone over it time and time again until I drove Larry to disctraction. But there was something not right about it all. That wasn't the

Charlie I knew. But then, like I said, did you ever really know anybody, deep down?

I jumped as I heard Larry come in from his golf and call up to me. 'Elsie, I'm home. What's for dinner? I'm starving.'

I had made his favorite, steak and kidney pie. Larry and I had a good marriage, and at sixty-seven years of age, he was still a good-looking man. Only lately, since he had retired, he had taken to being very, um, demonstrative again, in the physical sense, if you know what I mean. We had always had a good sex life, perhaps because children had never come along to interrupt it, and we only had each other. But for the past six or seven years that had simmered down pretty much, and I had to say I was rather relieved. At my age, I found I liked going to bed for other reasons, apart from sex. I did even wonder occasionally if he had been taking Viagra. I knew a friend of his was because he had told me, joking about it. I said I thought it was absolutely ridiculous. But I wouldn't put it past Larry, he'd try anything once. I sighed, finished my last email and got up. To be honest, I was finding this renewed passion a little tiring. Charlie would have had a good laugh at that, I thought to myself – not that I would have told him.

And that's when it happened, when I heard the *ping* of a new email arrive and had to sit down again suddenly. It was from jame.s.bond, at an address I didn't recognise – but then, I didn't have to. *Moneypenny*, it read, *you have to read this.* There was only one person who ever called me Moneypenny. Dear God, I thought as all the breath was sucked out of me. And then I heard Larry call again and his footsteps coming up the stairs, so I shut it down, quickly. There was only so much I could cope with at the moment, and getting through dinner without letting slip about this extraordinary develop-ment would take all of my concentration. James Bond, and whatever he might have to say, would have to wait.

'There you are,' said Larry, bending to kiss me hello. 'Steak and kidney pie, how did you guess that was what I'd been dreaming of?' he smiled at me as he pulled off his golf jumper and headed for the bathroom. 'I'll just jump in the shower and I'll be down.'

'I have a nice bottle of red waiting too,' I said. 'I'll just go down and dish up.'

'What did I do to deserve you, Elsie?' I heard before the shower roared into action.

I wouldn't drink any, of course. I had to keep my wits about me, and with a bottle of red inside him, there was a good chance that Larry would actually fall asleep tonight, and soundly. Then, if I could summon the strength, I would read that email.

Lukaz

Why not Ireland? I say to myself. Thinking about it, is very clever suggestion of my friend Leo. Too many oligarchs in London – more than can throw stick at. London known as Moscow-on-Thames now, good joke, yes? No oligarchs in Ireland – none worth talking about, anyway.

This aeroplane very cramped, I am thinking. But I fly economy occasionally, just to remind myself. Of course, that is not total truth – I fly economy because it is the best introduction you can have to a country and its peoples. You can learn a lot from a plane ride. My smaller jet, the Gulfstream, will be flown in later, after nightfall, better for security this way. Not so many private jets in Ireland these days, I hear. Celtic Tiger got no claws no more – also good reason for coming to Dublin.

Russia not good for oligarchs now. Too many tax audits, criminal invstigations and so on. Besides, I have Irish ancestor. My late mother very proud of this and she tell me, Lukaz, never forget you have Irish great-grandfather. He come to Russia in 1920s, dissillusioned with Irish revolution, dominated by Church and bourgeois, as usual. But he had sad story. He ended up prisoner in Stalin's gulag. His crime? He was a foreigner and presumed capitalist. He lasted three winters – most men barely lasted one. That's minus forty degrees winter. Of all the family, my grandmother say I am like him. I have his spirit – may he rest in peace. Now, I go to see his country. My countrymen! Is very emotional for me. Of course, I don't tell nobody nothing about being an oligarch, not yet. For now, I am just ordinary tourist person.

I call air hostess for vodka. I must toast my visit to this new country. When she bring drinks I give her fifty euro note and say, 'Keep the change, honey.'

She look at me strangely and say, 'No, no, I can't do that.'

'Can do whatever you want, baby. Give it to charity if *you* don't want it.' I wink at her. She blushes. I like girls who blush. It's cute. Means she likes me. I spend lot of time in America, so I know how to talk to Western women. But Irish women more like Russian, I think – we both share peasant heritage.

'Hey, baby?' I say to her before she pushes trolley away.

'Yes, sir?' She looks cross, but I know she's flattered.

'You got Mr Ryan's number?'

'Excuse me?'

'Mr Ryan – his name is on aeroplane. I want his number.'

She looks worried. 'Er, Mr Ryan, who founded the airline, died some time ago. A man called Michael O'Leary runs it now.'

'Then give me Michael O'Leary's number,' I say.

'I'm afraid that's not company policy. Why, is there something you would like to comment on regarding your flight? If so, I can pass it on to management.'

'Pity. I just want to tell him he has very pretty air hostess. Very important.'

'Er, thank you, sir. I'll pass that on.' And she move away.

I pour my vodka and man next to me who smells a bit, wakes up. 'May I offer you drink?' I say, handing him one of my vodkas.

'Thanks very much,' he says. Not many teeth, he has.

'This is my first visit to your country,' I say. '*Sláinte!*' I clink glasses with him (this is Gaelic toast – it means 'good health').

'Is that so?' he says. 'And what brings you to Ireland?'

'I come to buy horses – and big country estate.'

He is impressed. 'You're into the horses, are you?'

'Yes,' I say, 'very big into horses.' This is true.

'Well in that case, let me give you my card. I have a cousin who works in Goffs, he'll be the man to help you out.'

'Very kind of you,' I say. I know Goffs, is famous blood-stock agency. Prices down now, is very good time to buy bloodstock.

'And what kind of a place are you looking to buy?' he asks.

'Big country estate, with stables.'

'Well,' he says, 'the man who set up this airline, Tony Ryan, his country estate is up for sale, but it's pricey.'

'How much?' I ask.

'Eighty million yoyos,' he grins. 'A snip.'

'Yoyos?' I am not familiar with this expression.

'Euro,' he explains. 'Would you be spending that kind of money?' he seems to think this is a good joke, so I laugh with him.

'No problem!' I say. And he laughs even more.

We are coming in over sea now, land approaching. It is very green, pastoral, I like this. Beside me, the man crosses himself, so I do the same. Is important to adopt a country's customs.

'Are you a nervous flyer too?' he asks me.

'No,' I shake my head, 'but I prefer when I am in driving seat.'

'You're a pilot then?'

'Yes,' I say, 'but only fly my own planes, and these days, don't even have time for that.' He looks at me strangely. 'Lukaz,' I say and hold out my hand to him.

'Johnny Mac,' he says, shaking it. 'Well, Lukaz, welcome to Dublin.' And the plane hits the runway.

Johnny Mac gets up to go, and I wait while people dis-embark. Of course I don't tell him my other reason for coming to Dublin. Dublin is where Charlie Fitzgibbon lives. I invested lot of money with Charlie a few years ago. His company was performing very well, buying landmark properties in London, when we met. Charlie is fun guy, I like him, I tell my people to go ahead with deals. Now, though, I hear things not so good for Charlie. In London I hear bad stories. It's not that I need the money, although things are bad in Russia too – I am down to my last 4.6 billion – but I want to talk to Charlie – it is point of honour with me. So when Charlie's people not return emails to my people, I smell rats. Same time, I have to leave Russia – silly disagreement over the ownership of 2 million acres of forest with little bit of oil underneath it and some silliness about some tax I may or may not owe. So when I discuss with my friend Leo, and he suggest Ireland – I think, why not Ireland? Is good idea. I have great love of land, I am hunter, horseman, lover of arts – I am also ex-Spetsnaz. Spetsnaz make SAS look like ladyboys. So I don't worry about finding Charlie. I come to Dublin to rest for a while and see how I like Ireland, and also to honour my great-grandfather. Charlie can help me – we have good time together.

Plane is almost empty now, I leave my seat and go to exit.

'Thank you for flying Ryanair,' says air hostess at door.

'No problem, honey,' I say to her and swat her bottom. She blush again and looks cross, and her colleague beside her laughs, putting hand over mouth.

I like these Irish people, I decide. They have good sense of humour.

I go through passport control; my luggage and personal effects will be flown in later on the Gulfstream. For now, I see sign held up, with code name *Mr Smith* written on it. It is Olag, one of my people who has come for me. He takes me outside where my blacked-out Hummer is waiting. As we begin the drive to the city, I turn on my phone. Of course there are already ten messages from Natascha, my current girlfriend, but I am not in mood to ring her now. Instead I ring my grandmother, my last living relative. 'I am in Ireland,' I say, and she cries.

'Already I like this place, Grandmother, soon I bring you here for visit.'

It is important to honour the family. Honour very important to Russian peoples.

'Take me to the best bar in city, Olag,' I say to my man. 'I want to celebrate coming to Dublin.' This is true. It is also the best way to find helpful locals. You buy enough drinks, you make friends very quickly – in any country. Simples.

Shelley

February's the shortest month of the year, but this one was interminable. And after that, there would just be another month, and another one.

It was as if I had stepped into a parallel universe. Hell, maybe. The seventh circle. That's what it felt like, some bizarre *Groundhog Day* starting over and over, a weird movie – the set unfamiliar, the script stilted and the charcters clumsy and flunking their lines, tripping over props and tongues alike.

Mornings were the worst. I woke early and would lie rigid in bed, straining to hear Vera get up and make her first foray to the bathroom. This occured at a quarter to seven on the dot, when her morning routine began. Vera was a creature of habit, I quickly learned, long adhered-to habits no doubt, and the thought of disturbing these filled me with horror. It was bad enough we had landed on her, intruded so forcefully upon her life, her daily routine, despite all her continuing protestations to the contrary. 'You must do exactly as you please, Shelley,' she had said to me that first day. 'You are to treat this house as your own home, and follow your own rules and regulations. I know we're all a little crowded, but with a bit of give and take I'm sure we'll figure it all out eventually,' she had said, her face taut with forced brightness.

So I would wait until I heard her come out, go back into her bedroom and get dressed (no lounging about in dressing gowns in this house), and when I heard her make her way downstairs I would hurl myself into the bathroom and have a half-hearted attempt at a tepid shower, holding the tele-phone shower head in various strategic positions. (Oh, how I yearned for my power shower, or even showering at my erstwhile gym – the glorious luxuries I had taken for granted. My friend Sal had very kindly said I could use her shower(s) any time I wanted, but there's only so much you can ask of friends, and she was a good one, my only true one, perhaps.) Then I would pull on a pair of jeans and a jumper and begin the herculean task of getting the kids up. The girls were first in line. 'C'mon, get up,' I would hiss, pulling curtains and duvets back, 'quickly, quickly, hurry!'

Emma got it. She would oblige – slowly, mind you, but at least she moved. Not only that, but she went on to rouse Mac, which involved a trip up the trapdoor ladder, some-thing I couldn't even contemplate, not at that hour anyway.

Olivia was another matter. She would curl into the foetal position, eyes squeezed shut and hold on to her duvet with the strength of an arm wrestler. Once she even told me to 'fuck *off*, Mum' through gritted teeth and I almost slapped her.

'Don't you dare use that kind of language,' I snapped. 'You're in your grandmother's house now.'

To which she replied, 'Don't we all fucking know it,' and shot me a look of such loathing I almost recoiled. This time Emma did slap her, and punched her in the arm as well.

'Emma!' I protested, but secretly I was glad. I was turning into a witch.

'Bitch!' hissed Olivia, scrambling to clutch at Emma's hair. But it had worked. She was up.

Then we would troop down to the kitchen for breakfast. Vera would always be taking a last sip from her cup of tea and look up with the same expression of mild surprise, and say, 'Gosh is it that time already? I really must be dashing. There's fresh coffee in the pot, Shelley. Have a good day at school, dears.' And she would gather up her handbag and coat and exit, quietly closing the front door firmly behind her. The collective sigh of relief we breathed was indecent, followed by a gut-wrenching twinge of guilt – on my part, at any rate. Here we were, counting the seconds till she was out the door, and every morning she would leave a fresh cafetiere of coffee for us before she went. Of course it was undrinkable, but how you like your coffee is a very personal thing, isn't it? So I would remake it, but the effort inherent in Vera's gesture made me want to cry. Speaking of which, I was doing rather a lot of that lately. I would have to pull myself together.

It was the small things at first.

The bathroom arrangement, obviously. Emma was talking about drawing up a timetable and pinning it on the door, and Vera thought this was a teriffic idea, but listening to them both, and thinking of my beautiful bathrooms in our old house, I just wanted to bawl.

Watching Mac flee up to his hideaway in the attic the minute he came home from school as if he were being pursued by terrorists, instead of dragging his overladen backpack into the kitchen, sprawling at the table and regailing me with every detail of his 'skanky' school day. Now it was Emma who followed him up the trapdoor ladder with a mug of hot chocolate and a muffin she had brought home from school for him. He didn't seem to want to talk to me.

Not being able to relax, even for a second, was making me want to scream *and* cry. Well you can't, can you, in someone else's house? There was the moment of blessed relief when Vera would leave for her charity shop three days a week, but that was almost immediately replaced with anxiety as to how to avoid her later on in the day. How I had taken for granted the bliss of being boss of my own roadshow. I really couldn't take it in, just how much your life can change in a split second.

And not being able to drink. I could have, I suppose, but it didn't feel right somehow. I couldn't quite work up the courage to breeze in from the shops and open a bottle of wine and say to Vera, 'What about it, old girl? You an' me setting the world to rights, sod the dinner, we'll just order a takeaway.' Come to think of it, I never *had* seen Vera take a drink – perhaps she never had. I would imagine she would disapprove of it. Although there was a drinks cabinet in the front room. I had examined its contents thoroughly one day, down on my hands and knees, and it held a bottle of Harvey's Bristol Cream, a half-empty and very sticky-topped bottle of Creme de Menthe, some rather flat-looking tonic and a bottle of Gordon's. I backed off quickly, before I was tempted to pour myself a large one.

Then there was dinner, which was a nightmare all on its own. So far, Vera and I split the cooking, although I would gladly have taken it on on my own. After all, it wasn't as if I had anything else to do apart from get the kids to and from school.

'I'll do Monday, Wednesday and Friday and you can do Tuesdays, Thursdays and Saturdays, hmm?' she suggested briskly the first week. 'What about that, Shelley? We have to get a routine going. It'll be fun, a surprise every evening.'

'Of course.' I smiled my best rallying stiff upper-lipper.

'And we'll have to work out the grocery shopping too. Perhaps you could make a weekly list of everything you need and I'll do the same and we'll come to some sort of arrangement. No use in us both of us trawling through the supermarket.'

'No,' I murmured, 'none at all.' I wondered wildly if I would ever be able to grocery shop online again, or would that be considered a selfish and slovenly habit? Not that there was broadband in this house, never mind wifi, although the kids still clutched their laptops as if they were life rafts. I know because I had asked, without a lot of hope, but it was worth a try. Vera could have been a mad internet hacker for all I knew.

'Don't you mean hifi?' Vera tilted her head to one side. 'Arthur had a very good system installed in the sitting room, although I must say I rarely use it. I'm more of a radio person myself, but the sound quality is very good.'

I watched Emma stifle a grin and decided to leave the computer conversation for another day. One technological innovation at a time.

Vera did dinner first, as it happened, it being Monday. I had bottled completely at the thought of even trying to begin to explain to her the never-ending saga of what my lot would and wouldn't eat – and that wasn't even counting Olivia's varying whims/diets/allergies. In the end, I just said nothing and prayed they wouldn't show me up, or worse, make a scene.

At six-thirty sharp, we were summoned to the tiny dining room, where the table had been set with crisp, freshly starched white linen napkins beside each place. 'Well, go on, sit down!' Vera's face poked through the serving hatch in the wall, making the kids jump. 'Shelley, I've carved and dished up in here, would you give me a hand to bring the plates in?'

'Of course,' I said, jumping to attention. In the kitchen, on the counter, expertly carved, sat the pickings of a plump, perfectly moist chicken with all the trimmings: crispy bacon, chipolatas, mountains of stuffing and roast poatoes. For veggies there were creamed parsnip and turnip and tiny, lusciously glistening petis pois. Suddenly I was faint with hunger. 'This looks wonderful, Vera, you shouldn't have gone to so much trouble.'

'Nonsense. Since when was sticking a bird in an oven trouble? And everyone likes chicken, don't they?' she asked hopefully as we trooped into the dining room laden with dishes.

'Everyone loves it,' I said firmly and shot a laser-like look of warning around the table, particularly in Olivia's direction, just daring her to even think of being on one of her vegan trips. She ignored me, of course, but I saw her nostrils twitch, which boded well.

So far, so good, even though Mac, bless him, went bright

red with fright when Vera asked him briskly if he prefered breast or leg. 'Um, I dunno, thanks,' he mumbled, studying his plate intently.

'What about a bit of both, then?' said Vera, totally ignoring any implied insinuation as Olivia leaned in to him and said, 'Closest you're ever going to get to the real thing, muppet.' And poor Mac went even redder. Olivia really could be vile sometimes, and then, without any help from anyone, she tripped herself up perfectly by tucking in to her dinner.

'Ahem.' It was Vera. Around the table, cutlery froze midair, although Oivia was already munching. 'Aren't we forgetting something?'

'What?' chorused my heathen children, collectively dropping me in it.

'I'm so sorry,' I blurted, 'it's just that it's been such a long time, and—'

'Never mind,' Vera said kindly. 'I know it's considered old-fashioned, but we always said grace around this table and I think it's a nice tradition to continue. It's only giving thanks, nothing wrong with that, is there?' I felt my cheeks flame and my children's eyes widen. 'So if you don't mind,' continued Vera, 'I'll just go ahead.'

We all bowed our heads and listened to the words I couldn't remember last hearing, and then everyone mumbled 'Amen.' Vera smiled approvingly and even more broadly when Mac added a spontaneous, 'and God bless the cook!', making Emma and even Olivia giggle. There was very little said at all for a while, as we all tucked in to a proper, home-cooked family meal, and tried desperately not to think about the one family member who really, *really* should have been there.

'This is really nice,' Mac said after a while, mid mouthful, sounding mildly surprised, and I wondered if Vera appreciated the understatement.

'Don't talk with your mouth full, Mac, how many times

do I have to tell you?' I was uncharacaristically sharp and he looked wounded.

'Thank you, Mac,' said Vera. 'I'm glad you like it. Although it's not altogether a surprise. Roast chicken was your father's favorite at your age, and remained an enduring one, as I'm sure your mum knows all too well.' She smiled in my direction, seemingly oblivious to the weight of silence that suddenly descended. Olivia scowled, Emma chewed her lip and I felt the familiar threat of simultaneous tears and rage.

But Vera went on, undeterred. 'We *can* talk about him, you know. In fact, we should. It's not as if he's dead, is he?' Her eyes swept the table and were unmet. I felt sick.

And then Mac piped up again. 'What was he like, my dad, when he was, like, my age, you know?' The look of hopeful eagerness that flooded his face tore my heart.

Vera paused, considering his question with deliberate weight, and then looked straight at him. 'He was an awful lot like you, Mac, now that I see you up close. In fact, you're the spitting image of him,' she grinned. And for the second time that evening, Mac went bright red. But this time it was with sheer delight.

Did I say mornings were the worst? I lied. Night-time was the real beast. Vera would retire early, at about half nine. Olivia and Mac retreated to their respective lairs almost immediately after dinner, Emma would study in the kitchen and I would eke out the time sitting in front of the the TV until about ten o'clock, when I would give in and go to bed. I would trundle up the ladder to say goodnight to Mac. Despite his air of studied indiference, I knew he still enjoyed our night-time cuddles. 'Get *off*, Mum!' he would growl when I kissed him and hugged him far too tightly. I would pick up his discarded clothes and set out fresh ones for the morning.

'Mum?' he said now, and I stiffened, mid-clothes trawl.

'Mm-hmm?'

'Have you heard anything from Dad?'

I couldn't lie to him – I had done enough of that to myself. 'No, darling, there's no news, I'm afraid.'

'Do you think he's really alive, or was Granny just saying that? Because if he was, he'd contact us – wouldn't he?'

'Oh, Mac, darling, of course Daddy's still alive,' I sought to reassure him. 'It's just really difficult for him right now. He'll be in touch any day soon, I'm sure of it.'

'But how do you know?' he persisted. 'How do you know he's alive?'

'I just do, honey. You have to trust me on this – I promise you, Daddy's alive.'

'Honest Injun?' It was our code of honour.

'Honest Injun.'

'Okay,' he said, his voice sounding a shade more robust. 'If you promise, I believe you.'

'Go to sleep, baby.'

As I made my way down that damn trapdoor ladder, I wondered if it was true – if I was right – because I really and truly knew nothing for sure anymore. Was Charlie still alive? I assumed he was – I had heard nothing to the contrary and there had been rumoured sightings. But one thing was for sure – if he was, then I wanted to kill him for what he was doing to his kids. I didn't care about me and him any more – 'us' – I mean, what was that anyway? Some dim and distant other lifetime. Death would have been easier – there would be closure, sympathy even. But this, this hideous whirlwind of disasters he had put in motion, had taken everything we knew and devoured it – even my memories, such as they were, could no longer be put in any kind of sentimental context. They seemed as false now as the man I had loved and lived with – the man I thought I knew.

But there was still a sliver of relief, however bereft, in finally closing the bedroom door on the day, and on any further interaction with anyone. But it was only for a few moments, those mechanical moments when I would wash my face, brush my teeth (there was a basin and wash stand in the room), pull on a nightdress and fall into bed, lying there numbly while my brain made a few unsuccessful attempts at computing the situation. I suposed Vera had meant well, putting me in Charlie's old room – plus there weren't a lot of options bedroom wise in the house – but the irony was rather more than I could manage. I would lie there, my eyes roving around the walls, the floor, the ceiling, taking in the Man United posters, the stacks of car magazines, the mororbike annuals, even the prized collection of model cars sitting on the shelves. It was a boy's room, a room that Charlie had left for his first flat at twenty or twenty-one, if I remembered correctly, and the room looked as if it had been preserved as it was on the day he left.

'I never got around to clearing it all out,' Vera had said to me, settling us in that first day. At the time I had been too shell shocked to take it in, let alone comment. 'Of course, I'll get all this stuff put away, Shelley, and you can arrange the room however you wish.'

That had been six weeks ago. Only now did the room strike me as rather macabre. Charlie was forty-eight years old, wherever he was, gone from this house for almost thirty years, yet his room looked ready for his younger self's imminent return.

How could I make this room my own? The very thought was slightly ludicrous, and worse, it implied time – that I – we – would be here for how long? The only way I could cope, could endure it, was to somehow pretend it was all temporary, just a minor upheaval that we would all laugh about in a few months, when we were in our own home again, wherever that might be. I had to believe that, however unlikely it was. Otherwise I would go out of my mind.

So I gritted my teeth and repeated the mantra I had adopted every night. *Soon this will be over. Soon we will be in a house of our own again. Soon Charlie will be back and explain this has all been some terrible mistake and he'll make everything better.* In the meantime, I would have to be strong. I could do this, put a good face on for my children, be an appreciative daughter-in-law to Vera. I would ignore the terryfying abyss that Charlie had left me gazing into as best I could and try to pretend, as I lay in his old bed that was neither a single nor a proper double, that I didn't yearn for him, that I wouldn't give everything in the world to feel his arms around me one more time. But even there I failed miserably. Because the ache of his absence was a physical presence all its own.

Emma

'Tell me again about the bathroom!' Sophie demanded, hugging her knees as she sat and I reclined on the vast space that was her kingsize bed, in her equally kingsize bedroom.

I used to have one of those, I mused, folding my arms behind my head on softest duck down pillows. Funny how you noticed these little details when they were suddenly wrenched from you.

'Go on,' she urged, her eyes alight with anticipation, like a small child wanting a favorite story.

'Well,' I began. 'It's a sort of prosthetic pink.'

'Eeeuuuw,' she squealed obligingly. 'Must have been fashionable back in the day.'

'And the tiles are kind of square and all the same.'

'No design?'

'Uh-uh'.

'Mosaic?'

'Get real. And there's lino on the floor – pink and black diamond pattern.'

'Lino's cool, it's making a comeback, I think.'

I shook my head. 'Not this one.'

'Shower?'

'Not so's you'd know it. There's a kind of telephone shower attatchment on the bath that you can lift off its hinges, but it's really weak and sprays all over the place, and a plastic shower curtain with . . .' I screwed my eyes up to visualise the exact pattern, 'fish swimming through weeds under water.'

'It sounds really retro,' she offered uncertainly.

'No, not retro. Definately not retro. And there's a basin, with a dodgy mirror and a kind of built-in cabinet around it.'

'Is that good?' she asked hopefully.

'Nope. Mum has one in her room, though – so has Gran.'

'A mirror?' Sophie looked worried now.

'No, a basin thingy – apparently they were all the rage in the fifties and sixties so people could wash their teeth and stuff if someone else was in the *only* bathroom in the house.' I emphasised the *only*.

'And no loo – in the bathroom, I mean?' She wanted further confirmation.

'No. There's a separate loo, next door.'

She shook her head in wonderment. 'I mean, why?'

'So if someone's hogging the *only* bathroom in the house having a bath or whatever, it means someone else can still get into the only *loo* in the bloody house.'

Sophie was digesting this. 'I suppose it makes sense,' she ventured. 'If there's only one. Are you sure?'

'Oh yes.'

I watched her do the maths. 'What happens if, you know, if someone *else* wants to use the loo too?'

'Ah.' I played my pièce de résistance. 'Then you go outside.'

'What?' She looked aghast. 'Now you're winding me up.'

'Not a bit.'

'But that's barbaric. That's, like, against the laws of hygiene, surely?'

'Not exactly,' I explained. 'There's an outside loo – for the gardener, or workmen, next to the shed.'

'Outside,' she repeated.

'Outside. As Mac discovered the other morning,' I grinned, remembering the incident. 'Olivia was in the loo and Mac needed to use it. He was just about to leave for school and he was going mental, bursting for a pee.'

'What did he do?'

'Gran shouted to him to go outside – meaning to use the outdoor one, or the gardener's loo, as she calls it. But poor Mac didn't know about it – he just thought she meant him to go outside – so he did, and weed in the rose bushes. Mum saw him out the window and roared at him and then Gran saw him and realised and tried to explain to Mum it wasn't his fault. They've both been too embarassed to refer to it since.'

'Poor Mac.' Sophie shook her head.

'It's not so bad,' I grinned. 'You just have to work out a routine, a sort of timetable. I go at school most of the time – it's easier.'

Her eyes widened. 'Jeez, that sucks. You can go here any time, you know.'

'Thanks.' I looked at her ensuite wistfuly. 'But I doubt I'd make it in time.'

'If you ever want to, you know, have a proper shower or get ready for anything.'

'Thanks, Soph, I might take you up on that occasionally.'

I told her lots of other stuff too. In fact, I was becoming quite the class clown, a celebrity of sorts. I was dining out on my surreal exepriences.

Other girls had had to 'cut back' a bit, and sure, everyone's family was feeling the effects of the credit crunch – some weren't even going skiing this year – but no one seemed to have had their life turned upside down like ours had been.

Having to share a room with an odious older sister when we had always had our own bedrooms was a particular brand of hell. The other stuff I could manage, but sharing with Olivia was awful – I wasn't sure how much more I could take. But my accounts kept people entranced. Having to live together in a kind of regimented commune, in such close proximity. Having inherited a grandmother I only barely knew about. Those were the stories, the little accounts of our days

I kept the girls in stitches about. I had to make it funny, and in a mad sort of way it was. I had to laugh, because otherwise . . . well, I just had to laugh.

That was what I told Sophie anyway.

What I didn't tell her was about the other stuff.

I didn't tell her that I could hear Mum crying herself to sleep some nights. It's not that I was listening or anything, but I had a headache one night and I was going to ask her for some asprin or something, and just before I was about to open her door I heard the muffled sobbing. My hand froze on the door handle. I didn't know what to do so I just went back to bed. It was really weird. I couldn't get to sleep that night.

I didn't tell her either that Mum had stopped wearing make-up – not that she ever used to wear that much, but now she didn't even bother with mascara. And I didn't tell her that her size twelve jeans were hanging off her, even though she was eating as much as we all were. I know, because we sat down to dinner every evening – and I was putting on weight.

And I certainly didn't tell her about the day Mum had gone to meet her friend Sally for lunch – and had come back completely pissed. I wasn't going to tell anyone *anything* about that, not even Sophie, because that had really scared me.

Jackie had given me a lift back from school because Sophie had a drama lesson and they were going in my direction. That's what Jackie said, but really I knew she just wanted to snoop, to see exactly where we were living now. I know that sounds mean, but it's true. Anyway, I was home earlier than usual and the house was empty – which was cool. I was upstairs, dumping my stuff, when I heard Mum come in – or should I say *fall* in – the door.

'Hell-ooo-oh?' She called loudly (too loudly) before she slammed the door. 'Anyone ash home?'

I hurtled downstairs.

'Em,' she smiled, swaying on her feet. 'I've jusht had lunch with Sal, a really lovely, lovely lunch.' She threw her bag on the hall table, scattering a small china figurine. Horrible visions of that movie *Misery* immediately sprang into my mind, and Gran bursting through the door demading to know, *'Where's my little penguin that always faced due south?'*

'Mum!' I hissed. 'You're completely pissed.'

'I know,' she beamed. 'It was jush like ol' times. Haven't had a good lunch sinch . . . can't remember when.' She tried to take off her coat but seemed to be getting tangled up in it.

I wrenched it from her. 'You can't do this, Mum,' I was gibbering. 'Gran will be home any minute – you can't let her see you like this.' I propelled her into the kitchen and pushed her down on a chair. 'You'll have to drink some coffee and sober up.' Wasn't that what they always said – drink coffee?

'Don' want any coffee – yuck. Want another glass of bubbly, hic.'

The kettle was finally hissing to a boil and I'd poured a ton of instant coffee into a mug when the front door opened again and Gran came in.

'Somebody left their key in the door,' she called out reprovingly before coming in to the kitchen armed with Tesco bags.

'Ooops,' said Mum guiltily.

I saw Gran look at her strangely.

'Mum's not feeling well, are you, Mum?' I said quickly, going to help unpack the bags.

'I'm nosh?'

'No.' I was firm. 'Food poisoning – she ate something off at lunch.'

'S'right. Not well, got a bish of a headache coming on.' Mum smiled weakly.

'You poor thing!' Gran exclaimed. 'You are looking a bit peaky, Shelley, now that you mention it. Em,' she said, 'I think you should help your mother up to her room – have a bit of lie down, hmm?'

'Good idea,' I agreed, grabbing Mum by the arm and hauling her out of the chair.

'All right?' Gran followed at a respectful three paces, waiting to see if we made it up the stairs. She looked worried.

'Fine,' I smiled encouragingly. And it was – until the door opened for the third time and Olivia materialised, complete with two Brown Thomas shopping bags, I noticed.

'What's the matter?' she demanded, her accusatory glance sweeping us all in.

'Your mother's not feeling well. She's going up for a little rest,' explained Gran, looking at Olivia's bags with interest.

'Hi Liv!' Mum peered down from the third stair. 'Oooh, Brown Thomas, what'd you buy?' There was a pause, and then, 'But we haven't any money . . . hic.' She giggled.

'You're pissed.' Olivia was outraged. 'She's completely pissed!' She repeated disbelievingly to nobody in particular.

'No, no' Gran said. 'It's a nasty bout of food poisoning, very unpleasant.'

'Migrane,' offered Mum, leaning over the bannisters not at all helpfully. 'S'eadache, thumping.'

Olivia's face darkened. 'You've never had a migraine in your life. It's disgusting, that's what it is.'

That was it. Pushing Mum upstairs with one hand, I leaned back to face my obnoxious sister. 'Sometimes, Olivia – in fact, make that *most* of the time – you're one thundering bitch.'

I thought I might have been imagining it, but I'm pretty sure I didn't. I'm almost certain I saw Gran put a hand to her face and turn away – but not before she had time to hide what was plainly a very definite grin.

Later that night, at about eight o'clock, Gran handed me a bowl of soup and a small glass of something dark that looked like wine. 'For your mum,' she said. 'Why don't you take it up to her, Emma, she might be hungry now – and port and brandy is marvellous for settling the tummy.'

I didn't think that Mum would look at food, but I brought it up anyway, knocking gently on the door before I went in.

'Oh, Em,' she said, sitting up in bed. In the light of the bedside lamp she looked pale and sort of blotchy. 'I'm so sorry,' she whispered. 'I never thought.'

'Gran sent this up. It's some soup and port and brandy, she said it's really good for an upset tummy.' I handed the bowl to her and put the glass down on the bedside table. 'If you don't want them, I'll bring them back down.'

'No,' she said, sounding more like her old self. 'Actually, I'm quite hungry, and Gran's right – port and brandy is just the ticket for a dodgy tum.' She smiled at me and downed it in two gulps. Then she demolished the slice of baguette and hoovered down the soup. 'Mmm, I feel much better now. A good night's sleep and I'll be grand.'

'Are you sure?' I was doubtful. 'That you're okay, Mum?'

'I'm fine, Em, really. Just went a bit overboard at lunch. It was silly of me. Do tell Gran I'm feeling much better now, and thank her for sending this up.' She handed me the bowl and glass to take back down.

'Okay. Night, Mum.' I kissed her and headed back downstairs.

'Well?' asked Gran when I went to the dishwasher.

'She said she's feeling much better, and to say thank you for the soup and port thingy.'

'I'm very glad to hear that. Upset tummy's a horrible thing. The port and brandy never fails. She'll be right as rain in the morning.'

'That's what she said.' I straightened up, but I was still doubtful.

'Of course she will,' said Gran. Your mother's had an awful lot on her plate lately – as you all have.' She looked at me keenly. 'I'm not surprised she's feeling a little bit under the weather, not at all surprised.' She began to put the breakfast things out for the morning and smiled at me. 'Now if you've any sense, you'll get off to bed soon yourself – don't stay up too late studying.'

I would have gone to bed a lot earlier every evening if it didn't mean sharing excrutiating space with Olivia, who, I had almost forgotten, I had to quiz about the Brown Thomas bags – where had she got the cash to shop in *there*? Maybe she'd taken to shoplifting, the thought gleefully crossed my mind. Either way, I felt a little bit better about things. Gran didn't seem to be shocked or even put out about Mum's lunch episode, although I'm pretty sure she could tell Mum was pissed – but then again, maybe not. Old people probabaly hadn't a clue how much everybody drank nowadays.

All the same, I was still scared and I didn't exactly know why. I mean, everything bad that could possibly happen already had – hadn't it? It was just that I had this creepy feeling that we were somehow falling apart. Us. Our family. We needed something to happen to bring us back together. So I did something I hadn't done since this nightmare had begun – because since Dad had gone, I decided I really hated God.

I said a prayer. Just a tiny one, not even a prayer, more a sort of desperate, silent, angry yelp. *Look,* I said, *for God's sake – if you're up there, do something to keep us together. It's bad enough we can't have Dad right now, but don't let us fall apart as a family, not now, when we need each other more than ever – and more importantly, when Dad needs us all to pull together, wherever he is.*

It struck me even then as sounding particularly pathetic, like something you'd hear on *The Waltons* or maybe *Little House on the Prairie*, although right now I wouldn't have minded being a part of either of those families, however pathetic they were considered these days. At least they had dads – at least they actually talked to one another and worried about each other. And no matter what happened, either a mum or a dad or an old person always sorted everything out. I could hack that.

But all the same, that prayer must have worked, although it didn't seem like it at the time. Something happened very soon that did exactly what I had asked for.

Vera

'They think I'm stupid.' I was talking to myself again, muttering as I added some new clothes to an already crowded rail. I was referring to young people in general, but if I was honest, it was the young people I was sharing my house with in particular.

'Who's stupid?' It was Roger, the twig, dressed today in a chameleon-like brown jumper and cords. He blended so artfully into the walls that he made me jump when he spoke. I had only been thinking to myself (or had I actually spoken?), but that was the trouble with young people – their hearing was so accute, they could practically hear your thoughts. In fact, knowing Roger, he could probably lip read.

'Never mind,' I said crisply, 'not you anyway.'

'I should think not,' he replied indignantly, manouvering a pair of Lycra shorts onto the rail, which were equally smartly taken off by a rather effete-looking young man. Roger looked after him speculatively. 'I think he fancies me,' he said.

'Whatever gives you that idea?' I was surprised, shocked, even. 'You're not that way inclined, are you?' Normally I wouldn't ask such personal qustions, but lately I found I was coming out with the most extraordinary comments, not to mention observations. It was unnerving me. Clearly I had unnerved Roger.

'Of course I'm not,' he said huffily. 'But that's the third time he's been in this week. Not that I've anything agaist them,' he added quickly, 'but anyone can see I'm a red-blooded heterosexual.' He rattled a few hangers to illustrate his strength of feeling on the subject.

Personally, I wasn't so sure – not that he was gay, but that people would be so sure he wasn't. It wasn't as if there was anything terribly masculine about Roger – not that that meant anything, I knew. Why, some of the most delicate men I knew over the years turned out to be the most prolific womaniers, but back in those days nobody thought about being anything other than thoroughly nondescript and normal. Neither I nor any of my women friends would even have *considered* anyone being homosexual – it simply didn't enter our heads. I'm not even sure when I found out exactly what the word meant.

To distract myself I decided to unpack a few black bags and sort through even more piles of clothes, and then after that I needed a cup of tea. I hadn't had a break all afternoon, and although it was almost time for me to knock off, I wandered into the kitchen, where as luck would have it, Tom had just brewed up. He was looking as dapper as ever today in what I would bet was a bespoke charcoal grey chalk stripe suit, complete with pale pink double-cuffed shirt and a perfectly chosen navy tie with rather jaunty pink foxes on it. At least, I think that's what they were. His still plentiful grey hair was swept neatly back from his brow. He really did look awfully well for his seventy-five years. Not for the first time did I wonder if, as Maura put it, he was a bit 'special', meaning, of course, gay. There I went again – I was obsessed with who was gay. Roger, and now Tom – I must be going mad. At that very moment Roger came in to join us, and looked, I thought, rather longer than he might have at Tom. 'Nice suit,' he commented, taking the words from my mouth.

'I was just about to say the very same thing,' I added.

'Thank you,' said Tom, beaming. 'I still think it's important to take the trouble. Just because we're getting on a bit doesn't mean you have to forego being a natty dresser – like you, Vera,' he said approvingly. 'You always look lovely. I like a lady who takes a bit of trouble with her appearance – after all, we're still on show, aren't we? Until they put us away in some awful home or other,' he shuddered.

Roger looked at us both as if we were mad.

'Tea?' Tom was pouring.

'Oh, I'd murder one,' I said, sinking into the more battered of the three chairs. I felt we were well matched. I felt old and rather beaten up at that moment, and I wasn't quite sure why.

'How's it going, Vera?' Roger enquired, munching through a flapjack. 'With the new family?'

'Remarkably well,' I said, lying through my teeth. 'Of course it's a big change for all of us, but we're adjusting – slowly.'

'Respect, man,' he nodded dutifully towards me, and although I had no idea what he was getting at, I felt it was meant commendably.

'Yes, Vera, what you're doing is a wonderful thing – we all think so.' Tom confirmed the general consensus. 'Families are supposed to stick together, especially in tough times. Blood is thicker than—'

'Yes, yes,' I snapped uncharacteristically. They both looked first shocked, then sheepish.

'I'm sorry,' I said, suddenly chastened. 'I didn't mean to snap, it's just that actually, it's proving quite a strain – for everybody.' There, I had said it, and a slow breath escaped with the relief of uttering the beginnings of truth.

'Bound to be,' said Tom, nodding sagely.

'Must be weird.' Roger dunked his flapjack assiduously, regarding me with renewed interest. 'You've all lost your space, man.'

'I feel as if – as if – they all think I'm stupid.' I took a gulp of tea, and then, once I'd started, there was no stopping. 'What is it about young people, even adult younger people,' I asked, listening to the note of escalating despair in my own voice, 'that they think we don't *know* anything? We've lived longer than than they have – our generation was arguably just as permissive as theirs.' (Not that I got a chance to engage in that sort of thing before marriage, but the sixties were definitive.)

'Absloutely!' Tom agreed heartily.

'But they think we know nothing, see nothing and understand less.' I paused, to inhale deeply. 'Just because we're old.'

'The arrogance of youth,' mused Tom. 'I suppose we were like that too, once. I know I thought I was going to take the world by storm,' he grinned.

'And did you?' Roger asked.

'In a small way,' Tom said intriguingly. 'In my own small way, which is all that matters, of course.'

I thought about last week, and Shelley coming home from lunch clearly six sheets to the wind, and how my heart went out to her – and even more to poor Emma, so valiantly trying to cover up for her mother. That girl was a gem, a real brick. Not that the others weren't wonderful, of course they were, but there was just something special about Emma, and I had the feeling she was taking on far too much for her fifteen years. Some people are like that from the start, always taking on too much, but I didn't want her to be one of them.

Her sister Olivia, on the other hand, was in no such danger. She was the difficult one. Spoiled and conceited and clearly finding her new surroundings a real come down. She wasn't working or studying either, which was a worry, and I didn't feel it was my business to enquire as to why not. Not at the moment, anyway. They had all been through so much. There had been references to modelling and trying to break into TV presenting, but so far there didn't seem to be any sign of any gainful employment. She seemed to spend all day in her room, except when she went out (God knows where) and returned with the inevitable shopping bags.

And Shelley . . . I was worried about her, truly worried.

She was being terribly brave and pulling her weight more than was necessary in the house, but I knew how difficult it must be for her. Well, that wasn't strictly true. I didn't *know*, could only imagine what it must be like to lose your husband, your home, your life as you knew it. And yet, in my own way, I had done all of those things, just in different circumstances. It was so long ago now, but it had been the same conflicts, the same gut-wrenching emotional turmoil. But that was then, and each person's situation was entirely, well, personal. But still, I could empathise with her. I just didn't think it was appropriate to instigate a discussion. It didn't seem fair. I guessed that I'd be the last person on earth she'd want to talk to, to open up to about it. After all, I was Charlie's mother – albeit an estranged one. It would be a bit like fraternising with the enemy. Bad enough she had to live with it.

I listened mindlessly to Tom and Roger chatting about their favourite soap operas and crime dramas and finished my tea.

'The body language one, have you seen it? Brilliant!' proclaimed Roger. 'There's nothing I can't tell now about a person's body language.'

'Or psychological profile,' agreed Tom, '*Criminal Minds* is superb!'

'Speaking of which,' observed Roger, 'you're looking a bit twitchy, Vera.'

'That's because if I don't get a move on, I'll miss my Dart,' I said, making a move to get my coat and bag. 'See you on Wednesday, all.'

'Bye, Vera, take it easy, old girl.' Tom smiled and waved an admonishing finger at me.

'Something tells me you've got a few interesting stories stashed away yourself, Vera.' It was Roger, looking speculatively at me over the rim of his cup. 'You never tell us anything about your life, and I for one would love to hear. Your body language is very guarded, you know,' he grinned.

'Is that a fact?' I replied lightly. 'In my day it was called ladylike.' I shot him a reproving look.

'You don't deceive me for a minute, Vera. I bet you were a real humdinger in your day, you're too good-looking not to have been – but your secrets are safe with us. Don't you think so, Tom?' he continued infuriatingly, but Tom just smiled. He was on my side.

'Dream on.' I resorted to one of Emma's favourite put downs, and they laughed. But underneath I was rattled. Roger had no idea just how close to the truth he'd come.

I made the Dún Laoghaire station just in time. As I descended the steps, the train pulled in. It was dusk now, but still before the after-work crowd would pour out, and the train was relatively empty. As we trundled along, I looked out at the varying degrees of grey – sky, land and sea – and the flickerings of first lights coming on across the bay. It struck me how little had changed, in many respects. I remembered the same view as a girl, the same landscape – trips to seaside towns, visits to relatives and neighbours, the excitement of a summer's day brimming with promise and the darker, electric thrill of Christmas shopping, all taken on the same route – in, out, in, out – all those years, and what was it all about? What were we supposed to learn? To keep with us?

I roused myself from my musings just in time not to miss my stop. It was barely a five-minute walk from the station to my house. That at least was a bonus for the new inhabitants, especially Mac, who could now get the Dart to school, which apparently increased his street cred no end, or so Emma informed me. Emma got the bus and usually a lift home with one of her friend's mothers. Olivia, well, I knew as much about Olivia's chosen mode of transport as I did anything else about her. The cars – hers and Shelley's, and of course earlier Charlie's – had been repossessed, rather unceremoniously, I gathered. It wasn't a subject that was raised for discussion very often.

Shelley, of course, had the use of my Nissan Micra if she needed it – I used it so rarely – but I was damned if I was putting it at Olivia's disposal, never mind put her on my insurance. It was high time that girl came down to earth a bit.

I was just turning in my driveway when I noticed a figure almost huddled in the porch. For a moment I stopped in my tracks, afraid it was another reporter; I had had my fair share since this awful business began. But catching sight of me, the figure straightened up and called out my name.

'Mrs Fitzgibbon!' she called. The voice sounded vaguely familiar, but it wasn't until I was almost beside her that I realised it was Caroline. And no wonder – I would hardly have recognised her. Not that I saw her often; why, it must have been close on five years since I'd seen her. She and Charlie worked together a lot, apparently – she was a real go-getter, a whizz kid like him. He was always quoted as saying she had the most astute business mind he had ever come across, and that was saying something. Charlie didn't bestow praise lightly – or at least that was what I used to read in the papers.

'Caroline?' I took in the pale face and darkly shadowed eyes along with their guraded expression, although she seemed relieved to see me. Very relieved.

'Mrs Fitzgibbon—'

'Vera, please,' I tutted. 'Honestly, Caroline!' I reproved her, simultaneously proffering my cheek and a one-handed hug while searching for my hall door key with my free hand.

'I'm so sorry for turning up like this, Vera,' she said, shivering in her oversized coat – or was it that she had lost that much weight? I certainly didn't remember her face looking that gaunt. But then, she must be affected badly by the current circumstances – we all were. 'But I just had to talk to someone. I'm going out of my mind.'

'Well, you've come to the right place,' I said briskly, although I shot her a worried look. 'Any news?' My heart paused.

'Nothing.' She shook her head as we went in to the narrow hallway in single file.

'You?'

'No, absolutely nothing.' I ushered her into the kitchen and put the kettle on as we took off our respective coats.

'What about Shelley? Surely . . .'

'No, nothing. It's terribly hard on her, on all of them.'

She put her head in her hands and took a deep breath. She seemed about to say something and then thought better of it.

'Coffee or tea?'

'Whatever you're having.'

'Tea, then. I'm afraid we're all out of sympathy.' I tried to make a little joke.

'How is Shelley? How's she . . . coping?' Caroline chewed her nail.

'As well as she can under the circumstances.' I brought the teapot over and poured. 'She's being strong for the children, of course.'

'Of course,' murmured Caroline and she gave a little involuntary shiver.

'Dear me, are you cold?' I got up to check the radiator. 'It's just that it takes a few more minutes to come on. No one's here much during the day and I've never felt the cold.' I smiled, sitting down again. 'She'll be sorry to miss you.'

'Who?' Caroline looked alarmed.

'Shelley, of course. She's gone over to her friend Sally's house for dinner – a girls' night, I think – and won't be back till much later. Isn't that who you wanted to talk to? I know you couldn't possibly have known about any of this business, but it might help Shelley to talk about it with someone who knew Charlie – worked with him.'

'No – no, I don't think so, Vera. Actually, it was you I was hoping to see.' She replaced her cup on its saucer carefully.

'I can't think why!' I said, rather surprised. 'Although when I saw it was you I was hoping *you* might have some news, any news. Are you sure?'

'I wish I had.'

'And you, Caroline, are things very bad for you?' I knew her job was gone, of course.

She shrugged. 'Could be worse. I still have my house. Not sure how long I'll manage the mortgage for. Oh, and I have my mother living with me now.'

'I thought your mother lived in her own place?'

'Used to. She sold it..'

'Oh, I see.' Again she seemed about to elaborate but didn't.

'I'm talking to people in London. There's a couple of interested companies – not much chance of anything in the financial sector here.'

'London!' I said with forced gaiety. 'Well that would be good, wouldn't it? I do love London, and you've worked there before, haven't you?'

'A long time ago.' Her voice was flat.

'And you've no children, so you're free to go, aren't you?' I added brightly, knowing the minute the words were out of my mouth that they were the wrong ones. What was the matter with me?

'No – no children.' She drained her tea.

'You'll have another cup?' I lifted the teapot but she declined.

'No thank you, Vera. I'd better be getting on.'

'But you said you wanted to see me – to talk about something?' I was confused. I hoped I hadn't offended her.

She smiled and shook her head, pulling on her coat, which was, as I had thought, way too big for her – and yes, she was certainly too thin, much too thin. 'I was just hoping you might have had some news.'

'I'm so sorry, Caroline. Really, if I do hear a thing, I'll let you know.'

'Would you?' She looked pathetically hopeful.

'Of course – it's the least I could do.' I hugged her briefly. I felt for her, I really did. She must worrry about Charlie. Sometimes I even wondered if she'd ever got over him. They were joined at the hip, that pair, together for five years. She had been his girlfriend, his only really steady girlfreind. I had been sure they would end up together, but that was before . . . well, before a lot of things. Before Shelley came along, anyway. I think Caroline had been very cut up about that, but of course I wasn't told anything, Charlie and I weren't speaking at the time. But you didn't have to be Einstein to know that Caroline had been mad about him – and he her. Funny how things worked out. I had always been fond of her, even before that awful incident. And she had been so nice about it, so kind and understanding. I was fond of her – of course I was. I wondered if she had ever met anyone else, but I didn't like to ask, even in my current tactless mode.

'Goodbye, dear, do drop in any time. I'm here most evenings.'

'Thank you, Vera, it was good to see you. Take care.' She made her way out the door and slap bang into a large man with an armful of flowers.' Roses. Red ones. Two dozen at a glance – and then it dawned on me. Valentine's Day had escaped me completely. I had clean forgotten about it.

'Sorry, ma'am' the chap said, stepping back from Caroline, flustered at the collision. 'Shelley Fitzgibbon?' he asked hopefully.

'No. No,' she said brusquely and pushed by him – but not before I caught a look of the bleakest despair on her face.

Of course there was a card with the flowers. The chap handed them over to me and I signed for them with a trembling hand. He must have thought I was mad. As I laid them carefully on the hall table in their pristine cellophane and elegantly tied ribbon, it took every shred of self-control I posessed not to rip the small white envelope open. Instead, I just stared at it, and prayed.

When she came through the front door, Emma showed no such restraint.

'Omigod!' she said, stopping dead in her tracks and flinging down her schoolbag. 'They're for Mum, aren't they?' She looked wildly at me. 'Please say they're not for Olivia.' She went over to the table and stroked them wonderingly.

'No, I can safely say they are not for Olivia,' I smiled. 'They're for your mother, of course.'

'So that means they're from Dad, doesn't it?' Her excitement was palpable.

'Well,' I said carefully, it didn't do to take anything for granted, but I was hoping against hope. 'We must wait and see. They could be from anyone, after all.'

She threw me an 'as if' look and chewed her lip.

'Don't even think about it,' I said to her as she looked longingly at the card, running her finger along the sealed lip.

'Where is she?'

'At Sally's, I think.'

Emma whipped out her mobile and sent the fastest text message I've ever seen. Almost immediately, her phone rang.

'Mum,' she said breathlessly, 'you've got to get back here – yes, everything's fine, but there's a massive bouquet of roses here for you. Mum? What? Of course they're for you, you've got to come home *now*, Mum. Look, you tell her, Gran.' She thrust the phone into my hand.

'Shelley? Yes, dear, it's me. Emma's rather excited, but it's true, they arrived not ten minutes ago, two dozen red roses ... Are you there? What? Oh, right, see you shortly, and Shelley, do drive carefully.'

'Well?' Emma demanded.

'She's on her way.'

'Thank Christ for that!' She sank to the floor, where she sat, hugging her knees, back against the wall.

'Emma!'

'Sorry, Gran, but I'm not sure if I can stand the suspense.'

'I think I'll put the kettle on.' I went into the kitchen, feeling rather shaky myself.

It can't have been more than twenty minutes, but they were excrutiating ones before we heard the car door slam and Shelley's keys turning in the lock. Both Emma and I rushed into the hall.

Shelley was looking at the huge bouquet as if it might jump up and bite her. I didn't blame her. And what if they weren't from Charlie? But I banished that ridiculous thought from my head, although Shelley had every right to have any number of secret admirers. It was absolutely none of my business – but two dozen red roses?

'Go on, Mum,' Emma said through gritted teeth, 'open it, for God's sake! We're dying here!'

So she did. She took the envelope from the cellophane with shaking hands and tore it open. Then she slipped the card out and looked at it, then she bit her lip and tried to speak but couldn't. A sort of gulp came out instead.

'Shelley, dear?' I prompted her.

'Oh for God's sake!' Emma snatched it from her, but Shelley didn't seem to mind, it was as if she had gone into a sort of trance. 'It's from him!' Emma shrieked. 'It's from Dad – I knew it!' she said triumphantly, jumping up and down. 'Look, Gran!' she handed it to me.

I took it gingerly, hardly daring, or indeed liking, to read it. 'May I?' I asked Shelley, who nodded mutley, but she was smiling now.

To my darling Shel, it read. *Happy Valentine's Day, all my love, now and always, C.*

It didn't say a lot – it didn't have to. All that mattered was that the flowers were from Charlie. Our Charlie. Wherever he was. And suddenly we were all hugging and laughing and crying. And that's how Mac found us, huddled together when he came in, and said with a worried frown, 'What's going on?'

'Dad's just sent Valentine's Day flowers to Mum, that's all,' said Emma, infuriatingly dismissively – but she was grinning like a Chesire cat.

'How do you know?' Mac looked bewildered.

'Doh! Even you couldn't miss those!' Emma pointed at the masses of roses.

'Emma!' Shelley had come to her senses and put her arm around Mac. 'There's a card with the flowers, darling, from Daddy.'

'A card?' he repeated blankly, and then asked hopefully, 'Is there anything for me – a message?'

'Oh Mac, darling—'

'Don't be so stupid, you muppet!' Emma shook her head in mock disbelief. 'Even you must know Valentine's Day is for people you love – or fancy.'

Mac's face fell. 'I just thought, maybe if there was a card, he could have.'

'Hang on a sec,' Emma said, making suddenly for the door. 'We haven't checked the letterbox, have we?'

It was outside at the gate, an old-fashioned one but perfectly adequate. It had been a gift from an American client of Arthur's many years ago – a 'mailbox', he called it. Emma hurtled towards it now, yanked it open and rummaged inside, returning with a fistful of white envelopes. 'Look,' she shrieked, 'there's one for everyone – even you, Gran.'

And there was. I didn't recognise the writing, no one could – it was carefully crafted capitals and had been posted locally – but there was a card for everyone. Olivia, Emma, Mac and, as Emma pointed out, myself. All were signed from 'Guess Who?!' or 'A secret admirer'.

Mac was deflated. 'He didn't send us anything!' he wailed.

'Who else do you think they're from?' Emma gave him a shove. 'Of course they're from Dad!'

'Emma's right, Mac – they're from Dad,' Shelley said gently.

'Are you sure?'

'Positive.'

'Then why doesn't he just say so?' He looked mutinous – and then as if he might cry.

'It's what you're *supposed* to do, Mac,' Emma explained painstakingly. 'You're supposed to make people guess who the cards are from. Who else do you think would be sending *you* a Valentine's card?'

Mac shrugged, then grinned. 'Dunno.'

'Precisely.'

'We mustn't forget Olivia's,' said Shelley, placing the card with her name on the hall table. Just at that moment, she appeared – in our excitement we had left the hall door open. She stood there with one of her designer handbags and her arms full of flowers. For a moment I softened towards her. *How thoughtful for her to bring home flowers for her mother on Valentine's Day*, I thought – I had been too hard on her.

Clearly Emma thought the same thing, because she said, 'Dad got there before you, Liv – look what he sent Mum! There's a card for you too.' She pointed towards the table.

'What?' Olivia asked, looking at us as if we were dim.

'These flowers – they're from Dad. Isn't that wonderful?' Shelley was beaming.

'Oh? And that makes everything all right, does it?' she said scornfully.

It wasn't quite the reaction anyone was expecting. I tried to pacify her. 'Olivia, it's wonderful news, for all of us. And it's so nice of you to bring flowers too, isn't it, Shelley? I'd better go and polish up my vases. I do hope I'll have enough, that's an awful lot of flowers for one house!' I made for the kitchen.

'But they aren't for Mum, are they?' Emma had snatched the card from the rather ostentatious bouquet as quick as a flash and was reading it.

'Give me that back, you cow!'

But Emma was reading out loud now in a mock saccharine tone. 'To my darling Tiggypoo, my little—'

'Give it back, you stupid bitch!' Olivia snatched it from her.

'Olivia!' Shelley said.

'Sorry, Mum,' she mumbled, 'but you're not the only one who can get flowers sent to them, you know.' She looked defiantly at Emma, who was looking at her speculatively. 'And no, it's none of your business who they're from.' She stomped off upstairs, flowers and all.

'You're forgetting your card from Dad.' Emma said in a low, rather threatening tone, I thought.

'Give it here, then.' She held out her hand over the bannister and took the card from Emma.

'And you needn't think I'm going to share any space in our room with you and those – those *things*.' Emma regarded Olivia's flowers as if they were insects.

'Don't worry,' Olivia shot back. 'You won't have to – for long.'

I really didn't think any more about it – I don't think any of us did, we were just so excited to have had contact from Charlie. Shelley's face was a picture of happiness. Suddenly I wanted to celebrate. 'Well seeing as it's St Valentine's Day, what about getting a Chinese takeaway?' I asked, knowing how partial they all were to it. I'd never had one – and to date had declined their invitations to try one – but tonight I thought I'd give it a go.

'Great idea,' beamed Shelley.

'Brill,' said Mac.

'And we'll tell them to send along a bottle of champagne, too.' I made for the phone in the hall. 'Emma, would you get the number for me, please?'

'Cool,' said Emma, a wide grin beginning.

Much later – well, it felt much later, although it was only ten o'clock, but late enough by my standards – I looked at the Valentine's card sent to me, presumably from Charlie, and turned it over and over in my hands. He hadn't sent me one since he was a little boy. Arthur used to send them, of course, from the boys when they were very small. He was so thoughtful like that. Such a good husband. The postmark on the envelope was local, so unless Charlie was here (which was unlikely; there had been rumoured sightings in both Spain and South Africa), he must have had someone send them on his behalf – his solicitor, perhaps, or a friend? Who knows. But thank God he had made contact – not for my sake, of course, although I was glad, glad and thankful for it. No, it was Shelley and the children who needed to hear from him, to believe he hadn't left them entirely – whatever was going on. I sighed as I undressed, cleansed and washed my face and got into bed. I was suddenly dog tired. Must be all the excitement. Downstairs I could hear them still up, chattering and laughing. Everyone except Olivia, that is, who had preferred to stay in her room sulking – even the champagne and Chinese takeaway hadn't tempted her down. 'All the more for us, then,' Emma had proclaimed, tucking in. And I must admit, it had been tasty. I would even go so far as to say I might try it again – that chicken with ginger and spring onion. Of course I didn't have any champagne – it doesn't agree with me, I don't drink alcohol these days – but Shelley and Emma polished off the bottle between them, and Mac was allowed a glass too. All in all it had been a very jolly evening.

I was sleepy now and hardly able to read a word of my

current book. As I reached over to turn off the bedside light, I looked again at the photo of Arthur staring down at me from the chest of drawers where it held pride of place, and the card, standing beside it. 'Goodnight, Arthur dear,' I said, as I always did, and he smiled back at me. That card might have been signed by 'A Secret Admirer', and it might very well have been from Charlie – or indeed a well-intentioned friend. But I knew without a shadow of a doubt that Arthur had sent it to me – he had arranged it from wherever he was, looking down at me. He had always been a romantic. What was it he used to say on all his cards? *I love you to distraction, my darling Vera, yours for all eternity, Arthur, your loving husband.* And he *had* been a loving husband. I had kept them all, every single one of them, in my special drawer. This latest one would join them in good time. After all, what's a little bit of time and distance between souls who really love each other? And with that comforting thought in my mind, I drifted off to sleep.

Caroline

I bottled out – as usual. I so wanted to tell her, get the whole thing off my chest, open my heart – and then something made me stop. It was halfway through the first cup of tea, and I'm still not sure why. I knew she was pleased to see me, Vera and I had always got along well, even after the mind-blowingly awkward incident way back.

But she looked so worried beneath her immaculately groomed exterior, it sort of took the wind out my sails. I mean, what was it going to achieve, me telling Vera I had been having an on-again-off-again affair with her son? And maybe, just maybe, she already suspected as much.

Perhaps it was her various references to Emma and Mac, whom she clearly adored. Or her mentioning that Shelley was out with one of her girlfriends, and what good she hoped it would do her, her telling me how awful it had been for Shelley, this dreadful, awful abandonment. *Tell me about it*, I thought. It was nasty, I know, but that's how I felt. *Had* been feeling for longer than anyone could know. And I had no one to blame but myself.

I turned him down, you see. Charlie had asked *me* to marry him – begged me, even – and I had turned him down. That was how stupid I had been. How unbelievably stupid. Arrogant, too – naturally, I thought he would wait for me. Although back then, I wasn't sure if marriage under any circumstances was for me. I was a trailbalzer following some distant, beckoning star, happily ignoring the one that was there, right under my nose for the taking – the only one that would ever mean anything to me. I know that now, of course, but then . . .

'Marry me, Caro.' Charlie rolled on top of me again, taking me by surprise in more ways than one. We had just spent a wonderfuly lazy Sunday morning in bed, read the papers, had the croissants and coffee, made love, and now – this. He looked down at me, those mesmerising blue eyes scanning my face, his hand gently stroking my cheek. 'Will you, please?'

'Charlie,' I began, already seeing the retraction in his eyes. 'I love you, you know I do, but you know what my plans are. I'm doing Harvard, my Masters – I haven't even thought about marriage. I don't even know if marriage or children are what I want. I haven't even thought it through.'

'So think about it now.' He leaned his face on his hand, eyes boring into mine, but something else had entered his tone – rejection had hit home already, I could feel it.

'Can we please not do this now?' I was already adopting Americanisms. I wanted so badly to spread my wings, my talents, my ambitions. Marrying Charlie, however we would have done it, would have meant abandoning my Masters (he wouldn't have been able to postpone things once his mind was set on it), getting married to the man I adored, getting pregnant, giving up work and playing supportive wife to his rising star. I couldn't have done it. Not then. Not when I had my whole life in front of me, that glittering future that lay ahead. And Charlie knew that. He knew that if I got to the States and spread my wings, there was a very real chance I wouldn't come back to him. And I knew that he knew that. His proposal may have been genuine – I don't doubt that it was – but it was also calculated. Charlie didn't like things getting away from him. He liked to be the one saying where, when and how.

So I said no. I refused. I turned him down. And part of

him never forgave me. But worse, much worse, was the fact that I never forgave myself. That was what I had to live with – and it had come to be a very heavy burden.

Elsie

I did as he asked. I sent the flowers and the cards and I never said a word to anybody – not even to Larry. Especially not to Larry. He'd mean well, of course, but this nugget of news would have been been too much for him to keep to himself. And who could blame him? It would have made headlines – and for all the wrong reasons. To be honest, I was so relieved to hear from Charlie, I didn't really think beyond that. It meant that he was alive and well and thinking of his family. It was a start – however precarious – and one I wasn't going to jeopardise. Although I did buy a card for Vera too, and that *hadn't* been on his list of requests. I mean, why not? What possible harm could it do? They were all living together now, for heaven's sake. I couldn't have everyone in the house getting a Valentine's Day card apart from Vera. Could I? It would have been cruel. All the same, I'd love to have been there when the flowers arrived for Shelley. I hoped at the very least that they had brought a flicker of light into the awfully long, dark tunnel she must have been living through lately. I felt for them all, I really did, and for Charlie perhaps most of all. Oh, I know he'd been cast as the villain of the piece, but it wasn't as simple as that. I was sure of it. Charlie would never, ever walk out on his family like that, whatever about his business commitments, without some-thing awful prompting it. I just knew it in my bones. It's easy to make a scapegoat out of someone – easier still if they've run away rather than face the music. But Charlie wasn't a runner. He'd face any number of showdowns, particularly when his own flesh and blood were involved, not to mention his reputation. What was it the Indians said? Never judge a man until you've walked a mile in his moccasins. Well, I'd walked a lot of miles beside Charlie, in a manner of speaking, and walking out on his wife and family like this just wasn't in his character. I didn't know what was going on, but I was damned well going to make it my business to try and find out.

In the meantime, I would have to do everything in my power to keep the lines of communication open, and that would include finding a way to keep a discreet eye on his family again. I had met Vera at Charlie's wedding of course, but she wouldn't remember me. Shelley however, would. The children, well, they had all been tiny tots really, but I had to find a way to get to know them again, make sure they were all right. I had promised Charlie on my life that I wouldn't break his trust and tell anyone he had been in touch with me. But I could still keep an eye on them all, couldn't I? There was nothing wrong with that. Who knew what could happen at any moment? Suppose someone became ill, or heaven knows what.

But something told me I should watch this situation closely, and that meant making sure Larry didn't get so much as a whiff of what was going on. If his cronies in the golf club got hold of the fact that Charlie Fitzgibbon was in touch with me – *me!* – well, all hell would break loose. Luckily that wouldn't prove too difficult. Larry was either wrapped up in his golf or worrying about his non-existent health problems, and like most men was happy to regale me with details of both ad nauseum.

In the meantime, I would send Charlie an email. I had set up an alternative online address for that very purpose.

From: moneypenny@bmail.com
To: jame.s.bond@hailmail.com
James,
What on earth is going on? You really must give me some idea.
Everyone is extremely worried about you. If I can do anything
to help, I will. Running away never accomplished anything.
    Delivery carried out as per your instructions.
Moneypenny

I had no idea where he was, of course, or whether there
was a significant time difference involved, but I had to keep
this correspondence going, whatever it took and however
tentative. Charlie had to know there was someone he could
talk to at this end and he had chosen me – I couldn't abuse
that. I hoped and prayed that I would hear from him again.

Ping! I almost jumped out of my skin as a new message
slid onto my screen.

From: jame.s.bond@hailmail.com
To: moneypenny@bmail.com
Thanks MP, knew I could rely on you. Keep an eye on the
family for me.
James

That was it. Nothing more. How frustrating. I closed down
my email with a heavy heart. I would have to be patient. The
slightest wrong move on my part could ruin everything.
Although all things considered, the Fitzgibbon family's
prospects weren't looking too good on that front.

Charlie

How do you know when your life's falling apart? Financial problems? Business going under? Marriage on the rocks? Inability to cope? To sleep? To barely function? Well, I ticked all the boxes – and then some.

It's not really done for a guy to admit he's buckling under pressure, and I genuinely didn't think I was, but suddenly, the only thing that seemed to make sense was for me to go. And once I left the house, well, it just seemed easier to keep on going. I didn't think – thinking wouldn't have been a good idea right then, even if it had been an option. The trick was *not* to think. So like Forrest Gump, I just started running, and then I began thinking that maybe, in one guise or another, that's what I had been doing all my life. It brings you up short, that kind of realisation. Not one I wanted to reflect on until I realised that was the only thing I *had* to do – the only way forward. Because from where I was standing, there was certainly no going back.

Pretending had always come easily to me. I was good at it. Not with the intention to deceive so much as to make the truth a little less unvarnished – easier to digest. For myself, that is. The trouble is, pretending (even to yourself) can get you into trouble, and I had become so good at it I could hardly tell where the truth began and I ended.

Sure, I had done well, and so had most of the people I worked with. I was one of the success stories of the Celtic Tiger – wasn't that what it was all about? But honestly? All that stuff never mattered to me, not really. Sure, I got a buzz out of it, and yes, the money was nice, but I was self-made, and I could cope with having nothing again if I had to. What mattered to me was my family. My wife and children. And that's why, that fateful day, I had had to go. I had had to get out of there.

I've gone over and over that last scene before I left, like a bad, surreal movie, one that seemed endless until the final scene, which is what floored me. The straw that broke the camel's back. I could handle the other stuff, or try to. I could even manage failing, as I so obviously had – and spectacularly. But I always thought Shelley and I were solid, that we could make it through anything. I sure didn't see that one coming.

So I came out here, to Cape Town, because there's something I have to do, some family business I have to take care of. And bit by bit, I'm trying to get some perspective on what's happened. Maybe out here I can do that – I certainly couldn't do it at home.

Cheeky Charlie, they called me, even at school, and the name stuck. It was easier that way. I learned that early on too. Boys are expected to be tough, even when they're confused and hurting. Anyway, it worked for me – or I thought it had.

Except now everything else has come unstuck. But I couldn't think about all that right now.

Instead, I pulled my baseball cap down firmly, turned into the infamous Camp's Bay wind and walked back down the beach, just like any number of the many tourists enjoying a holiday in sunny Cape Town.

I missed it all, of course I did – my family, my mates and home. My life in Dublin, such as it was – or rather, how it had seemed.

Crossing the busy road, I hardly noticed the open-topped cars that drove by lazily, the beautiful people sitting outdoors in the cafés and bars or lying on sun loungers in the baking sun. At least I could be relatively incognito out here – here, my picture wasn't plastered on every newspaper I opened. And for now my family was better off without me.

It was March and the season was coming to an end. The Christmas crowd had long since gone and the others, plane-loads of them, many of them Irish, were following suit, suntanned now and happy to have escaped the harsh weather and harsher realities of home for a couple of weeks while they could.

Walking up the steep incline, around the corner and on up the winding road that led to the house one of my few remaining friends had loaned me, I let myself in and checked my messages. One was from Dave, the local golf pro, reminding me I had a lesson that afternoon. The other was from Annika, saying she would meet me at the restaurant that evening half an hour later than previously arranged. Things could be worse, I tried to tell myself. I was in a beau-tiful house, in a beautiful part of the world and having dinner with a beautiful woman tonight.

Looking out at the stunning view, the sparkling blue of the ocean spreading out beneath me, it struck me how cleverly the house had been designed. Hidden from passers-by, a simple entrance gave way to generous parking space that was the only visible clue to its existence. When you descended the steps carved out of rock, however, the pristine white, architect-designed modern house was revealed. Inside, expan-sive sheaths of glass looked on to the bay beneath that today stretched blue and unblemished into the horizon. If you looked up from the steeply winding road below, it seemed as if the house was suspended precariously over the cliff, about to fall at any moment, mirroring, rather uncannily, my own particular situation. But that wasn't quite accurate – my life had already come crashing down around me.

Olivia

'What's going on, Liv?'
I came back into our manky bedroom to find Emma examining my new Gucci spangled one-shoulder top as if it were forensic evidence.

'Don't touch that! I'm wearing it tonight and I don't need your grubby paw prints all over it.' I snatched it from her and hung it back on the door of the cupboard that passed for a wardrobe in this woeful house.

'Where're you going?' She sat on her bed in that ridiculous fluffy pink fleecy dressing gown with dripping wet hair that was already beginning to frizz nicely – thank God mine was straight. Thanks to her sneakily hogging the bathroom before me, I would now be even later than I'd already planned. Guy would be pissed off.

'What is this, twenty questions?' I sat down, turning my back to her, and angled my magnifying mirror as best I could on the bedside locker with the Argos bedside light to do my make-up. Luckily the modelling course the agency had sent me on a couple of years ago taught you how to apply your make-up under the most basic of circumstances – you had to be able to do your own make-up if you were, say, stuck in some grotty location and the make-up artist didn't show. Naturally that didn't happen very often, but the training came in handy now – as grotty locations went, I had struck gold. And just as well I'd had my hair blow-dried earlier in town.

Behind me I could feel Emma's penetrating gaze. Sharing

a room with any sister must be hard work, but with Emma it was hell.

'Only two, and you haven't answered either.'

'Get a life, Em. And shut up, will you? I need to concentrate when I'm doing my eyes.'

'But seriously, Liv, all these new clothes . . . are you lifting?'

'I *beg* your pardon?'

'Are you stealing them? Shoplifting? You don't have the money for this kind of gear – none of us do now – and it's not as if you were ever a saver.'

'You really are pathetic, Em, you know that? Shit, now you've made me blob my eyeliner.'

'I am not pathetic. It's a perfectly reasonable deduction, a lot of girls do it out of stress, or for a rush – it's an addiction. And since Robert dumped you—'

'He did *not* dump me. He just couldn't cope with the press.'

'Oh please, Liv, once he realised your trust fund was history, he was gone faster than Hussein Bolt, and good riddance if you ask me. I mean when did he ever, like, *ever* put his hand in his pocket? Everyone knows you paid for everything when you went out.'

'I so did not!'

'Yes you did. All the girls in my year knew 'cos Annie's sister told them.'

'Annie was always jealous of me and she fancied Rob for years, made a complete fool of herself over him.' I made a mental note to get my former friend back for that little morsel of information – the bitch. 'If you must know,' I said, making sure to sound deliberately bored – I hadn't planned on breathing a word about Guy to anyone, let alone Emma, but with nasty speculation like that doing the prospective rounds it was time to set the record straight, 'I'm seeing someone else.'

'Who?'

'His name's Guy, not that it's any business of yours.'

'What sort of a muppet is called Guy?' she sniggered. 'The only one I've ever heard of is that sleaze Dad was in business with for a while, Guy Whatshisname,' she frowned.

'Guy Richards. And he is not sleazy, he's sophisticated, not that you could tell the difference.' I could see realisation beginning to dawn. There, that would shut her up.

'No.'

'Yes, Emma. A very definite yes, actually.'

'I don't believe you.'

'Whatever.'

'Liv, please tell me you're joking – this is a wind-up, right?'

'Oh, get over yourself, Emma! I'm going out with Guy Richards and I'm having a fabulous time – and it's only going to get better.'

'The clothes.'

'Yes, Guy's incredibly generous. He really knows how to treat a girl.'

'But Liv, he's an old man. And he's married!'

'Separated – and he's only forty-four.'

'But he's as old as—'

'Dad is forty-eight, so don't you dare compare them.'

'Mum then.'

'Mum is forty-five, nearly forty-six. Guy's just turned forty-four, he's in his prime.' I blotted my lips together and applied another coat of Mac lipgloss. In the mirror I could see Emma's mouth opening and closing like a fish.

'Seriously, Liv, I mean you're not *really* going out with him, are you? I mean, are you having sex with him? Because if you are—'

'God, Emma, you sound like Gran.' A quick slick of gloss and I turned to face her. For a moment I almost felt sorry for her. She looked about twelve, and had that expression on her face that kids get when they want you to reassure them the bogeyman isn't really under the bed – he lives in the wardrobe instead. Only kidding, but you get the drift. Emma had always been naive, but you'd swear I'd admitted to dating a terrorist. I reached for my top and wriggled into it, enjoying the reassuring feel of expensive fabric as it slithered to a hip-hugging halt. Leggings, suede thigh-high boots, my new short shearling jacket and I was ready to go.

'Are you?' she demanded, and before I could reply, said, 'You are, aren't you? Liv, how could you? That's disgusting. It's repulsive. I can't bear the thought of being in the same room as you if you're, you're . . .'

I grabbed my bag and delivered my parting shot. 'Well you won't have to for much longer. I'm moving out. Guy's letting me have a flat of his, he has loads of them.'

I thought that would shut her up – and it did – but then she looked as if I'd hit her and sank down on the bed.

'Liv, you can't.' Her voice was a whisper. 'You can't go, not now, not when Mum needs us all. You can't mean it.'

'Em,' I sighed, 'I can't stay in this poxy place for a second longer. It's doing my head in. Anyway, I was living away from home before all this.'

'But that was different.'

'You're telling *me* it was different.' My hand was on the door knob. 'Look on the bright side, Em. At least you'll have this lovely room all to yourself – and one less person to race you to the loo.' I flashed her a smile. 'Don't say anything for now, I'll tell Mum myself when I'm ready.'

'When are you going?'

'Next Friday.'

After that she didn't say anything at all, so I went out and closed the door quietly. I thought it would feel good, telling her like that, but it didn't. It felt sort of weird. But then, everything in this family was weird these days. I hurried out of the house, and waved down a passing taxi. I couldn't think about it all now. I needed a drink, champagne preferably, and knowing Guy there would be a bottle with my name on it waiting in the Four Seasons. We were meeting in the old bar, or the residents' lounge, as it was correctly called, but ever since the Ice Bar had opened at the other end of the hotel, it was referred to as the old bar. Guy preferred the old bar. He said it was more intimate, but I knew it was because that's where his mates would be, other businessmen and developers like himself. We had only just started to go out in public and he said he wanted to show me off.

That's what I loved about Guy. He really made me feel good, special, and he didn't care about what other people thought. At first I was a bit worried about bumping into people my parents probably knew, but Guy told me to relax, that they would just be jealous of us. Anyway, I didn't care. I had done enough of this poverty thing – it just wasn't me, and I wasn't going to pretend it was. I wanted glamour and excitement. I was only twenty-four, for God's sake – my whole life was ahead of me. I sure as hell wasn't going to let it pass me by being holed up in that manky house of Gran's and end up working in a shop or something. Recession or no recession, there were still people out there having a good time – I'd seen them, and I intended to be one of them. Anyway, even if I'd wanted a job there weren't any to be had, so I might as well enjoy myself. I'd heard one of Guy's friends, an older man, say the only thing you needed to survive this recession was to have youth on your side, and Guy had winked at me and said, 'Well I certainly have it on mine,' as he pulled me closer. 'Mind you, Dave,' he added, 'I have a few other tricks up my sleeve as well.' That was another thing I loved about him – Guy never talked about the R-word. 'Life's short, baby,' he told me. 'You've got to squeeze every second out of it. No point thinking about the depressing stuff.'

I did ask him once, when we were in bed together. And that was another thing. Guy was totally amazing at sex – like, *really* amazing, much better than any of my other boyfriends – and much more romantic. I used to think Rob was good in bed, but Guy would totally blow him out of the water. When I think of Rob now, I laugh – he was so immature. I don't know how I didn't see that before.

So I asked him what had happened with Dad. How had he lost all his money? How could something like that happen if he was supposed to be so clever? How could we even lose our home?

'He took his eye off the ball, baby.' He shook his head and looked serious. 'You can't ever do that in our game. I tried to advise him, warn him even, but he wouldn't listen to me. Charlie can be a stubborn son of a bitch when he sets his mind on something.' I liked that Guy treated me as an equal. He never tried to patronise me or make me feel stupid. Like calling Dad Charlie when he was talking about him, never 'your dad'.

'But why—' I wanted to know more, but Guy silenced me with a kiss.

'Don't think about it, baby, it'll wreck your head. Anyway, you've got me now, I'll take care of you.'

I knew he was right and that he would take care of me. Guy made me feel a lot of things – sexy, glamorous, important even – but most of all, he made me feel safe. And after everything that had happened, I didn't think I would ever feel safe again.

No one tells you how hard it is being the eldest in the family. You're the one parents cut their teeth on and mostly fuck up with – the experimental guinea pig. Dad even used to call me Piggy 'cos he said I went on about it so much – even though Emma had been the fat one. Well, not fat, really, Mum said it was just puppy fat, but I don't remember ever having it. That's why it really irritated me when Dad used to call me Piggy, although he could always make me laugh. Dad could make anyone laugh. He had a really good sense of humour, not embarrassing like most parents.

But it's true, you know. I used to argue with him about it – I wasted so much emotional energy breaking the rules just in time for Emma and Mac to get it easier, and no one ever thanks you for it. 'That's your job, Piggy,' Dad would grin, and I used to say it was easy to see that *he* hadn't been the eldest in his family. The youngest one is always the most spoiled – I mean, look at Mac, he was practically carried around in cotton wool. Dad had an older brother, Uncle Patrick, who used to live in Canada, but he had been killed in a car accident years ago. Dad didn't talk about it much, but I remember visiting his grave when we were in Toronto 'cos he brought us with him, but I didn't like graveyards, they really creep me out. And Gran never talked about it either, about him being dead. She used to talk about him almost as if he was still alive, as If he was just sort of travelling on his gap year: *Patrick would have loved that. What a shame Patrick isn't here to see this. Nobody could tell a joke like Patrick . . .* But it had been his old room that Emma and I were sleeping in – that was another good reason to get out of that house.

Apparently Patrick had been the golden boy, mum told me once, and that Gran and Granddad had worshipped him. He had been really clever, came first in everything at school and was really brilliant at sport. He'd done law too, just like Granddad, only then he went off to Canada and decided to stay there. Mum said Dad told her his parents never got over that. And then he was killed, much later. I hadn't really thought about it till now, but it must have been really hard for Gran. Anyway, I bet things couldn't have always been easy for him because he was the eldest, like me. It's never easy, even if it looks as though it is. People, especially old people, always say the first baby has a special place in parents' hearts – yeah, right.

I was a honeymoon baby, but then after me, Mum and Dad ran into problems (sorry, too much information maybe) and Mum had to have IVF to have Emma and then Mac came along. When I wanted to annoy Em, I'd tell her that I was the only *natural* child in the family, a proper love child and not just a test tube baby, like her, and she'd say that she had been much *more* wanted than me because I had just arrived and Mum and Dad had gone to such a lot of trouble to have her. When she was younger it used to drive her mad, but later we used to laugh about it. Em can be really funny sometimes. And Mac, well, no one really knew where Mac came from. He could have been a natural, or a sort of hangover bonus from the IVF thing, so we used to call him the Hybrid. Mum heard us one day and went mad, but Mac didn't care. I don't even think he knew what we were talking about, but Mum said we were being disgraceful, and then she sat Mac down for a long talk about how loved he was and not to listen to anything his mad sisters said to him. Then that led to 'the talk' about babies and everything with Dad, and Mac came out of the room looking a lot more traumatised than when we'd just been winding him up. That's parents for you – they just don't know when to leave it alone.

But I really didn't want to think about my parents now. In fact, they were banished from my mind until further notice. But I couldn't get Em's face out of my head when I told her I was leaving. It was the prospect of me leaving Mum that she used to make me feel guilty, but I knew deep down it was *her* who would miss me, and that did make me feel guilty. Em was so transparent, and so naïve for her age. Still desperately wanting to play happy families. But we weren't a happy family, were we? And Mum and Dad hadn't been happy either for ages, even before he went. For about a whole year before that they had been rowing, or worse, not speaking. Then Mum would be deliberately extra nice to all of us, and that always made me mad. It was so obvious and irritating, and done purely to get up Dad's nose when he was around. Well, I guess it worked.

But I wasn't going to think about any of that now. The taxi had pulled up outside the Four Seasons and the doormen all greeted me as I walked through the lobby. Guy was waiting in the bar, smiling at me and tapping his watch. Apart from two other couples, we were the only people there.

'You look gorgeous, baby,' he said, leaning in to kiss me as he handed me a glass of bubbly. 'Well worth the wait.'

'Sorry I'm late, I got delayed telling Emma I was moving out. I didn't want her making a scene after I'd gone,' I explained.

'Will she?' He arched an eyebrow.

'Not now. But it's better she knows. After that there's only Mum to tell.' I thought I saw a flicker of worry in his eyes. 'Don't worry, it's not like I haven't moved out of home before.'

'I know, Liv, but I wouldn't want to be the cause of any friction in the family. Are you sure this is what you want?'

'I've never been more sure of anything in my life. I'll go crazy if I have to spend a minute more in that house.'

'Well, as long as you're sure, and nobody thinks I'm pressurising you.'

'Relax,' I said, a trifle sharply, as I slipped onto the barstool. Then to compensate, I gave him my most flirtatious from-under-lowered-lashes look, which seemed to get things back onto a more promising track. 'I *am* over the age of consent, you know,' I grinned.

'Don't I know it,' he said, looking a lot happier, and rested his hand lightly on my thigh.

Annika (Cape Town)

You were a surprise, that's for sure. But when I look at you now, paddling out to catch a wave, shrieking and laughing with your friends, hauling golden, skinny limbs upright and riding your board along the building swell, I shudder to even contemplate a life without you. You arrived two weeks early on 15 August 2000, and after that everything else suddenly made sense. The shackles of my old life fell away and the future was a place of promise instead of fear. Days were filled with purpose, with meaning, joy and laughter. I had finally discovered what it truly meant to love.

That's not to say I was exactly overjoyed to realise I was pregnant. As I recall, it preceded throwing up for the third time that day, this time in the loos of the wine bar where I had arranged to meet Marge, who now waited outside with bated breath.

'Is there a line or not?' I was vaguely aware of her hissing through the door while I squinted at the stick trembling in my hand.

But I was too stunned to take it in – and too sick to reply.

Looking at my face as I emerged, Marge immediately took charge. That's what she always did, and anyway, she said she needed a drink to cope with the news.

'Two Sauvignon Blancs, Nick,' she told our friendly bartender. 'And don't be stingy, I've had a bitch of a day.' She watched eagle eyed as Nick duly filled one glass well above average measure.

I stopped him before he filled a second. 'Just sparkling water for me, thanks.'

'Are you kidding?' Marge looked at me, eyebrows raised. 'If I need a drink to digest this, then surely you're entitled to one.' She nudged me in the direction of a just-vacated outdoor table and we sat down. 'One glass of wine won't hurt, surely?'

'I'm pregnant, Marge.' I took a swig of my water.

'Yes, we know that,' she looked at me archly, 'but not *staying* pregnant. Anni, I mean, tell me you're not . . . oh God, I don't believe this.' She struggled to sound patient, but exasperation flitted back and forth across her face as she waded in to rescue me. Except this time I didn't want to be rescued. Or stage managed. This time it was about me – and, as it turned out, about you. I had already known we were inextricably linked – for keeps. 'I'm keeping it,' I told Marge.

'But Anni,' she protested, massaging her temples and then joining her hands together as she looked at me intently, 'you can barely take care of yourself. I mean, you're hopeless. You really can't be serious. What about your career? You're a model, for heaven's sake, or have you forgotten? And speaking of forgetting things, might I remind you there is no prospective father on the scene, unless I'm missing a trick here? Is there?' She raised her eyebrows. 'I'm guessing from what you told me you didn't swap addresses. Did you even get his name?'

'I don't care about that, we'll work it out. I can manage,' I scowled, not wanting to remember the hazy flashbacks of the all-night party on the beach that had led to your conception.

'Please, Anni,' she tried cajoling. 'You have to think this through. Think of the reality, it would be a disaster.'

But I didn't need to think. Some things in life you just know. And even though everything else was a mess, I knew we'd be okay, that somehow I would manage to take care of us. Although sometimes I wondered, and still do, just who rescued who.

The party lifestyle was the first to go – late nights, hangovers and foggy heads have no place in the life of a single mother. I was on duty twenty-four seven and loved it – loved you. Nothing else mattered. I had enough money in my account to get through the first six months, and after that I went back to work, taking only local jobs. Luckily, there was plenty of work here in Cape Town. I got my figure back reasonably quickly and Betsy, our neighbour from across the hallway, looked after you if I had a job.

You were such a good baby, never a problem, almost as if you knew how scared I was that I wouldn't be able to cope, that I wouldn't be a good enough mother to you.

Then later, with your blond hair, blue eyes and big gaptoothed grin, the agency found us even more work in the mother and baby catalogues. You were a natural in front of the camera, and still are, although I knew it was only so long before you got fed up of doing the kids' TV ads that were so lucrative. The long hours and mind-numbing boredom of being on set when the sun was shining outside wasn't fair to you, so we gave that up. But it didn't matter, because by then Greg had come into our lives, and we found ourselves falling in love with him, just as he did with us.

Vera

What makes a good marriage anyway? That was what Zoe had asked, or rather aggressively demanded, yesterday in the shop. She had sounded almost angry as we were pricing items in the back room before putting them on display, her little elfin features cross as she held up a tarnished mirror in need of a good polish and stuck her tongue out at it. I got a flash of the dreaded tongue stud and had to turn away; really, I couldn't look. She had so many of the awful things she looked like a pincushion. Barbara, the overweight girl who seemed to take charge whenever Joan wasn't there (although no one could ever remember her being *put* in charge), had previously informed us that, in her opinion, such a lot of body piercings was a sign of self-loathing. I had looked at her curiously then as she went on to inform us that she herself was attending Overeaters Anonymous, which, she explained, was a twelve-step meeting for people with food issues. As a result of this, and her experience, she was very well up on issues of every kind, she told us with a certain air of self-importance.

I was glad Maura wasn't there to hear this train of thought. A retired nurse, Maura had very little time for what she called waffling about issues and the like, and a lot of time for what she liked to refer to as hard-core common sense. 'The only disorder that girl has,' she said to me privately one day as she eyed Barbara shoving not one but two biscuits into her mouth as she continued to talk and spray crumbs at people, 'is too much time and money on her hands. Why hasn't she got a real job?'

This was a fair question, I thought, especially after Maura had told me that Barbara lived in an apartment of her own and drove a BMW. Plus she was only twenty-five, although with the extra weight and all those strange clothes she wore she looked a good deal older.

'Poor little rich girl,' Maura had proclaimed, nodding knowingly at me.

'Well,' I added mischievously, 'perhaps not so "little".' Maura had laughed heartily, although I had immediately felt remorseful.

'I blame the parents,' she continued. 'These days they think parenting means throwing money at them, and now they're paying the price. In my day, we all lived at home until we got married.'

'That's a trend that's on the up again.' I reminded her wryly.

'And there was no money for constant chocolate and biscuits and what not. They were considered treats, at the weekend maybe, or on a Sunday. And,' she was warming to her theme now, 'there was none of this central heating turned up at full blast either. What do they expect? If you walk around in a T-shirt in the middle of winter, of course it's going to be bloody cold. That's what jumpers are for, not central heating! The body's built to keep itself warm if properly clothed – it burns calories too. No wonder they're all putting on weight and running to gyms these days. All they need to do is turn down the heating and get out of their cars and actually *walk*.' She paused to draw breath. 'I guarantee you whatever problems that girl has could be sorted out with a good dose of common sense, and I'd be only too happy to give it to her.' Maura wasn't too keen on Barbara, who could, in fairness be very irritating, but

I tried to remain non-judgemental. After all, who was I to cast stones?

But back to Zoe's question – what makes a good marriage? Well, there's no easy answer to that, is there? Arthur and I had had a good marriage, as good as anybody's, better even, but no one could have predicted what would happen, me least of all. That's why whenever anyone asked that question (and you heard it all the time these days; every magazine and TV show was trying to analyse what made a good marriage and, good Lord, some of the nonsense they came up with!), I always said the ability to forgive was the most important thing. At least that's what had turned out to be the most important thing in our marriage. If Arthur hadn't been able to forgive me, I hardly like to think what would have transpired. But he did, thank God, and we had struggled through together and eventually got through our Bad Patch, and although I could never quite believe he could or had forgiven me (he had to reassure me constantly, poor man), eventually I came to believe he had. That should have been the end of it, of course, but in many ways it was only the beginning. Arthur forgiving me was one thing, but Charlie forgiving me was quite another. That's the trouble when you play fast and loose with those you love – even innocent bystanders get caught in the resulting fall-out. But all that was so long ago. I hated still to think about it, and indeed was encouraged not to by the few people who still knew about it (now all gone bar one, of course). Charlie never mentioned it, but from that day on, he never, ever forgave me for it.

I wielded the hoover with a little more force than was necessary, I supposed. I always found housework therapeutic these days, and now that we were a full house, there was a lot more of it to be done. A house doesn't clean itself, even if all in it are reasonably tidy. Of course Shelley and Emma helped out – not Olivia, I hasten to add – but really I preferred to do it myself. So we came to an arrangement: Shelley was in charge of the bathroom, loo and sinks, I dusted and hoovered and we all did our own ironing – even poor Mac, which I thought was a bit much, but his sisters insisted, although he took so long and made such a to do about it that I saw Shelley take over for him on a reasonably regular basis. At least he knew how to plug in the iron and set up the board. In my day that would have been beyond most men, unless you were in the army or something. I supposed it was a good thing. But on days like today, when I had the place to myself for a bit, I liked to give the house a good old going over.

Shelley had managed to get a job, which was wonderful. It was part-time, so she could still be there for Mac and Emma when they came in from school, although between us, someone was usually at home. Emma had decided that it was a good thing for Mac to be a 'latchkey kid', as she now called him, though he didn't like that at all. He considered himself to be quite the young man, even though he was only eleven. I couldn't help wondering if that was because his father wasn't around at the moment. Was poor Mac feeling abandoned? They say the youngest is always overprotected, don't they? Even in my day they said it, but I thought they suffered in other ways. That had certainly been the case with my boys, only we never realised it until it was too late.

Shelley

The job was a lifesaver. Not, obviously, for the amount of money it brought in (the salary was barely above minimum wage), but because it got me out of the house, and the hours weren't too much. Ten till three, Tuesday, Wednesday and Thursdays. Perfect, really. A friend of Vera's had mentioned it to her, a woman who was a friend of my employer's wife, who had told her to keep a lookout for 'someone suitable'.

Since the job was in a small private art gallery, tucked away off Grafton Street, I had dressed carefully and agonised a lot. I knew a bit about art – I had studied Art History at college a million years ago – but I hadn't worked since I married Charlie and I knew nothing much about computers except how to shop on eBay, which was another occupation I had given up, along with manicures, pedicures and attending charity lunches. If I was honest, avoiding the lunches was a relief. I had never quite felt I fitted in anyway, and armies of women had always scared me, particularly since I had the distinct feeling they were only being friendly to me because I was married to Charlie, back when he was a mover and shaker in Dublin business circles. Since he'd left town, my invitations had dried up. Not that I cared. I had hated all that stuff and the entertaining clients and endless dinner parties that went with it. There was just something so terribly fake about it all. Most of the people attending couldn't wait to gossip about each other the minute a back was turned. Well, they must be getting a good laugh out of me, I thought grimly.

Not that that mattered a jot – it was how the kids were coping that concerned me.

So far there didn't seem to be any major problems, thank God, but then again, it's not as if they would necessarily tell me, would they? In fact, these days, Emma and Mac seemed to chatter away with Vera, though Olivia didn't seem to be on speaking terms with anyone at the moment, apart from the odd monosyllabic comment. Anyway, she was hardly ever there. I really would have to sit her down and find out what was going on with her. She was keeping ridiculous hours and obviously thought that, in my currently deranged state, I wouldn't notice that, or the endless supply of new clothes she appeared to be acquiring. I noticed that Emma had been throwing everdarkening looks in her sister's direction, but I didn't have time to dwell on all of that now that I had the gallery to look after. And I loved it, once I had got over my initial nerves.

The prospect of the interview had reduced me to sleepless nights and cold sweats, to the extent that I even had Vera rattled about it, and Emma and Mac were constantly shouting at me to just chill. In the event, I needn't have worried. Ernie, my prospective employer, seemed even more distracted than I was, if that was possible.

'Sorry, we're not open yet.' He peered suspiciously around the door I had duly banged on after there was no reply to the bell.

'Are you sure?' I asked tentatively. 'You see, I've come about the interview.' I smiled in that fixed way nervous people do, taking in the ample frame, bald head, sideburns, glasses and disapproving glare that was being aimed directly at me. Even though I was in high heels and my feet were already protesting, I wanted to turn and flee. 'I'm Shelley,' I offered hopefully, 'Shelley Fitzgibbon – Vera's daughter-in-law.' Now I *was* going to run. I allowed myself to count to three . . .

At two, the frown lifted and was replaced by a broad smile,

and at three he barked – a short, sharp sound which I gathered was laughter, and Ernie, I later learned, laughed a lot, which just goes to show appearances can be deceptive.

'Of course!' He smacked his forehead with the heel of his hand, which sported a very large, impressive-looking signet ring with a heavily embedded family crest on his pinkie finger. 'Come, in, come in, I clean forgot, my dear. How rude of me, you must think I'm an absolute boor.' He ushered me inside to a space the size of a generous sitting room with pristine white walls on which were hung works of various modern artists. An eclectic selection of sculpture was displayed on various plinths and alcoves. The collection was as modern and cutting edge as its caretaker was Dickensian. Ernie Huggard could have walked straight out of *A Christmas Carol* – all he needed were the coat-tails. As if reading my thoughts, he took a pocket watch from his waistcoat and peered at it, pulling idly on a bristly sideburn. 'Now Melly,' he looked up and beamed, 'you'll have a cup of tea with me and we can go over a few little details.'

'Shelley,' I corrected him gently.

'What? Yes, I shall remember that. My grandmother was called Melanie, and a very lovely name it is.' He disappeared from view to what I assumed was the kitchenette, and after a few minutes of sitting alone, listening to a series of clatters, I thought I'd better investigate.

'Can't find the blasted teapot. I'm afraid I'm useless at this sort of thing. I suppose I could . . .'

'Why don't I make the tea?' I said, locating a couple of clean cups and saucers and finding the tea bags that were clearly eluding him.

'Oh, jolly good, that's the spirit. I like mine good and strong, if you'd be so kind.'

Half an hour later I had managed to establish a few details, one of which was that Ernie Huggard was one of life's true gentlemen. I hadn't thought there were any left. How he had managed to operate a thriving business was beyond me. Because he had, a very lucrative one, and had sold out handsomely, he told me. And now, in his retirement, he was able to indulge his little hobby, which was collecting and dealing in modern Irish art.

'There's the computer, of course,' he indicated a state-of-the-art iMac. 'Never touch them myself, but we're all wired up and so on. Dorothy, the girl you'd be replacing, was a bit of a whizz.' He looked over his glasses expectantly at me.

'Ahem,' I cleared my throat. 'About the computer . . .'

'Yes?'

'I have to tell you I'm pretty useless at that sort of thing. I can send emails, just about, but—'

'Oh, don't worry your head about that, my dear, we'll get the computer chappie to come in and show you how to work it, give you a few lessons, apparently there's nothing to it,' he beamed. 'And a young thing like you will be up and running on it in no time!'

Suddenly I felt myself tearing up and bit my lip hard. I wasn't sure if it was the huge relief I was beginning to feel for the first time in weeks, or the fact that it was the first time in longer than I cared to remember that anyone had referred to me as a 'young thing'. My girls would have a good laugh at that.

'So it's not a problem, then, me not being a whizz on the computer?' I wanted it confirmed.

'My dear,' he looked at me over his glasses again as if I was a bit dim, 'as long as the days and hours are acceptable to you, anyone who makes as good a cup of tea as you clearly do is at the top of my list of candidates.'

'I suppose there are lots and lots.' My hopes were immediately dashed. There were bound to be any number of hot young things in the art world after a position such as this.

'What? Good Lord, no. I can't abide all this interviewing

nonsense. I have to see a few others, but I'll have made my decision by lunchtime, and if you'd be so good as to give me your telephone number, I'll let you know by then.'

'It's there,' I pointed to my considerably padded-out curriculum vitae, 'right at the top.' He barked – sorry, laughed – again.

'So it is.' He stood up and we shook hands, and then he said something that took me quite aback. 'I'm so sorry about all this business with your husband – Charlie, isn't it?' He went on before I had a chance to reply. 'It must be very difficult for you. I met him a couple of times, you know, thoroughly nice chap, helped me out of quite a pickle with my business at the time. I owe a lot to him, very clever chap.' He looked at me kindly and I managed to mumble a thank you and then I fled to the door, knowing if I stayed a second longer I really would cry.

'I'll give you a tinkle after lunch, Melly,' he called after me.

'Oh, right, thanks,' I said.

'Toodlepip!' I heard him call as I closed the door behind me.

After all that, I needed a stiff cup of coffee. I certainly wasn't ready to go home yet and face the well-meaning enquiries of whoever might be about, most likely Olivia, since it was approaching eleven. She didn't usually stir before lunchtime.

Making my way across Grafton Street, I hurried down Clarendon Street and turned left and quick right and found the little restaurant I remembered. It was empty, the lunch crowd yet to descend, but I knew they served coffee in the mornings, so I slid into a corner table and ordered a large cappuccino. When it arrived, accompanied by the glass of water I had also asked for, I took a long drink, and then a gulp of the coffee. I was suddenly feeling shaky, but why? The interview was over and it had gone well, if unexpectedly, so what was the problem?

The problem, a little voice told me, *is that old Ernie hit a nerve, mentioning Charlie like that. You weren't prepared for that, were you?* And the truth was, I hadn't been. He had taken me completely unawares.

In Vera's house we had got used to tiptoeing our way around the subject. The kids mentioned him now and again to me (what they said to each other, God only knew), but 'Dad' didn't have nearly such an effect on me as 'Charlie', and certainly nothing as much as 'your husband, Charlie', as Ernie had said. 'A thoroughly nice chap,' he had added. And he was right, of course, Charlie could be thoroughly nice, but then again, he could be thoroughly difficult – and the last year of our marriage had been sheer hell.

I pulled myself up short then, cup poised in midair, before replacing it carefully on its saucer. Was that what I really thought? That our marriage was done and dusted? That it was over? I swallowed hard, forcing myself to remember the last time I had seen him and spoken – or rather, shouted – at him. I didn't want to think of it now, because that ugly scene was the last thing I thought of every night before the sleeping pill dragged me into a fitful sleep, where, in dreams ragged with remorse, every hurtful, vicious comment I threw at him was replayed.

'You all right there, love?' It was the waitress, taking my cup and looking at me with kind, knowing eyes. 'Fancy a top-up?'

'No thanks,' I said quickly, fumbling in my purse for change. 'Just the bill, please.' I found a tissue and blew my nose, surprised to find that tears were rolling down my face.

I had been putting my head in the sand. I was very good at that, not good at all about facing things head on, especially scary things. That was one of the lovely things about marrying Charlie – I had felt safe with him. I knew he'd take care of me no matter what. I was madly in love with him, of course; it would have been hard *not* to love Charlie. Women were mad about him, even the ones who hardly knew him. He just had that effect on them. When I met him first, I couldn't believe he was interested in me. I thought it was my considerably flashier girlfriend Sasha he fancied as he chatted to us both at the party, but it was me he called, me he asked out to a movie and a bite to eat, and me he continued seeing for the following eight months until he proposed to me. At the time I couldn't believe that either – well, it *was* kind of unusual. A letter arrived at our house. I wasn't used to getting much post other than the odd postcard, but it was addressed to me, so I opened it. Inside was an A4 page, and centred in the middle were typed the words WILL YOU MARRY ME? Underneath were two boxes, one marked YES, the other NO and the instruction to tick the appropriate one and return to sender, with Charlie's address at the top of the page. At first I thought it was joke and I was annoyed. Then my mother had looked at it and got all misty eyed and told me to ring him up immediately. 'Don't you dare keep the poor boy waiting on tenterhooks, he doesn't mean you to literally reply in writing. Ring him up now. What a thoughtful way to propose.' She went off to find my father to tell him.

'Don't go telling Dad,' I yelled after her. 'For all I know this could be his idea of a joke.'

She came back and put her head around the door and gave me one of her looks. 'Shelley dear, one thing men never, ever joke about is a marriage proposal, never mind one in writing,' she said, then disappeared again. (At least I thought she had. I later learned she'd been listening outside with her ear to the door the whole time I was on the phone to Charlie.)

But she was right, as it turned out. Charlie had been thrilled when I rang him, even though he was at work.

'Are you serious?' I asked him. 'Because if this is your idea of a joke . . .'

'Just answer the question, Shelley.'

Then I got a bit tongue tied, because it dawned on me that he *was* serious, and I was suddenly overcome with nerves.

'Shelley?' he prompted me.

'Yes, yes, I'm here,' I said stupidly, fiddling with the telephone cord.

'Yes, you're here, or yes, you'll marry me?'

'Both,' I squeaked. 'I mean, yes, yes Charlie, of course I'll marry you – I'd love to marry you!'

'Phew!' I heard a long breath escape at his end of the line. 'I was hoping you'd say that. For a moment there you had me worried.'

Hoping? I remember even then feeling bewildered. Charlie Fitzgibbon hoping that any girl would marry him? It was mad. Charlie could have had anyone. He was the sexiest man in town, and a catch to boot. My mother's reaction alone was testament to that. She went out to have her hair done just so she could casually drop the good news into general conversation that afternoon over coffee with her girlfriends, she claimed, but really I knew it was because Charlie was coming around that evening for celebratory drinks.

Later that night, when Charlie and I were finally alone, he made me tick the box anyway. 'I want it in writing, just so you can't renege on me.' As if. So I did – I ticked the YES box, and Charlie grinned and folded up the piece of paper carefully and put it in his wallet. I never knew what he did with it after that – had he put it away somewhere safe, or was it long gone? He wasn't usually sentimental about stuff like that. Anyhow, I reasoned with a sudden pang, it wasn't as if I could ask him now.

After all, it was me who had told him in no uncertain terms to get out of my life – out of our lives. 'Go on,' I screamed. 'Why don't you just fuck off out of our lives and off to your bloody South African hoor!'

It's just that I never in a million years thought he would.

Charlie

Like I said, I didn't think. It was all I could do to function. I had been trying to tell Shelley for days, but she didn't seem to want to talk – or listen, for that matter. There was always something else, and truth be told, it was easier for me to bottle out, to put it off for just one more day. It's every man's nightmare – telling his wife that their life as they know it is over, or as good as. But I'd had no choice.

The Russian investment had been a godsend at the time, bought us at least another year, but that year was up and nothing could be done to stop the banks from pulling the plug. That was when the game was finally up. But Russians aren't noted for taking it well when their investments don't perform according to plan, especially in the current climate, and 30 million is a lot to be down on, even for an oligarch. So I did the only thing I could at the time – I forged Shelley's signature on the deed of sale and made the house over to Tolstoy Investments, the company fronting the deal. In the good days our house, Summerton, had been valued at 10 million. Now it was anyone's guess what you would get for it. But it was a gesture, and it was all I – all we – had left. It would go to the banks or I could sign it over to the Russians. Neither option was appealing, but I knew which one made screamingly obvious sense. My life might have been falling apart, but I still had one – other people who had got on the wrong side of the big boys hadn't been so lucky.

I had met Lukaz Mihailov through an Irish wealth management expert called Gareth who had been making quite a name for himself on the international scene, particularly since the acquisition of a major chain of high street stores and real estate in West End London had catapulted him into the big time. When I put feelers out for extra investors, it was Gareth who immediately suggested Tolstoy Private, and I arranged to fly over later that week so he could make the introductions and I could take things from there. And a very memorable night it had turned out to be.

I booked into the Lanesborough, which apparently was popular with Russians doing business in London, and which was where the meeting would take place. At seven thirty sharp I was in the bar, as instructed. Gareth arrived about thirty seconds later.

'Charlie,' he slapped me on the back, 'good to see you, mate. I wanted to have a quick word before they get here.'

I told him again how much I was looking for, and he grinned. 'No problem to Lukaz Mihailov – it all depends on whether he likes you or not. They're funny like that, and very superstitious.'

'About thirty mil?' I quipped. 'Can hardly blame him.' I wanted to order a pint but Gareth warned me to wait for them. 'It's expected,' he explained. 'And that's another thing – no matter what they do, act as if it's perfectly normal. Laugh when they laugh, look serious and concerned when they do. I'm warning you, if they like you, you're away on a hack. If they don't, it's goodnight Irene. But don't worry,' he added quickly, grinning at my face, 'they're gonna love you – just be yourself.'

'But you've just told me not to be – to be like them.'

'It's easy, believe me. Just go with the flow, and whatever you do don't look shocked and don't refuse a drink.'

I raised my eyebrows. 'Have you ever known me to?'

'It's a bit like being on a school tour, except unsupervised and with unlimited funds.' He immediately straightened up and ran a hand nervously over his scalp. 'Righty-ho, here they come.' He smiled confidently, but I could see beads of sweat breaking out on his forehead.

'I thought it was just the three of us,' I murmured.

'The other two are bodyguards,' he said under his breath, still smiling. 'Like I said, just act normal. Lukaz!' he boomed in a hail-fellow-well-met fashion, and once the greetings and introductions were over, we were ushered to a table where out of nowhere (or so it seemed) ice buckets of Stoli vodka appeared accompanied by chilled glasses. And that was just the beginning.

'First, we do business,' announced Lukaz, 'then we eat.' He raised his glass '*Sláinte!*'

Gareth replied smartly with something impressively guttural, which I took to be a Russian toast, and we knocked back our first shot of vodka. The bodyguards, I noticed, were on Diet Coke.

While Gareth went over in broad strokes what we were hoping to achieve, Lukaz leaned back and rested one arm casually along the back of his chair, but he was listening intently.

He was a handsome guy. I was pretty sure women would find him attractive – quite apart from the fact that he was rumoured to be worth billions. I think it had something to do with him owning about half the aluminium resources in Russia. He stood about six foot two, although his build was stocky, and his immaculately cut designer suit failed to hide impressive muscles. This was a guy who worked out – he was in mega shape. I guessed he was early forties, although it was hard to tell, he could have been younger. His skin was sallow and unlined and stretched over wide, slanting cheek-bones. When he smiled his teeth were white and even, although the smile never quite reached his heavily hooded eyes. I would bet his genial gaze missed nothing, and though he appeared relaxed, easily contained tension emanated from every pore, like a lazy big cat ready to pounce if provoked.

I wouldn't like to try it, I thought.

'So, Charlie,' he looked at me expectantly, 'tell me about yourself.'

I knew Gareth would have already filled him in on my general business background and obviously furnished him with any necessary details for his own people to go over, so this was the cue to get personal. Ludicrous though it might sound, I even produced the photographs Gareth advised me to bring – of my offices in Dublin, our home, Summerton, and of course, photos of Shelley and the children. As I watched Lukaz examine them carefully, they seemed to be having the desired effect. He handed them back to me and smiled broadly. 'Very nice, very nice. Your wife, she is very pretty, nice children too.' He nodded approvingly. I immediately enquired about his family.

Before he replied, we drank another toast – to family, naturally.

'I have two children, Katerina and Olga. They both went to school here, in London – this is also where my ex-wife like to live. So I buy her a house near Harrods. This makes her happy. Happy ex-wife is good, yes?' He laughed, we threw back another toast, and the bodyguards, taking Lukaz's cue, grinned. 'But,' he paused dramatically, 'I have Irish great-grandfather. Dead now, of course, but one day I vow to myself, must go to Ireland.'

'Well of course you must.' Gareth was practically rubbing his hands with glee. This was a good sign, clearly.

Before we set off for dinner, I had learned of his estate in Surrey, his house in Mayfair, his villas in Sardinia and Cap Ferrat and his *dacha* in Russia. Then of course there were the two yachts and the two private jets, which he liked to fly himself, time permitting. There wasn't a lot that was discreet about Lukaz but, in a way, I guess it was rather refreshing.

Luckily we didn't have far to go. Dinner, it turned out, was downstairs, in the Wine Cellar, named after the original was discovered by chance in the hotel's last renovation and which had now been reincarnated as an impressive and intimate dining room. We were joined by eight others – two colleagues of Lukaz and their respective entourage. I was seated on Lukaz's right, which was another good sign, Gareth told mè.

Dinner was another production, with mountains of caviar (which I hated), but which I manfully threw down with more vodka. The main course was greeted with much back slapping and indeed cheering. I understood why when I learned that the Kobi beef had been flown in from Japan earlier that day on Sergie's (one of the colleagues) Gulfstream. He proudly informed us it was 300 dollars a kilo – and that was without including the transport. This was accompanied by a Mouton Rothschild '48 (at least three grand a bottle, even I knew that) reverentially introduced by the sommelier, who poured and waited for Lukaz to taste and signal his approval. This was duly given and his glass was filled, and although the same sommelier's regal bearing never flinched, I'm quite sure he wanted to cry when he saw a liberal splash of vodka being added, because I know I did.

After dinner, there was a lap-dancing club, although not like any I'd ever been to. I'm not a great fan myself, but they were a regular feature on the menu at these sorts of boys' business dinners. I'm quite sure we could easily have walked the short distance in Mayfair, but that's not how it's done, apparently. Instead, three Maybachs and a blacked-out Hummer were lined up outside the hotel on Hyde Park Corner, out of which jumped yet more bodyguards. Gareth and I were hustled into a Maybach, Lukaz leaped into the Hummer, the 'meat' jumped on board and we all did a few laps around

Hyde Park before being deposited all of a hundred yards from our starting point. If my head hadn't already been spinning, it would have made me dizzy. 'Whadidishell you?' slurred Gareth rather charmingly as he stumbled out onto the pavement and rapidly straightened up. 'Is this fun or whash?'

I wasn't sure that was the word I'd have used, but I grinned to show I concurred with the general idea.

Inside the club, which was the interior of a thoroughly dignified Georgian house, we were ushered to the 'drawing room', which was handily located beside the gambling tables, and once we had made ourselves comfortable, a parade of the most beautiful girls I have ever seen came in, in various stages of undress. My memories of what followed are very sketchy, but I'm pretty sure they included more vodka – this time poured into Château Pétrus. I'm also pretty sure I remember someone snorting coke off the ridiculously toned abdomen of a Ukrainian girl, but at this point I may have been hallucinating. I think at some stage shortly after that I must have passed out. I do remember waking up with a feather boa around my neck and seeing Gareth snoring loudly on the sofa opposite. Lukaz was at the gaming table still surrounded by women and the bodyguards were standing at a respectful distance. I already knew my hangover had started.

We were taken back to the hotel, and somehow I made it through the lobby. I think I may have been leaning on Lukaz. 'Goodnight, Charlie, my new Irish friend,' he said, laughing, as he hurled me into the lift, followed by Gareth, who was deposited by one of the bodyguards. 'Sweet dreams. We must do business more often. Next time in Dublin, yes?' And then the doors closed. Gareth promptly sank to the floor. I have vague memories of him crawling on all fours along the corridor to his room. Just as he reached it and managed to pull himself upright by the door handle, he called after me. 'I think he likesh you, Sharlie.'

He must have done, because after that, Tolstoy Investments put 30 million euro into the project. Things were looking up.

But now, just over a year on, they couldn't be much worse. Whatever about the business, I wasn't about to let my family go, my children. Shelley might hate my guts – she had certainly made that much abundantly clear – they were all entitled to hate me after what they'd been through. But there was one thing that had astonished me beyond all else, something I still couldn't quite get my head around. When I found out from Elsie I had thought she must have got it wrong, but she was adamant. Shelley and the kids had moved in with my mother. Whatever else I had expected, it certainly wasn't that.

Elsie

To do list

Merrion Centre:

Tesco — pick up shoulder of lamb + veggies for Saturday.

Peter Mark — hair appt, 11 a.m.

Call in to Mary and borrow dog to walk.

It was the only thing I could think of and, believe me, I had racked my brains over how to keep an eye on Charlie's family, as he had asked me to. It may have sounded like a casual request, but I knew Charlie had invested enormous trust in that one-liner email and I wasn't going to let him down.

I'll get to the dog bit in a moment, but before I explain about that, I got what I call a lucky break. I ran into an old acquaintance, a woman I vaguely knew who had been friendly with my sister when we had all been younger. Anyhow, we were in the Merrion shopping centre and she seemed delighted to see me and suggested we go for a coffee. Normally I wouldn't, as I don't like getting sidetracked on my plans for the day, but something made me agree. I was feeling tired after doing the Tesco shop and the idea of a coffee sounded reviving. So there we were, chatting about the usual things, the unseasonably cold winter, the recession (of course) and so on. It must have been the recession that triggered it, because before I knew it, she was talking about a woman who worked with her in the charity shop where she, Maura, worked – a good friend by all accounts, whose son had lost a business, disappeared and sold the house from under his wife's nose.

'Imagine,' said Maura. 'This *poor* woman at her age – a widow, you know, having to take in the family into her own house. That's what she's done, her son's family have had to move in with her lock, stock and barrel.'

'How many of them?' I asked, being careful not to appear too curious, but my antennae were immediately up.

'Well, there's her daughter-in-law, obviously, a boy and two girls, and the eldest one's a bit of a madam by all accounts,' Maura said archly.

'Isn't it wonderful for them they could turn to her,' I said, taking a sip of my coffee. 'Does she live near you?' I ventured.

'Actually, she lives very near here.' Maura mentioned the road, which I immediately made a mental note of.

'Really? Which end is she at?' I enquired. 'I have a friend who lives on that road.' (I didn't, of course, but it was worth a try.)

'Number twenty-two. A lovely house, but only three bedrooms and one bathroom. It's a huge upheaval for Vera.'

I nodded sympathetically. 'Well, they won't be alone, Maura. Families are losing their homes all over the country, as we speak.'

'Dreadful business.'

'Goodness, look at the time – I really must be going. My husband's having his cronies around for a bridge party tonight and I'm doing a bit of baking for it.'

So we paid up and went our separate ways, promising to meet again soon. Back in my car, I took a detour and drove around to the road where Vera lived. It was a quiet little road, conveniently near a Dart station, with well-kept semi-detached houses, although number twenty-two was one of the more old-fashioned ones. Clearly a lot of the others had had work done to them (what part of Dublin hadn't?), and weren't we all paying dearly for *that* now? At twelve o'clock there was no one much about, just a man walking a rather fat dog. And although I slowed down passing the house, there was no sign of any life.

That's when I got the idea of walking a dog. A dog would be the perfect alibi, only I didn't have a dog. But I knew Larry's sister did. And since she'd got her hip done recently, I guessed she'd be glad of an offer to walk her dog. I wasn't that keen on dogs and I couldn't remember what hers was, but it seemed like a good idea to have a bit of a stroll up and down the road – who knew what family member I might catch sight of? The more I thought about it, the more convinced I became. It was the ideal solution. Feeling like a sprightly Miss Marple, I hurried home to set my plan in motion. Being an amateur sleuth couldn't be any harder than being a first-rate PA – could it?

Charlie

Children know things from a very early age.

Like whether or not they are loved. Whether or not there is tension in the home. Whether or not they or another sibling is indulged – or preferred. Despite any protestations to the contrary to pretend otherwise, these are just some of the things a child instinctively knows, just as he or she will know when a parent or adult is lying to them. But we need those lies. We depend on them. Like a comfort blanket, they wrap around us, a fleecy reassurance, a protective layer against our deepest, darkest fears. That Santa Claus might not exist. That the Bogeyman just might really be under the bed, that the Tooth Fairy will forget us. That we are not good enough, that we are somehow to blame.

They are also very good at playing along with these lies. Because were they not to, the unthinkable might happen, and their little world (which is anything but little to them) might come crashing down. Of course, the irony is that they're far too young to fully comprehend this. Like I said – they just know.

I knew, for instance, without a shadow of a doubt, that my elder brother Patrick was the favourite. I could also clearly see why he was. He looked like my father, he thought like my father and he excelled at everything without ever seeming to have to try very hard. My father pretended not to notice or indeed applaud these achievements very much, but the very inflections in his voice were a giveaway. The gruff, sometimes intimidating tone would soften when Patrick was around and tenderness would rearrange features normally set in stern, unrelenting lines. My mother's face lit up at the sight of Patrick. A boy notices these things, just as he notices their absence in his own parental interactions.

I was two years younger, and I adored him too. He was my playmate, my champion, my aspiration. I was also his opposite in every way. We were chalk and cheese. Where Patrick was methodical, I was mercurial. He was demonstrative, I was reserved. He was assertive, I was easily distracted and stubborn. When I was little, I thought he was the cleverest person in the world. As long as Patrick was around, life looked okay to me. I didn't mind that the hugs he was given were always longer and tighter than mine, or that his questions were not met with thinly veiled exasperation, or that when we were kissed goodnight at bedtime, it was Patrick whose hair was stroked tenderly, whose bedside my mother always lingered at a fraction longer. Because that's just the way it was. We all idolised Patrick.

But looking back, Patrick didn't know everything, not like I thought he did. I assumed that one day he knew there was something wrong, like I did. Something different was there beyond the normal fussing and frustrations of normal, everyday life as we knew it. An underlying silence had crept into our house, the kind of silence that speaks volumes to a watchful child. Conversations were held as normal, time-keeping adhered to, school runs undertaken, but now, especially around my mother, there was a palpable energy beating. I couldn't see it, but I could feel it.

My mother was beautiful. I know every small boy thinks that, but she really was. Later I understood she had been considered a beauty in her day. Her and Dad made quite the couple, his dark looks complementing her blonde. I especially liked it when she drove us to school and all the other boys, even some of the bigger ones, would stare at her as she waved us off, or giggle and blush and start shoving each other around awkwardly. I think she liked it too. But when I was sick and had to stay off school, that was the best of all. That was when I had her to myself. I think it only happened once, when I was seven. I had chickenpox and was contagious, and even though I was really sick and really hot, I remember thinking I never wanted it to end. She got me my favourite comics, *The Dandy* and *Beano*, even though Daddy didn't really approve of comics. And she read stories to me too, sitting on the side of my bed, putting on special voices and making me laugh, checking my temperature every now and then, resting a cool hand on my forehead. When I was getting better she made me special soup to eat, and even ice cream. I thought I was in heaven. When I was strong enough to get up but not well enough to go back to school, she would let me come into their bedroom, after Dad had gone to work, and I would watch her, fascinated, as she brushed her silky hair and put on powder and lipstick. Nobody, I thought, could ever have a mother as beautiful as mine.

All too quickly, of course, I got better and was back at school with Patrick, under strict instructions from my father to make sure to catch up on any work I had missed. But I didn't worry about that. Patrick had already got notes from my class teacher and said he would help me with it. I was far too busy being miserable to worry about silly old school. The person I craved attention from most in all the world seemed no longer to be specially devoted to me. Things were back to normal. But I would never forget that magic time, when it was just us – just me and my mum.

Which was why, a few weeks later, when I was sent home from school after falling out of our favourite tree in the playground (I was bruised and scratched, but not hurt), just for safety's sake, I was delighted at the chance for even a few precious moments to be alone with her again, to have my mum's sympathy and have her tell me how brave I was and how she would make all the nasty cuts and bruises better. My school-teacher dropped me home – she was on a half day herself – and waited while I found the special key that was always left outside under the backdoor flowerpot for emergencies (this was 1969, remember). When I appeared at the front door to wave at her and she knew I was safely inside, she drove off.

It was a beautiful day, early summer, May, probably, when we had one of those balmy weeks that lured us into a false sense of tropical weather to come. 'If only we could rely on the weather,' older people used to say. 'If only there was even one month, just one, when we knew it would be good. Then, with our beaches and coastlines – well, it would just be sheer heaven.' But that was just it. You couldn't rely on the weather in Ireland. You still can't. We have some of the most beautiful beaches in the world, but apart from the odd day when the gods smile, the clouds part and the mist lifts, they mostly appear grey and damp.

That day was not one of the grey, damp days. This had been a week that sparkled and shone, a week that demanded ankle socks and sandals, trips to rock pools and beaches where picnics were hurriedly concocted and deckchairs and wind shields stood solidly against the wild Atlantic salt-ridden gusts, a week when children skipped and climbed trees (or in my case, fell out of them). When old people smiled fondly at us and parents complained of the heat (we're not equipped for it) and women ventured into summer dresses, light as an evening's breeze. Some men even wore short-sleeved shirts. My father was not one of them. He disapproved strongly. What next? Knotted handkerchiefs? Rolled up trousers? Dear God.

It was three o'clock. I remember that clearly because I had been proudly wearing my new Mickey Mouse watch that my godmother had sent me from America. Luckily, it had emerged unscathed from the fall. My wrist was sore though, and I had two fairly big cuts on my knees that had been cleaned and bandaged at school and would scab up nicely. I had a good scratch over my right eye too, which had dried up now, but which had bled quite pleasingly at the time. I was pretty sure I looked much worse than I actually felt, which was bound to produce a good result.

Inside the house was quiet, but Mum's car was outside and I could smell her perfume, so I knew she was home. I wandered into the kitchen but it was empty, although the door to the garden was open and I could see our small summer table and two chairs had been set up on the patio. The table was covered in a white cloth and two brightly coloured cushions sat on the chairs. There was some food left on the table, I remember that, some cheese, I think, and the long thin bread that I didn't like. There were glasses too, nearly empty ones, that smelled of something bitter and when I took a gulp the fizzy liquid went up my nose, making me splutter. A radio was playing, sitting on the low wall behind the table, but there was no sign of Mum. She must be upstairs.

Inside, the house smelled of furniture polish, and I remembered just in time not to grab at the stair rail with my hands so I wouldn't leave fingerprints all over it; Mum was always giving out to me and Patrick about that. On the landing, all the bedroom doors were shut. I remember thinking that was strange, because usually they were left open. 'Mum?' I called softly from outside her door, but there was no answer. Maybe she was asleep; she went for an afternoon nap sometimes. Now I was torn – would I be disturbing her? But no, she would want to see my cuts and bruises, I knew she would, even if she was asleep, and maybe, just maybe, she would let me climb in beside her for a while and cuddle up, or maybe read me a story. So I turned the handle and pushed the door ajar, just enough to peep through.

I'm not sure how long I stood there, frozen, both hands still clutching the door handle. But however long it was, I knew they hadn't seen me. Or heard me. I closed the door, quiet as a mouse, and just as quietly went downstairs. Then I went outside and down the road to Mrs Buckley's house and rang her bell.

'Charlie,' she said, her face breaking into a beam. 'What is it, love?' She ruffled my hair and, although I hated it, I let her. Mr and Mrs Buckley adored Patrick and me because they didn't have any children of their own.

'Could I stay with you for a bit, Mrs Buckley? I've been sent home from school early 'cos of these cuts, but my mum will be out for a while. I forgot she's shopping in town this afternoon. She'll be back later, though, and Patrick will be home in about an hour.'

'Well of course you can, I'm only delighted to have a visit from you. Now how about some lemonade and a slice of sponge cake while I take a look at those cuts?'

'Thanks very much, Mrs. Buckley,' I said, as I had been taught. 'That'd be lovely.'

I followed her into their kitchen, which was a lot like ours, and the back door was open too. Only outside, in their garden, there was a swing-seat, and Mr Buckley was sitting on it reading the newspaper, smoking his pipe. When he saw me he put the paper down and spoke out of the corner of his mouth. 'Well, well, well, who have we here?'

'Charlie's gone and fallen out of a tree,' explained Mrs Buckley. 'Vera's out for a bit and Patrick will be home in an hour. I said we'd be only delighted to have him for a while.'

'And so we are,' agreed Mr Buckley, patting the seat beside him for me to sit down while his wife went to get the lemonade. 'Now, young man, tell me, what class of a tree was it that you fell out of?'

So I told him in great detail about the fall, making sure to leave nothing out. I even repeated bits of the story without knowing I was. It felt reassuring, you see. It was something that *had* happened, something I could explain, and more importantly I could relive it in my head as I told it, scene by scene, blocking out the other, unwanted, inexplicable ones that had found their way inside my head.

'Slow down, Charlie, slow down,' Mr Buckley chuckled. 'You're talking so fast I can hardly keep up with you. Now, look – here's Frannie with the lemonade.' He made room on the table in front of the swing seat as Mrs Buckley set out the cake and lemonade for me. 'I think young Charlie might need something stronger than this,' he said, winking at us both. Then he looked at his wife and said, 'I think the poor little fellow's still in shock.'

Later, of course, I did go back home. I made sure to wait for Patrick as he walked back from the school bus that dropped him off after games at the end of our road.

'What are you doing here?' he asked me, hauling his bag over his shoulder. 'Weren't you sent home because of your fall?'

'Yeah,' I shrugged, 'but I didn't want to go home. I called in to Mrs Buckley instead and had lemonade.' And then I remembered that I had left my school bag at home. Someone would have seen it, I was pretty sure I left it in the kitchen. I had to think fast. 'I mean, I went home, but Mum must have been out or something. Anyway, there was no one there so I went to Buckleys, then I thought I'd meet you off the bus and we'd go home together.' We were nearing our house, just footsteps away. I felt my heart begin to thump. Patrick broke into a run.

'Last one in's a sissy.'

But my feet had suddenly become as heavy as lead. I thought I was going to cry.

'What's the matter?' Patrick stopped, puzzled. 'C'mon,' he said, waiting till I caught up with him. 'If you're that sore, you'll get ice cream for sure and Mum will kiss it all better.' He was mocking me now, but I didn't care.

I didn't want ice cream. I wanted everything to be exactly

as it was before I'd left home that morning. I certainly didn't want my mother – not now.

'Patrick, and Charlie!' The door was flung open before we reached it. 'Thank God,' she exclaimed, running out to meet us, 'you had me worried sick.' I couldn't look at her. It wasn't my mother at all – it was some strange woman who looked like her and sounded like her but had taken my mother away.

'Charlie,' she was saying, bending down to look at me and my scratches while Patrick dumped his bag in the kitchen. 'You scared the life out of me. When I found your bag and rang the school, and then rang Mrs Buckley and she told me you'd left – oh, your poor, poor knees, let me look at them!'

But I didn't want her to look at them – not her. It was then I started to cry, loud, wailing sobs, but I beat her away with my fists.

'Don't mind him, he's just being a baby,' Patrick said, reaching for a biscuit. 'Sure, he was fine when he came to meet me at the bus, not a sound out of him then.'

'Leave me alone,' I wailed. My mother stood back and shook her head. 'I don't know what's got into him.' She looked genuinely worried, but I knew it wasn't so.

'What's all this?' It was our father, home from work.

'It's my fault,' said Mum, bending down again to look at me. 'Poor Charlie fell out of a tree and they bandaged him up and sent him home, and I wasn't here when he got in, poor mite.'

'Where where you?' my father asked mildly, putting his briefcase on the hall table and taking off his jacket. He looked tired, and hot.

'Una dropped in for a bite of lunch. It was such a nice day we sat out in the garden, and I said I'd drop her home to save her catching the bus. I needed to pick up some groceries anyway. Poor Charlie here had to go to the Buckleys, the pet.'

She said all this while she was looking at me – not Dad.

'Well.' He came over to us and Mum stood up. 'What's the damage, son?'

I looked him in the eye. 'Nothing,' I mumbled. 'I'm fine.'

It had been the right thing to say.

'That's a good lad.' He headed upstairs. 'I'm going to have a shower, Vera. Have I time, before dinner? This blasted heat will kill me. The court was like an oven, and the drive back from Kilkenny was worse.'

'Of course you've time,' she called after him. 'Dinner won't be for another half an hour.' Then she turned to us. 'Why don't you boys go and play outside while it's still nice and warm. No rough and tumble, mind. And I think there might be ice cream for dessert – especially for a brave boy like Charlie.' She smiled at me, but I wasn't taken in. I would never believe her again, this woman who pretended to be my mother.

Later, when we went to bed, our parents came up to say goodnight. 'No climbing trees in your dreams tonight, son!' my father said, smiling as he bent to kiss me. 'We don't want you falling out of bed too!'

'Are you sure you're all right, pet?' It was her, smoothing back my hair and running her thumb along the scratch above my eye. 'If you're sore anywhere I can get you an aspirin.'

I shook my head and turned away from her.

She put her hand under my chin and gently turned my face back until I had to look at her. 'Charlie, pet, what's the matter?' Something flickered across her face I had never seen before. Later, when I was older, I recognised that look in people's eyes – it was fear.

But now I had to lie. 'Nothing,' I said. 'Nothing's the matter.' And I curled up tight and closed my eyes.

'What did I tell you?' I heard Dad say as he turned off the light and closed the door. 'He'll be right as rain in the morning. He'll have forgotten all about it.'

I never heard what she said in reply. I didn't want to. I just wanted to go to sleep and stop the scary images that kept coming into my head, so I picked at the scratch above my eye instead, until it bled and stung like a nettle. And bit by bit I could feel nothing else, not even the sorest part of me, the part no one could see somewhere in my chest, so sore that it hurt to breathe. I knew even then that that particular pain had nothing to do with falling out of the tree.

Like I said. There are some things children just know.

Lukaz

Hotel suite is good, but not as good as own house, I think. That's why I rent townhouse here in Dublin until I find my country estate and maybe stud farm. Olag says estate agent peoples he approach very excitable when he instruct them to find residence for me. He has done well. They offer me house of Irish businessman to rent, 6,000 square feet in town. It is near embassies – I like this. But I do not like the furniture or paintings. They are not of my taste. So I tell agency peoples, take it all out and I will rent the house, get my own furniture and art. Art is very personal thing I think, and I like to collect.

So far, I like this little city. Peoples are very friendly. Even when Olag drive me in the blacked-out Hummer, I see them looking at us everywhere. Some even wave at us, so I let down window and wave back, which surprises them. I think it is safe to do this occasionally, here – although all the windows and car are bulletproof. Personal security is very important to oligarchs. Some of us even buy our own personal firms.

I like to get to know a city, so while agencies are finding suitable properties for me to view, I behave like tourist person. I walk around Dublin and visit Christchurch, the Liberties and the Guinness tower, which I like very much. Dublin Castle too, and of course Trinity College and Kelly's Book. I stroll down Grafton Street and am told to have coffee in Bewley's, which is Dublin equivalent of Russian Tea Rooms in New York, I am guessing. Then, after coffee, I feel like doing some shopping, so I go to small store called Brown Thomas and pick up some casual clothes. I get a lot of attention. I am good-looking guy, even if I say so myself. I am tall, I have blond hair, which I wear closely cut. My face is nice, I think, and I have a good smile – from my Irish great-grandfather, my grandmother tell me. I keep in good shape too, work out every day, not as fit as I was in my Spetsnaz days, but I still have six pack. Still can lift 500 pounds. For forty-two years old this is not bad, I think. After clothes shopping I tell the shop salespeoples that my driver will pick up clothes later – I cannot carry around parcels, that is for women! So now I go to find some galleries, I think, and see a little Irish art.

It is nice day here, mild, sun is shining and peoples are stopping and talking to each other in the street. This is not like London, I notice. Irish talk a lot – Russians too. Peoples always rushing in London. I turn a corner and cross a street, then look down small alleyway. A sign catches my eye. It says Ernie's Eclectic Art. So I decide to go there and have a look. It is twelve forty-five, almost lunchtime, but gallery is open. Small, but open. I look through window and see woman dusting sculpture. From behind she look very nice. Good figure, even under gypsy skirt and white blouse she wear, I can tell this. Hair is tied up loosely. Her hands, which carefully stroke the bronze figure, are firm yet gentle. I smile to myself. A man likes to indulge these kinds of speculations.

I open the door and she jumps – I have taken her by surprise. I am guessing things are not so busy here during recession time.

'Can I help you?' she says. She has turned around, and I congratulate myself. She looks just as nice as I thought from the front. Very nice smile, she pushes lock of hair behind her ear and looks nervous. I like her immediately. Her voice sounds like breathless caress.

'Yes,' I say. 'I hope so. I am looking for some art. Mind if I have a look around?'

'Of course,' she say. 'If you need any help, just let me know.' And she goes over to desk and sits behind it. Studies computer. I think she is shy.

I look around, and I like what I see. This is interesting collection, modern but soulful – it speaks to me. I go upstairs. Look around some more, bigger pieces are here, paintings stacked against wall – more sculpture – life sized. I inspect all of them. There are names I recognise and some pieces which are quite innovative. I think I have come to the right place. I go downstairs and ask the woman who the buyer is.

'The man who owns the gallery is Ernie Huggard. He selects all the work, it's a lifelong passion.' She smiles, and it is a lovely smile. I get the impression immediately that this is a woman who does not realise how attractive she is – and this, for a man, is extremely attractive. I find myself smiling back at her, and noticing how her eyes crinkle. She blushes. Very cute.

'Your husband?' I ask.

'I'm sorry?' She sounds confused.

'Ernie – your husband, yes?' I am still looking her in the eyes, and smiling.

'Oh, er, no,' she laughs a little. 'No, I just work for Ernie – he's my employer, the boss.'

'He is lucky man,' I say.

'Er, was there anything you wanted to ask about?' Now she is looking serious, as if it is wrong to have fun while you work. Maybe she is afraid of Ernie person – maybe he is tough boss. But not for long, I think.

'Yes, actually,' I reply. 'I like what I see here.'

'Oh,' she says, looking pleased. 'Which piece?'

I look at her and smile again. 'All of them.'

'Um, all of what?' she ask.

'Everything. Paintings, sculpture. I like it all.'

'Oh,' she says again. 'Well, that's very nice of you to say so.'

'No problem,' I say. 'So . . .' I leave a significant pause. 'How much?'

She looks pleased now, and hopeful – eager, yes, that is the word I am searching for.

'How much for what? Which piece?'

'All of them.'

'I'm sorry?'

'All of them, honey,' I say. 'I want to buy everything. Everything in here.' I watch as she tries to understand this.

'You want to buy everything?' she repeats.

'Yes. Everything. On one condition,' I add.

'I – I'm not sure if that would be possible, Mr . . . ?' She looks at me, her face is a question mark.

'Luke – just call me Luke.' I smile. This is the English for Lukaz.

'You want to buy everything in the gallery?'

'Yes,' I repeat. 'And it is always possible.' I smile again. I am patient man, but determined, and clearly this is going to take some time. 'Why don't you call Ernie?' I suggest, and I look at my watch. This seems to bring her back to her senses – for a moment I think she is lost in understanding. English people are used to oligarchs' purchasing ways, maybe Irish people not so used to this. 'Now,' I add, tapping my watch. 'No time like present, yes?' I add, making joke.

'Yes, of course,' she say, looking nervous again, 'just one moment, if you'd like to take a seat, please.' She gestures towards the seat in front of the desk.

I wait while she dial the numbers, but I notice her fingers are trembling. I feel immediately protective of her, poor baby, this Ernie must be bad boss – but I think he will be happy with her very soon. I look forward to meeting him. It is inevitable, they always want to meet with me.

'Hello, Ernie? It's me, Shelley, can you talk? I'm not inter-rupting you?' She sounds anxious. 'No, no problem, not at all, it's just that I have a buyer here, a Mr . . . Luke.'

I smile at her and nod encouragingly. 'And he wants to make a rather sizeable purchase.' She pauses. I like the way she puts this – *a sizeable purchase*. I make a mental note to remember this phrase. She pauses and listens, and then says, 'Well, everything.' I sit back in my chair and watch. It is always the same.

'No, no, I'm quite sure. In fact, he's sitting here in front of me. Would you like to talk to him?'

I shake my head at the idea. I don't want to talk to Ernie, is much more fun to watch Shelley talk to him. I remind her. 'Of course, don't forget – there is one condition,' I say.

She continues to talk into the phone. 'Hang on a sec, Ernie, he says there's one condition.' She puts her hand over phone and ask me, 'He wants to know what the condition is.'

'You have lunch with me now – that is the condition,' I smile.

Now she is really looking worried. I think it is time to take charge of things. 'Here,' I command, 'give me the phone.' And she hands it over.

I briefly tell Ernie my intentions. I also give him my refer-ences in London art world. I tell him to check them out and ring me back. In the meantime, I say, I take his very helpful employee out to lunch. With his permission, of course. He tell me to put Shelley back on phone.

'Yes,' I hear her say. 'Of course I'll have the phone on me.' Her voice is sounding weak. She hangs up.

'So,' I ask, smiling, 'you will have lunch with me now?'

'Yes, if you'd like,' she says, chewing her lip. 'Ernie said he'll ring back.'

'He also told me you could take afternoon off,' I say, grinning. 'Close up shop, Shelley, we are going to have very nice lunch.'

She laughs nervously. 'Um, where are we going?' she ask, and then, 'I need to freshen up, if you wouldn't mind waiting a few minutes.'

'No problem,' I say. 'I think we go to Guilbaud's, yes?'

'I think you have to book,' she says doubtfully, 'and I'm not sure if I'm appropriately dressed.' She smoothes down her gypsy skirt and looks at her cowboy boots.

'You are perfect,' I say, and I mean it. 'And there is always table for me at Guilbaud's.'

I wait for her as she goes to bathroom – and I realise my heart is beating. This is not because of imminent purchase, I think. I realise with pleasant surprise that this has not happened to me for a long, long time. I am looking forward to talking now with this Irish woman. I must tell Grandmother, this will please her. For now I put my phone on silent. Natascha has already phoned me six times this morning and I don't want lunch to be interrupted. I look at my watch, it is one fifteen. I hear Shelley's footsteps as she reappear and I smile at her. 'Let's go, baby,' I say, and I hold the door open for her.

Caroline

I'm a fighter, you know. I don't just sit back and let things happen to me – that's for losers. It's all a matter of perspective. And although it might seem as if things had gone belly up for me, I knew it was just a matter of applying the same positive mental attitude to the current situation that I had used to get me through the other sticky moments in my life thus far – and there had been a few, I'll admit that, but like the song says, too few to mention. From a practical point of view, the worst part, of course, was having my mother living with me, or as she would have it – *me having to move back in with her*. Rich, isn't it? It was my bloody house. Which is why I had to get out of it on a regular basis – being cooped up with her there was driving me quite insane.

I was running now across the bridge on the motorway, heading for the campus of University College Dublin, my old alma mater. Four miles on the running track would clear my head and keep me in shape. It always calmed me. This is not the end of the world, I repeated to myself. I can get through this, come out the other side – just like I did when I came back from Harvard to discover Charlie was marrying Shelley. I had thought that was the end of the world then, but it hadn't been, had it?

I remember even then, all those years ago, thinking what a stupid name Shelley was. And who the hell was she, anyway? And how had she managed to get her grasping little claws into my Charlie? All right, we weren't exactly going out together then. We were on a sort of break – after all, I had turned down his marriage proposal in favour of going to Harvard to do my Masters – but it had been me he wanted to marry, not her. He should have waited for me, sown a few wild oats if he had to, sure, but get engaged? Get married? It just wasn't possible.

I vividly remember getting the phone call – from my mother, of course, who else? She was in a right state when she rang. I thought someone had died or something.

'Caroline,' she said in a tremulous voice as I picked up the phone and my Harvard roommate groaned in protest. It was five a.m. in Boston, way too early for a social call.

'What is it, Mum?' I struggled to come to. I had exams all week and had been studying late every night.

'It – it's Charlie.' Her voice was breaking.

Oh God, I thought, as a cold hand of fear clutched my heart. Oh no, please let nothing have happened to him. 'What – w – what's happened to him?' I whispered.

There was a pause, and then, 'He's getting married, Caroline,' she sniffed – a stifled sob. My mother was crying? She never cried, not even watching *Casablanca*. 'Charlie's getting married. I'm looking at the engagement notice in the *Irish Times*, I'm holding it in my hand as I speak. As God's my witness, I'm—'

'Okay, okay I get the picture,' I snapped, rage and relief flooding through me in equal measures. Relief because he was alive, not dead or paralysed; rage because I knew my mother was milking the drama content of this little scenario for all she was worth. She didn't fool me – she was *enjoying* this. This one would run and run.

'Well there's no need to be like that! I'm only going to the trouble and expense of ringing you, making a transatlantic phone call – or would you rather hear it from one of your so-called friends? It'll be the talk of Dublin, you know, and you've no one to blame but yours—'

'Shut up,' I hissed, a little uncharitably, but along with the shock, I could see where this was going. 'When?' I barked. 'When exactly is the wedding?'

'How should I know?' she shot back at me. 'This is the engagement notice, it doesn't say.'

I let out a long breath. There was still time. Term finished in ten days. I had planned to hang out in Cape Cod with my friends for the summer, but that wasn't important now. I would go home instead, tell Charlie to stop this madness. We were meant for each other, everybody said so. I would forgive him this – this rebound fling or whatever it was with the Shelley person. She would understand. She would have to, although it might be hard for her. It wasn't her destiny, because Charlie couldn't marry anyone else. He just couldn't, because quite simply, Charlie belonged to me.

I met him when I was in my first year at college. And no, it wasn't love at first sight. Although looking back there was always something compelling about Charlie, even then. We met at a local rugby club disco – well, local for Charlie, not for me – but it was the one the girls and I decided to go to for a laugh, on the posh side of town. We thought we'd show the saddo spoiled kids up with our street cred and couldn't-care-less attitude. In fact, looking back, it was amazing that anyone ever did come over to talk to us or ask us to dance, we were that rude. But we looked good. We had made sure of that, which in itself was quite a feat, seeing as it was 1978, not an era memorable for its flattering styles. I noticed Charlie before he noticed me, but I didn't let him know that. Instead, I drank vodka from a brown paper bag that my mate Julie had smuggled in. Then we (there were three of us) took to the floor, giving off aggressive vibes and lurching around to pop music.

From under the fringe of my heavily permed hair, I could see Charlie watching us – watching me. But even I didn't expect him to walk over to us and actually ask me for a dance.

Normally at these things the girls danced together until the guys got so plastered they might stagger over and start lurching around on the edge of the group until one or other of you sort of shuffled into each other's general orbit. It wasn't really done to actually ask anyone to dance. You either did or you didn't, and rejection (which would have been decided upon hours before) was indicated by the general derision of the collective group of girls. Hideous, really, when I think of it, but back then we didn't know any better – and none of the guys complained. At least not to our faces. Just as well we didn't have mobile phones and text messaging – that could have gotten tricky.

So as I said, I was surprised when Charlie came over and asked for a dance, although if it had been anyone else they would have looked like a nerd. But even my mates, who were trying hard, couldn't quite manage to snigger at him, so I started to dance with him and bit by bit we edged away from the rest of the group.

That was what I liked about Charlie, although I didn't know it back then – he had natural confidence, something I would have killed for. And out of all the girls there, even some really classy-looking ones, he had chosen me.

When we started going with each other (no one called it *dating* then, or even *going out with*, or *seeing* somebody – you were just going with them), there were mixed reactions. My mates were surprised, but it was masking envy – I knew that because I'd have reacted exactly the same way. Raised eyebrows, slight disbelief, followed by disinterested shrugs. He's not one of us, they were saying. Suit yourself, but he won't fit in – and you won't last.

My brothers laughed at him and then radiated resentment when Charlie got first a motorbike, and later a car.

My mother's nostrils flared with pride (she couldn't help it, it was a genetic thing – an attribute, thank God, I've managed to avoid). *Her daughter's boyfriend was the son of a judge.* She never got over it – still hasn't, but that's another story.

And improbable though it may have seemed, we did last, for five years. You see, although we may have been very different on the outside, Charlie and I had a surprising amount in common. We were both terrifically ambitious, for one thing, and both equally determined to hide the fact. I quickly discerned that in Charlie's case it was because it would have looked like he was trying too hard, and he had an older brother, Patrick, who already ticked that box. So for Charlie, success had to come about seemingly effortlessly. But that never happens, not really – clever people just make it look that way. But when you're younger that doesn't seem so obvious.

In my case, I would have been ridiculed. My mother never worked a day in her life. She did a course in Domestic Science before marrying my dad and made a career of waiting hand and foot on him and my two brothers. Working outside the home was not something she would have aspired to, never mind understood. Marrying a man who could 'keep you' was all.

We weren't poor or anything, though there wasn't much money in evidence. I suppose we would have been described as lower middle class, if you were that way inclined. My father worked in an administrative position in an insurance firm, eventually reaching the giddy heights of manager. My brothers were doing their best not to work at anything at all, but were being pushed respectively into the civil service and the post office. The ambition gene had escaped them – but not me. I wanted university, and I wanted it badly enough not to mention it to a single living soul. Not even my teachers, who were equally in the dark about my agenda. I didn't get great results at school in general, but it wasn't until the final two years, when the Leaving Certificate loomed, that I started working properly and studying hard at home, where in the privacy of my own room (there had to be some bonus to being the only girl) I vowed to attain the results needed to go to UCD. I was an outsider, of course, an unlikely contender. No one in our family had ever entertained thoughts of going to university. But outsiders have this uncanny knack of becoming winners – any bookie will tell you that.

So I went to university and studied economics. Charlie was a year ahead of me, doing commerce, and we helped each other through our finals. But it wasn't just about academic results – that was the least of it for me, really.

I learned so much just from being with Charlie. And I loved spending time with his family, observing them, listening to what they spoke about, conversations that were a million miles away from anything I'd ever hear at home. I'd been afraid, meeting his parents and his brother Patrick for the first time, not that I let on – but I needn't have worried. They were posh for sure, but reassuringly normal. Their house was normal looking too, a nice semi-detached one and well kept, of course, but it was in what my mother would have called A Very Good Area. I hadn't told her I was going around for my dinner to Charlie's house (we called it tea). She would have driven me mental about it and probably tried to get me to wear a twin set and fake pearls or something mad like that. But I was determined to be myself. It was all I had to offer, and so far Charlie, at least, was liking it.

Inside the house was different, though. Even before I noticed the tasteful furniture and elegant paintings, there was just a different sort of atmosphere, I suppose you'd call it – sort of calm and, well, solid. The sense that things ran well and easily here, and had done for generations. Charlie's mum, Vera, came out to the hall to meet me when she heard us come in. She was nice and friendly and not overly interested, not looking me up and down on inspection like some mothers might. I liked her immediately. She told Charlie to take me into the sitting room and told him to get me a drink, then she disappeared off back to the kitchen where she was cooking dinner.

'So, what can I get you to drink?' Charlie asked in mock gallantry while I started to giggle. 'Sherry, perhaps?' A gin and tonic?' I settled for a Coke.

Then his dad arrived, came in and shook hands with me, muttered something about tax and went out again. And finally Patrick thundered downstairs and showed none of his parents' considered restraint as he barged into the room.

'Hiya Caroline,' he said, grinning broadly. 'Good to meet you.' He flung himself onto the couch where we were sitting. I had to hold on to my glass so it didn't topple from the arm it was resting on.

'Well, you've met her now, so get lost,' said Charlie, only half joking, but I could tell what Patrick thought was impor-tant to him, just by a subtle shift in his expression, an eagerness in his eyes.

But Patrick didn't get lost (which I deduced correctly to be a good sign). He sat and chatted with us and made me laugh as he flicked channels on the TV, and then their mum poked her head around the door.

'Caroline, boys, dinner's ready, come along.'

It was the first of many pleasant evenings I would spend over the next few years in that small dining room, and surpris-ingly quickly, I felt at home there, although, as I said, it was all a million miles away from dinner in our place. There, I actually felt like someone who mattered. A person in my own right. Even Charlie's dad, Mr Fitzgibbon, who I thought was pretty scary, him being a judge and all that, was really nice and interested in me, especially when he heard I was studying economics. He even asked me about an element of an important case that had come before him recently and listened as if my opinion really mattered.

This, surely, was how things were meant to be. I had always suspected as much. People, families, sitting down around a table and conversing, discussing interesting topics, parents actually enquiring how a day went, and a mother who calmly, efficiently presided over dinner and cleared it away (of course I offered to help but I was refused) with, mind-bogglingly, the help of her sons. That was an eye-opener for me, I can tell you.

I now knew for sure that there was a better way to live, a way of life worth working for, aspiring to, however long the journey might take. I secretly called it the Clockwork House, because everything seemed to happen so perfectly and on time there, like a Swiss railway station. (I'd never been to one back then, but it seemed an appropriate analogy.)

Which was why, when the timing faltered that day and everything went so horribly out of kilter, I could never really feel the same about that house, or Charlie's mother, Vera – no more than she, I imagined, could ever feel the same way about me, although almost immediately afterwards and in the years to come, we both achieved a remarkable degree of denial about the whole episode. It wasn't that we disliked each other – far from it. I had always liked Charlie's mum. It's just that when you've seen someone stripped bare like that, seen raw pain flare in their eyes, followed almost immediately by horrified fear and humiliation – well, you can never be quite the same around each other, never quite at ease, even though you yourself had nothing to do with what happened.

I had walked in on it unawares, you see, the time bomb that was ticking away in that family, especially between Charlie and his mother, and like any other (reasonably) innocent bystander, I got caught in the crossfire.

I recovered after the initial shock, but I'm not sure if Charlie ever did. And knowing what I know now about life, I'm pretty sure a part of Vera withered away that day too.

But isn't that what life is about, as some wise person once pointed out to me – a series of little deaths, of letting go? I'm still not very good at that – the letting go business – but no one said it would be easy.

Even at my age, as a grown woman, I find it hard to think about, to dwell on that day at all, although as teenage exploits go it was a reasonably innocent one, even back then. It was just our choice of venue that had been unwise. Of course, that was what had made it so much part of the fun – the forbidden element.

'C'mon, we'll go back to my place.' Charlie dragged me up from the grass in Herbert Park where we were celebrating our respective exams being almost over. Anyway, we had a break of a couple of days, so there was a reprieve from frantic cramming.

'What?' It was only three o'clock, and still sunny, and I was enjoying our beer and Tayto cheese 'n' onion crisp picnic. 'Why?'

'Because . . . I feel like it.' Charlie slid a hand under my T-shirt and his thumb traced circles on my skin.

I shivered. 'But . . .'

'They've gone away, they left at lunchtime, remember?'

Actually, I had forgotten, but I was getting the general drift of things.

'What about Patrick?'

'He's in Munich, with his au pair friend, Greta, working on his language skills, I'm sure.'

'So.'

'There's no one home – except me – for the whole weekend.' He was kissing me now and I giggled. 'So what are we waiting for?' He blew a stray tendril of hair out of my eye.

'Are you sure, Charlie? I mean, what if . . . ?' A whole series of undesirable possibilities ran through my mind. I was the adventurous one, it was usually me egging Charlie on, me pushing all the boundaries, but suddenly I was cautious. I actually liked his parents and I knew they liked me, and it dawned on me that I didn't want to jeopardise that and risk losing that elusive respect I seemed to have found both for them and from them. I certainly hadn't experienced it with any other adults I knew, especially not my own parents, who along with the rest of them thought I was either wild, deluded or unreliable, when in fact, as I discovered many years later, I was just very, very clever. But I had no idea about that back then. Even then, I thought getting into university had been a fluke, and I had yet to get my first year top-class honours.

It wasn't done to admit to actually working for results anyway; they were always supposed to be some mad accidental joke that surprised you more than anyone, seeing as you had supposedly spent all year missing lectures and tutorials along with your mates in favour of hanging out in the student bar getting smashed. No one ever admitted to actually doing any work – it just wasn't part of our pre-Celtic Tiger ethos – which is why I always suspected so many Irish people did well abroad. It was safe for them to be seen to be working, admired, even, and the more jobs the better – two, even three job shifts weren't unusual. Finally there was an outlet for all that energy that had been put into getting drunk and having *craic*. Although a surprising amount of my mates *did* get their exams anyway, so we must all have been great actors as well.

The point I was making is that although Charlie and I were sleeping together, not living together, this was Ireland in 1980 and we were both city students – it wasn't done to move out of home unless you were going to an out-of-town university, so for anyone from outside Dublin, who came up to town to go to UCD, well, the world was their Dublin Bay oyster, but the rest of us were stuck at home. Which meant we were at it like rabbits at any opportunity we could get, and believe me, they were rare enough.

Which is why the prospect of an afternoon and evening spent in a real bed, in a real house that we had all to ourselves was enough to make me throw caution and any other reservations I might have had to the wind. And there was a whole weekend of it looming. I wouldn't be able to stay the night, but I could spend the following two days there, which was just as good.

'Are you sure they're gone?' I tugged Charlie's arm.

'I'm positive. I know they were leaving at one o'clock at the latest, Dad had it all arranged – he wanted to be on the course at four o'clock for a quick nine holes, and Mum had a hair appointment there for the dinner dance this evening.'

Charlie's parents had gone to a popular hotel on the west coast for a golfing weekend – they wouldn't be back until Monday evening.

So home we went to Charlie's house. It was only a fifteen-minute walk anyway, and Charlie laughed at me for ringing the bell 'just to double check'.

'Can't you see?' he said, putting his key in the door and turning it. 'The car's gone, they're well on the road by now. Relax, will you?'

I did try, and no one was more surprised that I, always the wild child, was now discovering a hitherto well-suppressed sense of decorum, possibly even guilt emerging. But seeing the look on Charlie's face, I happily ignored it and followed him quickly upstairs to his parents' room, where he threw himself onto the bed and then pulled me on top of him. I remember then thinking how lucky Charlie was, and wondering if he knew it. Did he have any idea? Liberal parents who trusted him, even let him drive the car, and this house, with its tall ceilings and well-kept rooms – even this bed, whose sheets were clearly freshly ironed and curiously silky (of course I would make sure they were freshly washed and immaculate for his parents' return).

'It's starch, I guess,' said Charlie when I commented, immediately going back to kissing my stomach and trailing a hand along my thigh.

'How do you know that?' I was genuinely curious.

'Because Dad's always going on about it. How there's nothing in the world like freshly starched sheets.' He grinned. 'But I can think of something a lot better.'

'What?'

'You an' me in them.'

I laughed, and then stopped, as Charlie reminded me why I spent so much time thinking about him when I wasn't with him. He could make me feel amazing. With him, my body turned into something wildly exciting, responsive and joyful. And if that sounds a bit over the top, it's just that now I have the right words to describe it – back then I just thought *oh God, this guy is incredible*. It was as if he knew exactly what to do and when to do it without the slightest prompting. Almost as if he could hear a running commentary from somewhere deep inside me that I didn't even know existed – and followed it. Later, of course, years later, I would just admit to myself that he was a naturally gifted lover, and although I knew he had slept with a couple of other girls before me, back then I assumed I'd be the last. We were that good together. So good that neither of us heard the front door opening, nor anyone's footsteps coming up the stairs, not even anyone calling my or Charlie's name although they must have, even softly. We never heard a thing, so blissfully engaged we were in our lovemaking, barely registering the warm breeze and the gleeful shouts of children playing in the distance that floated through the open window as we lay entwined.

'Charlie! Oh my God!'

I always thought in a situation like this that I would sit bolt upright, clutching a sheet protectively to my bosom, like they do on TV. Instead I froze and lay rigid with fright while Charlie disentangled himself from me and looked around, although there was no mistaking who the voice belonged to. He sat up slowly.

I must have reached for the sheet. I have never before or since felt so exposed.

Silence.

Something made me look. I forced myself to. And like an out-of-body experience I witnessed Vera at the door, one hand clutching the door knob, the other clutching her throat.

'Haven't you heard of knocking?' It was Charlie, in an astonishingly measured voice, one I didn't recognise.

When she spoke, her voice was strangely high. 'We came back. Your father forgot his blood pressure pills,' she was babbling. And then, 'What the hell do you think you're doing?'

Here it comes, I thought. The shock was wearing off, and anger kicking in.

'How dare you?' she cried. 'I – I can't believe this, in my – in our bedroom – in my own bed.'

Her voice was beginning to falter. *Oh no*, I silently begged from under the sheet, which I had retreated under, *please don't let her cry*. I could cope with anything but Vera crying.

'And you, Caroline,' she said chillingly. 'How could you? I thought so much more of you. How can you both degrade yourselves and our house like – like—'

She never got any further.

'Shut up.'

'Charlie,' I whispered, disbelievingly, 'please, don't.'

'What did you just say?' Vera sounded puzzled.

'I said shut up and I mean it. It's a bit late now to be barging in here with your hypocritical crap and self-pity. You might be able to fool yourself, but you don't fool me.'

'What? How dare you? I – I'm going to call your father right now.'

'Yes, go on, why don't you?'

I didn't know what was simmering beneath the surface, but some instinct told me it wasn't good. I scrabbled for my clothes, thankfully in a discarded puddle by the bed beside me, and although it felt interminable in the loaded silence that filled the room, seconds later I was dressed. I sat on the bed with my head in my hands. Charlie, however, was still lying up against the pillows, a sheet to his waist, but I could tell that underneath the sheet, his feet were crossed. This relaxed pose struck me as faintly ludicrous.

'Caroline,' Vera said, 'I think you'd better go, please.'

'She's not going anywhere.'

'I will give you three minutes – three minutes – and when I come back I want you both out of my room and downstairs.'

'I'm so sorry, Vera,' I whispered, and looking at her caught a flicker of sympathy in her eyes.

'I saw you.' It was Charlie, in that strange measured voice again. 'I saw you with him, here, right in this very bed. That's what this is all about, isn't it? It didn't seem to bother you then, bringing a strange man into the house, into this bed. Didn't seem to bother you at all.'

'What? What are you talking about?'

Now my head snapped around.

'You heard me. I saw you, I saw you both, that day I was sent back from school. You never even noticed me, never heard me come in either. It's a long time ago now, but that sort of image is pretty memorable to a kid. Why don't you go down and tell Dad *that* while you're about it?'

'Jesus, Charlie,' I said. I looked in horror from him to Vera, who looked as if she had been hit. She was struggling to speak but there were no words, only strange gasps. I thought she might be having a heart attack or something, but I couldn't move, and the way Charlie was looking at her would have made anyone shrivel up.

'I'd better go,' I said, making for the door. 'Sorry,' I said as I slipped by Vera, but I don't think either she or Charlie heard me. They were both locked in their own memories.

'Ve-ra-a-a,' Arthur called up the stairs. He must have followed Vera inside to see what was taking her so long.

I hurtled down the stairs and past him where he stood in the hall, looking mildly surprised.

'Caroline!' He seemed concerned but pleased to see me.

But I ran. I ran out the door and kept running till I reached the end of the street. I never wanted to see that house again.

Vera (1966–72)

I never knew what depression was, not really. I'm not sure anyone else did either in those days – it was all rather haphazard, to put it nicely. None of those sorts of things were discussed then anyway, not like they are now. Women can be experts on anything now, especially their own health and emotions – which is exactly as it should be, of course.

It wasn't done to talk about your feelings, not even to close women friends, certainly not within the context of a marriage, and it certainly wouldn't have gone down well to admit you simply wanted to die because your foreign lover had been wrenched away from you. No, definitely not that. Not under any circumstances.

We were the generation who grew up with a war in progress, for heaven's sake, a world war, even though here in Ireland it was quaintly referred to as The Emergency. We were neutral, you see. Non-committal, which is how a lot of things were conducted in this country long after the war was over. No confrontation and no talk. Talk was the great evil, the ultimate threat, the unutterable sword hanging over everyone's head. Anything could be got through as long as there wasn't any talk about it. If it wasn't talked about, it never happened.

It was an Irish solution to an Irish problem. An ongoing, long-adhered-to method to ignore and hopefully cull any untimely, unruly emotions that might rise up, eat into our minds and souls and ultimately destroy us.

So you just got on with things. That's the way it was – and

that's exactly what I did. Or tried to do. Except I found that I couldn't. I tried, I really did, desperately hard, and for a while I thought maybe, just maybe I could continue in the mindless routine, wrapped in the numbness that was itself a blessed protection. I thought I could pretend my way through it, a bit like I had pretended my way through the whole affair and its likely consequences, but I hadn't reckoned on the enormous, immutable, impenetrable wall that surrounded me. Later I would learn it was grief – not just for the end of the affair, although that surely was the trigger, but grief for all the unspoken unhappiness of what felt like generations. I felt as if they were all trying to speak through me at once, a veritable collective of female misery. Wave after wave, it kept on coming, until finally even Arthur had to admit there was something wrong. And still we didn't talk about it.

I knew, of course, whatever they said or didn't say. It was simply a broken heart. A shattered, useless thing, no good to me or anyone, least of all my long-suffering husband and children. It wasn't anyone's fault, it just got broken. Hearts do that – all the time. And when they come back together and are pronounced better, yes, they are recovered, yes, they will work well and efficiently again. But there is scar tissue to consider. A different beat to follow, one that can take some time to decipher. And yes, it's true what they say – what doesn't kill you makes you stronger. Only they don't tell you that you may have to die a few slow deaths to get there.

I met him in June of 1966. As if I could ever forget – though Lord knows, I tried to often enough. The Douglases, a couple I was very fond of, had invited us to a tennis party at their place in Wicklow, a lovely Queen Anne house with acres of beautifully tended gardens and, of course, a tennis court. What's more, they had just installed a swimming pool, so we were all instructed to bring our swimming togs as well. I couldn't wait. We were just back from a holiday ourselves.

Arthur had taken myself and the boys to Le Havre on the ferry and we had driven to the south west of France, the Cote Basque, eventually pulling up at a lovely small family hotel called Les Roches, near Saint-Jean-de-Luz, right on the prettiest little beach. The boys were in heaven. They came back brown as nuts and I had quite a nice tan myself from playing with them on the beach all day. Arthur was looking well and relaxed too, although he preferred to stay in the shade and read. I never met anyone who could read as much or as quickly as Arthur, but on holidays he used to get through masses of books, and nothing light either, they were all historical or political tomes. It used to make me feel quite stupid sometimes, sitting beside him with my love stories or my favourite *The Whiteoaks of Jalna* series that I so loved. But Arthur never made me feel stupid. When I asked him if he thought I was reading nonsense, he used to smile at me and say, 'Vera, darling, it's love that makes the world go round. I enjoy a good love story myself, only I'm lucky enough to get to live mine.' He said that, he really did. That's the kind of man Arthur was, kind and appreciative to the end. Which is why what transpired was so dreadfully unfair. A man like Arthur deserved so much more. And yet, if I'm ruthlessly honest, I wouldn't change a thing, because if I hadn't gone to the tennis party that Saturday afternoon, I would never have met Felipe.

It was a gorgeous day and the boys were staying with my mother, who spoiled them rotten. That's why it was such bad luck when Arthur drove a nail through his thumb putting up a picture and had to rush to the doctor to get it disinfected and bandaged.

'Well, Vera, no tennis for me, I'm afraid,' he said ruefully when he got back to find me searching in the hot press for his tennis whites that I'd ironed specially.

'Oh, Arthur darling, your poor hand. Is it terribly sore?'

'It's thumping a bit all right, but the worst is over, though I must say I went a bit green at the gills when old Denis yanked it out!'

I winced at the thought. 'Poor darling,' I kissèd him. 'Never mind, you can umpire, you know how no one ever wants to, and Maggie will be thrilled to have you all to herself for a couple of hours!' Our hostess, Maggie Douglas, was quite a *femme fatale* and harboured the most enormous crush on Arthur. It was an affectionate joke in our circle, one which her charming and very attractive husband William took utterly within his stride, being quite a flirt himself.

Now it was Arthur's turn to wince. 'Actually, Vera, would you mind if I didn't?' He looked sheepish. 'I really couldn't bear two hours of undiluted Maggie, and I'm quite sure I couldn't possibly concentrate on the games in this heat with my thumb throbbing away.' I felt immediately remorseful and selfish. 'I thought I'd have a bit of a quiet read here in the garden, in peace, and drive down in time for the party after-wards, about seven-ish. What do you think? Would you mind terribly? You can get a lift down with Declan and Pam.'

'Well of course, if that's what you'd like,' I said, folding away his shorts again and feeling a bit disappointed. But then I cheered up. Arthur wasn't that keen a tennis player at the best of times, and he would join us before I hardly had a chance to miss him. And Declan and Pam were good friends of ours, so going down with them would be fun. 'Be a dear, Arthur, and go and ring the Douglases now, will you? Tell them you'll be coming later and then ring Pam and get her and Declan to pick me up on the way, that way I can get ready now instead of fussing around.' I retrieved my own freshly pressed dress and tennis shoes and checked my watch. 'I'll have to get a move on, look at the time!'

While Arthur went downstairs to use the phone, I slipped into my tennis gear and tied my shoes, doing a little twirl in the mirror. I must have been quite vain in those days and I was pleased to see I looked well. I was nicely tanned and looking slim and trim after the holiday, and there was nothing like a short tennis skirt to show off browned post-holiday legs. I pinned my hair back and found the dress I had selected to wear that evening and lifted it carefully on its hanger. It was a plain shell pink linen shift with a scooped neckline and which hugged my figure in all the right places. With my pearl earrings and necklace and the little dress watch Arthur had bought me last Christmas, I felt I could give Grace Kelly a run for her money any day. Married women all modelled ourselves on either her or Jackie Kennedy in the mid-sixties. Miniskirts and flowers in your hair were for young, braver, single women, and as I was blonde and blue eyed too, I spent an awful lot of time copying her outfits as best I could. This latest one I had made by a wonderful dressmaker I had discovered. In fact, it was my friend Pam who had given me her name, and I'd had a few summer dresses copied from magazines that I was very happy with. Arthur loved them too, which was just as well. He could be very particular about clothes. If he didn't like something, well, that was it, I could forget about wearing it. But he had marvellous taste anyway, so it was rarely a bone of contention between us. I slipped the dress and shoes into Arthur's suit carrier and told him to bring them down when he was coming – it was one less thing to worry about.

I heard the doorbell just as Arthur called up to me. 'Vera, Declan's here!'

'Right,' I called back, 'coming in a jiffy.' I ran down the stairs, where Arthur was waiting to hand me my tennis racquet and Declan kissed me.

'Don't you look edible,' he said, grinning at Arthur. 'Surprised you're letting her out on her own in that very fetching outfit, Arthur, she'll put everyone off their game.

The women will be jealous and us poor chaps thoroughly distracted!' he chuckled. 'Pam would kill to tan as easily as you do, Vera. She'll look like a porcelain doll next to you!'

'Pam is always the chicest woman in any room, as you know perfectly well,' I retorted, smiling, 'and so does she.'

'Right, off with you, then, or you'll be late. And drive carefully, Decco – precious cargo!'

'I will,' Declan assured him, ushering me out the door. 'See you later, old boy!'

'Bye, love,' I said. 'And Arthur, for heaven's sake don't forget my dress.'

'I wouldn't dare,' he said and waved us off. 'See you later.'

'Hello, Pam,' I said outside and kissed her as she got out to allow me to clamber into the back of the car.

'God, Vera, you look amazing,' she said enviously. 'And so brown – I sincerely hope I don't have to play doubles with you, you'll make me look like a ghost! How was the holiday?'

We chatted easily during the drive to Wicklow, which took about an hour but felt like much less. Pam and Declan were good friends of ours and I was really fond of them – they had a wicked sense of humour.

'At least we're not the first to arrive,' said Declan as he rounded the curve in the impressive tree-lined driveway. We saw several other cars already parked and others being frantically directed into a field by the Douglases's gardener, who was clearly on parking duty for the afternoon.

'Oh look,' said Pam, 'there's Maggie now, at the door. Dear God, I do believe she's got even thinner. If she turned sideways I swear she'd disappear.'

I chuckled, but it was true, I thought, looking towards the doorway where Maggie lounged, then seeing us, waved delightedly and ran towards us.

'Hello, Mags, you're looking ravishing,' Declan said as he

wound down the car window. He always knew just what to say to women.

'Hello, darlings!' Maggie was in her tennis gear too and she had a new haircut, a sleek, sharply angled bob. It looked super on her. I was still wearing mine long and straight, the way Arthur loved it. 'Pull up over here, Dec,' Maggie said, 'I kept a place outside the house specially for you.'

We followed her through the house and outside to the wonderful terrace overlooking manicured lawns and beyond, the sea, which today was delphinium blue. The place really was magnificent, having been refurbished exquisitely – at what expense, I hardly dared to think. It had been the talk of Dublin when they bought it. But seeing as how they owned a significant motor agency for Ireland, the Douglases were pretty rich. I think Maggie's parents were very well off too, so no expense had been spared doing up the house, and of course between them, William and Maggie had wonderful taste.

There seemed to be about thirty of us outside, and more people were arriving all the time. Some were already sitting or lounging against the balustrades, drinks in hand, and not all of us were dressed for tennis, but there were enough for me to wonder how Mags and William were going to organise things.

'Best of three games.' It was Will, putting his arm around me and pulling me in for a kiss. 'You look divine, Vera,' he said, smiling appreciatively. 'I hear Arthur won't be joining us until later?'

'That's right.' I explained about the nail mishap. 'He was feeling a bit miserable, so he said he'd join us afterwards instead of watching us all have fun on the courts.'

'Very sensible,' Will nodded, his blue eyes twinkling as he pushed a lock of blond hair off his forehead. 'Or risky, depending what way you look at it. I must say I wouldn't let you out of my sight for a second, Vera, even before you got that glorious suntan – hope you'll be showing it off in a bikini later? That's the only reason I put the pool in, you know!'

He really was incorrigible, Will, but somehow he got away with it. I think it was because even though he was a dreadful flirt, it was so plain that he idolised Mags that nobody ever took any notice of him – although it did do a girl good, particularly if her boyfriend or husband was taking her for granted. Will just couldn't pass any woman without complimenting her, and I for one wasn't complaining.

I laughed at him and asked how he was going to organise the tournament.

'Mixed doubles of course, unless numbers don't add up, and then whatever boys or girls are left over will have to partner up. We'll be drawing names from a hat, two hats to be precise, one for chaps, one for chapesses. Maggie's drawing the girls' names, so when your name is drawn then you pick a name out of the men's hat and that's who your partner is. Then it's the best of three games, otherwise we'll be here all bloody day! And I have every intention of going for a swim and downing a couple of martinis before getting stuck into the grub.'

I immediately felt relieved. Although I enjoyed a game of tennis and I was a reasonably good player, mixed doubles always unnerved me, especially when you didn't know your partner. Some men could be frightfully competitive and make the whole thing a bit of a nightmare. This arrangement sounded like fun, and not too taxing. Anyone could manage three games. Will carried on chatting and I must have been chatting back, although suddenly, out of the corner of my vision, I was aware of a movement and a subtle shift in energy around us. A man had come through the French doors, strolled casually down the steps to the terrace, and my breath caught. He was tall, about six four, and dark, very dark, with jet-black hair and olive skin. He was broad shouldered, dressed in immaculate whites and his long well-muscled legs were, well, magnificent.

I must have looked distracted, because Will followed my gaze and laughed. 'Ah,' he said, 'I see Felipe has arrived. He's Maggie's latest acquisition, third secretary with the Spanish embassy. Quite a specimen, eh?'

I didn't have time to reply because just then Maggie spotted Felipe herself and raced over to claim him, announcing at the same time that the draw for team partners would begin and for everyone to gather round and pay attention. So we did, and there was a bit of a flurry as people quickly finished off their drinks and searched for their abandoned racquets. I lost sight of him then, and it seemed ages before Maggie held up my name and called it out. I duly went up to fish a name out of the men's hat that Will was waving at me.

'Wonder who the lucky chap will be?' he called out and there was a murmur of appreciative laughter. I put my hand in and pulled out a piece of paper, unfolded it and read out the name – Felipe san de Segovia-Suarez.

'Quite a mouthful, isn't it?' I looked up to find him in front of me, holding out his hand, which I took. He had the darkest eyes I had ever seen. They had a definite twinkle to them, and something else flickered there too, but I was far too flustered to work out what. I was saved from looking like a complete bumbling idiot by Maggie, who materialised instantaneously by his side. 'Don't tell me you haven't met Felipe, Vera? Why, he's been guest of honour at every party for the past three months since he got here. Haven't you, Felipe?' She linked her arm through his and smiled coquettishly at him. 'And you can certainly see why, can't you, Vera?'

'I am sure I would have remembered if we had met previously.' His voice, when he spoke, was deep and rich, with only the barest hint of an accent. 'But I am very honoured to be your partner.' He seemed to be finding something amusing, but I wasn't sure what – in hindsight, it was probably my expression. I'm pretty sure I must have looked like a stage-struck schoolgirl.

In any event, Maggie rattled on. 'Felipe's a superb player, you'll be in good hands. Won't she, Felipe?' I shot Maggie a look. She could sail pretty close to the wind sometimes. 'And I shall be keeping a close eye on you both,' she continued. 'Arthur, Vera's husband, will be joining us later. Lorenza, Felipe's wife, is in Seville, visiting her parents,' she explained pointedly to me. 'Such a shame she couldn't be with us, but maybe next time. Do tell her I was asking particularly for her, won't you, Felipe?'

'Of course,' he said, inclining his head. 'She was most upset to hear she would be missing this wonderful invitation, although she would confess herself that tennis is not one of her favourite pastimes. Lorenza is not the sporty type.' He smiled, and my stomach lurched alarmingly.

'Well, off you go, the umpire is calling,' said Maggie as we heard Will's voice calling us to the court, although her eyes remained glued to Felipe. I couldn't say I blamed her.

'After you, Vera.' Felipe stood back and held out his arm, his hand hovering somewhere in the air behind the small of my back. It was just a gesture, a small, chivalrous movement – he never even touched me – but I swear I felt as if I'd been hit by 10,000 volts.

As I said, I wasn't a bad player, and I'd been practising for a while too. Arthur and I had been having the odd game at weekends, and I played now and again with some girlfriends of mine at the local club. But now, inexplicably, my legs felt like a pair of Donnelly's sausages, my hands had developed a trembling life of their own and my new Wilson racquet might as well have been a cricket bat. My game, if you could call it that, fell to pieces. As Emma would say, it was your worst nightmare. Never had I wished so fervently that Arthur was with me. How he would have laughed, made light of the whole thing, teased me and all of us girls unmercifully and made some witty but not disparaging comment about 'smooth continental aristocrats'. I knew within seconds he and Felipe would have been chums, and I could have gazed at one or both of them admiringly without this horrid feeling of my whole body being suddenly out of control, as if at any moment I might fling my racquet down and run screaming from the court – which is exactly what I wanted to do. But even then, I knew that sort of reaction was beyond the bounds of reason. I may have lost my body to some strange affliction, but I was determined not to let my mind follow suit, or any other part of me that was harbouring that sort of inclination. So I gritted my teeth and stood awkwardly or ducked, as required, and missed shot after shot until those three interminable games were up. Then, with trembling fingers, I went and shook hands at the net with our opponents like a normal person might – even if I was feeling anything but.

We won, of course, and even though Felipe tried to kiss me on both cheeks, I stood rigid with primness and held out my hand to him instead, which he duly took and bowed over. He was, as Maggie had pronounced, a superb player and chivalrous enough to allow the women an attempt at a decent rally before wiping their male partners off the court. I know this because I was so mortified by my own behaviour that I demurred any more matches, claiming I had reactivated an old sports injury and couldn't attempt another game. Thankfully, Maggie immediately stepped into the breach, and she and Felipe went on to win the tournament, although he very charmingly credited me with his first win as he opened the bottle of vintage Krug that was the winning team's spoils to a round of applause. I wanted to die with humiliation, but

I smiled gamely and waved from my spot on the terrace. For the umpteenth time I looked at my watch and prayed Arthur would be there within the hour. 'Where on earth is he?' I demanded from an amused Pam and Declan as we leaned against the balustrades sipping our drinks.

'Hang loose, Vera,' Declan grinned at me. 'He'll be here any moment. It's only six, we've barely finished up the tournament.'

But Pam, who had more feminine intuition, patted my shoulder. 'Don't worry, darling, he'll be here before you know it, looking as gorgeous as ever.' And then, to her husband, she said, 'She's been Felipe'd, darling – we all have. It's only natural she's feeling a bit unnerved. And Vera, he's clearly smitten with you too,' she went on mischievously. 'He hasn't been able to take his eyes off you since you abandoned him on court! We've all been watching.'

I gave her a 'don't be ridiculous' look and swigged back the remains of my gin and tonic. It *was* utterly ridiculous. He was married. I was married – and happily. The fact that this complete and utter stranger was having this ridiculous effect on me was insane. I just needed Arthur to be there at my side, reassuring and supportive. That was all it would take to get me over this maddening episode. I knew it in my bones, even though every molecule in my body was protesting otherwise.

Thankfully Arthur did arrive shortly after that and joined us on the terrace, where Maggie hugged him and thrust a martini into his hand. 'Now that's what I call a welcome,' he said to her, grinning. 'Vera, I hope you're taking note.'

'You're looking as handsome as ever, darling,' Maggie purred, 'but I must warn you, you have serious competition today.' She grinned impishly.

'Oh?' said Arthur, raising an eyebrow.

'It's that Spanish chap from the embassy, Felipe whatsit,' said Declan. 'He's turned all the girls' heads, I'm afraid. He was playing tennis with Vera earlier. They made a very dashing couple on court, I can tell you.'

'Any man would look dashing with Vera standing beside him,' Arthur said gallantly and winked at me.

'Darling, you did remember my dress, didn't you?' I was anxious to change the topic.

'Of course I did, it's inside, and your bikini too – you forgot that.'

'Oh, I don't think I'm going to swim.' The thought of undressing and revealing my body to the world, however tanned, seemed suddenly terrifying, though I couldn't think why – I had been looking forward to a swim all day.

'Well, I am. I've been looking forward to it all day,' Arthur said firmly, echoing my thoughts. 'C'mon, Vera, you'll love it once you're in – you know you will.' He looked at me expectantly and of course I couldn't refuse. Anyway, he was right. I loved a swim, I was just being ridiculous. I looked down to where the pool sparkled in the sinking afternoon sun and smiled at the shrieks of laughter and fun that floated up on the breeze.

'All right then, let's go and change.' We went upstairs to the room where our things were and hurried out of our clothes and into our swimming togs. I couldn't help watching Arthur surreptitiously as he undressed. He was forty-six, ten years older than me, but he was still in pretty good shape, still tall and reasonably well muscled and not too much of a tummy. But of course you couldn't expect – particularly a hard-working man who was either at a desk or standing in court all day – well, you couldn't expect them to have the body of an athlete, could you? It was just silly. I was being ridiculous again. I didn't know what had got into me. I had just spent a wonderful two weeks with Arthur in the south of France and I hadn't been going over his body with a magnifying glass then, had I?

I fastened the strap of my pink and white gingham bikini and pulled on my matching pink bathing cap with the pink and white flowers that I'd bought in France. It really was rather sweet, and although bathing caps were a curse, they were better than the alternative – having wet, sticky hair to contend with, particularly at a do like this, with so many glamorous women around, and not all of them had been playing tennis or swimming. They were the sensible ones. Arthur handed me my towel wrap and we headed back downstairs and out to join the others. As we drew closer, I could already see the little group of admirers, both in the pool and out of it, watching Felipe execute a perfect dive and ripple through the water as smoothly as a dolphin. A few of the men were attempting to do the same (you know what men are like) and looking pretty pathetic. This was Ireland in the sixties, and not many people were strong or competitive swimmers.

'Last one in's a sissy!' said Arthur, diving straight in at the deep end, which was pretty much empty, so I followed him, throwing off my wrap and diving straight in after him. I was a good swimmer, and the water felt delicious after the heat of the day and all my awkward lurching about on the tennis court. I did a couple of lengths of front crawl and was relieved to see that swimming, at least, seemed to be something that was still within my capabilities. I paused for breath at the deep end, the end farthest away from Felipe, who was standing in the shallow end surrounded by at least four women and Arthur, who had clearly been introduced to him at this stage – or knowing Arthur, he would have introduced himself. I felt unaccountably relieved, so I pulled myself up on my elbows at the pool edge and took a little breather, allowing my legs to float lazily behind me.

He was beside me in what seemed like three seconds. Even though the pool was at least twenty metres long he had swum it underwater, so I had every reason to be surprised when

he surfaced beside me, shaking off water and slicking back
his black hair. His eyes were dancing and his teeth (oh, those
teeth!) gleamed impossibly white against his dark skin, where
droplets of water clung to the sleekest muscles I had ever
seen. He was quite simply beautiful. I had never used that
adjective before to describe a man, and I never have since.
Very few of them warrant it, in my humble opinion.

'Well, Vera,' he said, and it made me shiver the way he said
my name, the way the *r* rolled deliciously against his tongue.
'You are a very good swimmer, I see. You have a very good
stroke, almost as good as your tennis.' He was teasing me
now and I immediately felt ridiculous again.

'Actually I'm quite a good tennis player normally, you can
ask my husband, Arthur. I don't know what happened to me
today, it was that old pulled muscle acting up.'

'Yes, I know.' He was still smiling. 'Our bodies can always
let us down when we least expect it. But swimming is a very
good release for any sort of tension, muscle or otherwise,
don't you think?'

'So they say.'

'That's a very pretty swimming cap you have. It shows off
your beautiful face.' He wasn't teasing now, but the smile had
changed, and he was dangerously close to me, balancing with
one hand lightly on the pool edge, inches from mine. 'And
yes, I met your husband, Arthur. He is a very charming man.
I look forward to getting to know you both a lot better. It is
always, how do you say, disorientating settling in to a new
country, new customs – even for us diplomats – although
already Lorenza and I love Ireland.'

'That's good. I look forward to meeting her sometime.'

'Yes, I'm sure we will bump into each other again – Dublin
is a small town, is it not?'

'Aren't you the two water babies!' It was Maggie, wearing
a very daring cutaway black one piece, sitting down carefully

and dangling her legs in the pool. I was heartily relieved to see her.

'I must get out, I'm beginning to feel cold,' I said to no one in particular.

'You can use my bathroom to shower, Vera, there's lots of towels. The food should be ready buy the time you're back. Will's shouting at the barbecue as we speak!'

'Thanks, Maggie, I will.' I swam back up to the shallow end and waded up the steps. And then, of course, I remembered I had foolishly left my towel wrap at the other end, where Arthur and I had dived in earlier, so I had to walk back down, trying to look nonchalant when I had never felt so naked in my life. It didn't matter that everyone else was too. I pulled it round me quickly and walked back to the house, feeling Felipe's eyes on me every step of the way.

The party afterwards was lovely, it really was. It had all the right ingredients – wonderful hosts, terrific company, delicious food and an idyllic setting. I remember taking a mental snapshot as I looked around at all the happy faces, relaxed, laughing and having fun. I knew even then that I would always remember that night vividly. But for some reason my appetite had deserted me, even after all that activity, and I toyed with my food, which was most unlike me. Of course Arthur noticed immediately, and I had made sure to wait until he had eaten, and heartily; after all, he'd driven down specially.

'What's up, love?' he murmured to me as I discreetly hid my plate among a table already groaning with food. 'Aren't you hungry? The salmon is delicious.'

'It's not the food, Arthur, I know it's all gorgeous.' I was suddenly feeling hot and clammy and sort of claustrophobic, even though we were outdoors, and it was a beautiful, warm evening. 'I've just got a terrible headache. I must have got too much sun out there this afternoon. I think I might have to go home.'

'We'll leave right away, darling. Why don't you slip out to the car and I'll make our excuses to Mags and Will, then I'll grab our things and meet you in the car.' He handed me the keys.

'Would you? I'm not dragging you away?'

'Of course not. I'm ready when you are.'

'It's just that I really couldn't stand making any fuss. Tell Mags I'll ring her tomorrow, and Pam, of course.'

'Will do. Are you all right, Vee, or shall I walk you out to the car first?'

'No, I'm fine,' I assured him, 'see you there in five.'

I slipped away and into the house, through the drawing room and into the vast, dimly lit marble tiled hall, and breathed a sigh of relief. My footsteps echoed eerily as I made for the front door and then I froze as a figure, an exceptionally tall figure, half emerged from the alcove where the phone was. It was Felipe, rattling something off in Spanish, but he turned and saw me and held out his free hand, palm up, gesturing for me to wait. *Oh God*, I thought, *how hideous* – he must think I'd followed him inside, when he was the very person I was desperate to get away from. I'd last seen him surrounded by a group of admiring women and indeed, several men, laughing uproariously at something he had said. It had made me feel quite annoyed at the time, though I had no idea why. Then he caught my eye and I turned my back abruptly.

Now I stood, immobilised despite myself, and watched as he finished off the call and took a step towards me. 'Vera?' He was close to me, close enough for me to smell his cologne, and something else, entirely of him, beneath it.

'I'm leaving.'

'So early, surely not?'

'I have a headache, I – I need to go home.'

He reached out then and gently stroked my cheek, trailing a finger along my jaw. Our eyes locked and I felt my lip tremble as his thumb brushed across it. 'Vera,' he murmured, 'beautiful Vera.'

I'm not sure what would have happened next if I hadn't heard Arthur's footsteps on the stairs and then the landing above us. He must have gone up through the back stairs. I simply wrenched myself away and fled to the car, which thankfully was right outside the door. At any rate, I had a few minutes to compose myself, and then Arthur was there, putting our bag into the back seat and joining me in the front.

'Sorry I took so long, I got cornered by old man Duggan, must be eighty if he's a day. I had to chat to him for minute or two. Are you all right?' He looked concerned.

'Yes, I'm fine, two aspirin when we get home and I'll be as right as rain.'

The drive home seemed much longer than it had on the way down. I felt utterly drained. Arthur chatted happily all the way.

'I must say, that Spanish chap is thoroughly nice, bit of fun too, I'd bet. I was chatting to him for quite a bit while you were getting dressed after your swim.'

'Really?'

'Yes, he was telling me all about Rome. That's where they were before here. His wife adored it apparently, and they have four children, three boys and a girl. I think one of the boys might be about Patrick or Charlie's age – or maybe it was the girl, can't remember. But he's certainly a handsome chap, reminds me of some movie star, can't think which one. No wonder you girls were all a flutter.' He glanced at me and grinned.

'I've always thought those continental types were very over-rated,' I said, a touch witheringly, I have to admit.

Arthur just smiled and patted my knee. 'You know I love you to distraction, Vera, don't you? Sometimes I think I don't tell you often enough. And you looked ravishing today – everybody was saying so.'

I smiled back. 'I do know, Arthur darling, and I love you too.'

'I know,' he said, rubbing my thigh lightly. 'And that's what makes me the luckiest man in the world.'

I took his hand then and held it, resting gently on my knee, and we were quiet for the little that remained of the drive.

But it was Felipe's touch I was thinking about, the imprint of his hand still burning on my face.

Olivia

I keep trying to find a moment to tell Mum I'm moving out, but the time just never seems right. She's got this job now, three days a week, and on her days off she's either organising Mac and Emma or constantly talking to Gran about The Job. It's only something in an art gallery, but the way they go on you'd swear she was giving Michael O'Leary a run for his money. I mean, how hard can it be, answering the phone and doing a bit of dusting? Speaking of which, I'm now having to leave the house myself on a pretty regular basis during the day, or else Gran will expect *me* to start cleaning and hoovering. Well, she can whistle. I didn't sign up for any of this crap, and I'm not going to start acting the hypocrite now. What you see is what you get with me. I call it like it is. Dad used to say that's a very good quality to have, saves everyone a lot of BS, but that sometimes you have to temper it. But that's just it – that defeats the whole purpose, doesn't it? See, that's being a hypocrite. And I can't *stand* hypocrites. That's why I'm so pissed off. 'Cos it turns out that both my parents are major hypocrites. Of course I more or less knew that already – most parents are – but you don't tend to think of your parents objectively while things are still normal. But when they turn your life upside down, well, normally I'm a pretty easy-going person, but this is just *way* past acceptable. I should probably be getting counselling, but I can't be bothered. What good is talking about it going to do now?

And besides, I'd rather spend the money on make-up or

a blow-dry. Guy would probably pay for it if I asked him to – the counselling, that is – but he'd think I was a loser, and I'm damned if I'm going to become a whinger just 'cos my parents have fucked up. I can look after myself, thanks very much. In fact, I'm better off without them. They didn't exactly make a success of things, did they? As far as I can see, neither of them had a clue what was going on. Maybe Dad did, but he sure as hell kept the rest of us in the dark. And Mum? Well, she obviously didn't want to know, and look where that's got us all.

Jesus, I'll never forget it, that day I lost my apartment and had to hand over the keys. And then trying to explain things to people, my friends and stuff, which wasn't easy when they could read all about it in the papers. And Robert, well, he had been a real tower of strength – *not*. He's a total jerk – I can see that now, of course, Emma got that one right, not that I'm ever going to admit that to her. He was around for about ninety seconds after Dad did his runner before he announced he 'needed some space' himself. That's men for you, or should I say boys. He's dating some loser model now, Amanda something or other, but I could care less – I'm with a Real Man now.

I met Guy at Iniquity, an exclusive members' only club where you can have dinner or just lounge around on sofas and check out the different bars on the three floors. I was there with my friend Ginny, who had invited me out with her the week of the family meltdown. It was nice of her, because a lot of my so-called friends were sniggering behind my back, I could just tell. Part of me didn't blame them. I'd probably have laughed myself if I didn't have a starring role in this bad movie that was turning out to be my life. But Ginny's cool. I met her when I was doing my marketing degree (that's what I did after leaving school, but only 'cos I was forced to), and like me, she did a modelling course on one of our summer breaks. But she got lucky – a year later she was taken on by Dublin's top agency. I wasn't with her the night she says she was 'discovered' – actually, she wasn't discovered at all, at least not by a talent scout like she says. But her current partner, Rick, *did* discover her. Rick's a lot older than Ginny. She says he's in his forties, but everyone knows he's fifty-four at least. He's also not properly divorced, like he says he is. But he's loaded, something to do with gaming halls, and that's how Ginny got taken on by the model agency and got loads of work, while I got taken on by a promotions agency and got stuck handing out leaflets or promotional drinks in gammy pubs. I don't think Mum was very impressed with that at the time, but Dad said it was good for me. 'It'll teach you the value of a proper job, Piggy,' he said. God, he had some nerve, looking back.

After that, Ginny got a really brilliant job as a TV presenter (Rick again – his brother owned the station, or most of it), so she has, like, a really perfect life. She even gets a clothes allowance as part of her job. Ginny says it's really important to have a career, even though Rick wouldn't care if she never worked at all.

'Why?' I asked her.

'Cos it's important to have your own money and stuff.' Ginny gets this really serious expression on her face when she talks about money.

'But you said Rick gives you all the money you need,' I said.

'Yeah, well, he can be tight sometimes, y'know. He doesn't always come through,' she said, looking evasive.

'What, like a kind of allowance?'

'Yeah,' she said, 'kinda.'

It sounded good, whatever it was.

I'm not sure where Ginny's from in Dublin. She hasn't been to school with anyone I know, and a lot of people say she's a chancer and a gold-digger. To be honest, her accent does slip occasionally, especially when she's had a few drinks. But she lives with Rick now, and she never talks about her family. Anyway, I liked her, even if people said she only hangs around with me 'cos she's a social climber. If she is, it hasn't got her very far, has it? But she's fun, and she's really pretty, and I always have a good time whenever we go out together, which isn't as often as we used to. Rick doesn't like her going out without him, especially on girls' nights, and I can't say I blame him. Men are attracted to Ginny like bees to a honey pot. That's another reason I like going out with her. Like I said, I'm not a hypocrite.

So that's how I met Guy. Ginny and I were in Iniquity, in the downstairs bar, having a quiet drink, when a couple of guys came in, older but good looking, and they looked like they intended having a good time. One of them knew Ginny (he was a friend of Rick's), and the other one was Guy. They insisted on buying us champagne, and of course we let them join us. It was fun, and fun was exactly what I was after that night. It turned out that Guy knew my parents (which was a bit of a downer). He knew Dad through business, but he seemed much more laid back than they were, and younger, or maybe it was the champagne, who knows? But at least he didn't go on about what had happened, didn't start to commiserate with me – he just said, 'These things happen all the time in business, you just have to move on.'

I had to bite my lip to keep from pointing out that that was exactly what my dad *had* appeared to do. Move on, that is, unbeknownst to any of us. I was still trying to take the whole thing in. It was common knowledge by then, of course, but like I said, Guy never referred to it. That's why I liked him straight away. We had a good time that night, and later that week Guy phoned me to ask me out. Of course, I said yes.

He and his wife are separated, and he lives in this really amazing penthouse apartment overlooking a beautiful park, just minutes from the city centre. Going out with Guy is fun – he makes it fun. It's an escape, however brief, from this crappy scenario unfolding in our family. He's good to me too, really generous, buys me fabulous clothes and stuff – anything I want, really. Which is also great, 'cos I'm not really a chain store girl and I was afraid I'd never be able to afford designer gear again. In fact, I don't know if I'd have gotten through those first few weeks without Guy. He made it all bearable.

But now, well, there's just the little problem of telling Mum. I've already decided to move in with Guy. He's as up for it, as I am, so I think telling Mum will be quick and painless. I'll just come right out with it – say I'm moving out again, into an apartment. It makes perfect sense. I can tell her the rest bit by bit. But even though I've worked out exactly what to say, every time I try to say it, the time just never seems right. I feel guilty. Why, I don't know. It's not my fault, any of this. Dad obviously doesn't care about us or give a damn, he'd have talked to us if he did. And I hate this house. Apart from it being out of the Dark Ages, it's scary. And so is Gran. I catch her watching me when she thinks I won't notice. And although she's always polite to me, I can tell she thinks I'm trouble. Disapproval is written all over her face. And she's never once offered me her car to drive, even though she practically never uses it. But apparently it's all right for Mum to drive it. Jeez, who'd have ever thought my life could change like this? It's beyond scary. And I hate Dad for doing this to us. I really, really hate him.

Elsie

To do list

Walk dog

Pick up prescription at chemist

Email Charlie?

I still hadn't heard anything more from Charlie – not a peep. But I *had* begun walking the dog, which in itself turned out to be a challenge. His name was Buddy, and he seemed harmless enough when I went to meet him. He was a typically overweight, friendly Golden Labrador. This affable charade was maintained until we were halfway through his front gate, having been waved a cheery goodbye by Mary, my sister-in-law, when Buddy hunkered down to best adjust the force of gravity in his favour, thrust his head forward and with the power of a pair of shire horses, lurched forward, towing me helplessly in his wake. Stopping him was impossible, unless, of course, he wanted to stop, which was an equally unpredictable experience, usually involving trees, where he would dig in to a halt and inspect the specimen thoroughly before marking his territory. Within minutes I looked quite windswept, my recent blow-dry blown to bits. And that wasn't the worst of it. He seemed to take particular pleasure in stopping to do his business right outside, or in view of, the most elegant houses in the neighbourhood. And he wasn't discreet about it at all. Of course I was ready and prepared with plastic bags to pick it all up, but I had no idea, none at all, just how much one dog could produce. It was all very mortifying. However, I did at least achieve my desired result, which was a couple of sightings of the Fitzgibbon clan. It was Vera I saw first, hurrying towards the Dart station. I recognised her from Charlie's wedding, although she wouldn't have had a clue who I was. She had barely been introduced to me, and that was over twenty years ago now. She looked older, of course, and a little more frail, but she was beautifully turned out, and beneath the headscarf she wore, her face still retained those enviable cheekbones. I always told Charlie they were wasted on him – a woman would have appreciated them so much more.

Another day, in the afternoon, I saw Emma being dropped home. It must have been Emma, because she was about the right age – a lovely looking girl, with such a strong look of her mother as I remembered her. She seemed a bit downcast but, then, she was weighed down with a huge schoolbag and no doubt had a ton of homework to fill her evening, poor kid. I saw Shelley too, a few days after that, in the morning, leaving the house. She was heading in the direction of the Dart station and I quickly turned away in case she recognised me. She looked very thin and rather worried, but just as lovely as ever. It made me feel terribly sad, suddenly. There was no sign of the older girl, Olivia, even though I was passing by now on quite a regular basis.

I was to learn very soon why not.

I had returned Buddy to his delighted owner and got into my car, feeling nicely cocooned in the enclosed space with four wheels underneath me (a lot easier to control than Buddy), to set off for the chemist. I wasn't sleeping well lately and had reordered an old prescription of mine. It wasn't entirely for my own use either, if I'm honest. I found that if I occasionally added a crushed pill to Larry's nightcap of a glass of red wine, he was asleep the minute his head hit the pillow. Slept like a baby the whole night through, too, which had its advantages. Just knowing I wouldn't be 'disturbed' meant I automatically slept better too. I'm sorry, but I don't feel in the slightest bit guilty about it – I was dealing with a very tense situation here and I had to have my wits about me. And Larry was in wonderful form. He kept remarking on that fact that his golf swing had improved dramatically, and couldn't work out why. I assumed it was the relaxing effect of the sleeping potion contributing, but I didn't comment.

After the chemist, on my way home I stopped to pick up a few groceries and a couple of new magazines. It was much later that evening, after dinner, when I got around to flicking through them. And that's when I saw the article. I didn't recognise her initially, but the name leapt out at me instantly. *Olivia Fitzgibbon*: *How to Get the Look*. It was one of those silly fashion articles profiling some model or other and asking them about their fashion style. There was a picture, of course, and it was one of Olivia with a much older man who looked vaguely familiar. When I read the name I knew why – he was a small-time property developer and on the few occasions I had met him, I hadn't liked him. Good-looking chap, but sleazy. You know the type, I'm sure. But what I read under the photograph horrified me. Olivia referred to this chap as her 'partner' and was gushing about 'living with him' and how she couldn't have coped with her demanding career without his support. Her job title was marketing manager for somewhere called Iniquity. That sounded promising, until I realised it was some sort of nightclub. And she appeared to be no more than a glorified waitress there. After that, I closed the magazine quickly. I really didn't want to read anymore. A lovely fresh young girl like that – she couldn't have been more than twenty-four – shacked up with that sleazy old . . .

well, I became quite angry just thinking about it. Poor Shelley, I immediately thought, and then I wondered if she even knew. And as for Charlie, he would have gone around and killed that Guy with his bare hands at the thought of . . .

I actually had to pour myself a glass of Arthur's red wine and take a couple of deep breaths. I had been going to email Charlie that night, wherever he was, just to tell him every-thing looked all right as far as I could make out. But now I found I couldn't. I would wait a few days until perhaps I heard from him again. Tonight, all of a sudden, my heart just wasn't in it.

Emma

Well, she's gone. So now we are four: Gran, Mum, me and Mac. I wonder who'll be next? I should keep a journal. This entry could be titled *Fitzgibbons: The Incredible Shrinking Family.* Even though she was hardly ever here, it's really weird without her. I know Liv had moved out before all this and was living in one of Dad's apartments, but that was different. She was always popping in for stuff or coming round to eat – it didn't seem as if she was really gone. But this is, like, serious. I mean, I know I never liked Bob the Builder, but jeez, he was better than Guy. Anyone would be better than Guy. I just can't get my head around it. Neither can Mum, by the sounds of it. I thought Gran would be the most shocked of all, but she's been strangely quiet about it all. I guess she's worried about Mum. If you'd seen her when Liv told her, you would be too. I thought she was going to self-destruct.

Of course Liv's timing was impeccable – *not.* She waited until Mum had been about a wet week at her new job and was all happy and upbeat for the first time in, like, years, and then while we were all sitting at dinner (shepherd's pie and peas, my favourite), she drops her little bombshell.

'Have some more,' says Gran, nodding at Liv to help herself.

She's finished first because she'd only taken about a spoonful and has been pushing that around her plate and gazing at it like it's a work of art or something.

'Er, no thanks, Gran,' she says. 'Actually,' she clears her throat, 'I have something to tell you all.'

Only Mac goes on eating. Not a lot disturbs him these days – or if it does, he's not letting on. The rest of us look up, but I'm the only one who knows what's coming.

'I'm moving out. Tomorrow,' she says brightly.

Silence.

'What?' That's Mum.

'I'm moving out – of here. I'm, um, getting an apartment. Like before – you know?' She looks way too innocent.

'But why?' Mum again. She's looking puzzled, sad and shocked, all at the same time, and I can see her brain whirling into action. 'That's nonsense, Olivia. You don't have any money. You don't even have a job – how on earth are you going to get an apartment?'

'Social housing?' I quip.

Liv narrows her eyes at me.

'What's going on, Olivia?' Mum dabs her mouth with a napkin, then sits back and folds her arms. I settle into my chair. This is going to be good.

At this point Gran gets up and makes a great show of clearing away the plates and tells Mac to help her bring them in. 'Come into the kitchen with me, Mac, and we can see what you'd like for desert, pet,' I hear her whisper loudly as Mac trots after her.

'Nothing.' Olivia's eyes widen. 'Why should there be?'

'Come off it. This is me you're talking to, your mother, remember? I know you, Olivia, and you might as well come clean right now. What is going on?'

There is quite a bit of noise coming from the kitchen, plates and cutlery being clanked about, but I know Gran is listening 'cos she keeps loitering about by the serving hatch on the other side.

'Nothing's going on,' Liv says sulkily. 'I've got a new boyfriend and I'm moving into an apartment of his. That's it. No big deal.' She raises her eyes to heaven. Big mistake.

'I'll be the judge of that, young lady, and do not roll your eyes at me! Emma,' she barks and I jump. 'Did you know anything about this?'

I hate it when she does that. I was just enjoying the scene unfold and now I'm a suspect too, apparently.

'Um, sort of.'

'What do you mean, "sort of"?'

I shrug and look at Liv meaningfully. This is her mess. 'I share a room with her. I notice things,' I say enigmatically.

'What things?' Mum's eyes are boring into me now.

This is becoming uncomfortable. 'Stuff . . . you know, clothes and things. I knew she had a boyfriend, otherwise she had to be lifting.' I think maybe this will seem like a worse alternative scenario, but it doesn't seem to do the trick. And now Liv is glaring at me. 'And Valentine's Day – those flowers,' I offer.

'I'd forgotten about those.' Mum's eyes revert to Liv.

'Hard to if you were sharing a room with them,' I mutter.

'What?' Mum's head is whipping back and forth now like a Wimbledon spectator. 'Don't mumble, Emma.' She's getting rightly steamed up. 'Yes, I remember those now, it was a very ostentatious bouquet. Just who is this boyfriend of yours, Olivia? Have we met him? Is he anyone we know?'

Silence. Olivia is chewing her lip. I can tell she's bottling, frantically thinking what to say.

And then Mac saves her the trouble. 'His name is Guy.'

'What? How the hell would you know?' Olivia rounds on him, not surprisingly. She stares at him as if he's sprouted horns.

'Do not speak to your brother like that! Mac,' Mum turns to him and says more gently, 'how *do* you know?'

I watch, riveted, as Mac extracts a card from his back pocket and immediately recognise it as the one that came with the flowers. I wonder how long he's been keeping it there.

'It says it right here,' he pipes up. '*To my darling Tiggypoo. My little tigress in the bedroom. All my love, Guy.* What's a Tiggypoo, Mum?'

And then all hell breaks loose.

I look at Mac in wonder as he is told to leave the room, and Gran comes in to escort him out. He's either beyond stupid, or very, very clever. But if he wanted to get Liv back for all the countless times she's humiliated him, he's played a blinder. That kid has a future after all, I'm thinking.

But now I'm told to leave the room too. So I get up, shrug helplessly at Liv and close the door quietly behind me. It's just her and Mum.

I join Mac and Gran in the sitting room, where the television is turned up loudly. Mac is digging into a bowl of ice cream, his normal vacant expression resumed.

I actually feel kind of sorry for Liv. When Mum's on the scent of something, you don't stand a chance. And she wasn't going to be happy about all this.

I join Mac on the sofa and look at him with new regard. I shall have to be more careful around that boy.

Shelley

Thank God for the job. I've said it a thousand times, but I swear, if I wasn't able to get out of this house and realise that there actually is a relatively normal world going on out there, with relatively normal people in it, to take my mind off things, I'd have swung for someone by now. Not that you could call Ernie particularly normal, but at least he was nice, and decent. He had a heart of gold, though mad as a brush most of the time. But his little gallery was my escape, briefly, from the shambles that had become my life. Our lives. It stopped me wanting to kill people. Like my daughter, Olivia. Or that vile man she had taken up with, Guy, who was old enough to be her father, for heaven's sake. Dear God, I remember on the few occasions I had met him with Charlie, he had even tried to flirt with *me*. And now . . . well, I just can't bear to think of it. My lovely little Liv. My baby. Our little girl. *Just wait until your father gets to hear about this*, I had automatically raged in my head, and then . . . Oh, what was the use? What was the point of anything any more?

And Caroline! That bitch! Having the nerve to actually call around to the house (when I wasn't there, of course) and 'talk' to Vera. I nearly dropped the plates I'd been carrying in the kitchen at the time when Vera casually mentioned it. But before the anger kicked in, my initial reaction was one of sheer, blessed relief. Caroline was here – in Dublin. She didn't know anything either. Most blissfully satisfying of all – he hadn't taken her with him. That was what I had feared above all – Charlie and Caroline, in a little love nest tucked away from the rest of the world. Anything was better than that. I was almost grateful to the South African girl, whoever she is – at least she's not Caroline. If it wasn't for Caroline, Charlie and me would still be together, I know we would. I know things hadn't been great between us this past eighteen months or so, but every marriage has its good, not so good and bloody awful years, don't they? But we'd have got through it somehow if it wasn't for her ruining everything.

Still, she had some nerve calling to Vera's house. But then, I should hardly be surprised – it was clearly something she made a habit of. I sure as hell would never forget the day she called around to ours.

I had never liked Caroline, right from the first moment I met her – and I had tried to like her, I really had, for Charlie's sake. It wasn't surprising, really, because I knew she hated me long before she ever met me. She was Charlie's ex, his long-time girlfriend before he met me. And she never got over the fact that he had married someone else – particularly someone without a brilliant mind or a brilliant career, like she had.

Back then, she had been working in London in some high-flying firm, earning a fortune. She was the Irish career woman success story, and God, she never let anyone forget it. You couldn't open a magazine or watch a business programme without Caroline bloody O'Donnell showing up. I'd been curious about her, of course, the way you always are about a spouse's previous long-term relationship, and I had always wondered why they split up. I know Caroline had gone off to Harvard to do some business degree, but Charlie said they would have gone their separate ways anyway, that she was too driven, even for him. It didn't stop him getting her a job, though, when she came back a couple of years ago from London – and that was before I had any clue about the apartment he set her up in. God, I was so stupid, so pathetically naive and trusting. All along I believed him, that she had just been his first love, that they had had great times together as kids – but that they never would have worked out. Seems he changed his mind about that one. Or maybe she did, and that was all it took. First love – they say you never forget it, don't they?

Then I had arrived on the scene. I heard from a friend of mine who knew a friend of Caroline's that she had been completely devastated when she heard Charlie was getting married. Couldn't believe it, apparently, and that's why she went to London all those years ago – to make a life without him. She never married, though, and that's when I knew, somewhere deep down, that this girl hadn't quite gone away, that she was going to be trouble sooner or later, whether Charlie realised it or not. She might not have wanted Charlie back then – perhaps she had taken him for granted – but there's nothing like seeing your ex in a happy relationship with another woman to make him seem awfully attractive again. And clearly Caroline had been prepared to wait, to bide her time, even if it had meant waiting over twenty long years. Charlie used to tell me I was silly, but I never underestimated her – not for a minute. And now I had been proved right. But it hadn't worked out for her, her little plan. I wasn't the only one who had been taken in by Charlie, and when she had discovered that – well, hell hath no fury like a woman scorned, and Caroline had turned her fury on me.

Hard to believe it had only been four months ago. In many ways it seemed like another lifetime, and yet I could replay the scene in my head as if it was yesterday.

She had returned from London about two years previously and was working on a consultancy basis with Charlie's firm. I wasn't happy about it, but what could I do?

'She's the best in the business, Shelley,' Charlie said. 'Her experience is invaluable, it would be silly of me not to use her.' I mean, what could I say to that? We'd been married for over twenty years by then and I had no reason not to trust my husband, but let's face it – who wants their husband's ex-girlfriend who has never fallen out of love with him, and never married, working side by side with him, intimately, possibly travelling on business with him? It was my worst nightmare. All right, I admit it – I'm insecure. Actually, I can border on the paranoid sometimes, especially regarding other women – Charlie is so damned attractive and they love him, always have.

That's why I could never quite believe it when he chose me. Charlie could have had anyone. And all those high-flyers he mixed with . . . I often felt as if he must have found me really dull and predictable to come home to, although to be fair, he never made me feel that way – it was just my general perception. Sometimes, nice though the money and success were, I wished Charlie could have been something normal and humdrum – but then, I suppose I wouldn't have fallen under his spell. Charlie was always meant for the big time. It's just that I wasn't ever really cut out for it. I just wanted to be a wife and a mum, and that's what Charlie wanted for me too. He said it was the most important career in the world, being a mum, and of course he was right about that. It's just that when that starts to involve entertaining endless amounts of high-profile businesspeople and going to never-ending 'functions' and always having to look your best – well, that in itself becomes a full-time job. And I wasn't getting any younger, yet the women seemed to look more dewy and more and more glamorous every year. I tried to keep in shape, but I'm hopeless about discipline. I was forever signing up for this class or that personal trainer and never persevering with any of them. Charlie used to laugh at me about it. I remember him saying to me once, 'Shelley if you got all those books and DVDs you have about getting a flat stomach and lay down and put them all on your stomach – then it would be flat.' I think I probably threw one at him then. He was – I mean, *is* – funny.

'Anyway,' he said, 'you're perfect. You look great the just the way you are.' But that's what they always say, isn't it? Just for the sake of a quiet life.

Anyway, I must have been doing or just back from one of my new classes, or maybe I was doing a bit of hoovering, because I was wearing a T-shirt and sweatpants and I had my hair all tied up and no make-up on when I heard the doorbell. I wasn't expecting anyone, so I assumed it was a delivery or something. When I opened the front door, there was Caroline on the step, looking immaculate and very, very thin. For a moment I almost panicked, thinking there might be something wrong, that something might have happened to Charlie – Caroline had never shown up at the house and Charlie wasn't there. And there was something odd looking about her, I remember thinking – her colour was up, she looked sort of feverish.

'May I come in please, Shelley? I need to talk to you.'

You'd think I would have said something along the lines of *Actually no, Caroline, I'm afraid it's a very inconvenient time,* or *I'm awfully sorry, Caroline, but actually I have a rendezvous with my illicit lover* – anything – but no, I just stood back and said something really lame, like *Of course, Caroline, come on in.* Caroline was always very authoritative, and I was secretly scared of her, hugely in awe of her and that oversized brain of hers that everyone kept talking about. So I led the way down to the kitchen and put on the kettle. 'Sit down,' I said, overly brightly. 'Would you like tea or coffee?'

'Neither, thank you. And I won't sit down, if you don't mind,' she said, although she did take off her coat (toffee-coloured shearling; I had my eye on exactly the same one, but it looked so much better on her, she had the extra inches in height) and threw it carelessly over a chair. I almost wanted to hang it up for her, but instead I started to chew a nail while she paced back and forth, her eyes sweeping around the room. She was making me nervous.

'Nice kitchen,' she commented. 'New?'

'What is it?' I eventually managed to ask.

She threw me a glance and laughed. A short, sharp sound. 'Charlie, of course.'

And that's when I felt everything slow down – except my heart, which began to beat double time. I remember doing the automatic mental maternal arithmetic then. You know, ticking off the kids and their whereabouts one by one. *Olivia* – modelling course – check. *Emma* – school – check. *Mac* – school and soccer – check.

We were alone. All clear.

'What do you mean?'

She looked at me then, pityingly – or was it witheringly?

'He's been a very naughty boy. Surely you've guessed by now?'

'W – what?'

'Oh, come on, Shelley, even you can't be that dim. I know you like playing the helpless little girl card, and maybe it's worked with Charlie, kept him tethered to you all these years, but it won't wash with me.' She tossed her head, and her hair, styled in glossy black layers, immediately rearranged itself flatteringly around her face – which looked, in contrast, tight and mean.

'You've been having an affair.' I wondered, even then, why I uttered the words as a statement – not a question. I suppose they'd been lurking there for years, hovering on my lips, just waiting to tumble at the inevitable moment.

'Very perceptive,' she grinned. 'Ten out of ten.' She was pacing again.

'Why are you telling me?' I asked listlessly.

'Oh, for God's sake! Why do you think? Because *he* wouldn't. Or couldn't. He could do everything else, though.' She was ranting now. 'The car, the apartment, even working together – everyone knew, of course. Everyone except you. He couldn't tell *you*. *I can't do it, Caroline,*' she mimicked nastily, '*not to Shelley, she couldn't cope. And the kids – I just can't do it to them.* Always the bloody kids.'

She paused to draw breath and something inside me unleashed itself.

'Don't you dare bring our children into this, you bloody leech,' I said coldly. I was holding on to to the back of a chair to steady myself. Shaken though I was, the wave of anger that surged through me was making me fight for breath.

'What did you call me?' She looked disbelieving.

'I called you a leech, Caroline, and that's exactly what you are – a slimy, grasping, bloodsucking leech who can't or won't let go of a man who didn't, and doesn't, want you. It was *me* he married, remember? All those years ago? He didn't want you then, and he doesn't want you now.' I was winging it, and didn't know where the words were coming from. I had suddenly found another voice – resurrected from another lifetime, presumably, seeing as I obviously realised this one was over – or at least as I knew it. Put it this way – I had nothing left to lose.

Caroline suddenly looked as if all the breath had been sucked out of her and sat down shakily. 'So you did know all along.'

Silence. I didn't trust myself to speak. Of course I hadn't known, but I wasn't going to tell her that, not when this inter-pretation of events seemed to be producing a more dramatic, sobering effect.

'You knew he was seeing someone else.' She was speaking

to the wall opposite her, not looking at me at all, thinking aloud. 'I suppose you had him trailed?'

'Don't be ridiculous. I don't spy on my husband.' (I want to, but I don't. There are limits. Now I wished I had.)

'Then how did you know about her? Were there others?' Her voice was disjointed, edgy.

'I beg your pardon?'

'*Her.*' She spat the word and fumbled in her bag. Then she threw them at me, scattered sheets of printed-out emails. 'He didn't even try to hide them. Perhaps he wanted me to find them. But somehow,' her mouth was curling now and she paused, 'I doubt very much that he wanted *you* to. Which is why I'm giving them to you. A parting gift for Charlie. Have a look, Shelley – they make rather interesting reading.'

'I don't doubt it.' My voice was trembling now and I felt sick. I couldn't take any more in, couldn't listen to another word of her vitriol. 'But I'd like you to leave now, Caroline, our children will be home soon.' I mustered every ounce of self-control I had and walked out of the kitchen to the front door, which I held open for her.

'You're going to ignore this?' She pulled on her coat and looked at me, shaking her head. 'Stay with him still, after *this*?'

'What Charlie and I do about our marriage is absolutely none of your business.'

I thought I saw a flicker of admiration in her eyes, but I was wrong, because then she smirked. 'You're an even bigger fool than I took you for, then,' she said. 'Play the supportive wife all you like, Shelley, but it's too late. I could have ruined Charlie for this – and I would have – but I didn't have to. He's done that all by himself. Your cosy little world is about to blow sky high, Shelley. Charlie Fitzgibbon was never a man to do things by halves.' And with that cryptic comment she swept out the door, leaving me alone with the tatters of my shattered life.

I must have walked back down to the kitchen then, although I have no memory of that. But I do remember standing staring at those emails, which stared contemptuously back at me from the kitchen table. *Go on*, they seemed to be saying. *Pick us up. Have a read. We dare you.*

So I did. I sat down, and feeling more terrified than I could ever remember, I began to read.

From: annika23@coolmail.com
To: charles.fitzgibbon@celticcrestinvest.ie
Subject: Jack
I'm so sorry for barging into your life like this again, Charlie, and you've been so kind to agree to discuss everything. I wouldn't be doing this unless it was a matter of life and death − I do hope you understand.
   My number is + 27 (0) 21 791 2014 Ring any time − the sooner the better.
Annika

From: annika23@coolmail.com
To: charles.fitzgibbon@celticcrestinvestments.ie
Subject: Jack
When can you come out? Jack and I are so excited. He can't wait to meet you!
Annika

From: charles.fitzgibbon@celticcrestinvestments.ie
To: annika23@coolmail.com
Subject: Jack
I'm not sure when I'll get out, Annika. I'm under a lot of pressure here at the moment, but of course I'll come. Nothing

is more important to me than family. Jack must be a very brave
little boy. It can't be easy not having his real father around.
This has all come as quite a shock, I'm sure you can appreciate, but I'll call you tonight to talk. Take care of yourselves.
Charlie

There were others in the same vein, all dated the past two
weeks, but my hands were shaking so much by the end I
could hardly make out the type. No wonder Charlie had been
behaving oddly. No wonder he had hardly been at home for
the past three months. It was a wonder he could keep track
of this lot, I thought bitterly. My head began to swim. I was
fighting to make sense of it all, but I couldn't. Not Charlie,
my Charlie. He wouldn't do this to me.

But he had, hadn't he? I'd heard it from the horse's mouth.
You're always the last one to know, that's what they say. How
could I have been so stupid?

I wanted to be angry. I wanted to get up and hurl things
around the kitchen, or scream, but that would come later. At
that moment, all I could feel was the devastating knife twist
of pain that made breathing impossible. So I put my head
in my hands and wept instead.

Charlie

I should have seen it coming. And maybe I did, at some inexpressible level. But denial is a very easy thing to slip into – especially when everyone else is. The first warning signs were like the rumblings of a distant earthquake – a little bit shaky, but not enough cause for serious alarm, not until the big one hit, and then there was financial mayhem. You all know what happened at this stage, so I won't go into the well-worn details. In our case the banks closed in; even Tolstoy's cash injection hadn't been enough to stave that off. But I did make sure everyone was paid off, every single one of our suppliers – except Alan, the guy who put in our kitchen. But since the house had to go anyway, what use was the kitchen? So I told him to go ahead and take it back.

Funnily enough, that was what was uppermost in my mind the evening I came home to tell Shelley the house was gone – our home – that I had lost everything. The kitchen that had been so laboriously and meticulously installed just months ago would have to go back. It's funny, the kind of details that bother you when your life is turned upside down, like how we were going to manage without a kitchen, not *where the hell were we all going to live now?* As it turned out, though, that was the least of my problems.

Feeling beyond weary (I have been working around the clock for the past six months, desperately trying to salvage anything), I took a deep breath and put my key in the door.

How bad could it be? At least it would be a relief to finally share the burden, I reasoned. Carrying it alone had all but finished me off. I couldn't sleep, couldn't eat and spent all of my waking hours at the office or frantically setting up meetings where everyone looked and felt as stressed and hopeless as I did.

Enough. It was over. I had done everything humanly possible to avoid this, but the fight was over. And to be fair, Shelley had never been motivated by money. Things hadn't been good between us for the past year or so – I had been working too hard. I guess I kind of shut down on her, withdrew, but I was just trying to protect her. It was bad enough that I was worried sick – there was no point in having her worry too, or the kids, particularly when there was absolutely nothing anyone could do. I hadn't been spending enough time with her or the kids, and that had become a problem. I almost laughed – there would be plenty of time to address that particular shortcoming. They'd be seeing an awful lot more of me now. Whatever else, I told myself, we were still a family – we could get through this together. Or so I foolishly thought.

So in I go through the front door. It's two p.m., and there's an unusual stillness in the air – or possibly it's my imagination. Despite the quiet, I know Shelley's home because her car is outside. We have an hour or so to talk before any of the kids get back, but she won't be expecting me. I didn't call; what would have been the point?

I take off my coat, throw it on a chair in the hall and walk towards the kitchen. Then I see her. She's sitting at the kitchen table with her head in her hands. She hears my footsteps and looks up and I catch my breath. Her face is ravaged, raw from crying, but there's something else there, some un-uttered howl of sorrow has etched itself in her expression. She appears to me at once unbearably sad, hopeless, brave and unbelievably vulnerable. She must know. But how? Who would or could have told her? It doesn't make sense. I want to take her in my arms and rock her as I would a child, soothe her, protect her, tell her it will be all right. I will promise anything. In that moment I hate myself more than any other person ever could.

'Shelley,' I begin. But I don't get any further.

She gets to her feet, and now I see rage take over – I don't blame her – and she goes for me. The blows rain down from every direction. She is beating me with her fists, pummelling me, and I let her. Anything is better than looking at that face, that bleak, bereft expression. That is not my Shelley, not my beloved wife. So I let her vent, and then I catch her wrists. She is incoherent, crying still and shouting, 'How could you? How could you? You bastard, I trusted you,' over and over until eventually she stops and it's just the tears.

'I was going to tell you,' I say. 'I've been trying to, so many times, but I couldn't. I was trying to protect you all, seeing if there was something, anything I could salvage.'

'Salvage?' she shouts. 'You want to salvage something? You've thrown it all away, you miserable bastard. Everything – me, our children.'

I'm beginning to feel alarmed. There is something amiss here; she's out of control. 'Shelley, please, just calm down, will you? I'm trying to explain – we'll get through this. You and the children are all that matter to me. We're a family – we're still a family, aren't we? Sit down, please, Shelley, we have to talk about this.'

'Oh, you want to talk now? Typical,' she says bitterly. 'It's a bit late for that. Caroline's already told me all I need to know.'

This throws me completely. Caroline knows, of course she knows, she works with me, but why would she say anything to Shelley?

Shelley sits, wearily now, but still rigid with rage, her hands trembling. I'm torn between sorrow, self-hatred and a building exasperation. I need her to listen to me.

'When were you talking to Caroline?' I'm puzzled. 'Why didn't you talk to me? I would have told you everything.'

This inflames her further. 'Because I didn't fucking know, did I? I didn't know you were having an affair. I didn't know I wasn't enough for you. I didn't know you were a cruel, unfaithful bastard! I didn't know you were so unhappy with me – that I had *tethered* you to me for all these years.' She is sobbing again and her hand slams the table. But now I'm speechless. I recoil. And there is something building inside me, something incomprehensible, something that grips me so fiercely I have to fight to control my every movement. When I speak, it sounds as if from very far away. An icy calm.

'What did you just say?'

'Don't.' She is shaking her head now, an ugly sneer curling her mouth. 'Don't you *dare* have the gall to look aggrieved at me.' She stands up again, clutching the table, leaning over it. 'She told me everything.'

'Just what exactly are you accusing me of, Shelley?' My voice is cold.

She looks at me disbelievingly, as if I'm an imposter. 'You're unbelievable. You're not even the slightest bit contrite.'

'Answer me, Shelley!' I bark.

She jumps. 'Don't you dare speak to me like that! You might be able to talk to your bloody mistress in that tone, but I don't work for you, Charlie. I'm your wife, remember? An annoying little detail in the scheme of things, I know, but still your wife.'

'You're accusing me of having an affair? Is that it?' I'm fighting to get my head around this surreal mess.

'So you're admitting it? Or should I say admitting to one of them, at any rate.'

'One of them?'

She takes a sheet of paper and crumples it into a ball and throws it at me. 'The emails, I've read them all. I know every-thing. All about her – them.' She is shouting again now and I'm backing away, literally in disbelief that Shelley could think of me this way. I thought at least – well, what I thought clearly didn't matter anymore. I'm quiet now, but unspeakable anger is building. I keep my mouth shut and let her rant.

'Go on,' she screams. 'Why don't you just fuck off out of our lives and off to your bloody South African hoor, whoever she is.'

And then it's suddenly all too much. 'I don't have to take this,' I say thinly. My head is spinning, reeling. I turn and walk away. Upstairs, I throw a few clothes into a case, grab my wash bag from the bathroom. I leave the envelope of cash in Shelley's underwear drawer where she'll find it. Then I go downstairs, take my coat and go. And that's when I began to run.

Some people jump off buildings.

Some people shoot themselves.

Some people, the lucky ones, lean on their family, their friends.

Me? I got on a plane. I'm not saying it was the right thing to do, but at the time it was the only thing I was capable of doing that made any sense to me. I had to get away. I had to try, somehow, somewhere, to get some kind of a handle on all of this – get some perspective.

There was also the matter of a little boy who needed my help.

I didn't need to think twice about where I was going.

Vera

I was worried about Shelley, very worried. It wasn't that she was falling apart or anything; in fact, she seemed to be coping admirably – on the outside at any rate. But I knew better. She had lost her husband, her home, their business, and now Olivia had upped and left. I think that had shaken her badly. Not that everything else hadn't, but we could all row in together to help with the other mess, at least on the surface. But this one, well . . .

I was so annoyed with Olivia. Talk about putting the cat amongst the pigeons. I was trying very hard not to judge her. We all have to make our own way in life, make our own mistakes – I knew that better than anyone – but I think it was the last straw for Shelley. She must have felt as if she was losing everything and everybody, bit by painful bit. I blamed myself too. It must be awful for them all having to come and live with me, a grandmother they hardly knew in a strange house that wasn't their own home, but I thought we had been doing surprisingly well, all things considered. Or were we all just in denial? Getting through the days with our heads down, firmly avoiding voicing the obvious?

Well, I had been *there* before.

I was aching to talk to Shelley about it all, to ask her what on earth had really happened between her and Charlie, but then, what business was it of mine? I would have to wait and hope she wanted to talk to me. Sometimes I thought she was about to open up, and then something would change her mind.

Thank God she had her job. She seemed to genuinely enjoy it. Her boss, Ernie Huggard, seemed to be a jovial sort, and they had sold an enormous amount of art to some mad Russian billionaire who appeared to be keeping them in business, and who, reading between the lines, seemed to be taking quite an interest in Shelley. Her boss was thoroughly encouraging it – and I couldn't say I blamed him. Good Lord, in these recessionary times, it was a wonder anyone was buying anything at all, let alone art, and this chap appeared to be in the process of acquiring several homes which needed adorning with various ongoing collections. And it was good for Shelley to be out and about, to have someone her own age to mix with. She was a very good-looking woman, Shelley, in a lovely, natural way. I could certainly appreciate how men would find her attractive.

And then I would want to kill Charlie all over again. What on earth had come over him? Why had he gone away like this? I was the last person who could expect to know, sadly, but to leave a lovely wife and his children – none of this was making sense. I began to wonder then if he had had some sort of breakdown, but he'd had the presence of mind to send the flowers and cards to Shelley on Valentine's Day. It was all most peculiar – and deeply, deeply upsetting. I was worried sick about Charlie. You never stop worrying about children, you know, no matter what age they are or how long it's been since you've spoken to them – and I was largely responsible, of course I was, for making Charlie the kind of man he was today. I was still his mother, whatever he may feel about me. Parenting doesn't come with a handbook, and I suppose Arthur and I had done our best. Well, Arthur certainly had. I just did the best I could with what I had.

But the guilt. It still hit me like a sledgehammer when I least expected it, sneaking up on me when I could be up to my eyes with things to do, and inevitably at night-time, when only the blessed relief of sleep brought some escape.

I didn't know what had gone on in Shelley and Charlie's marriage – how could I? But whatever it was, I could understand. I would not judge them. Who was I to judge anyone?

But I did desperately wish that I could do something – anything at all – to help.

'Vera?' It was Joan, interrupting my reverie. I must have been miles away, mindlessly folding clothes into piles. 'Would you go and help Zoe out on the till? It's got really busy out there. I'll look after this lot.' She bustled about, taking the black bag of donated clothes from me. 'Thank God you were able to come in today. Are you sure you're all right?' She was concerned but sounded frazzled.

We were short staffed this week with both Maura and Barbara out with the dreaded swine flu – or wine flu, as Emma had taken to calling it.

'I'm fine, Joan,' I reassured her. And I was, in that respect at least. I was blessed with a strong constitution and I always had a good walk every day and made sure to eat reasonably healthily. I made a mental note to ring Maura later. As a retired nurse she was more than qualified to handle her health, but this flu was a bad one, and she lived with and took care of her younger brother, also retired, who suffered from increasing dementia. Life could be bloody tough for people. I wasn't the only one with problems, I reminded myself sternly as I went out to the front of the shop to man the till.

Joan was right – it was busy. There were at least ten people queuing to pay, with two little old ladies insisting on having a detailed conversation with Zoe about the weather, delaying things interminably. Zoe, bless her, was too kind to hurry them up. A young chap sidled up quickly when he saw me. 'Got any more of these?' he asked, holding up a very nice Ralph Lauren polo shirt (it was amazing some of the nice clothes we were given).

'I'm afraid I can't tell you. Whatever we have is out on the floor, but we get new clothes all the time. You'll have to have a root yourself,' I said briskly. Honestly, what did he expect? A personal shopping assistant? I must have sounded exasperated, because he immediately grinned and looked me up and down in a manner I most certainly did not appreciate. Not at my age, anyhow.

'What's a good-looking woman like you doing working in a joint like this, anyway?' he asked cheekily, leaning on the counter while I gave him his change and put the shirt in a bag.

'Where do you think I should be working?' I retorted.

'Dunno.' He thought for a minute, looking speculative. It wasn't something he did very often, I'd bet – think, that is. 'Somewhere classy,' he ventured, 'like a hairdressers or something.'

Behind me, I heard Zoe stifle a snort of laughter.

I looked at him hard, but on reflection I didn't think he was being smart. He probably thought he'd made my day.

'I'm phobic about scissors,' I said and left it at that.

'Don't mind him,' said Zoe after he'd ambled off, shaking his head. 'He's in here all the time, always trying to chat us up.'

'Yes, well,' I said dryly, 'you I can understand, but really, Zoe, I'm seventy-nine, not seventeen.'

'Really?' She sounded genuinely surprised. 'You don't look it, you know. You're a really good-looking woman, Vera,' she said, considering me. 'I hope I look half as good at your age. What's your secret?'

I just smiled. There were a lot of things I had the answer to, but I suspected the really important things always eluded you. That's one of the things you discover when you get to my advanced age – none of us really know very much about anything at all. And good looks in a man, or indeed a woman, could bring their own set of problems.

'Well, Zoe, it's not something you'll ever have to worry about,' I said and she blushed. She really was a dear. I just hoped against hope she'd grow out of all those horrid piercings and studs she insisted on wearing. They really were quite terrifying. But then perhaps that was the effect she was hoping to achieve. After all, what did an old woman like me know?

Vera (1966–68)

Of course I met him again. It was inevitable, although not for a while – two months or so later. Time for me to have become complacent, to convince myself I had forgotten all about him and the effect he had had on me.

We mixed in the same circles, you see. Arthur, being a successful young barrister, managed quite a busy social life. We were always being invited to this supper party (fork suppers were all the rage then amongst young marrieds) or that cocktail party. People give out yards about how much everybody drinks these days, especially young people, but I really don't think they could drink all that much more than we did – it was just under very different circumstances. We could put it away, you know, our set, and nobody batted an eyelid. And it wasn't just white wine and champagne, not at the parties anyhow. No, it was Martinis and gin and tonics (gin and anything, in fact), although it all seemed so innocent looking back. There was always some old duffer making a bit of a show of himself, but you rarely (in fact I never) saw a woman getting drunk – it just wasn't done. Not in public, anyway. But someone, somewhere, always seemed to be entertaining, certainly at the weekends.

So we were bound to bump into each other, Felipe and I.

At first, it was at a couple of cocktail parties. Arthur did quite a bit of work for some international companies and we had always known a few of the diplomats. They were always such charming people and threw the most marvellous parties

– well, it was part of the job, wasn't it? So I was quite prepared to bump into him again, presumably with his wife next time. I was looking forward to seeing under normal circumstances, where everything would be, well, normal, and I could forget all about that ridiculous day when we must all have been a bit squiffy and had probably had too much sun to boot. But I was wrong.

I sensed him before I saw him. I know that sounds terribly melodramatic, but it's true. It was Horse Show week in Dublin, early August, and the French embassy was having a drinks party at the residence. I had always loved that house, still do, and to this day I can't pass it without so many bittersweet memories flooding back.

Arthur and I were there early, in plenty of time. He always insisted on being punctual and I remember thinking how glad I was the week was almost over. Horse Show week was always madness in Dublin – drinks parties, lunches, hunt balls, the lot. We used to be complete wrecks after it. The room was already filling up a good bit and all the usual crowd were there – the Douglases, Pam and Declan, all our friends, although I hadn't got around to talking to them yet. I was chatting to a very nice couple, an art dealer and his wife, when I felt it, a sudden change in energy in the room, a sort of feeling as if all my cells had shifted imperceptibly to high alert. My arms had suddenly broken out in goose bumps although it was a perfectly warm evening, and I automatically looked around. It was Felipe. He and his wife had just arrived. He was standing just inside the door and his eyes scanned the room before locking with mine in an instantaneous exchange that was quite electric. And ridiculous though it might sound, I was suddenly afraid.

I immediately excused myself from the little group I was chatting with and went to search for Arthur. We were both good mixers, not the type to stay joined at the hip at a party, but now I desperately needed his solid, reassuring presence beside me. I found him, not surprisingly, talking to the ambassador, Alain, a tall, austere-looking man whose demeanour belied a marvellous sense of humour and oodles of Gallic charm, and hurried through the room to join them.

'Vera, my dear,' Alain said, making a great show of kissing my hand. 'I was just boring your charming husband to death with tales of the riots in Paris. You have joined us just in time – and how lovely you look, as always. Am I mistaken, or is that Chanel you are wearing?'

'Perfume or suit?' I quipped and he roared with laughter. (Actually, I'd had the suit copied by my dressmaker, and I *was* wearing Chanel No. 5 – it would take a French man to notice.) And then I added quickly, 'I do hope I'm not interrupting?'

'Of course not, I'm delighted you and Arthur could join us. Will you be going to the Aga Khan tomorrow?'

'Depends how well you treat us tonight, Alain,' said Arthur mischievously. 'If my memory serves me correctly, the last time we were here for drinks from six till eight, as your delightful invitation indicated, we didn't get home until after four a.m. Isn't that right, Vera?'

'When in Rome, Arthur, when in Rome,' our host chuckled. 'Ah, speaking of Rome, here is my good friend Felipe, he's with the Spanish embassy, just posted here. He was in Rome until recently – have you met him? Charming fellow. Felipe!' he called.

I managed to take a discreet gulp of my gin and tonic before he was beside us.

Once introductions had been made and we established that yes, Arthur and I had met Felipe, but not Lorenza, his wife, I was able to stand back and have a good look at her. Surprisingly (or not, really), she was not the mantilla-wearing, moustachioed creature I had clearly imagined or perhaps longed for her to be. On the contrary, she was very attractive, in a striking, dark, continental way – not unlike Maria Callas, but with a larger, rather hooked nose and without the sparkle or softness. But she was very charming, and Arthur seemed more than happy to chat to her, Alain too, which left Felipe free to talk to me.

I'm sure we all appeared like any normal little group at any drinks party, but it felt like anything but. I can't even remember what Felipe said to me – I was too busy drinking him in, mesmerised by his beauty, his deep, resonant voice, his dark, laughing eyes and something else, something that hovered around his mouth, his lips, that even now I can't find words for. I suppose it was chemistry. That's what you'd call it nowadays, but back then we called it animal magnetism. Whatever it was, he had far too much of it. Luckily, Mags arrived over just then (I knew it wouldn't take her long, but I was relieved, honestly), looking as thin and dramatic as ever.

'Darlings,' she said gleefully after kissing me hello. 'My two favourite men in one corner – how lucky can a girl get?' Thankfully, I was able to slip away and circulate in safer groups and conversations.

There were a few other meetings like that one, social, convivial, harmless. And then one day when I met him in our local village, outside the grocers. And that wasn't at all safe or convivial, although at the time it was entirely innocent. It was the beginning, in fact, of my complete and utter undoing.

I had parked around the corner (in the days when you could throw your car pretty much anywhere in Dublin) and picked up my groceries, which was last on my list of things to do. It was a beautiful warm, late summer's day, about noon, and I was planning to do a bit of sunbathing in the back garden, make myself an alfresco sandwich and listen to the radio before picking up the boys from school. And then, box of groceries in arms, I ran slap bang into him.

'Vera!' he exclaimed. 'What a pleasant surprise.' He gently took the box from my arms. 'Please, allow me. I insist.'

'Well, thank you, Felipe,' I said, 'that's very kind of you, my car's just around the corner. I must say, I wouldn't have expected to run into you here. How's Lorenza?'

'Lorenza is in her parents' villa in Sardinia for a family reunion,' he said, looking ridiculously handsome in a crisp white open-necked shirt and Raybans. 'The children and I are fending for ourselves.' He smiled disarmingly.

'With the help of your staff, I'm sure.'

'Of course,' he inclined his head, 'but we have a shortage of tomatoes in the house – and I promised my daughter, Marysol, that I would make my special gazpacho for her tonight.'

'You cook?' I couldn't help sounding impressed.

'Rather well, if I say so myself.' He grinned and I felt that odd sensation again in the pit of my stomach.

'Well, here we are,' I said, relieved, as we arrived at my little car. I opened the back door for him to deposit the groceries. 'Thanks so much.'

'Not at all.' He waited, moving around to hold the driver's door open for me as I slid in behind the wheel.

'Well, goodbye. Nice to see you,' I said, about to pull the door closed when he stopped me.

'Your dress, be careful.' He reached down to move a fold of material that would have been caught in the door.

'Oh,' I said, 'silly me.' And pulled the door shut. I put the key in the ignition and turned it – and that was when I heard the ghastly wheeze. *Dear God, not now*, I prayed, *please, not now, not here*. I tried again, frantically pressing the accelerator, but it was no good. After a few feeble splutters the engine coughed and died completely. I looked up and he was still there, watching from the pavement, an eyebrow raised in question. I sighed and opened the door. 'My car seems to be refusing to start.' I said, colour flooding my cheeks.

'So I see. Would you like me to try?'

'Oh, would you?' I got out, feeling very foolish. 'Maybe I'm doing something wrong, but it's never happened before.'

So he got in after he'd manoeuvred the seat back about a mile to accommodate those long legs of his and tried, unsuccessfully, to start it. 'Flat battery, I suspect, but I'm no mechanic.' He shrugged.

'Oh dear.'

'Never mind, Vera, I'm parked just across the way. If you can wait for me to collect my tomatoes, it would be my pleasure to give you a lift.' He got out and leaned in to take out my box of groceries. 'At least your car's not in the way here. If you lock it up, you can phone your garage and have them tow it, I'm sure. In the meantime, let me get you settled in my car.'

Well, what could I say? It would have been completely churlish of me to refuse his kind offer, although every instinct I possessed was telling me to run. Instead, we crossed the road, Felipe carrying my groceries, and I waited once again as he opened the door to his car, put them in and then opened the passenger door for me.

'I'll be just a moment,' he said and set off across the road to the grocery shop, which he seemed to manage in about three long strides. I couldn't help noticing then, as I sat there cocooned in the sleek black Mercedes, how women's heads turned when they saw him, even a few elderly ones, and I smiled to myself. Felipe certainly wasn't the type of man you expected to see crossing the street in Dublin, and certainly not shopping for tomatoes in a village grocery store. He would look more at home striding off a yacht or a movie set.

Then I reproved myself. I really was being ridiculous again. But all the same, as I sat there in the car, with its CD sign discreetly on the rear beside the number plate, I did allow myself, just for a second, to wonder what it might be like to be married to a man like that. A man that women stopped to stare at, helplessly, and who even men glanced at admiringly, respectfully. One with a glamorous career, travelling all over the world – and one who could even cook for his children. I tried to imagine Arthur rustling up anything for the boys in my absence and only got as far as sausages and canned beans. But then, that wasn't fair – continental men were much better in the kitchen. It was part of their upbringing, their culture, I supposed, although there was something very appealing, rather sensual about the whole idea.

I saw Felipe about to cross the road again, tomatoes in hand, and pulled myself together. How on earth could I compare Arthur to him? And Arthur was a good-looking man. It was terribly disloyal of me, but that was the trouble about Felipe, I suspected. I'd bet there wasn't a woman alive who just couldn't help comparing any man in her life to him, even for a split second, and always, I'd bet equally certainly, that poor man would come up short.

That's what fantasies were all about. Just pure silliness.

And then he was beside me, starting the engine and pulling out onto the road. Immediately, despite the roominess of the car, I felt suffocated. 'So you got your tomatoes, then?' I asked brightly, desperate to focus on the banal, the imme-diate facts, to dispel the growing feeling of combined elation and trepidation I felt at being in such close proximity to him.

'I did,' he said, glancing sideways at me and smiling. 'And some other things too.'

'Oh?'

'I got some peaches, and strawberries.'

'How lovely,' I said inanely. 'I love strawberries, and they've been particularly good this year. If you could take a left here, Felipe.' I indicated a turn coming up.

'Of course. But first, Vera, I am going to suggest a detour.'

'A what?'

'Only if you agree, of course. But it is such a beautiful day, and we are neither of us in a hurry, are we? I thought we would go to the beach, have a walk and eat the strawberries – what do you say?'

'Oh, I don't think so, I—'

'Sometimes it is good not to think, Vera, just to be spontaneous, no? One day, we will both be old and grey, and what better way to fill our time then than with a few charming memories? And a walk along the beach with you on this lovely summer's day would certainly be a memory I would hold very dear.'

When he put it like that, I suddenly thought, why not? He was absolutely right. We had nothing pressing to do and I was fed up with always being predictable. Why not go for a walk on the beach and eat some strawberries and peaches? It was a perfectly reasonable suggestion.

'I promise to have you back home within the hour.' He looked at me hopefully.

I hesitated for only a split second. 'Yes, let's do that.'

'Wonderful.'

And we were off. There were several beaches near us, Dublin being on the coast, but we decided to drive out to Killiney Bay, which is often compared to the Bay of Naples, and go to a beach called White Rock. Once we had decided, something between us lifted, and instead of being uncomfortable, we were like a pair of teenagers, chatting and laughing easily for the twenty-minute drive.

When we arrived, even Felipe was taken aback by the view that spread out beneath us. 'I had no idea how beautiful this place is.' He shook his head as we got out and strolled along. And it *was* beautiful. The sea was a deep blue beneath a cloudless sky and you could see all the way to Bray Head. I showed him where the entrance from the road was and we crossed the bridge over the railway track and began our descent down the hundreds of little steps along the winding path that led down to the beach. At the bottom, we took off our shoes, put them behind a rock and began to stroll along. Despite the glorious weather, there weren't that many people around. It was a weekday, after all, and most people, men at any rate, would be at work. Apart from a few scattered groups of mothers and children, whom we soon passed, we pretty much had the place to ourselves. We reached the far end and found a perfectly flat rock to sit on and eat our fruit, which was delicious.

It's surprising what you can learn about a person in a few short moments. I was fascinated to hear about his life, which seemed so completely different from my own. I learned that Felipe's father was also a diplomat, his parents based now in Buenos Aires, that Lorenza's parents were old Spanish nobility, and that in families of that ilk in Spain, marriages were still pretty much arranged.

'Not insisted upon, you understand,' he smiled at me, 'but encouraged. Marriage is still very much an alliance of sorts, don't you think? It is considered very important in Spain, particularly in aristocratic circles, to make an advantageous alliance with a similar family. Lorenza and I have known each other since we were small children.' He smiled, but there was a fleeting sadness in his eyes. 'And you, Vera, tell me about you – I want to know everything.'

I didn't think there was much to tell, honestly. My life had been so ordinary, or until I'd met Arthur anyway. I was from a perfectly respectable family, I had gone to school, then college, and had only worked for three months as a radiographer before Arthur had proposed and we had been married. Arthur was ten years older than me and from a pretty posh family, and it was really only after I'd met him that I began to feel I was learning about life. He was a wonderful teacher too, and so generous, always wanting to show me new things and places. He had brought me on some wonderful holidays, and our honeymoon, travelling to Paris, Rome and Vienna, had been enchanting. Then the boys had come along, and we were a proper little family. I was a traditional wife and mother, and that was all I had ever aspired to be.

'But you, Vera, what are your dreams, your deepest desires?'

'I have everything I could possibly want,' I said primly. And it was true, I thought. 'A wonderful husband and two terrific, healthy little boys. What else could I want?'

Felipe was looking out to sea. He seemed to be lost in thought, and then slowly, and very gently, he turned, hooked his hand around my neck, leaned in and kissed me.

I shall never forget that moment. It was at once unbearably tender, filled with unspoken longing, and yet I was appalled, shocked, though if I'm honest, I knew right at that moment I was lost. But I couldn't admit that to myself – not then.

'You taste of strawberries,' he said, caressing my face. 'And I have been wanting to do that since I first set eyes on you.'

'We should go,' I said, collecting myself, not allowing myself to think.

'Don't be sorry, Vera,' he said, smiling. 'Some moments in life are given to us by the gods – that was one of them.'

'I don't think either of our spouses would think of it quite like that,' I said abruptly. I was being sharp, but I was scared now, not even about who might have seen us, but at what I had done, what I had allowed to transpire, and most of all, the effect it had on me. 'Please, Felipe, take me home.'

We walked back in awkward silence and collected our shoes, then back up all the steps to the car that was waiting by the road.

'I'm so sorry, Vera, if I have offended you, but I—'

'Don't,' I said. 'Please don't. I really would rather forget all about it, and I certainly do not want to talk about it.'

We drove back in silence, save for the radio playing some irritating pop song. The journey couldn't have been more different from the lovely, cheerful, innocent run out.

When we neared my house, I made him stop the car and let me out at the end of the road, around the corner. I couldn't get out of that car fast enough.

'But Vera,' he said, looking genuinely distressed. 'What about your box of groceries? Let me at least—'

And do you know what I said? 'Hang the bloody groceries!' And with that, I slammed the car door shut and walked as fast as was decently possible back to my house.

Once inside, with the door firmly closed behind me, I went into the kitchen, put the kettle on and burst into tears. It was ridiculous, I know, but suddenly I felt about twelve years old, confused, helpless and in turmoil. And even then, in the midst of all my righteous self-pity, I heard that little voice that was to taunt me, saying *You're not a bit sorry it happened. You're just like the thief who's awfully sorry he's been found out.* And it was right, that voice, because it wasn't the kiss that had shocked or appalled me, but my own behaviour. That's why I was so furious with Felipe, because until I met him, I was able to believe I was just a happy, fulfilled, housewife and mother. I didn't want to confront this other, awful part of me that was suddenly making itself known to me, and loudly. The part that had come alive with longings, desires and a terrifyingly cavalier attitude to what might happen or what people might think, even though they knew nothing at all – because now *I* knew. And it didn't matter how fast or where I ran to – I was to learn, all too soon, that veritable piece of wisdom that you can never run away from yourself.

For the next few days, I stayed in the house as much as possible, which was easy, as the car was being fixed. It felt safer, and after a predictable return and embracing of routine, I could almost pretend to myself that I had imagined the whole thing and I deleted it from my mind. I refused to think about it. And then, it must have been on the Friday, there was a delivery. It was from the grocers, not one but several boxes of fruit and vegetables, enough for a family of twenty. I didn't need to ask who it was from, and once he had deposited the boxes, the delivery man from the grocers handed me an envelope.

When he had gone, I opened it and read it.

My dear Vera,

I am so terribly sorry for upsetting you as I did and have been overcome with remorse ever since. I fully understand your outrage, and hope you will at least allow me to replace your lost grocery order, which I trust has been delivered if you are reading this.

I cannot, however, change what happened, nor would I want to. As I said, I have been wanting to take you in my arms since the moment I set eyes on you – madness, I know – but it's the truth and nothing else seems to make any sense.

I will be at that same spot on the beach on Monday at twelve midday. I need to see you, to talk to you, to explain. If you can find it in your heart to meet with me it would mean the world to me. If not, I fully understand and apologise once again for my inappropriate behaviour.

It will never happen again.

Felipe

That was it. I searched for my cigarettes and lighter and lit one shakily (yes, of course I smoked back then), then carefully set light to the note before washing the ashes down the sink.

How presumptuous! How typically male! What did he think I was? Mad? Available, more like. A willing target for his smooth continental charms. I never wanted to set eyes on him again.

I did, however, stow away the vegetables and fruit in the larder – as much as we would use, at any rate. I put the remainder, which was quite a lot, in my car and drove to our local convent of Poor Clare sisters, who were always grateful for some nice fruit and vegetables. I didn't go in, although I knew one of the sisters quite well, the one who used to answer the door and appear from behind a grill to speak with visitors, who inevitably were asking the community to pray for their many intentions. I had done so myself regularly over the years, and would continue to do so. Instead I just rang the bell, dropped the boxes inside the door and fled. I remember feeling quite envious then of how those wonderful women were cocooned (all right then, imprisoned) behind closed walls. Safe from worldly temptations – from themselves. Because although I was outraged at Felipe's letter and his even hinting at the suggestion that I would meet him again, and covertly, part of me (that awful part) knew that I would.

I tried, I really did. All weekend I convinced myself that it had all been an episode of utter madness, one which I had been lucky to escape unscathed. I reminded myself how lucky I was, how fortunate. I cooked, baked, had a lovely time with Arthur and the children (we went to the zoo, always a fun outing) and slept soundly and happily through Sunday night. By Monday, when I had dropped the boys to school and Arthur had gone to work, I had organised to meet Pam in town for lunch. And then, at eleven thirty, she rang to cancel, something about a plumber arriving. I couldn't hide my disappointment, but even Pam couldn't have understood why.

'But we'll do it next week, Vera, I promise. I know it's irritating of me to cancel like this at the last minute, but I just have to be here. Same day next week?'

I put down the phone with a heavy heart. I would go into town anyway, I resolved, but of course I didn't. Instead, I got into my car, and hating myself, turned left instead of right, heading for the coast road, my heartbeat accelerating with every mile. Perhaps it was a trick. Perhaps he wouldn't be there at all. Perhaps he did this to women all the time. But already I was powerless to escape the pull – I had to know.

I parked along the cliff road. There weren't many cars that day, it was grey and overcast though still warm. When I saw his car parked ahead, I found it difficult to breathe. I crossed the bridge, and from my vantage point could see no one but two elderly men strolling along on the beach below, and a dog scampering by the water's edge. Down the steps I went, those never-ending steps, and then I saw him. It couldn't have been anyone else, even in the distance. Then, overcast and grey though it was, the world suddenly lit up for me, as if someone had turned on a switch, one I had been searching for my whole life. And as I got closer and he began to walk towards me, his face breaking into a huge, joyful smile, I ran, straight into his outstretched arms.

Emma

Remember I said I should start a journal? Well, I've started a blog instead. I kinda like the idea of being able to be honest on the internet the way I can't be at home. And I'm wondering if I'll get any interesting feedback from anyone out there. I've called myself Copergirl ('cos that's mostly what I do) and nobody *ever* posts their real name. That's the whole point – to be anonymous. Here's my first post.

blogspot.com
Posted by Copergirl
15/03/09, 20.30 GMT

Friends are God's apology for your family – true or false?

Are all families weird, or is it just mine? My dad's gone AWOL. He lost his business, and then, like, just disappeared. Our house was taken from us and we're living with a grandmother we never knew we had. Well, hardly. There was some big fight between her and my father years ago and they became estranged.

It was really nice of Gran to take us in. I realise that, and I'm grateful, of course, it's just that it's such a weird feeling losing your home and everything that you're used to. We all had our own rooms in our old house, but in Gran's house I have to share a room with my 24-year-old sister, only she's left now 'cos she couldn't hack it, so she's moved in with her 'boyfriend' who is 44 (I know). Although it was hell sharing a room with her, I miss her. My mum has got a part-time job and me and my brother (11) are still at school. I thought it would be really hard going back to school after all this stuff happened, 'cos it was all over the papers here in Ireland, which is where I live, but school has been the easiest bit. I don't have to think about stuff then – I can just concentrate on my work. In fact, my grades have gone up, which surprised me as much as anyone. Also, my friends have been brilliant, especially my best friend, I don't think I could have got through all this without her. I've known her since we were five years old, and I hope we're friends forever. I spend a lot of time at her house. Her mum often picks us up after school, and it's kinda strange because although it's nice to hang out in a really cool house, it also reminds me of everything I've lost. Like my dad. Especially my dad.

Anyway, tomorrow is my friend's birthday and I've made her this really neat collage of photos and had them printed onto one sheet, and pasted it onto a self-supporting board, I really hope she'll like it. Later we're going to a Beyoncé concert which should be totally amazing. At least it'll take my mind off things – like my weird family. Anyone else out there got one?

Views: 110
Comments: 21

Comment posted by bulletproofbabe:

Y'all speak strange over there, Copergirl, but I've always wanted to visit. One of my granddaddies was part Irish and it looks real pretty. Wanna hear weird – or wired? My parents are both on their fourth marriages – lucky for some – not. I have so many step-siblings and half-siblings I've lost track.

One of them even has the same name as me. My mom's 2nd husband tried to shoot her, yes ma'am. My dad's first wife stabbed him with a carving knife. My parents both met in rehab. My younger brother's already an addict and both my parents are in denial about it. Might interfere with their drinking. My younger sister's pregnant for the second time, she's fifteen, practically an old maid. I don't remember ever having a nice house, and three of us are bunked up in my room, not counting the roaches. The shack we live in now is about to be repossessed, so we're moving on again, I guess. My mom says my dad's a lazy good for nuthing piece of sh**t. Next week she says she's going to visit with her sister in a trailer park outside of Biloxi. I don't think she's coming back. Y'all sound like you have a good scene going on over there – so quit whinin' is my advice. Your dad going missing could be the best thing that ever happened to you. Wouldn't care if mine did. My boyfriend's doing time for a crime he did not commit – he gets out in nine months. I'm in between beauty pageants then so we're planning on doing Europe. Maybe we could meet up and y'all can tell us where we should go in Ireland?

Comment posted by salvationarmygeezer:

You are not alone, Copergirl. Jesus loves you. Wot you is goin thru is the trials He sends to those He loves. He has taken away your earflie father because He wants you to turn to your Heavenly Father. Commit yourself to Him and try to save your sister's soul who has obviously hooked up with a person of The Lie. Your grandmother too needs to heal the rift wiv your father. Be assured I am remember you in my prayers. Join our web of prayer NOW on www.bornedagain.co.uk. Be strong in Jesus.

Comment posted by mylittlewhitedove:

Copergirl, you do not say how old you are? Every child is precious, and here at www.parentsright2guns.com we provide support for each and every child who is feeling vulnerable. Do not fear, we are just a link away. Click on virgindove in the left-hand column of our site and we can discuss your situation. Has it crossed your mind that your sister might be in some sort of trouble? If so, click on nestingdove in the left-hand column. Your mom sounds like she could do with some support too (click on motherdove). We aim to help every family, no matter where, with interpersonal problems. Coping alone is not the answer. Talk to us. Soon.

There were others, but that was enough for me. So my experiment with blogging is over. I had to show it to Soph, though, and she fell about laughing.

'You bloody mentaller!' she said. 'What are you like? You even said where you lived, you mad cow.'

'No I didn't, just what country.'

'Great,' she said. 'Don't blame me if you find the Salvation Army and a mad bunch of Americans with machine guns lined up outside your house – or rather, your gran's house. That'll be fun.' Then she looked at my face and said, 'I'm only winding you up, Em, but really, there are some scary people out there – you need to be careful.'

'You sound like my mum.'

She was quiet then for a moment, which is most unlike Sophie, then she looked at me and said, 'You really miss your dad, don't you?' And I had to look away, 'cos I couldn't answer that. 'Em?'

And then I began to cry, and once I started I couldn't stop. I stayed that night at Sophie's house. Jackie gave me the guest room, which was like a hotel suite. Both she and Sophie sat with me for ages while I cried and eventually fell asleep. When

I woke up and said I had to go home because of Mum and Gran, Jackie said, 'It's okay, Emma, I've talked to your mum and she says it's fine if you stay here tonight, I'm going to drop you home tomorrow.'

Later, when she had given me some warm milk and honey and turned off the light, I heard her whisper to Sophie, 'She'll be fine in the morning, Emma's a strong girl. This has been coming for quite some time; that poor kid has had a lot to cope with. You make sure you're looking out for her now.'

'I *always* do,' muttered Sophie indignantly. 'Em's my best friend, for Christ's sakes, Mum.'

'I know,' said Jackie. 'Sure, haven't the pair of you been inseparable since your first day at school?'

And even though I had cried my heart out and was beyond tired, I got a nice warm feeling as I drifted off to sleep again.

Lukaz

I am watching Natascha weave herself around the pole in my bedroom. She is very good, very provocative. But my mind is elsewhere. Not even Natascha's sexy moves can make me focus. I think she knows this, but wisely says nothing. No worse question in the world for men than a woman asking what are you thinking about? We hate that. So I smile at her encouragingly, because she is trying very hard. It is not easy to be girlfriend of oligarch. We are rich beyond most people's dreams – even rich peoples – and everywhere women chase us. This also is very unattractive to men – all men. Men are the hunters, we like to have to work to make a woman ours, even oligarchs – perhaps especially oligarchs.

I meet Natascha when she was just eighteen in a Moscow club. She is working as dancer and cocktail waitress, and her gracefulness sets her apart from the other girls immediately. I learn she trained with the Moscow Ballet for some years – this is great honour – but was not quite good enough to become professional ballerina. So she does what all girls like her do, become dancer, waitress, maybe call girl. The lucky ones meet a rich guy, this is their aim. The others have not so good a life. Natascha is very pretty I think then – like fairy-tale princess, very delicate features, not broad faced as a lot of Russian women. She also has incredible bendy body. I talk to her and she is very shy, very respectful, and I feel protective of her. Of course she becomes my girlfriend. My wife is not so happy about this. Marika and I get married very young, eighteen and nineteen – I was a baby! Also, back then I was not rich – very poor, in fact, but hard working. Now I own a sixth of all Russian aluminium production. Those days are like other life. I am very good to Marika, very generous, she is the mother of my two daughters. I move to London for her, buy her nice house near Harrods, but I will not give up Natascha and this makes her angry. I tell her she is lucky woman – she has homes all over the world, yachts, planes – all she has to do is be nice to me, not be difficult. But this she finds impossible. So eventually we divorce. Since Putin came to power, a lot has changed. Putin watches us all the time, the oligarchs – he would like to take back everything we have worked for, but he needs us too. It is an uneasy alliance. But Putin does not like Russian peoples getting bad reputation abroad. He likes things clean. Does not like prominent Russian men to have obvious public mistresses while they have wife. So I knew it would be better if Marika and I divorced. Now she lives in her house in London and sends me all the bills. But I don't mind, I am generous guy, Marika and I are old friends. Even if she is angry with me now, in time she will forgive – we Russians are very sentimental people. I am fond of Marika, I look after her and her family very well, she can have as much money as she wants, do what she wants. I don't ask questions, although I think she has too much plastic surgery. That is another thing men do not like. You cannot capture youth. Women should understand this, I think. Silicone breasts, facelifts, lipo, whatever – none of them give you youth – that is only something for the young, it is like a sheen on their skin, something fresh and exciting that emanates from their pores. We all have it – we all lose it. That is life. Natascha is young. She is sweet girl, also clever.

But now, at twenty-three, she wants very much to get married. I understand this, but I tell her I will never get married again. It is better to be honest about this, I think. Women want to have babies, and for this is better to be young. But I would like a son, and Natascha knows this, so she is biding her time, hoping she will convince me to marry her. Young people can be very persistent, they have the energy, and this can be annoying. So I watch Natascha as she dance for me, but I am thinking of someone else. I am thinking of Shelley.

Shelley is not young. In her forties, I am guessing, but very beautiful. She has something unusual in a woman. Shelley is fresh, wholesome, like American apple pie. I find myself very attracted to her. At first, I do not know who she is. She is just woman who works in art gallery, so I buy art, a lot of it, to impress her, but instead this makes her afraid of me, I think. Her boss, Ernie, is nice guy, fun – old, but fun. Together we have been sourcing and buying a lot of art for my houses, my townhouse here in Dublin that I am renting, and the country estate with stables that I buy in Kildare. This keeps Ernie and Shelley very busy. But Shelley is sad. I see that right away from the very first lunch we had together. A woman as beautiful as Shelley should not be sad, and I want to make her happy. This woman I hardly know, I want to see her laugh and dance. I want to know why she is sad, because then I will be able to fix it and she will fall in love with me. This is what I am thinking since I have met her. But then – then I make the connection, and it happens quite by co-incidence.

When I move to Dublin and tell my people to make the necessary preparations, Olag, my right-hand man, tell me I already own house there. This is news to me! And then when he explains, I remember – Charlie Fitzgibbon, his company Celtic Crest Investments goes bust. Banks close in – *finito*! I am sorry to hear this at the time. Not just because one of my companies has invested heavily in Celtic Crest, but because Charlie did not think to come to me himself. I like Charlie. I remember fun night two years ago when we meet. I am sad for Charlie. I would have liked to help him – even banks listen to oligarchs – but now it is too late. But Charlie has signed over his house, Summerton, to Tolstoy, my company, as gesture. This is honourable thing to do, and we Russians appreciate honour. So when I arrive in Dublin I check out this house. It is very nice house, in south side of Dublin, on almost two acres. A family home, a happy house. Even without furniture in it I can tell this. It is very tasteful, very nice proportions – but strangely, no kitchen, just big space for one. Charlie must have run out of money before he could finish it. But the house is too far outside the city centre for me – I prefer to be in town. So I use it instead for my people. My security guys, they live there – this is good arrangement. Then, about two weeks ago, when I am out there, Olag says to me, 'Hey, Boss, what do I do with this?' He gestures to a box of stuff. 'I found it in the attic, must have been left behind by previous owners.'

So I take a look, and there are the usual things. Mementos, a few children's toys, a pair of tiny ballet slippers, some baby clothes, and some photographs. Looking at them I feel sad. It makes me remember my own family, my daughters as babies. I love looking at photographs, I am very curious like that. And then I see it. A family photograph, Charlie, his wife, two girls and a little boy. And I understand. There is no mistaking the woman, it is Shelley. Shelley is Charlie's wife. This is shock for me, and I have to think.

'So, Boss, what will I do – throw it away?' asks Olag.

'No,' I tell him. 'Leave it with me. I will take care of it.'

He shrugs and says no more. I take the box back with me, to my house in town, and I put it away carefully, and then I pour myself a vodka and I think. This is difficult situation. I make the necessary enquiries and my people in London tell me Charlie has left the country. This is a pity. I was hoping to meet with Charlie, he is only person I know in Dublin, I thought we could have had some fun together, maybe do a little business. Now, though, I think maybe it is not a bad thing that he has gone away. Although things must have been very bad for him to leave his wife and children – especially to leave a beautiful woman like Shelley. I do not understand this. I do not know Charlie well, obviously, but I am good judge of character, and something tells me Charlie is not the type of man to leave his wife and family so easily. I tell my people to find out where he is, where he is hiding out. When you are as rich as I am, you can find out anything.

But this explains Shelley's sadness. Now I will have to move carefully. I think about it for a while, and I decide it is best to be honest with her. I must tell her that I know her husband – that now I am the owner of her family home. This worries me. I do not wish to add to her sadness. Also I do not want her to hate me – I very much do not want that to happen.

So I have all this on my mind, and then Natascha ringing me ten times a day, saying always, *When can I come to Dublin, Lukaz? I miss you, I love you.*

I am settling in still, I tell her, getting houses ready, I will send for you soon. But last week, she say if I don't send my jet she will come anyway, and knowing Natascha, she will make big scene. Also she will attract attention at airport, behaving like celebrity and so on. So I give in, it is easier this way, for now. Also if I have girlfriend around, Shelley will not be so nervous of me, I think.

For now, I lie back on my pillows and I watch as Natascha finishes her dance and walks over to the bed, slowly removing her bra and cute little thong. Her body is like sculpture, covered in shimmering oil, legs long like racehorse and her breasts firm and high. Her hair, blonde and silky, hangs to her waist in waves. She climbs on top of me and trails that hair along my torso, her hands going to work quickly and skilfully. I reach for her secret place and she moans. 'Lukaz,' she murmurs, 'Lukaz, I have missed you so much.' Then she slides me inside of her, and I can feel those wonderful dancer's muscles contract with desire. So we make love, Natascha and I, thoroughly, urgently, but when I climax, it is Shelley I am thinking of.

Shelley

It was Tuesday, and I was sitting down in the gallery with my first cup of tea before I got around to checking emails and confirming a few orders we were expecting. I loved those early hours there on my own, although they were becoming increasingly rare. Ernie, who initially had been happy to leave me to my own devices, had taken on a new lease of life since Luke, the Russian, had bought the entire contents of the gallery that fateful day, and appeared to be on a personal quest to acquire as much art as Ernie could supply him with – probably money laundering, no doubt. I warned Ernie, but he brushed the idea off as ridiculous.

'Really, Melly dear.' I had given up on trying to get him to call me by my actual name – Melly I was and Melly I would stay. 'What do you take me for? I had his credentials checked with my London contacts, and they checked with New York too. He's a very well-known collector – and not just of art,' he looked at me meaningfully. 'He made most of his fortune in aluminium. All those chaps are filthy rich – they don't know what to do with the money, and I for one am not complaining that he's choosing to spend a bit of it here – and neither should you. Anyway, he's a thoroughly nice chap – got a good eye, too.'

Well he would say that, wouldn't he? I mean, it was Ernie who was sourcing and selecting all the art *for* him. So Ernie had gone from popping in for an hour or two during the day to now charging into the gallery all guns blazing, which was rather disruptive. Not that I minded, really, he was very good company and having him fussing around stopped me from thinking about my disintegrating life and family, at least for the days I was in there. Today, I was safe for a couple of hours because I knew he was checking the contents of a country house that had been put up for sale.

Against all odds, the kids and me were surviving pretty well, apart from Olivia's departure and her taking up with Guy Masterson, which I still couldn't bear to think about. I was completely stumped, still couldn't believe it – and what could I do? She was twenty-four; neither I nor anyone else could stop her once she had her mind set on something, but I was devastated. After she left (he had sent a car and driver, hadn't had the guts to show up himself – I might have had some smidgeon of respect for him if he had), I stayed in my room and cried and cried. I felt it was all my fault, that I must be a terrible, useless mother for her to do something so dreadfully lacking in any self-respect. And it wasn't as though Liv was a gold-digger, either. Oh, I know we'd lost everything, and yes, I suppose we had spoiled Liv in many ways, but deep down she was a good kid – I knew she was. I think she was just terribly confused and desperately trying to show us all how grown up she was, and by going off with Guy she was making some desperate bid to escape what was happening to her, to us all. And maybe, the thought occurred to me, just possibly, she was doing it subconsciously to hurt her father, even if he wasn't here. If he had known about it, Charlie would have strangled Guy with his bare hands. Which brought it all back to me again – if it wasn't for that awful day, that dreadful row, maybe Charlie still would be here. We still would have lost everything, but at least we'd have each other, we'd still be a family, and that was what caused me the most gut-wrenching guilt of all.

But then I would think of those emails, of Caroline's high-pitched voice and scornful expression, and I would writhe with anger. How could he? And where was he? Had he gone out to his South African woman and her child? Correction – *their* child. (I still couldn't bear to think about that either.) There were rumours doing the rounds, of course – this was still Dublin, and rumour mongering was recession-proof entertainment and cost nothing. My close friends, especially Sally, never mentioned them, but there had been at least one newspaper mention of him being spotted in Cape Town with a beautiful blonde. I know you shouldn't believe everything you read, but that had sent a knife through my heart, even when I thought I had no heart left. And still I couldn't confront any of it. It had been all I could do to cope with getting out of the house, packing up our old life and getting us all settled into Vera's. It was simply too awful. So how could I blame Liv? If she was living in denial, she had learned that lesson well and truly from her own mother.

And Vera? How must she be feeling about everything? She had been really wonderful to us, a rock. I really don't think we could have got through any of this without her. I had so much admiration for that woman, and to think I had been dreading living with her (it wasn't easy, but still). She was wonderful with the kids too, never intruded or asked any annoying questions, any more than she did with me, although I know she must have been dying to ask me what had happened between Charlie and me. That's why I had got such an awful shock the day she told me Caroline had called in to her. I thought she might have spilled the beans, told Vera everything, putting her own spin on it, of course. But apparently she hadn't, had just called in for a chat and a cup of tea. Perhaps it had been Caroline's way of warning me, though, a warning that if I didn't tell Vera, *she* would. I knew she and Vera had been close when Caroline and

Charlie had been dating all those years ago. Which was another thing that had been on my mind recently – knowing Vera as I now did, I couldn't for the life of me imagine how or why Charlie and she had fallen out, or why this rift had developed between them. Before, I had just sort of accepted it, the way you do when you take up with someone, that all their family baggage is just that. But now, well, it struck me as unusual. I couldn't ask her, although I was dying to. She was allowing me my privacy, and I equally would not intrude on hers.

At least Emma and Mac seemed to be holding up all right, although I know Emma missed Liv, even though they were almost always fighting over something or other. That's what sisters do, but even so, I knew she was as shocked as I was, more maybe, about Guy.

'Don't worry, Mum,' she had said to me that awful evening when I had eventually come down from my room, swollen faced and puffy eyed. 'It won't last – she's too old for him.' But even Emma's false cheerfulness couldn't raise a smile from me.

'You poor dear,' Vera had said, patting my hand as I sat down listlessly at the kitchen table. 'Try not to worry too much I'm sure it's just a phase and Olivia will come to her senses soon enough. The lure of an older man is usually just that, and one that wears pretty thin when you discover how little you have in common. He's what? Twenty years older than her, you said?'

I nodded miserably.

'Won't last kissing time, mark my words.'

'But it's what might happen *during* the kissing time that worries me,' I said to her. 'And it's such an appalling example to Emma and Mac, not to mention what her friends must think. No boy her own age will ever want her now.'

'You'd be surprised what people bounce back from, Shelley,

and Olivia has her whole life in front of her. People forget
very quickly.'

But nothing anyone could say made me feel any better. I
felt as if my family and I were becoming a floorshow for the
whole country. First my husband, now my eldest daughter,
and they didn't know the half of it – any more than I did,
by all accounts. Very soon I would have to sit Emma and
Mac down, have a talk, a family council of sorts, but what
could I tell them when I clearly knew so little of what was
happening myself? Thankfully they were both doing well at
school; that was something. Emma in fact, was studying pretty
hard, although she was spending far too much time on
Facebook, and Mac was also constantly on his computer.
Vera had succumbed and had wifi installed, and Mac was
instructing her on the joys of the internet. I would regularly
come in and find them both hunched over Mac's laptop in
the kitchen, Vera making notes and exclaiming from time to
time, *Well I never!* or *How remarkable!* She was taking to it
like a duck to water. I was too tired to bother. Besides, I had
never been into email on a social level, and I had the computer
in the gallery to use if I needed to. And since this whole business had started, being sociable wasn't exactly high on my
agenda. I was just trying to keep myself together, trying not
to think about how your life can change in just a split second,
how everything you took for granted can suddenly be whisked
away from you in a heartbeat.

I had gone over that day time and time again, trying to
watch it objectively, running it like a movie in my head.
Caroline's bombshell, those awful emails that rewrote my life
and marriage as I knew it. Then Charlie coming home later,
looking at me as if I was mad, talking about it all as if there
had been nothing he could have done about it, saying that I
should have talked to him. And then the blinding rage and
terror and how I had flown at him, wanting to kill him,

shouting, screaming at him until there was nothing left, nothing left to say except, of course, what I did say – to go, to get out, go to *her*. The look of total incomprehension on his face. And then afterwards, the dreadful silence, me going upstairs, to our room, realising that he had gone – had taken me at my word. Even then, especially then, I thought it couldn't be true, that he'd be back, that he had only gone for a night, maybe two to let me cool off – and then the next day I found it. It was staring at me as I opened the drawer the next morning after a tormented, sleepless night. An envelope with my name on it, nothing more, and inside was 15,000 euro in cash, and the note that said *This is all that's left, take care of yourselves and the kids*. That was it, that's when I knew it was over, but really it was only the beginning of the nightmare.

Then Edward, Charlie's solicitor, kind, concerned, looking as awkward as I felt, telling me what Charlie couldn't – that it was all gone, the business, the money, even, unthinkably, the house. All I had was fifteen grand in cash and a missing husband. And all the time I was trying to take it in, trying to understand, managing to speak coherently when all I wanted to do was scream. I could understand then, briefly, powerfully, Charlie running away – because I wanted to do exactly the same thing. Instead I went home and did the only thing I could think of doing, which was ringing Vera, my estranged mother-in-law, a woman I hardly knew and had met on only a handful of occasions. If she was shocked, as she must have been, she never said. I can't remember much at all of that conversation, of what I babbled down the phone to her, but I do remember the kindness in her voice, and the surprising, overwhelmingly welcome firmness in her tone when she said simply, 'You must come and live here, Shelley, you and the children. I know it will be an upheaval for you all, but we'll work it all out, that's all there is to it. We'll manage this one day at a time.'

When I said we couldn't possibly (ridiculous, I know; where else could we go? But I felt I *should* protest), she replied crisply, 'Nonsense, that's what families are for.'

And that's what we've all been doing ever since, getting by just one day at a time.

I got up to busy myself with dusting and polishing the sculpture. I'd found that manual work was the best for keeping the unwelcome thoughts at bay. The thoughts of Charlie, and how he must have been struggling, desperately trying to save everything, and how he hadn't even told me – or had I really not wanted to know? Just as I hadn't wanted to confront the fact that we weren't talking about anything much apart from the kids occasionally. He must have been going through hell. But before I could be overwhelmed by that particular wave of guilt, I would tell myself that the only thing he had been concerned with was what he could hide from me. No wonder the business went down the tubes – if he was carrying on with Caroline, not to mention his South African liaison, he can hardly have had time to be keeping his eye on the ball businesswise – he had been thinking of everyone *but* his wife and family, I reassured myself as the rage would build again.

And yet, at the bottom of it all, right at the back of all that searing, hateful anger, there was a small voice telling me I wasn't being quite honest with myself about this. I hadn't actually given Charlie a chance to put his own side of the story forward, had I? I had just flown at him, my husband of twenty-five years, the father of my children – I hadn't wanted to listen. I hadn't wanted to hear. But I couldn't think about that now, any more than I could think about what all this must be doing to the children. How they must be missing Charlie desperately, how none of us ever spoke about him any more, because if I did, I might fall apart completely. No, it was much easier, much more practical, to hang on to the self-righteous rage and self-pity. That was something I could do. And there was plenty of fodder for that if I thought about it, which was fairly constantly.

My dusting was interrupted by Ernie's arrival, announced by the door slamming and the slight responding shudder of the gallery. He blustered in rubbing his hands together and wearing a pair of tweed plus fours with bright red socks and a red scarf that matched his plump cheeks. He was looking particularly pleased with himself and produced a bottle of champagne from a bag under his arm. 'Melly,' he proclaimed, 'bring out the champagne flutes – we're celebrating!'

I checked my watch; it was a quarter to twelve. 'Not quite past the yard arm, Ernie,' I admonished him – not that that had ever stopped me before. 'This must be quite a triumph. What exactly are we celebrating?'

'All will be revealed, dear girl. Just get the wretched glasses, my hands are fairly quivering, and I'm not sure if it's cold or excitement.'

While I went to fetch the glasses, I heard the reassuring pop of the cork, and placing them in front of him, Ernie smiled infuriatingly as he filled two flutes.

'I hope you haven't got any plans for next Thursday and Friday?' he asked mysteriously.

'None apart from my usual maternal duties,' I said. 'Why?'

'Well you must cancel them, maternal or otherwise. We're going to London, attending Christie's 19th-century Russian art auction with Luke, and,' he paused and clinked his glass with mine, 'he's flying us over on his jet and putting us up at the Lanesborough.'

I took a moment to digest this. 'But there's no need for me to go,' I said, feeling a flash of panic. 'Surely you'll need me here to man the gallery.'

'Certainly not,' he retorted. 'I have the honour of bidding for not one, but five extremely coveted pieces in said auction, which will be a seriously contested bloodbath. I shall need you there to take care of all the administrative details and so forth. What's the matter with you?' He looked at me askance. 'I thought you'd be thrilled. Have you any idea how exciting this is, how much fun we shall have?'

'Well, I'm not sure,' I said doubtfully. 'I'll have to check with Vera, see if she's all right with me leaving her in charge of the children. Anyway, it doesn't matter if I can't come, you can hire any number of assistants for the day.'

'That's not the point, Melly. Luke specifically requested for you to be there, and I want you there as well, of course,' he added quickly. 'He fancies you, you know.' A wicked grin had spread across his face and his eyes were twinkling.

'Don't be ridiculous.'

'Oh he does, take it from me. He didn't actually come out and say as much, obviously he's too much of a gentleman, but any fool can see he hasn't been able to take his eyes off you.'

'That's absurd, you're imagining things.' I threw back a gulp of champagne and glared at him. 'And even if it were the case, I might remind you both that I am a married woman,' I said firmly.

It was only Ernie's lack of reply, apart from a discreet cough, the slightly sheepish look I caught crossing his face and the pinkness spreading from his cheeks to his ears that pulled me up short, and I quickly turned away. I sat down at the computer and surreptitiously twisted my wedding ring, which, along with my clothes, was considerably looser on me these days. Was I a married woman, in anything other than name? I didn't know any more, and with that realisation a feeling of utter bleakness suddenly swept over me.

Ernie came over and topped up my glass. His voice when he spoke was kind but firm. 'Melly, dear,' he said, 'you haven't had an easy time of it recently, I know that. Why not allow yourself a bit of fun? And this trip to London will be just that. If at any time you feel uncomfortable about anything at all, I shall fly you home myself. Well, not literally, of course, but you know what I mean.' He smiled.

He was right. Things hadn't been easy. But who's fault was that? And then I thought of Charlie, and that sighting of him in Cape Town with the blonde. I thought of Caroline, of my lost home, my disintegrating family. Why not? What harm could it do? *Just say yes.*

'You're right,' I conceded. 'It would do me good. I'll talk to Vera about it this evening and let you know tomorrow.'

'Attagirl,' said Ernie, smiling broadly. 'It wouldn't be any fun without you, Melly dear.'

Vera (1966–68)

In the beginning, we met once a month. And they were innocent, those meetings, even if our feelings were anything but. Walks, mostly, on our beach, as we called it, and other beaches. Trips up the Dublin Mountains, and farther afield, to Wicklow, and more beaches, more hidden woodland trails. Of course it wasn't enough, but we were grateful, deliriously, pathetically grateful, for any time we could spend together, finding out about each other, observing one another, uncovering with childlike delight mannerisms, turns of phrase. The simplest gestures enthralled us. That's what it's like when you're falling in love, although I'm sure I don't have to tell you. It's a form of insanity, they say, whoever 'they' are – and perhaps they're right. Whatever it is, we couldn't get enough of it – or each other. Before long we were meeting every fortnight, and then once a week. Never more than that. Felipe was like a drug to me, I was completely and utterly hooked – and that was long before we ever got around to the physical side of things.

They were extraordinary times, really, looking back. I was living somewhere in a parallel universe suspended between terror and bliss. Terror, of course, that we would be discovered, which I couldn't or wouldn't contemplate – the repercussions were too awful. And bliss, because I felt so completely and utterly happy and alive, at least when I was with him. The rest of the time (and I can still hardly bear to think of this), the time I was being the imposter, playing the dutiful wife and mother, was spent in a mixture of dread and exquisite longing to be with him again, to hear his voice, to feel his arms around me. It was nerve wracking, too. Remember, we had no mobile phones in those days, and I had warned Felipe never to telephone the house. I could, if necessary, ring him at the embassy and use the code name we had devised, but I avoided that where possible. Otherwise, if one or other of us couldn't turn up at our agreed rendezvous, the abandoned one had to take it on the chin. But we rarely missed our meetings. They had become entirely too important to us.

Then one day, Felipe said he had a surprise for me. I was to follow him in my car and not allowed any questions or clues. It was December, and a bitingly cold wind was slicing away what remained of the few surviving withered leaves. I kept one car behind him as we headed into town and pulled into a square full of Georgian houses from where a lot of doctors and dentists practised. Once we had parked, Felipe came over to my car, handed me a piece of paper with an address on it, told me to give him ten minutes and meet him there. It felt like half an hour, but when the ten minutes were up, I did as he said, pulling my headscarf tightly under my chin and praying I wouldn't run into or have to stop and talk to anyone I knew. As luck would have it, I didn't, and minutes later reached the house on the square with the ornately worked front door and overhead Georgian glass fan. The number on the piece of paper was clearly for the basement flat, so I went down the steps and pressed the bell on the small door. Immediately it opened and Felipe was there before me, laughing and pulling me into his arms.

'Are you mad?' I whispered, pulling away, horrified.

'It's all right, Vera darling,' he said. 'We are alone here – completely alone.' And we were. It turned out that the basement flat belonged to the embassy and was rarely used, mostly to put people up, extra staff and so forth, if needed, which was hardly ever. Felipe had the key to it now that it had been recently vacated.

'At last, Vera, we have somewhere that can be ours, for however short a time, somewhere we don't have to hide from each other.' He showed me around then, almost proudly, although the place was small and simply kitted out. There was a small kitchen, a sitting room and, of course, a bedroom, which I could hardly bring myself to look into.

Suddenly something had changed, and although I couldn't deny my delight and excitement, I was overcome with shame and guilt.

'Are you disappointed, Vera?' He looked worried, sadness flitting across his handsome features. 'I thought – I thought . . .'

'No, of course I'm not disappointed.' I sat down suddenly at the small kitchen table, a million thoughts whirring round my head, and none of them making sense. Inexplicably, I wanted to cry. It felt . . . sordid somehow, and not at all right. Well, how could it? Everything about what we were doing was wrong. But that was just it, that was what was so dreadfully sad – because alone, away from the rest of the world, Felipe and I were more right than anything I had ever known or dreamed of. But I knew in that moment, the way you do, that whatever happened, we could never, ever claim that right – it would always be wrong everywhere but in our own hearts and in the few precious hours we could steal together.

There was something else too. It was a shift, a move up to the next level, if you will. Here, safe, undisturbed and with a bedroom at our disposal . . . and suddenly I was filled with terror. I couldn't do this – I couldn't. Kissing yes, maybe, was bad enough, but anything more was unthinkable. So I sat there mute as he looked at me and then sat down beside me and took my hands.

'Vera, darling, please don't worry, please don't be sad, I

can't bear it,' he said, concern making his voice seem love-
lier than ever. 'I don't want you to do anything you don't
want to. You know that, don't you?'

'Yes,' I nodded miserably. But that was the problem – I
did want to. I wanted to do everything with him, not just
this. I wanted to live my whole life with him from beginning
to end. I didn't want a world without him – without us. And
I hated myself for it. So instead I made tea. I know it seems
mad, but I had to do something mundane, normal. I couldn't
think any farther than that. If I did, what I was about to do
would be smashed to a pulp with the promise of repercussions, consequences, that would kill me – or kill us. I couldn't
let that happen, not yet, so I made tea.

The little fridge was stocked, I remember that, just with
the essentials. Felipe watched me, bewildered and a little sad
as I bustled round that tiny kitchen, finding cups and saucers,
a teapot and tea, and listened to me as I prattled inanely
about nonsense. About how Pam was going to try Maggie's
new hairdresser and go for a similar sharply angled bob, and
how I was trying to talk her out of it. How our neighbours
had just got a new dog and he'd chewed their brand new
sofas to bits, and how before we knew it Christmas would
be upon us. And all the while Felipe listened and nodded
and made the appropriate comments. And slowly I relaxed,
feeling safer with the table between us, with my cup and
saucer in hand, with my silly, panicked conversation tumbling
out of my mouth. Then, when I got up to take the cups and
rinse them out at the sink, I heard Felipe get up from his
chair too. He came over to me and very gently took the cup
which I had been holding under the tap from my hand, and
took my hand, dripping wet, and kissed my palm.

'Vera,' he said with enormous tenderness, 'I know you are
afraid, and although it may seem unlikely, I am also afraid.'
He looked at me, really looked at me, and I could see nothing

but depths of honesty in those beautiful brown eyes as he took me in his arms. 'If you want to, we can go. We can leave here and never come back to this flat. I would never do anything to upset you. You know that, don't you, I hope?'

I did know that. I knew it without a shadow of a doubt, and I told him so.

'Do you want to go, Vera?'

Perhaps I could have escaped even then, but I don't think so. I was already madly and utterly in love with him. I shook my head. 'No, I don't want to go.'

And then he kissed me. I shall always remember that kiss, even though we had kissed quite a lot before that. This one was different – joyful, tender, passionate with promises – the fervent, hopeful, unspoken promises that all illicit lovers have made since time began, all the sweeter for the equally resolute certainty they ignore – that in the depths of their hearts and souls they know these same promises can never be kept.

That was also the first time we went to bed, that we made love. And no, I'm not going to tell you about the sex, except to say it was magical. Every generation thinks they invented sex or some new and daring way of doing it, but none of them did and none of them ever will do. My generation simply didn't talk about it much, whatever we were doing, so I'm not going to start now. In my opinion it makes it all sound rather coarse and vulgar, because you see, unless you're deeply in love with someone, sex can be rather, well, dispiriting. People talk a lot about chemistry these days, and yes, I have no doubt it exists to varying degrees between people, but there is no shadow of doubt in my mind that love, real love, is what elevates sex to the sublime. So as Forrest Gump (one of my favourite movies) would say, that's all I have to say about that.

Our love affair – and that's what it was, we were both of us deeply in love – went on for over two years, years of equal parts torment and delight that I still cannot rationalise. How did it affect my marriage, you must be wondering? Were we found out? Not to our knowledge, although you're always the last to know, aren't you? Dublin is such a small town and people may well have had their suspicions, but we were terribly careful, and as I said, only met once a week in our little flat, which became a sort of wonder world for me, a passport to adventure and delights I had never dreamed of, blissful escape from a life I hadn't even realised I wanted to escape from.

Once I had learned how to subdue the initial guilt (it's amazing how you can justify these things when you're in love), I used to live for the hours I could spend there with Felipe. Even if we had wanted to, I don't think we could have stayed away from each other. And it wasn't just the physical side of things, you know. I found him fascinating. He was intelligent, of course, but also warm, funny, terribly charming and just, well, the most gorgeous person I had ever imagined, so much so that sometimes I would look at him when he slept, or lie awake myself at night, thinking, wondering how God had thought him up, designing every perfect detail of him. That's how mad about him I was.

But I never stopped loving Arthur. That was the worst thing, although I didn't realise that back then. And I wished, sometimes desperately, that I could have. But of course I was out of my mind then, wishing for things that were not only improbable, but impossible. Fantasies that only love can feed to you, morsel, by tempting morsel. If Arthur knew about Felipe and I, he never mentioned it, never said a word.

I often wondered what it must have been like for him, what particular brand of hell I must have inflicted upon him. Of course he must have known. I know at one stage there had been an incident of sorts in the Law Courts. My dear friend Pam had very discreetly referred to it one day when we were having coffee together. She laughingly mentioned a well-known gossip who had said *her* husband had heard a barrister friend of *his* at the golf club talking about Arthur, and a rival barrister who had lost a case to him had made some snide comment along the lines of Arthur spending maybe *too* much time in court and not enough time at home with his very pretty wife. Of course I'm sure now, looking back, that there was a little more to the quote than that, but as I said, Pam was being discreet and just letting me know that clearly there was some kind of talk about it all.

I remember my blood running cold when she said it, and of course I brushed it off immediately, terrified that even Pam might ask or probe for details. But good friend that she was (she's gone twelve years now, cancer, and I miss her dreadfully), she never, ever asked – not then.

But Arthur must have known, or at least known that something was dreadfully amiss. It's the very fact that he never brought it up or asked me about it that makes me certain that he *did* know and that he just didn't want to confront it. Not unnaturally, neither did I.

You see, we had a good marriage, Arthur and I. We were terrific friends apart from anything else, and that was the worst part for me, the fact that I was betraying my best friend in the world. But I couldn't think about that, although it was always there, of course, always lurking at the back of my mind along with many other unsavoury thoughts. But I was burning too brightly. Everything that was happening with Felipe and I was feverishly consuming me. Nobody else stood a chance, not in any normal way, because of course I couldn't be normal, even though I was sure I was fooling everyone. I would talk too much or not enough at dinner and sometimes catch Arthur looking at me curiously or sadly, which would make me try to be even more chatty or witty, anything to elicit a smile, a reassurance that all was well.

I was looking well, too. I had lost a little weight – although nothing like what I would lose later on – and of course I must have exuded that glow that only a woman in love has, or can spot in another woman. I was overcompensating with the boys too, fussing over them, or if I was on edge, snapping, and then going to ridiculous lengths to make it up to them. I was giddy, unpredictable, and, I'm ashamed to say, I persuaded myself it was fun – that they were enjoying this new, exciting me, a mummy who was fun to be around, when it must have been awful and confusing for them, poor little mites.

And Arthur, who still said nothing, who dealt with this hideous intrusion into his life, his marriage, by retreating, knowing perhaps that this was exactly what I needed him to do, that I couldn't have coped with him being confrontational, or worse, overly affectionate or demanding physically. No, Arthur behaved as always with complete and utter dignity, and, I suspect, kindness, although I was too young and stupid to realise that then. I was just grateful that I could carry on my madness in continual denial, while Arthur slipped further and further into loneliness and threw himself increasingly into his work.

It couldn't go on, no matter how much in love Felipe and I were. There were a few salient facts we were careful never to discuss. For a start, we were both Roman Catholics. Divorce back then, in the mid-sixties, was not an option, certainly not for a diplomat, and most certainly not for a 'respectable' married woman with children living in Dublin. Then there was Felipe's career, and this was the part I really, *really* couldn't bear to contemplate. He would be posted in Ireland for a maximum of three years before moving on to another country, another diplomatic post farther up the ladder – and farther, forever, away from me. So you see, it was unthinkable that we might ever be together, even if either of us could have faced the thought of running away, divorcing, leaving our children – no, that was something that could never, ever happen, not in those days. So we simply never spoke of it. Perhaps it made our time together, those two and a half wonderful years, all the sweeter, infinitely more precious, this knowledge that this was all we had.

In a way, I suppose it was better that we weren't neighbours or social friends, where we would be forced to meet, to bump into and avoid one another long after the affair was over. This way, the end would be decided for us. There would be no long-suffering agonising about how or when we should end it. The end would simply come in a neatly dispatched order, a packing up of belongings and house and taking children out of school for Felipe to another country, another new beginning, and I would simply go back to life as it had been before him. That was what I convinced myself of on those pitifully rare occasions that I even allowed the thought to flicker across my increasingly unrealistic mind.

Because when the end came, as it inevitably did, it turned out to be the beginning of the most terrible period of my life.

Mac

They think I'm stupid, but I'm not – they're the stupid ones. Except Gran, maybe, she's quite good on the computer now. At least she listens. But I don't tell her anything of course, I don't tell any of them anything, not even Mum – especially not Mum. Anyway, they don't deserve to know. But I got Olivia back for all the times she made me look stupid, and now she's gone.

In the beginning I thought I'd hate it here, but it's not that bad really. I have my own room, sort of a converted attic with a trapdoor and folding stairs up to it, so no one bothers me, or if they do, I can hear them coming in loads of time. When we first came here there was no wifi, not even broadband or anything, so I couldn't use my laptop, which was crap – not the laptop, I mean, not being able to use it. Mum kept asking me if I was okay and giving me hugs and ruffling my hair – I hate that – but no one was talking, not really, they were just all being polite. Except Olivia, she just sulked in her room or went out to meet 'that muppet Guy', that's what Emma calls him. Now she's gone to live with him. I'm not supposed to know that, *doh*. Emma's okay. Sisters are minging but older sisters are the worst. Now there's just Emma and me left.

In the beginning, I had it all worked out. I was going to run away. I was going to find Dad and live with him; I didn't care where he was. But then things got better, so I've stayed – for now. But only 'cos that's what Dad wants me to do. He said I was to stay and be strong, and look after Mum and the girls until he came back and sorted things out. But I'm getting fed up of waiting, but I promised, and I won't break my promise, not without telling him anyway.

Everyone laughed at me that day those flowers came for Mum and they said they were from Dad, and I asked was there a message for me. And then Emma brought in those stupid cards with hearts and stuff on them. But anyone could see *they* weren't from Dad. Mine said *Happy Valentine's Day from Guess Who?* and there were a lot of Xs and Os. Dad would never have put that crap on a card to me. So when I finally got my laptop working and got that first message from him, I knew Mum had been lying all along – like I said, they think I'm stupid. But that first message was cool. That changed everything. I didn't recognise the sender address, but when I opened it and read it, I knew it was Dad even before I got to the end and saw his name – just like I had known he would contact me as soon as he could. This is what it said.

From: jame.s.bond@hailmail.com
To: macdenife@eirfly.net
Hey kiddo,
I need you to read this carefully, Mac, and try to be patient with me for a while. Your Mum and I are having problems, as I'm sure she's explained to you all, and I have to go away for a while, I'm not sure for how long just yet. I know you must be feeling angry and confused and probably hate me right now, and I know it's a lot to ask, but I really need you to trust me while I try to straighten out some really important stuff. I can't say where I am right now, but you and the girls can reach me anytime at this address — give it to Liv and Em for me and tell them I love and miss you all and can't wait to hear from you. As soon as I've taken care of things out here I'll tell you all about it. In the meantime I want you to be strong and look

after Mum and the girls for me. And remember, even if things seem really crappy, I promise I'll take care of everything — I just need some time to figure things out. Then I'll be back, I promise, I just can't say exactly when yet. Write soon and tell me you're okay — although I understand if you probably don't ever want to speak to me again.
All my love,
Dad

That's when I knew I was right. Dad hadn't left me, or any of us — he'd had to go. I knew that 'cos I'd heard Mum yelling at him to go. I heard her yell *Why don't you just fuck off out of our lives and off to your bloody South African sewer.* She doesn't know I heard that, but I did. You could have heard her halfway down our road.

I was at soccer practice that day, like usual, and Freddie's mum was picking us up, but it was cancelled 'cos our coach got sick and Freddie's mum took us all for a McDonald's instead and then left me home. Mum and Dad's cars were both there but I didn't want to ring the bell and look like a kid in front of Freddie. I don't have my own key but we always have one left out under a secret rock at the back door for emergencies, so I thought I'd use it. I locked the door carefully behind me, and that's when I heard the shouting. So instead of going in through the kitchen the way I usually would, I just went back out again. I put the key back, then I went up to my tree house right at the back of our garden and sat there for a while. Then, when I knew my friend Tim who lives next door would be back from school, I texted him to see if I could go around. He said yeah, come on over, so I did, and his older brother Kev had this brilliant new Xbox game called *Killer Zombies* that we weren't supposed to play but he let us. So we played that for about an hour and I won and then I went back home at the normal time. Emma was coming in then too, but Dad's car was gone. That was the day he never came back.

I hate it without Dad. Him and me were a team, us against the girls, that's what he always said. *You and me, Mac, us guys have to stick together, otherwise women run rings around you.* So when I got that email, I was really pleased. I wrote back straight away and this is what I said.

From: macdenife@eirfly.net
To: jame.s.bond@hailmail.com
Hey Dad,
I just got your email now cos I haven't been able to use my laptop for a while. Everything is fine. It's OK that you can't say where you are – I won't say where we are either, bet you couldn't guess. I'll look after Mum and the girls till you get back, but everyone's pretty pissed off with you, so I don't know if they'll want to write to you yet. You know what Liv and Em can be like. I'm the only guy here now in a house full of women. Our junior team won the league cup and Rocky Smith got three drop goals.
    It's lonely here without you, I really miss you so hurry back. Hope you're well.
Luv,
Mac

That was ages ago. I didn't tell anybody – why should I? They never tell me anything, so this is my secret. And it's Mum's fault he's had to go away like this. Dad wrote back and said he understood that everyone was still angry with him, that it was only natural. I don't get that. I mean, Mum told him to go – he should be angry with *her* – I am. But I just act like I don't know anything. They think I'm stupid, and that's OK. It can even be good sometimes. Dad said he's coming back, and that's all that matters. Then I can go and live with him and then they'll be sorry. Emma said she doesn't think he's ever coming back and that I should get my head around that, but what does she know? And she said I'm not to keep asking Mum 'cos it makes her upset. But like I said, they don't know everything – girls just think they do. So I keep emailing Dad just to let him know I'm OK. And he always emails me right back. I'm on his side. Dad and me, we're a team.

Vera (1968–72)

I call them the black years, because that's what they were. It was 1968 and a particularly bleak February when Felipe mentioned awkwardly that they would be moving him on in June. Only four months, four precious months left, such a paltry amount of time when even a lifetime wouldn't have been enough. We resolved not to speak of it. There was no point, absolutely nothing that could be done – we both knew that.

I think of that time before he left in snapshots, precious mental pictures I was constantly recording, imprinting on my mind. I wanted to remember every square inch of our little flat, as we called it – we didn't dare go outdoors any more. The small kitchen table with the wonky leg that rattled. The tiny sitting room, with the little velvet-covered couch that always seemed ridiculously small when Felipe's long legs were stretched out in front of it. The bedroom, with its modest double bed, which we always made up so carefully after unmaking it, disturbing it only with love, passion and increasingly wistful tenderness, lying there for hours, sometimes just talking and holding each other. I could have looked at him forever. A haircut I had, just brushing my shoulders, with a fringe, that Felipe said made me look like Julie Christie in *Dr Zhivago*, except more beautiful. Silly, useless conversations punctuated with the unspeakable – how I feared I couldn't go on without him, and didn't want to. Seeing my sadness reflected in the darkness of his eyes, every gesture, every touch, every squeeze of a hand, a silent support – *be strong, we have to be strong*. And looking back, I was, really, remarkably strong, but only because I couldn't have known or contemplated the horror that lay ahead.

Denial, I think sometimes, has its place. It props us up, supports the fragile places in our hearts and minds that, buffeted and torn by fractured love, would surely fall apart. It doesn't matter that it's an illusion – reality, whether we are deemed ready or not, intrudes in its own time.

In the end, I decided not to see him a month from before he left for good. It was simply too painful. And somehow, in my deluded state, I felt that by taking charge like this, being as decisive about the end as I was helpless about the beginning, would help me, protect me. I would feel some semblance of self-control returning. Felipe was as heartbroken as I was, but I was adamant. I would have to embrace this new, old life without him. And that's what I did, relentlessly. Arthur and I even went out to dinner with Pam and Declan a day later and I was the life and soul of the evening, chatty, witty, laughing uproariously at Declan's jokes and having far too much wine. I thought I was being charming, amusing, stoic, when in reality I was being horribly brittle – hardly surprising, since I felt I could snap in two at any minute. Arthur laughed along with me, perhaps a little too eagerly, but I saw Pam regarding me keenly, concern flickering across her lovely features, worry creasing her brow. Afterwards, Arthur helped me into a taxi and I hardly remember getting home before I collapsed into bed and passed out – which was exactly what I had wanted to do.

One day down, a lifetime still to go.

I got through that month because I knew he was still there, still around me. It didn't matter so much that we couldn't or wouldn't see each other, just knowing he was in Dublin, waking and sleeping and getting through the day like the rest of us, was a sort of ridiculous comfort. I still couldn't confront the reality that one day very soon he would be gone – from here, from me – never to return. I would remain here in my life, or what was left of it, while Felipe would be off to new beginnings, a carousel of countries, continents, all far away from me. I knew it deep down, I just couldn't face it – not yet – which was why on that fateful day when I did see him one last time, I was powerless to prevent what happened, wrong though it was – shamefully wrong. I had never been able to resist Felipe, even if, as then, it meant risking everything – my marriage, my family, my reputation, and although I didn't know it then, my sanity.

It was two days before he was leaving and I had been going about my usual routine, probably feverishly, wildly trying to keep busy, trying not to think – anything but to think. I had dropped the boys to school that morning and it was a beautiful day, one of those perfect June summer days which when they come to Ireland light everything up like a picture postcard.

Arthur was on his usual monthly stint in Kilkenny, where he stayed for a couple of nights on legal business he had there, and I was grateful to be alone. The week before I had invited Pam around on a vague suggestion of a garden lunch if the weather was holding up, but now I couldn't face the thought of seeing her, or anyone. I just wanted to be alone, but then scolded myself, telling myself it would do me good to see her, to chat. It was about midday, I think, when the doorbell rang. I wasn't expecting anyone and assumed it was the postman and went to answer it. When I opened the front door and saw Felipe standing there, I froze with shock, and then a myriad of emotions ran through me, overshadowed by fear.

'What are you doing here?' I gasped, both appalled and thrilled to see him.

'Forgive me, Vera, please,' he sounded distraught, 'but I had to see you, just one last time. I couldn't help myself.' He looked wretched. He had lost weight, and beneath his tan there was a grey pallor, new lines fanning out around his dark, troubled eyes. He had never seemed so beautiful to me. 'Please, may I come in, if only for a moment?'

I let him come in then, that last, that only time. He must have known Arthur was away (he was always away for those two days every month), but neither of us spoke of that, or anything much. I think we were beyond words – or sensible conversation, at any rate. Once I had closed the door behind him and we were alone, it all seemed perfectly simple. I rang Pam and cancelled our lunch, saying I would meet her next week instead. I took Felipe into the kitchen, where I assembled the makings of a basic lunch, Brie and some fresh baguette I had picked up earlier with my grocery shopping, and handed him a bottle of chilled white wine to open. Then we set up the small portable table outside on the patio, which I covered with a pretty cloth, pulled out two chairs, and for the few precious hours that remained to us, we tried and failed to pretend that we could be happy, even in the face of immeasurable sadness, of imminent parting – just one last time.

We drank the wine, smoked, talked, reminisced, even laughed with forced cheerfulness until my laughter turned to tears. Felipe's face was grim, taut with grief, and all the while he held my hand, stroking my face, murmuring, 'Vera, *mi amor, mi amor.*'

I don't remember at what point I decided to bring him up to bed, my bed. I just knew I couldn't let it end like this, let him go without holding him, being close to him, breathing him in one last time, so I could savour him, us, hoping that a sliver of that passion, that extraordinary love could be held in the memories that would be all that would be left to me.

It was madness, I know, stupid, reckless, selfish madness, but at the time I *was* mad – mad with love and mad with grief, whose hungry beginnings were starting to gnaw at the edge of the heart it would later devour.

So we went to bed, Felipe and I. I brought him to our room and closed the door. We had two hours left before the boys would be home from school – then later, Arthur.

But for now, for those minutes that I clutched at desperately, I could be someone else. And I *was* someone else. I was all the love I had ever felt or imagined I could feel, and ever would. I was consumed with love, desire – we both were – desperate, frantic for each other, and later, quietly, almost reverently, drinking each other in, tracing maps of tenderness wherever we touched, taking lingering, longing inventories, exchanging whispered, heart-wrung endearments – the loving before the leaving – that would have to last us the rest of our lives.

So it wasn't surprising, really, that I didn't realise we had been interrupted. That the door had been opened by little hands, if only a fraction, and that a small forlorn figure had stood there, however briefly, for what must have seemed like a lifetime before closing that door equally quietly and going away.

To say that thought fills me with shame and horror is an understatement, although back then I didn't know. I didn't find that out until many years later, until that dreadful day with Charlie and Caroline in our bedroom, encountering that eerily similar situation. Then I thought I really *was* going mad, hallucinating the same stage, but the cast had changed. I could finally understand Charlie's studied indifference to me, what must have been, up until then, the inexpressible anger he had held inside all those years.

To this day I still don't know exactly what my little boy saw, but I've imagined all the various hideous scenarios, though perhaps no image that day, imagined or otherwise, is more heart rending to me than Charlie's bandaged little knees, the cut above his eye that he was so brave about – the outer cuts and scrapes that masked the real wound, inflicted by his own mother, that was just beginning to fester.

Had I known that the day Felipe and I made love so desperately, I would have killed myself rather than meet him or ever begin our affair. But I didn't know. I wasn't to know anything properly, really, for the years following that.

Instead, I wanted to kill myself for another altogether selfish and stupid reason. I wanted to kill myself because of grief – heartbreak – which is perhaps, in hindsight, just as well. Because had I known that day that my little boy had seen us, I don't think I could have gone on, faced him or Arthur ever again. Maybe that would have been better. I don't know. But I did survive, in ignorance, yes, even years later until that awful day I discovered Charlie and Caroline in bed and Charlie told me. The day Caroline fled our house, and who could blame her.

I survived – eventually. It's amazing what you can survive, but I didn't want to. As I said, that day, the day Felipe left, was the beginning of the black years.

Olivia

It's been a month now since I've moved in with Guy and I have to say it's not quite as much fun as I thought it would be. The thing is, I've kind of backed myself into a corner here. At first it was great, really great. Long, lazy mornings in bed, loads of dinners out, but now Guy seems stressed a lot of the time, and believe me, he's no fun when he's stressed. It's partly the property collapse here, of course. For all his talk about my dad taking his eye off the ball, he can't exactly have been Donald Trump himself. He says the banks are giving him hell, but not nearly as much as his wife's lawyers. Apparently since I've arrived on the scene, she's taken a whole new interest in her 'separated' husband. I wouldn't mind, but all the woman does is shop. She's made a career out of it, Guy told me, and by all accounts she's educating the vile twins (that's what I call his eleven-year-old twin daughters) to exceed even *her* expenditure, if at all possible.

So to put it in a nutshell, Guy is feeling the pressure. I didn't appreciate quite how much until he suggested that I get a job the other day. Jeez! Who is he, my father? So I told him to back off, that I was entitled to take a gap year if I wanted to – all my friends are (well, most of them – if they're not travelling they're out of work; there's a recession on, remember?). What a downer, though – I've really started to go off him after that. But I did get a job, and it happened quite out of the blue. I was talking to my friend Ginny, and she said she'd heard they were looking for a marketing manager in Iniquity, so I rang them up, and to make a long story short, I got the job. Since it mostly involves trying to get more members to sign on, a large part of the job involves schmoozing people (easy peasy!) some phone work (hell-oo) and working three nights a week from ten p.m. till two a.m. Since that would be the time most of my friends would be there, it's not exactly hard work. But since it *is* work and I'm on duty, Guy isn't allowed to be with me on those nights, which is driving him crazy.

'Well,' I reasoned when he was whinging about it again, 'you wanted me to get a job and now I've got one. You should be happy for me. And while you're about it, why don't you tell your wife to get one too?'

We didn't speak for three days after that one, but he caved first. 'Forgive me, baby,' he said, putting on the puppy dog eyes he thinks fools me. 'You're the only good thing in my life right now.'

He bought me a present to make up – my favourite Agent Provocateur lingerie – and although I didn't say it, what I was really thinking was, *You'd better believe it, sunshine.*

All the same, I'm not going to do anything rash just yet. I couldn't face going back to the House of Horrors, and I haven't saved up enough yet to rent a decent place of my own. Anyway, if I moved out now, wifey would have won, wouldn't she? That's exactly what she wants me to do. I'd be playing into her hands.

Instead I decided to take Emma shopping. Her fashion sense is just awful, but with a bit of careful dressing, she could be quite a looker, my little sister. She's going to her first proper rugby club disco next week and she's out of her mind with anxiety and says she has nothing to wear. Well, that's what older sisters are for, isn't it?

Lukaz

So Shelley is coming to London. This is good. This is very good. For a while I worry that she will not come, but today Ernie tells me good news. Ernie is excited too, but for other reason. Day after tomorrow we go to Christie's, London, to special auction of 19th-century Russian art. It is my intention to buy five top pieces, maybe more, and Ernie, he will bid for me. I will remain absent – my presence would attract too much attention. But this auction is very important to Russian oligarchs – we like to compete, and all of us, the six big guys (can't tell you names, but anyone can guess), are very competitive. Afterwards, there will be big celebrations, but I have planned celebration of a different kind – just me and Shelley. Of course she don't know that yet. Also I am looking forward to London because I will see my daughter, Katerina. I love my daughters very much, am very proud of them. Katerina is twenty and very talented designer. People say she is good, although I think some of her clothes are a bit crazy. When she has finished in London College of Fashion, I will help her start her own label – but only for three years. If by then she has not made success, I don't help. It is important for children to have goals, but have to be able to make it on their own too, especially children of wealthy people. Otherwise they become lazy, think life is big picnic, so I say to my girls, I will help you, but only at beginning. After that you must succeed by yourself. If Stella McCartney can do it, can't be that difficult. But I don't worry about Katerina, she is like me, very focused.

Nikki, my youngest, is eighteen and studying in Paris, doesn't know for sure what she wants to do yet. That is okay, that will come. But Nikki is a bit ditzy, I think, more like her mother. When I was eighteen, I had already set up stalls to exchange vodka and cigarettes for Russian aluminium shares given out by state to the people. By twenty-three, I was sleeping at night in the aluminium factory beside the furnaces to protect them from competitors' sabotage. My boss make me partner – I have good head for figures, remember balance sheet like other men remember women's measurements. By thirty, I am already very, very rich. But I can tell you this – life is not a picnic, don't matter how much money you have. Always there will be problems.

Which reminds me, Natascha also want to come to London with me, but I tell her no.

'You have just come from London, baby,' I say.

'But I come from London to be with *you*, Lukaz, not to be here in Dublin without you.' She is angry with me, I know, although pretending just to be sad. I hope she doesn't cry. I really don't like women crying, reminds me of my grandmother, but she had good reason to cry a lot. Was very poor, had very tough life until I became rich, then I make everything better for her. I ring her most days to talk to her. She is lonely without me. Soon I will bring her to Dublin for a few days – Natascha can take her shopping and so forth.

'Is only for a few days, baby,' I tell Natascha. 'Go and see my horses, I want you to learn to ride. Have special instructor for you. When I come back from London, you can show me how quickly you learn, yes?' Is important for woman to be able to ride horse, I think. Also, riding clothes very nice on women. Very sexy.

Natascha doesn't like horses. She is scared of them, she says. 'Don't be silly, baby,' I tell her. 'Horse is noble animal. Anyway, only have two more legs than you, and you have legs like racehorse already – you will be natural.' This makes her smile a little. Of course she will do as I say. Natascha is not stupid girl. Young, but not stupid. So Natascha will go to my country estate and I will go to London.

My daughters do not like Natascha. This I understand. She is too close in age to them, and also my ex-wife Marika has encouraged them. Women are difficult, beautiful but crazy. Like thoroughbreds – but this is their charm, no? I will bring back for Natascha nice present from London, then she will be happy.

Now I must ring Ernie, make plans for trip. I am very excited. Like little kid. It is a long time since I have felt like this. But first I tell Olag to have Gulfstream ready, make sure papers are in order, because of course we are flying over in my jet. I wonder has Shelley been on private jet before? Possibly, I think – Charlie did not have his own jet, but probably timeshare hours in one, like most businessmen. But this is not the same as owning your own jet (I have two). So yes, perhaps she has flown by private jet before – but not with pilot who flies his own, I am betting. This I am looking forward to. This will impress her very much, I think. Like I said, I am very excited. It's no good being very rich if you can't have fun. This trip I am thinking will be a lot of fun.

Shelley

It's only one night. Just one night, not even two full days. I'm trying to think of it as a break, that's what Vera keeps referring to it as. 'It will be a lovely break for you, Shelley dear. Will you get a chance to do any shopping, do you think?' And then, of course, she looks embarrassed. Money's too tight to mention, as the song says. I'm trying not to think about that. The money Charlie left for us is running low what with school fees, clothes, sports equipment, although I'm being careful with it – downright stingy, in fact. And my salary, if you could call it that, would be nice as pocket money, but let's just say it wouldn't feed a family for long. Although Vera keeps trying to sneakily pay for everything when she can, which is making me feel incredibly guilty.

But when I mentioned last week that I might have to go to London on business for a couple of days and asked if she could hold the fort, she looked positively delighted. 'Of course you must go, Shelley, it will do you good. I used to love a few days in London, although I don't think I'd have the energy for it now. Will you take in a show?'

I told her I doubted it, but yes, a couple of days in London is always fun. And then it struck me – she would love to have the chance to have her house to herself again, even for one night. She must miss her own space dreadfully. How selfish I had become (more guilt).

When I suggested that Emma and Mac could stay with respective friends for the night and give her a bit of peace, she immediately said, 'Good Lord, what on earth for? Unless they'd prefer to, of course? Actually, I'd miss them. I've become very used to having you all about the place, I'm not sure I'd know what to do with myself now all on my own.' Then she went a bit pink and added hurriedly, 'But of course you must do whatever you want, Shelley, Emma and Mac too, but if it's Thursday, I think Mac and I have a computer lesson scheduled. I must check my diary.' And she did – I couldn't believe it! Imagine someone making an appointment in their diary to see Mac. Wait till I told him that!

And then it struck me, forcibly, that Mac and I hardly talked at all now. Not the way we used to. He used to tell me everything, couldn't wait to. There was only so much of his attitude I could put down to the forthcoming onslaught of teenage hormones, because he chatted away to Vera, I heard them, and not just when they were on the computer. I even heard him shrieking with laughter the other day with Emma, which had both delighted and unsettled me. Maybe it was only natural. Boys have to disengage from their mothers, don't they? It's all just part of growing up. But all the same, I felt he was deliberately avoiding me, shutting me out. He probably blamed me on some level for his father going away, even though he couldn't know anything. I was beginning to wonder what I knew myself on that front. But I still couldn't face all of that. Soon I would have to, but not just yet. One day and one family crisis at a time.

I hadn't heard from Olivia either, and she had been gone for a month now. We'd had the most awful row that day she told me she was moving out, and the next day she was gone. I rang her and left a message on her phone telling her to take care of herself and let me know she was okay, but I still hadn't heard from her. Emma had had a couple of texts, or at least that's what she told me. I trusted Emma, she wouldn't lie; it just isn't in her nature. At least Emma didn't hate me – not that I could tell, at any rate. But Olivia? And Mac too, if I was honest – what was I going to do? What could I do? What did it say about me as a mother that my eldest daughter had taken up with an older, married man (all right, separated, but *still*) and my eleven-year-old son would barely speak to me, yet had a grandmother who made special appointments in her diary to spend time with him? Vera was right – perhaps it was just as well I was going away for a couple of days. She was just too nice to say what I already suspected – that my family was probably better off without me.

It's the middle of the night, but my alarm clock is going off – *beep, beep! beep, beep!* And then I remember, as I struggle to sit up – five a.m., I'm being picked up at six. Ernie and I are being ferried to the airport to catch our flight to London. I haul myself out of bed and make my way blearily to the bathroom. A quick, tepid shower wakes me up (the water doesn't heat up before seven) and I get dressed and check my overnight bag. I still have no clue what to bring. I used to travel a lot with Charlie – trips, holidays – and I never could pack properly. He used to tell me I was hopeless, and then, out of sheer exasperation, he'd shut the case (sit on it too, more often than not) and tell me we could buy anything I'd forgotten when we got there. Well, those days had long gone. Now, I settled on an old reliable – a dark grey Donna Karen suit and crisp white shirt that I told myself made me look business-like, capable. I could wear it travelling and to the auction at Christie's. That was the easy bit – but what about for later this evening? What would we be doing? I had no idea, but Ernie had told me to prepare for something glamorous just in case. That could mean anything. In the end I reached for a black silk jersey wraparound dress, one that Charlie used to love on me – safe, elegant – and a pair of matching black suede high-heeled pumps. I pulled out my favourite black opaque tights only to find to my dismay that they had a great big hole in them. Never mind, I thought, I can a buy another pair when I get there. I didn't have time to fuss. Then I dragged my wheelie case downstairs and left it in the hall and went into the kitchen to make myself a cup of tea before the car arrived.

The breakfast things were out on the table as usual (Vera always put them out the night before), and as I put on the kettle, I noticed an envelope on the table with my name on it. Cup of tea in hand, I sat down and opened it. Inside was 300 pounds cash – sterling – and a note. *Dear Shelley, this has been lying around since my last trip to London and I'd like you to have it. Buy yourself something nice in London, you deserve it. Love, Vera.* I felt tears starting and blinked them away hurriedly. How kind of her, how thoughtful and generous – as if she hadn't done enough already, opening her house, her home, to us. I couldn't accept this – I just couldn't. But then, I thought, it would be churlish to throw it back at her, to leave it behind. I tucked it in my handbag and quickly scribbled a note of thanks on the envelope. I would buy something for her, for the kids and something for myself.

That was the kind of thing Charlie used to do – now I knew where his generous nature came from. But I couldn't think about that now. It was too painful.

Instead I forced myself to think about him and Caroline – about the secret life they had shared. Business trips, trysts no doubt, the apartment he had put her up in. The *other* Charlie that I never knew existed. The Charlie who thought nothing of having a mistress, of deceiving his wife and eventually deceiving that same mistress – the Charlie who had fathered a child I couldn't even bear to think about on the other side of the world. But I made myself think about it until I felt the familiar knife twist of pain. Then I threw back the remains of my tea and jumped as my mobile phone rang.

It was Ernie. 'We're outside, Melly dear! Your carriage is waiting! Chop, chop!'

I rinsed out my mug, pulled on my coat and, grabbing my case, went out the front door, shutting it quietly behind me while the house still slept.

Outside, a black Maybach slunk into the pavement and a man with bigger shoulders than I had presumed humanly possible leapt out with surprising agility to take my case and open the back passenger door for me. Ernie sat inside, a wide smile stretching from ear to ear. 'Morning, Melly! How's the form?'

'It'll be fine when I wake up.'

'Well, I for one am going to enjoy every minute of this trip – and I advise you to do the same.' He sank back further into depths of leather. As the car pulled away and we headed for the East Link Bridge, I nudged him, mindful of the driver, who was probably recording every word. 'Where's Lukaz?' I murmured.

'He's meeting us there.'

'He went over ahead of us?' I asked hopefully.

'No, silly. He's meeting us at the plane. Or so he said. I've never travelled by private jet before, have you, Melly?'

'Um, once or twice.' In the Celtic Tiger days, business-people were hopping on and off them like buses. Although I wasn't a great flyer at the best of times, I always felt hugely relieved when I was on terra firma again.

I checked my watch. 'What time's kick-off?'

'The auction's at eleven, which will give us time to check into the hotel and so forth first, and then we'll head straight to Christie's, won't take long. I can't tell you how much I'm looking forward to this.' He rubbed his hands with glee. 'Old Brompton Road, here we come! I hope they're ready for us.'

We sped through the city, still cloaked in darkness, along

the relatively empty motorway and before long the airport
loomed ahead of us, a mass of beckoning lights.

Instead of pulling up at the usual departures set-down area,
we swung around to the right, down another road and left,
and into the private aircraft area. I had forgotten how easy
flying private made travelling – no check-in, no security – all
the necessary documents had been cleared earlier that week.
The car slowed, and looking out, I noticed the place was
quiet, with no planes obviously on view, apart from a couple
of smaller ones, but no one revving up to go – and then we
turned and I caught sight of the sleekest jet I had ever seen.
Within seconds we had pulled up alongside it.

' G650,' pronounced Ernie, clambering out of the Maybach.

'What?' I watched as our small cases were taken by the
driver and secreted away.

'A Gulfstream G650, fastest business aircraft in its class –
Lukaz was telling me about it.'

'Please, madam.' It was the driver, waving us towards the
steps.

'Well go on, old girl – what're you waiting for?' Ernie
prodded me. I climbed the stairs and stepped into the plane.

'Welcome aboard, Mrs Fitzgibbon, let me show you to your
seat.' A stewardess (were they still called that? I wasn't sure,
but this one looked more like a supermodel) with a slight
American twang indicated a large leather swivel chair. 'May
I take your coat?'

'Thank you.' I sat down and tried not to gawp. I'd been
on a couple of private jets in my time, but most of them were
regular corporate jets, one's we'd been hitching a ride on, so
to speak, the odd company jet taking us to London or Paris,
even a couple of rugby matches. Charlie didn't have his own
jet, but he'd had plenty of access to them in his time. But
nothing like this. This was more like walking into a boardroom designed by Kelly Hoppen.

Across the aisle, Ernie winked at me. The cabin was about the size of a rather narrow boardroom, with suede-covered walls. At the far side was a conference table with four surrounding chairs. Further down were two sleek sofas and more chairs, and beyond, what I learned was the stateroom – and bathroom.

'May I offer you a glass of champagne, Mrs Fitzgibbon?' It was the supermodel, brandishing a bottle of Taittinger, my favourite.

'I don't think so, thank you.'

'Oh go on, Melly, one or two won't hurt,' said Ernie, beaming as his glass was filled by what appeared to be the double of the girl about to fill my glass. Like her, she was blonde, blue eyed and had an uncannily similar heart-shaped face. 'Are you by any chance . . . ?'

'Yes,' she smiled at me, 'Suzi is my twin sister.' And she glided away.

There was another stewardess, as dark and exotic-looking as they were blonde, and a male crew member, handsome but with a grim set to his face. His smile, when he flashed it, never reached his eyes. Four crew members to two passengers – that was pretty excessive by any standards. The steward began to lower the door and secure it. I turned to Ernie questioningly, who was also looking worried. 'What about Lukaz? Where is he?'

'I have no idea,' he said, his brow creasing, and he tapped one of the twins on the arm. 'Excuse me, Miss, but our host, Mr Mihailov, he should be here – is he delayed?'

She smiled disarmingly. 'No, no delay, Mr Huggard, Captain Mihailov is very punctual. We'll be taking off exactly on time, five more minutes – just sit back, fasten your seatbelt and I'll look after your drink until we're airborne.'

'What? Oh, of course!' Ernie banged his forehead and gave a shout of laughter. 'How stupid of me!'

Just then, a deep, resonant, accented voice came over the intercom, with a definite hint of a smile in it. 'Ladies and gentlemen, this is your captain welcoming you aboard our Gulfstream G650. Our flight time to London should be forty-five minutes. I hope you are sitting comfortably. Please ensure that your seatbelt is fastened, and if there is anything you need during your flight, please do not hesitate to let your cabin crew know.' And then, more abruptly, 'Cabin crew, take your seats for take-off please.'

While I was still trying to take it in, with Ernie grinning like the Cheshire cat, we taxied briefly, came to a halt, and then, with a massive thrust of Rolls-Royce engines we shot off down the runway and seconds later soared effortlessly into the air. As I looked down at dawn breaking over Dublin, painting it in a rosy light, all I could think of was how the kids would love this – even Olivia's studied disinterest would be shot to bits. But for now it was just me and Ernie, who was sitting in his chair toasting me with his glass of champagne. 'Drink up, Melly dear,' he said. 'This flight will pass all too quickly.'

He was right, as usual, and after what felt like no more than half an hour later we landed at London City Airport. The steward had told Ernie that we were to go ahead to our hotel and that Lukaz would catch up with us later. It was with mild regret that we were helped into our coats by Jenny and Suzi, the supermodel twins.

We were ushered quickly through customs, and outside another Maybach, identical to the one we had left behind in Dublin, was waiting for us. 'I could get used to this,' quipped Ernie, switching on his BlackBerry. I turned on my phone as well. There were no messages and I decided to wait until I had reached the hotel before calling Vera, just to make sure everything was all right and to thank her for her thoughtful and much too generous present.

We drove quickly through London, watching identical versions of pinstriped men and sober-suited women make their foray into the City, clutching coffees and newspapers alike. Then on into the West End and finally Hyde Park Corner, where we came to a halt outside the Lanesborough, our arrival causing a flurry of activity as doors were opened, cases grasped and hefty tips changed hands. Then it was inside to check in and be shown to our respective rooms. Ernie's was clearly below mine, as he exited the lift and followed the porter. 'See you downstairs in fifteen? In the lobby?'

'I'll be there.' And then the lift ascended again, quite rapidly, and came to a halt, and my accompanying porter strode ahead as the doors opened. I followed him along the corridor until he turned the corner, where only two doors remained, quite a bit apart, like two separate apartments, and waited while he slid the card into the door and opened it. Then I walked behind him into the most fabulous suite. 'There must be some mistake,' I said, looking around in confusion.

'No mistake.' He handed me the key. 'The Royal Suite is for you, Mrs Fitzgibbon.' He went on to explain the various features of the lighting, flat-screen TVs and 24-hour butler service, but I wasn't listening.

'Ahem.' It was a discreet cough as my small wheelie bag was deposited and I realised he was waiting for a tip. Luckily I had got some change in Dublin and I handed him a fiver. 'Thank you very much, Mrs Fitzgibbon.' And he was gone.

Alone, I wandered around in a daze. The place was spectacular – there was not one, but *three* bedrooms, a sitting room, a magnificent bathroom and a formal dining room. I almost laughed out loud. Instead I flung myself on the super king-size, heavily draped four-poster bed in the master bedroom and whooped. It was crazy – but it was bliss. A whole family could live in here. If only they *were* all here –

Vera, the kids (I couldn't think about Charlie) – we could have such a blast. But there was no point in thinking that. It was just me, and it was just one night, one I would make the most of I thought, eyeing the range of deluxe goodies in the bathroom. For now, I washed my hands, put a brush through my hair, reapplied some lip gloss and concealer and grabbing my bag and laptop, set off back downstairs.

'All set, Melly?' Ernie was sitting with the *Telegraph*.

'Ready when you are.' I suddenly found I had a spring in my step.

'Then let's go. I have an obscene amount of someone else's money to spend and it's burning a veritable hole in my pocket, as the man said.

Outside the Maybach waited for us, attracting not a little attention from curious passersby. Ernie and I slipped in and without a word the expressionless driver at the wheel pulled away.

'Where's Lukaz?' I asked Ernie.

'He'll be following the bidding online. Could be upstairs, in a private room, or maybe somewhere else entirely. He can get me on the BlackBerry anyway, but I have my instructions,' Ernie said confidently. We went in, announced ourselves and were shown into the Long Gallery where the auction was to be held.

'So what *is* on the shopping list?' I enquired, feeling a bit cross. Up until now Ernie had been mysteriously tight-lipped and had refused to divulge any details. I was wondering why I was there at all, and thinking of my lovely suite back at the hotel, languishing in my absence when I could be making such good use of it, was beginning to piss me off.

Ernie smiled and tapped the programme. 'The Ivan Aivazovsky, Konstantin Somov, Ilya Repin, Yuri Annenkov and Svetoslav Roerich before lunch,' he said casually, 'and the Evgeny Rukhin and Vladimir Weisberg after lunch.'

'But,' my mouth had dropped open, 'the last Svetoslav Roerich went for over 2.9 million dollars in New York.'

'Precisely.' Ernie looked at me smugly. 'So if nothing else, Melly, I'll need you to fend off the inevitable press onslaught that is bound to hound us when word of this gets out – which, of course, it will. Lukaz has told me I'm not to leave without them, no matter how tough the going gets, and I don't intend to let him down, I can tell you.'

'But that – that's . . .' I tried to work out the possible sum total that might be spent and failed.

'Better not to think about it,' advised Ernie. 'At least we're incognito. You never know with these chaps, you know,' he whispered, conspiratorially. 'They'd think nothing of bumping a rival bidder off. But what a way to go,' he mused dreamily.

'Thanks a lot, but I'd rather not. I have a family to get back to, in case you've forgotten.'

'Hush, hush, Melly dear. Let us take our seats. Into the lion's den we must go.'

The bidding started bang on time at eleven, and over the course of the next two hours, I saw Ernie Huggard change before my eyes. Gone was the affable, beaming, slightly dippy person I had come to know and love, and in his place was a poker-faced, intensely serious, combative individual with nerves of steel. Every piece he was going for seemed to boil down to the same last three bidders, all presumably on behalf of the other oligarchs, and the stakes were utterly mind-bending amounts of money. Across the room there were huddled discussions, tight nods and beads of sweat breaking out on various foreheads, but Ernie was as cool as a cucumber. We took a short break for lunch, and then it was back to the bidding at two p.m. By five o'clock Lukaz was 10.5 million pounds lighter and the proud owner of seven extremely coveted pieces of Russian art. I felt I had burned off at least half a stone in nerves alone. In the mêlée that followed, we were hustled quickly out through a discreet private exit and into the waiting Maybach and, breathing a huge sigh of relief, we headed back to our hotel.

'Don't know about you, Melly, but I think a large glass of champagne or several are on the cards. That was quite a day's work.'

I shook my head. 'You're telling me. I don't know how you did it!'

'It's always easy spending someone else's money, and that's not even taking into consideration the commission I'm going to get – out of which, I can assure you, you will receive a generous bonus. Just think, Melly, if you hadn't been there that day in the gallery, none of this would have happened. I knew it was a good thing, you turning up on my doorstep like that.' He smiled fondly at me.

'Don't be silly,' I said, blushing. 'It had nothing to do with me at all. But I will take you up on the champagne offer.'

When we got back to the hotel we headed straight to the bar, where there was already a bottle of Krug waiting to be poured for us, and several more on ice. But still no sign of Lukaz.

'Where is he?' I asked, raising my glass to Ernie's toast. 'I would have thought he'd want to celebrate.'

'Oh he will, don't worry.' Ernie took a gulp of champagne and we sat down while bar staff hovered at a discreet distance. 'He's in his London house, Pelham Crescent. He left instructions to meet him in the lobby at eight – he's taking us to dinner.'

'Oh.'

'I meant to ask you, Melly, how's your room? Mine's fabulous. I've got the works, flat-screen TV, feather-soft bed, wonderful bathroom.'

'Mine too,' I nodded, neglecting to mention that for some reason I was the inhabitant of a suite you could hold a summit in. Clearly Ernie had drawn the short straw in that respect. Thinking of which, I was anxious to return to it.

'If we're on for eight this evening,' I said, checking my watch, 'that only gives me an hour and a half to get ready, and I intend to spend a large part of that in a hot bath.'

'Jolly good idea. You go ahead, Melly. Shame to waste all this lovely champagne – I'll make do with a quick shower and spruce up, see you in the lobby later.'

So up I went and breathed a sigh of relief when I closed the door behind me. This was complete and utter luxury, and I was going to enjoy it. But first I rang home and got Emma, who told me yes, everyone was fine, Mac was on the computer and Gran was just clearing away dinner. 'I hope you're helping her,' I said.

'Course I am, Mum, and Gran says you're to have a really good time.'

'It's only one night, Em, I'll be back tomorrow.'

'You should have stayed for the weekend.'

'This is work, Emma, not a holiday,' I said, then immediately felt guilty, because it was beginning to feel exactly like a holiday – an obscenely expensive holiday.

'Is your room nice?'

'Gorgeous.'

'Bring me back any bathroom goodies, will you? We could do with some here.'

'Don't worry, I will.' I thought about telling her of the flight over and then decided to wait until I got home, otherwise I'd never get off the phone.

'See you tomorrow, darling. Say goodnight to Mac for me.'

'Bye, Mum, love you.'

'Love you too, Em.' And I did, I thought as I clicked off my phone. I adored all of my children, even Olivia, who knew exactly what buttons to press to drive me insane sometimes. I had been so lucky with them, so blessed. I just couldn't bear to think about what all of this was doing to them and to us as a family. Although maybe, hard though it was, we were beginning to learn what it was to *really* be a family, even if Olivia wasn't talking to me and Mac was shutting me out. At least Vera had come into our lives. My parents had both died when Liv was very young, before Emma or Mac had come along, and I hadn't realised how much the children were missing out by not having grandparents around. When all the time they had a wonderful one, we just hadn't got to know her. *Well, better late than never,* I thought, and I wondered again what on earth could have gone so wrong between Charlie and Vera for him to cut her out of his life like this. But I wouldn't think about that now. I could think about Charlie and all his mysteries until I had turned myself inside out – it wouldn't do me any good. Tonight I could take a night off, pretend I was on holiday. It was the closest I was going to get to one at this rate, and with that happy thought in my mind I turned on the sound system and went to run myself a long, hot, oil-scented bath.

I lay in it for at least half an hour, luxuriating in the oil, the foam, the steaming hot water that was dispelling the stiffness in my muscles, as I listened to Robert Palmer croon 'She Makes My Day' and 'I'll Be Your Baby Tonight'. Then, when I thought I was in danger of falling asleep (it had been an early start), I gave my hair a quick wash, climbed out of the sleek designer tub and swathed myself in fluffy white towels. I got ready fairly quickly (that was something Charlie *had* always liked about me – I was never particularly high maintenance), dried my hair, smoothed on a bit of base, some lipstick and gloss and I was done. Then on went the M&S underwear. I had dashed into a corner shop at lunchtime to buy a pair of tights, grabbing the first nearly black ones I could see. They didn't have any opaques, but at least these were the right colour and they had a nice sheen to them. I ripped open the pack and then realised that they weren't tights, but rather lacy-topped hold-ups – damn. Oh well, who cared? I rolled them on and smoothed them up around my thighs, hoping I wouldn't have a great big tell-tale bulge of flesh over the top, but I didn't. In fact, they looked pretty good on – I had lost weight, and in the black hold-ups and high-heeled pumps my legs looked longer and, dare I say it, really slim.

Charlie would love these, I heard a little voice say. *He loved you wearing stockings or hold-ups, used to say you never did often enough.* It was true. I had abandoned sexy underwear and stockings along with a lot of things over the past few years. For a moment I felt unbearably sad. How I wished he was here now, in this very room with me, and that I was going out to dinner with him. We used to have such fun. But then I thought of Caroline and Miss South Africa, and a reliable rage boiled inside me and I was glad I hadn't worn sexy underwear for ages – in fact, I wish I'd started sooner. If I'd known I wouldn't have bothered about make-up, about worrying about my weight, about – oh, what was the use? I took my dress off the hanger and slipped it on, tying it at the side, a quick spray of perfume and I was done. I grabbed my coat and bag and headed for the lift. I suddenly found I was ravenous. We'd only had a sandwich at lunch and that seemed like days ago now.

The lift, when it arrived, was empty and I wondered where Lukaz would be taking us. I remember Charlie talking about some Russians he did business with a year or so ago and he said they'd been completely mad. But I hadn't really thought about it at the time. I walked out into the lobby and looked around for Ernie, but there was no sign of him. And then the concierge approached me. 'Mrs Fitzgibbon?'

'Yes?'

'Mr Mihailov is expecting you in the bar.'

'Oh, right, thanks.' So that's where they were – Ernie had

probably never left it. There was still no sign of Ernie in the bar, but Lukaz was there, sitting down, a bottle of champagne open in front of him, and two glasses. I felt my step falter for a split second, then I took a deep breath, smiled and walked over to join him.

He stood up as soon as he saw me approaching, and at the same instant I felt an almost indecipherable flurry of energy ripple amongst the bar staff, who seemed intent on anticipating and no doubt delivering his every need.

'Shelley,' he said, bending to kiss me on both cheeks, 'I hope you will join me in some champagne before dinner? I hear you and Ernie had a most successful day.'

'That would be lovely, Lukaz,' I said as I sat down and a waiter filled my glass. 'It's not like Ernie to be late.'

'I am afraid Ernie will not be joining us,' he said. 'He is complaining of a migraine headache, and has opted for an early night. Too much excitement today, he says.' He smiled ruefully. 'I hope you don't mind if it's just you and me?'

'Um, no, of course not. What a shame – about Ernie, I mean.' I took a gulp of my champagne.

'Yes,' he agreed. 'It is a shame, but one we cannot afford to allow spoil the evening, no?' He reached across to clink my glass. 'We have a sizeable purchase to celebrate, Shelley!'

'Quite,' I agreed heartily, and equally heartily I silently cursed Ernie and his migraine, imagined or not, and then found myself wondering wildly if he had been drugged, or worse, maybe . . .

'Don't look so worried, Shelley.' Lukaz was watching me, and then smiled broadly. 'I have made sure the doctor has checked on him. He will be perfectly well after a good night's sleep.'

'Oh, good.'

'Are you hungry?' he asked after we'd been chatting for a while.

'Yes, actually, I am.'

'Me too,' he grinned, and I found myself relaxing. Perhaps it was the champagne, or maybe it was because Lukaz was actually very good company, and pretty funny without realising it, but suddenly I decided I was going to have a good time this evening. I couldn't remember the last time I'd been out to dinner on my own with a man who wasn't my husband, and this one seemed determined to show me a good time, so why not enjoy it?

'Good, then let's go. We are going somewhere very nice for dinner.'

He wasn't kidding. As we strolled outside and into the waiting Maybach, we drove the short distance to Old Park Lane, and pulled up outside Nobu, my favourite restaurant in London, and probably a lot of other people's too. 'Oh, I love it here,' I heard myself saying, 'and it's ages since I've been.'

Lukaz smiled at me then, and I couldn't help noticing how good-looking he was. But there was something else too, that aura of power, money – superficial things, I know, but people didn't half jump to attention when he showed up. It was fun, sort of like being with someone out of a Bond movie, and despite my earlier reservations, I was really beginning to enjoy it. *Pity Ernie is missing all this*, I thought vaguely, and then the car door was opened and I stepped out and was ushered through the restaurant entrance. Except we weren't going into the restaurant – instead, we were whisked up to the private dining room, where a line of attendant staff dressed all in black stood respectfully to greet us, and welcomed us with ice-cold cocktails.

Lukaz

Of course I have reserved the private dining room, and Nobu have done well, as always. The long, narrow room is lit perfectly, discreetly, the full-length windows look out over Hyde Park and it is a clear night – through the overhead atrium, we see the stars. The long table usually in place has been removed, as I instructed, and replaced by a smaller, circular one, big enough not to be crowded, but also intimate. The room is candlelit, dressed completely in white, and white orchids are everywhere. It is very nice, and I can tell Shelley is impressed, maybe a little shocked even, but she is pleased, she is not looking frightened anymore. This is good.

We go to the table and we sit down. I wait, of course, until Shelley is seated first, and as she sits, her dress (which is very nice, very elegant) reveals a flash of leg momentarily, and I notice she is wearing lacy stockings. This surprises me pleasantly, although she doesn't know I have seen this; I am very discreet. But now I am also hopeful.

We make a toast to a good dinner and then we eat. Food is very good. Shelley has Rock Shrimp Tempura with Ponzu and black cod with Miso and I have Salmon Tartar with Caviar and Yellowtail Sashimi with Jalapeno. Also we have caviar, of course. Shelley eats well, has good appetite, I like this in a woman. Men get tired of women always on a diet. This is not sexy. It is no fun. We are halfway through the main course, and I think it is time to be honest with her. She has relaxed, she is enjoying the wine, but is not drunk. Now

I think is the time, although I am very nervous about what I must tell her. I think, from my experience, to be direct is best.

'Shelley,' I say, 'I know your husband Charlie.' For a moment I think she doesn't hear me. She looks puzzled, then puts down her knife and fork and looks frightened again. This upsets me, but I must continue.

'Excuse me?' she says.

'I know your husband, Charlie,' I repeat. 'I have done business with him almost two years ago now.' And now, she is looking a little pale. 'I don't know him well,' I continue, 'I only met him on one occasion, here in London actually, and I have no idea who you are when I meet you – it is complete coincidence.

'So you've known all along.'

'No, not all along, I found out by accident.'

'Ernie.'

'No, not Ernie, although later, yes, he confirms this for me.' I take a deep breath, now comes the difficult part. 'But there is something else, Shelley. Your house, where you and Charlie lived? Summerton belongs to me now. Charlie lost a lot of money, Shelley – you know this, of course – and he signed the house over to my company, Tolstoy, as a gesture. It was an honourable thing to do, although at the time I did not know any of this, I have many business interests, obviously. My people explain this to me when I decide to come to Ireland. But I am sorry,' I say, 'I am sorry Charlie did not come to me himself, I would have liked to help him. Charlie is a good guy, I think. He must have been under a lot of pressure.' I pause to let what I have said sink in. I expect her to be angry, to maybe scream at me or to get up and leave, but instead, to my dismay, tears start to roll down her face and she begins to cry. This makes me very uncomfortable. I am not expecting this. I hate women crying, especially, now,

Shelley. The staff too are noticing this, they move away discreetly and leave us alone. 'Please, Shelley,' I say and I hand her my handkerchief, 'please do not cry, I did not want to make you cry. I wanted for you to have nice time tonight, nothing else. I know things must be difficult for you, Ernie has told me a little.' I signal the waiter to refill our glasses. 'Please stop crying, Shelley. Why don't you tell me about what happened, talk to me.'

Eventually, she dries her eyes (she has beautiful eyes, I notice this the first time I see her – they are green, with long thick lashes to which some tears still cling). And slowly, she takes a sip of her drink and begins to talk to me. I listen carefully as she talks, never interrupting, just nodding.

She tells me about losing the business, then finding out she has lost house and finally having to move in and share house with Charlie's mother (this is good, I think, it is important to be with family when life gets tough).

'But,' she continues, 'that wasn't the worst thing.'

Now she is talking faster, details coming quickly, some of which really surprise me.

'I discovered Charlie was having an affair with a – a – an old girlfriend – a work colleague.'

I say nothing.

'Actually, more than one.'

She sounds angry now. Still I say nothing. I am like priest in confessional.

'And if you're wondering how I know, the woman in question told me.'

I shake my head. This is not good. No wonder she is angry. Women do not like sharing their husband with another woman, but especially they do not like to hear about it from another woman, particularly the mistress concerned.

'So I told him to go, to get out of our lives – and he did. He left that day and never came back.'

'You haven't heard from him?' I interject here because this seems to me unusual.

'No. There were some flowers on Valentine's Day, but now I'm beginning to wonder if he even sent them.'

'And the children – they have heard from him?'

'Not a word. That's what makes me *really* angry.' She takes another drink. 'My eldest girl has left home to live with her "boyfriend", who is a separated married man of forty-four, old enough to be her father. In fact, he used to work with her father.'

I think briefly of Natascha, who is twenty-three – and I am forty-two. But only briefly.

'And Mac, my youngest, will hardly speak to me any more. He just spends all his time on his computer. But Emma, my younger daughter, has been marvellous. I don't what I'd do without her. And Vera, of course.'

'Vera?' I ask.

'Charlie's mother, the children's grandmother.'

'Ah, yes, of course. Grandmothers are very important, my own is still alive. She brought me up on her own. My parents and her husband, my grandfather, died when I was a baby – train accident.'

'Oh, I'm so sorry.'

'Thank you.'

'But it's Mac I'm really worried about. He doesn't talk about it. He doesn't seem to talk much at all, certainly not to me. And it's his birthday in a couple of weeks and I would so love to do something nice for him, something special, to take his mind off all this horrible business. He misses his dad terribly. He doesn't say so, of course, but I know he does, they all do.'

'So how old is he, your son Mac?'

'He'll be twelve on his birthday.'

'Hmm.' I am having an idea. 'Does he enjoy soccer?'

She smiles, a small smile, and immediately I know what I will do. 'He's fanatical about it. Eats, sleeps and breathes it.'

'Which team does he support?' I ask her.

And she says without hesitation, 'Chelsea.'

Now I smile. This will be even easier than I thought.

'Would he like to see them play?'

'How d'you mean?' She looks puzzled.

'Would he like to see Chelsea play at home, at Stamford Bridge?' I lean back in my chair.

'I'd say he'd like that more than anything in the world,' she says, then adds quickly, 'apart from having his father back, I mean. But how . . . ?'

'I think I can arrange for that to happen.'

She looks shocked. 'Are you serious?'

'I wouldn't joke about something as important as football,' I say, very seriously.

And then Shelley laughs. She throws her head back and laughs, and I think it is the best sound I have heard all day, even better than hearing I had succeeded in buying all those paintings from under other oligarchs' noses.

'I will have to make enquiries, naturally, talk to a few people. But as you know, Roman Abramovich owns Chelsea. I cannot promise anything just yet, but I will see what I can do.'

'Oh, Lukaz,' she says, very softly, 'that would be incredible.'

'Maybe he can bring some friends, not many, maybe two or three. And we can go over on my plane. I think that would be good birthday present, don't you? Even for oligarch,' I joke. But I am looking at her face, at how she lights up at the mention of her son, her children, and I am thinking this is a woman I would go to a lot of trouble for. To see Shelley looking happy again is very good, better than good.

But then she looks serious again. 'But Lukaz, why? Why would you do this?'

I shrug. 'Why not? I have a lot of money, I know a lot of

important people, some of them owe me favours. And – I like to make people happy.'

This seems to assure her, and she smiles again. 'I don't know how to thank you.'

'No need,' I say. And it is true. This is easy for me. Roman Abramovich is a fellow Russian, a fellow oligarch, we are very patriotic people. What I am thinking is that today I have bought painting that I know he wanted very much. He will not be pleased that I have won this painting from him. In order to get permission for match, maybe director's box, I may have to let him have this painting. But I will worry about this later. It is only a painting. No need to mention this to Shelley.

Instead, I change the subject and talk about London, about my favourite places in the world, my villa in Cap Ferrat and my *dacha* in Peredelkino, where I grow all my own vegetables and some fruit. I don't tell her what I am really thinking – that I am falling in love with her, this woman who is old enough to be Natascha's mother. This woman with the green eyes who is stealing my heart. No, I definitely don't tell her that.

Vera (1968–72)

I mentioned earlier, I think, that I didn't really know what depression was – I hadn't a clue. I'd heard of women having the 'baby blues' and some older women who went through an awful time during 'the change', but young, healthy women suffering? That wasn't talked about at all, particularly if you were a young healthy woman with a caring husband, two dear little boys and no money worries – what on earth was there to be unhappy about? It would have been considered monstrously selfish. So when Felipe left, I decide to wipe the whole incident from my mind, my life. It was the only way I thought I could cope with it. We had decided on a clean break (as if we had a choice). We couldn't telephone each other, and I certainly wouldn't have risked him writing to me and, anyway, what would have been the point? It was over. He was gone, far, far away from me, never to return. And now I had to live with the consequences. I was horrified enough at what I had done, what I had allowed to transpire – now was my chance to do penance, to put into practice the appalling remorse I felt and atone for it. That all sounds very Catholic, I know, but then, this *was* Catholic Ireland in the strictest sense, and the guilt I felt was enormous, crippling. So I decided to put the whole thing behind me, to never think about it, to make it up to Arthur (who had never once confronted me) and the boys – devote myself to being the wife and mother they deserved, who had been so immoral, so selfishly absent.

And I did try, back-breakingly hard. I cleaned, I worked, I shopped and baked – anything to keep active – because when I stopped, even for a moment, I would feel it approaching, that immutable weight descending, threatening to overwhelm me. But I wouldn't let it. I kept busy, kept running and frantically planning things – outings with the boys, self-improvement classes, bridge – and when it all felt too much, at the end of the day I would reward myself for getting through it and pour myself a large drink. I had to, I reasoned, because at the end of the day I would have to face another set of demons, which began when Arthur would come home from work.

There were two of us in it, you see, co-conspirators – although I wouldn't realise that until much later.

Arthur was hugely relieved, I could see that immediately. He would have known that Felipe was gone, moved on to another post, and I suppose he felt that was it. He thought, you see, that if he just sat it out and ignored the whole thing, that once Felipe was gone, once this intrusion into our marriage had been taken care of, that everything could return to normal – and I desperately wanted to believe that too, but that, if anything, was the biggest fantasy of the lot. He meant well, of course he did, and he'd been marvellous throughout the whole terrible saga, which must have been dreadful for him (I still can't bear to dwell on that), and I suppose he was thrilled and relieved to have his wife back, or so he imagined – back on terra firma and back to him. That might have been what happened in that lovely old film *Brief Encounter*, but it certainly wasn't what happened with us.

It began with Arthur suggesting a weekend away, three days, actually, in Paris. I think he was hoping for a second honeymoon of sorts – putting out feelers, offering an unspoken olive branch in the hope of new beginnings.

During the affair, we had (not unnaturally) retreated from

each other, in the physical sense, I mean. We hadn't stopped marital relations completely, but I avoided them pretty successfully, I have to say, and Arthur had been decent enough (or perhaps fearful of rejection) not to be demanding in that respect. But now – well, he was becoming very affectionate again, demonstrative and, to my chagrin, I found I just couldn't respond, which was awful. So I began to have a couple of stiff drinks when I thought it might be on the cards – it was the only way I could get through it. Because whatever I could pretend in my mind, my body, I found, had no intention of lying, of going along with this deceit – which is exactly what it was, ironic though it sounds. I could deceive my husband and be with (*long* to be with) a man I was completely and utterly in love with, but that same body was rigorously honest in its protest at succumbing to the renewed advances of the man I was married to, although I loved him dearly. So that weekend in Paris, which should have been a new beginning, wiping the slate clean, was in fact the start of a long and tortuous journey that would take me (and of course Arthur) to hell and back.

We got through the trip, or what little I remember of it, by me insisting on sightseeing, shopping, drawing out boozy lunches and dinners and avoiding bed at all costs, except when I could collapse pretty much comatose into it. And that was the beginning of the desperate attempt at denial and avoidance I would cling to at the cost of near self-destruction.

At home, it was easier – there were routines to embrace, friends to spend time with, rituals to hide behind. And all the time I convinced myself I was coping, fooling everyone admirably, although later I would learn that my close friends, Pam in particular, not to mention Arthur, were desperately worried about me. I lost weight, noticeably so, and I didn't need to – even though I was eating. But my stomach, or somewhere in the vicinity of my solar plexus, seemed to be constantly churning, and the only thing that relieved it was a couple of stiff gin and tonics.

I was constantly addled and agitated. I found myself snapping at Arthur and the boys, then feeling unbearably remorseful and trying to compensate, which only led to more desperate irritation. Pam tried to talk to me on several occasions, bless her, over coffee and lunches, but I clammed up and shut her out. I wouldn't, or couldn't, accept what was happening, to me or to my marriage. This was something I had to do alone, I reasoned. I had been the cause of all this deceit and misery and I alone could fix it. Ridiculous, I know, but I was resolute and stubborn and deluded enough to think that everything was still all right, that in time, things would settle down.

I must have been a complete and utter nightmare to be around, never mind to live with. But that, I'm ashamed to say, was the farthest thought from my mind at the time. Because I wasn't alone with this – I had my pain, which was indescribable. I knew it was there, but I couldn't *go there*, as you'd say today. It was too immense, too all-consuming, so I blocked it out any way I could, which in the beginning was with avoidance, aided and abetted by my new friend, alcohol. But on the occasions when it did surface, in a strange sort of way I clung to it. It made sense, you see, of what had happened – that I had found and lost the love of my life. Perhaps if we had rowed, or if, as might have been the case under other circumstances, the affair had ended of its own volition, for whatever reason, it might have been easier. But Felipe and I had been wrenched apart, still at the giddy heights of our mutual passion, which, if you've ever been in love, deeply in love, you are convinced will never waver. A love like that stays with you, vibrantly alive, stoked by precious memories, the yearning for never-to-be-fulfilled opportunities and the absolute certainty of bereft lovers, long after the enforced parting, never having to face what in all likelihood might have been its final, natural demise.

I couldn't sleep either. Even if I did manage to drink enough to fall asleep, I would awake on the dot of three in the morning and lie, tossing and turning, or on the worst nights, crying silently, accompanied by the reliable and rhythmic breathing of Arthur, who lay oblivious beside me. I would have given anything then to have had separate rooms, to have claimed that Arthur's snoring was keeping me awake, any excuse to make room for me and my clandestine, forbidden mourning, but by then the boys had taken a room each, and I couldn't face forcing them back to sharing when they were so delighted with their newfound autonomy. So I went to my doctor and was prescribed sleeping pills, another addition to the arsenal I would collect to get myself through my daily existence.

It wasn't just Felipe I had lost. I had become someone else with him, or so I thought, added a whole other dimension to my life, and when he went, he took that person, that joyful, sensual, blooming person, with him. Now it was just me, the old me, except I found I couldn't bear to be with *her*, not even for a moment.

And all that time, we never talked about it, Arthur and I. He never questioned me, never commented on my drinking (which I managed to keep to respectable levels, in public at any rate). If anything, he was probably hitting the bottle pretty hard himself in the evenings, but at least he had his work – that was his escape. So we went on together like that for a couple of years, carving out new and careful ways of circumventing each other, going through the motions, until one day, something happened that brought everything to a halt.

Pam and I were having lunch and had decided to see a film, *Ryan's Daughter*, that was the talk of the country – and not just for the wonderfully filmic scenery. Apparently there were some quite risqué scenes in it, by Irish standards anyway. I was looking forward to it, to any escape, as much as I could look forward to anything in those days. So we went to the cinema and settled down to watch the movie, which was mesmerising. But I hadn't reckoned on its storyline – the brilliant portrayal of the illicit affair between the newly married schoolmaster's wife and the shell-shocked British soldier back from the trenches caught me completely unawares. It was riveting, heartbreaking and all too close to the bone. By the end, and quite a bit before the end, tears were streaming down my face and I couldn't seem to stop them.

'Are you all right?' Pam asked me, looking worried. This wasn't the usual sniffles and overly bright eyes even the most sentimental movies brought on. I was fighting not to sob out loud. We waited at the end until the crowd had filed out and I had managed to compose myself.

'Look, let's go for a cup of coffee,' said Pam. 'I really want to talk to you, Vera. You're not yourself at all these days. I'm very worried about you.' That was the last thing I wanted to hear, I can tell you, so I quickly pulled myself together.

'No, Pam,' I said, 'I really can't. I have to pick up the boys from a school chum's birthday party, I can't possibly be late. I really must dash. And don't worry about me, I'm just a bit emotional at the moment, time of the month probably,' I fobbed her off.

But she didn't look at all reassured. 'Well, all right then, if you must. But I want to have lunch with you next week. We need to talk. You owe me that much, as an old friend.'

'I will, Pam, scout's honour.'

I hurried back to my car, which was parked nearby. What I had said was true, I did have to pick the boys up from a birthday party, and I was beginning to feel a headache coming on, probably because of trying unsuccessfully to fight back those ridiculous tears that overcame me in the cinema. But it brought everything back, not that it had ever gone away, and I found myself thinking of Felipe, of us together, wondering what he was doing, if he ever thought of me – so much so that I almost missed the turn to take to the road where the boys' party was being held.

I got out and rang the doorbell, and Sybil, the birthday boy's mother, answered the door. She seemed quite giddy, and from outside I could hear shrieks and shouts from the back garden. 'Vera, how lovely to see you, come in for a minute.'

I really didn't want to, I was anxious to get back home. 'I'm not too early, am I? The invitation did say pick-up was to be five thirty p.m. sharp.'

'No, you're bang on time.' She ushered me into a room where a few other mothers were waiting for their respective charges. 'The boys are just finishing off a game of football – have a drink with us and give them a few more minutes.'

I accepted a small sherry and got chatting to a few of the women I hadn't seen for a while. It was very pleasant, and I even had another small sherry before I said I really had to go, and Sybil went out and rounded up the boys.

We thanked Sybil, said goodbye and as soon as I got the boys into the car it become clear they were having some ridiculous fight about the football match and some imagined foul on Patrick's part, who had captained the winning team. They were like a bag of cats, squabbling and thumping each other in the back seat until I thought I would scream. We were halfway home on the Stillorgan dual carriageway when it happened. I looked around for a split second, to shout at them to be quiet or else, and when I looked back, a small dog had run out across the road and was heading right for us. I swerved to avoid it out of instinct, and then there was a sickening crunch and I was flung against the steering wheel as I crashed into a lamppost. There was an awful silence for a moment and then all hell broke loose. I was all right, shocked but not seriously hurt, and neither were the boys, but my swerve had been to no avail – the poor little dog was lying lifeless where he had run under the wheels. His owner, a young woman, was running over to him, distraught, and the boys jumped out of the car.

Suddenly Charlie started screaming, becoming quite hysterical. 'You killed him! You killed the dog, Mummy! You weren't even looking! You killed the dog!' he shouted, over and over again, until even Patrick was looking at him worriedly. By now a few people had pulled over and stopped to see what was going on and had very kindly come over to help. The little dog was carried to the side of the road and pronounced dead, his owner was sobbing, broken hearted.

'I'm so sorry. He ran straight out in front of me,' I said helplessly to the owner. A neighbour who had seen the whole thing confirmed this.

'He did,' said the man. 'I saw it myself, love, he ran straight under the car, the poor pet.' Then to me he said, 'You're lucky that's the only casualty, you could have killed yourself and your little boys swerving into that lamppost. Look at you, you must have got an awful shock.'

'I know,' said the dog's owner, still sobbing. 'It was a cat, he got out of the house before I could get the lead on him and ran straight after it. It's not your fault,' she said tremulously to me, which made me feel even worse.

Yet all the while, Charlie was still screaming. 'It is! It is your fault! Everything's your fault! You killed him! You did! You did!' He was crying now, angrily, and his fists were clenched. And suddenly it was all too much. I couldn't stand it. I put my hands over my ears and shouted, 'Stop it, Charlie! Stop it right now!'

But he wouldn't – he screamed even more and I couldn't take it. I felt as if I was going to shatter into a tiny thousand pieces if I had to listen to even one more high-pitched scream. So I walked over to him and I slapped him across the face – whacked him really hard.

'Mum?' It was Patrick, looking frightened now.

But I couldn't speak. I was way beyond that. I think if that nice man hadn't come over and taken hold of me, I might even have hit him again.

'Come on now, love, come inside and sit down and have a cup of tea. You've had a terrible shock, that's all, and the poor wee boys. Come on inside, love.'

But I couldn't move, I was rooted to the spot. I couldn't take my eyes off Charlie's horrified, hurt little face, the red welts where my fingers had struck – and then the look of utter loathing that came over it.

'I hate you!' he screamed. 'I hate you!' And then he took off, running down the road, followed by Patrick, trying to catch him. 'Charlie,' he was yelling, 'Charlie! Wait up, wait up, will you?'

I have vague memories of someone helping me inside to a neighbour's house while I sobbed incoherently. A kitchen. Someone making tea, more women appearing, all of them enveloping me with kindness, concern, trying to soothe me – but it was useless. I was beyond any consolation. All I could feel was immense, overwhelming grief, and I sobbed and sobbed and couldn't stop. When someone tried to put a small glass of brandy to my mouth, I flung it out of their hands. 'Leave me alone, oh, please, just leave me be.' I was unstoppable. The flood gates had finally opened – and there was no closing them.

A phone call. Hushed snatches of conversation. *Shock. She must have hit her head. The poor woman's lost her reason.* And then more hands around me, another neighbour, a doctor, the words *hospital* and *casualty*. And me, still sobbing, begging, 'No – no.' But an ambulance had been called, quite rightly, and I was helped in, struggling and shrieking. More crying, all the way to our local hospital, St Vincent's, where I was brought into casualty. They found Pam's phone number in my little address book and someone must have made the necessary phone calls, alerted Arthur. But I don't remember any of that. I do remember all the strength suddenly going out of me, feeling as limp and lifeless as a rag doll. I remember the doctors, and nurses, the necessary physical tests. I heard the words *just bruising, no internal damage, no bleeding*, and if I hadn't been so catatonic by then I would have laughed. My heart had broken long before, but I had held it together – now it shattered into a tiny million pieces, taking me with it.

And then the psychiatric resident was called, a nice young man with a kind face and gentle manner. 'Mrs Fitzgibbon,' he asked, 'can you tell us anything about what happened?' But I couldn't. I looked at him and I tried to find the words – just normal words – but they had gone and I couldn't speak.

I must have been sedated then, heavily, because I don't remember anything else until I woke up in a small room the following day, with Arthur sitting by my bed, holding my hand. 'Vera,' he was saying, over and over again. 'Oh, Vera, darling.' But I couldn't look at him and turned my head away to the wall.

I was in a private room, of course, in a private wing of a psychiatric hospital. I wasn't in for long – a week, possibly ten days – until they had pumped me full of drugs and pronounced me well enough to go home. Arthur had brought in a relative of a colleague of his, an eminent psychiatrist who specialised in women's 'nervous problems'. I didn't like him and I got the impression the nurses didn't either – female intuition.

'Don't worry, Arthur old chap,' he said in front of me a day or two before I was discharged. 'We'll have her right as rain in no time. Very common, this sort of thing, but we have wonderful drugs these days. I'll get her medication sorted out, and then I know a very good chap she can see privately – he'll take a look at her on a regular basis, once a month or so, just to make sure she stays on the straight and narrow.'

A couple of days later, I was taken home – to a house that seemed unnaturally quiet. The boys had been sent to my mother and were due back a day or so later. A housekeeper had been employed so that I could rest, which I was instructed to do in no uncertain terms. Pam and Declan were there to welcome me to my own home. I didn't feel anything. I couldn't. I was in a fog of Valium and other drugs. But that was all right. I didn't want to feel anything. I said what I knew would be required of me. That yes, I felt much better, just a bit tired. I thanked everyone for their kindness to me and the boys (someone had caught up with Charlie and Patrick that day and had seen they were taken home). Had a cup of tea with Declan and Pam that tasted like battery acid (the drugs) and was barely aware of the trembling in my hands until I almost dropped the cup, which clattered to the saucer in the nick of time.

Kind words, kind deeds, so much kindness – and once, fleetingly, Pam fighting back tears.

'I think I'd like to rest a bit, if you wouldn't mind,' I said and they left, quietly, discreetly, murmuring reassurances to Arthur.

So I went to bed, my limbs feeling like lead as I trudged upstairs, and into the bedroom where a freshly made bed lay waiting. I allowed Arthur to help me undress and tuck me in, as one might a child, and then tiptoe from the room. I slept then. I did a lot of that over the following weeks, months even.

As I said, I don't remember an awful lot of that time very clearly.

I do remember the boys being brought upstairs to see me. Patrick rushing over to the bed, Charlie lagging behind, a mixture of fear and mistrust written all over his face.

I apologised to them for my outburst that day, my strange behaviour. Patrick immediately said, 'It's all right, Mummy, we know you're not well, and we promise to be very good and quiet until you're feeling better. Don't we, Charlie?' He nudged his brother. His little speech wrenched my heart, although I must have seemed remote and unresponsive. But Charlie wouldn't meet my eyes. He looked down at the floor the whole time until Arthur took them gently from the room.

How did we manage, you must be wondering, for those years? Well, I'm not sure we did, is the answer. I recovered my strength, bit by bit, and with my darling friend Pam, who finally sat me down to talk when she felt I was able, I began to piece my story together for her. I found that with the drugs – Valium, Librium and a few other 'ums' – I had a repeat prescription, naturally – my feelings were numbed enough to at least talk to her about what had happened. She had known all along, of course, not exactly from the beginning, but soon after, and loyal friend that she was, she never said anything, never judged me for it. I suspect, although she never confirmed it, that quite a few other people knew as well. Poor Arthur.

'Of course I knew, darling,' she said to me that day when I opened up to her, hesitantly at first, then found I couldn't stop talking about it. 'It would have impossible for me not to know. The atmosphere when you and Felipe were in a room together was absolutely *charged*. You would have to have been deaf, dumb and blind not to see the two of you were madly in love. It made a lot of us quite jealous, I can tell you!'

So I told her everything, about our little flat, our snatched, stolen hours, how I loved him, desperately, and of my guilt, my relentless remorse. And then she said something quite unusual, something that I often think was the beginning of me turning the corner.

'Don't regret it, Vera,' she said emphatically, then waved a hand dismissively. 'Oh, I know it was wrong, technically speaking and all that, but what you had, you and Felipe, sounds like a once-in-a-lifetime thing, something incredibly special. Very few people get to experience that. We can't plan our lives, you know, we just think we can, but sometimes extraordinary people and events come into them when we least expect it – and I really do think it's for a reason. You and Felipe had this extraordinary love affair – it's over now, yes, but it's part of you, it always will be, it's part of who you are – why on earth regret that?' Then looking at me keenly, she asked, 'What about Arthur?'

'Well,' I said a trifle uncomfortably, 'we've never spoken of it. I never stopped loving Arthur. I know that sounds like piffle, but it's true – this was just a different kind of love.'

She nodded, understanding what I was trying to say. 'But I can't believe he's never mentioned it.'

'Not once.'

'Never even hinted?'

I shook my head.

'How awful. How dreadful for you both to have to live in the same house, the same – well, you know what I mean – and tiptoe around this big white elephant.' She looked cross then. 'No wonder you got sick, darling, the strain of it all – it must have been horrific.'

'Think what it's like for Arthur then.'

'I imagine it's not so bad for Arthur, Vera. You know what men are like. They'd do anything rather than confront some-thing that might damage their precious egos – even if it means watching the woman you love practically self-destruct before your very eyes.'

'It wasn't Arthur's fault, Pam,' I reminded her softly, 'it was mine. And Arthur has stood by me – he could have put me out, forced a legal separation.'

She harrumphed loudly at that. 'Arthur? A high-profile barrister who will no doubt become a judge when the time is appropriate? Arthur, who is always so correct, so – well, he can be quite judgemental, if you'll excuse the pun. I'm terribly fond of him, you know I am, but really, I've always considered him to be quite a controlling person. And this sticking his head in the sand, pretending to ignore every-thing, watching you tear yourself apart – well, I don't know that I would call that standing by someone. He was looking out for himself – like they all do.' Pam could be very outspoken at times, but I was quite surprised at this outburst.

'Oh, I don't think so, Pam,' I said, feeling I must defend him. 'Arthur's been marvellous, really marvellous to me.'

'Hmm. I'm not so sure about that, but let's not quarrel about it. The point is this dreadful mess is behind you and you can start to get your life back. Do you miss him dread-fully? Felipe, I mean.'

'Not a day goes by,' I said quietly.

'Oh, you poor darling.' She patted my hand. 'He must be devastated too, poor man. And I always thought that wife of his was a tough old boot – oh, charming as you like, but she didn't fool me. I always thought she was as cold as ice. So did Declan, but then he always very wisely agrees with me. Well, most of the time anyway.' She grinned. 'Hang in there, Vera darling, things will get better, I promise you, and I'm behind you all the way, you know that, don't you? Whatever happens.'

'I don't like to think what I'd do without you, Pam.'

It was true – I don't think I would have come through it all without Pam. She sort of made me her personal mission, but in a way that was never intrusive, never overbearing. In fact, it was through Pam that a couple of years later I met a wonderful therapist who would help me come off all the pills, talk through my various issues and finally make Arthur and I discuss what had happened. And that was no small feat, I can tell you. Remember, this was long before the days of

Oprah or Dr Phil, where these sorts of things are discussed so freely and openly. Back then in Ireland, the idea of seeing a therapist or shrink on a regular basis would have been considered loopy – or you certainly would have been. That sort of thing was only for people who were seriously mentally ill, or so we thought, and there was still a huge amount of stigma surrounding the whole thing. It was such a pity, you know, because there were a lot of us out there, bewildered, lonely women struggling to get through with mother's little helpers or alcohol, or whatever your chosen poison was. But actually confronting these things, talking about them, bringing them out into the light – well, that was for the very brave, or those coerced into it. I like to think I was part of the former group. Arthur, when he finally came to those few joint sessions after I had begged him repeatedly, was one of the latter. But he came, and it helped us tremendously. It helped Arthur understand and know what I was going through, trying to come off all those drugs, particularly Valium, which was hideously difficult. I had panic attacks and all sorts of anxiety, but slowly, with the help of my wonderful therapist, I got well again, redefined myself and emerged a new and altogether stronger person.

So dear old Pam was right. Things did get better slowly, sometimes very slowly.

But we got through it all, Arthur and I. It's the boys and those dreadful lost years when I couldn't be a mother to them – not the kind of mother they needed anyway – that upsets me so much when I think about it. What a dreadful effect it must have had on them both, especially Charlie.

And then later, that horrible incident with Charlie and Caroline, when Charlie confronted me with such cold, contemptible anger – and who could blame him? I can tell you I raced back to my therapist then for a few sessions. That really threw me, knocked me off my perch. And after that, Charlie never spoke to me again, which was devastating. He left home and made his own life, about which I knew little. Then, when he married Shelley, there was an invitation to the wedding, nothing more. So we showed up, Arthur and I. I was terrified but we went through the motions, and I don't think anyone was any the wiser. After that, when the children were born, we were invited to christenings, confirmations, that sort of thing, but that was it. Nothing more. It was all very superficial. When Arthur died, Charlie and Shelley came to the funeral, but little was said and they left early.

Then quite suddenly, and without any warning, Patrick was killed outright in a car accident. He was just forty years old and had never settled down, which I always thought was a great pity. He had emigrated to Canada fifteen years before and had done very well as a lawyer, but he never married. He had this on-again, off-again relationship with a Montreal girl. I met her once, very attractive, but a bit neurotic if you ask me. It had broken Arthur's heart when he left Dublin – Arthur had great hopes of him following in his own footsteps, but children have to go their own way, don't they? I was glad Arthur didn't live to know Patrick had been killed, it would have broken his heart – as if it hadn't been broken enough already. I went over for the funeral, of course. Patrick had left instructions that he wished to be buried there, in Toronto, where he had made his home, and in his will he had left quite a lot of money. As his next of kin, it went to me. I was deeply uncomfortable about that, but there was nothing I could do about it. I invested it carefully and I still haven't touched it. It doesn't seem right.

So you can see now, can't you, how grateful I am to have a family around me again? I feel as if God has finally forgiven me, even if I can't quite forgive myself, and I've been given a second chance. And it's one I'm going to do my damndest not to mess up.

Caroline

My mother is driving me mad. Stark, staring, howl-at-the-moon mad. She has taken to following me around like an incompetent detective, a one-woman mobile show of reproach and disapproval. I get out of the house as much as I can, but there's only so much exercise I can take. I can't avoid her indefinitely, much as I would like to. Then when I'm at home and trying to get some space, a little privacy, she creeps into whatever room I'm in on the pretence of something ridiculous.

Sitting room: 'Oh, are you watching television? That looks like an interesting programme,' and she plonks herself down beside me.

Kitchen: 'What's that you're sticking in the microwave? You really should be more careful about what you eat, Caroline, that packet stuff is very bad for you.'

Bathroom: 'I think I'll just use the power shower in your en suite, Caroline. I don't feel like a bath this evening, and the shower in yours is so much better.' And she thinks I don't hear her rummaging around having a good old snoop in my bathroom cabinets.

The other day I even found her in my office, if you could call it that, – the tiny third bedroom where I've set up my computer, desk and filing cabinets. 'What are you doing?' I demanded, and she jumped out of her skin, looking as guilty as a schoolgirl caught smoking behind the bicycle sheds.

'Nothing,' she said defensively. 'I was just having a look at that computer of yours and thinking I must learn how to do the email and everything. There are classes in the village, I believe.' And she sidled out.

I know full well that was a blatant lie. Apart from a refusal to learn anything of use in her entire life, except how to nag her late husband and achieve an unrivalled degree of reproach, silent or otherwise, and general negativity, my mother has no interest in computers and has been quite vocal on the subject. Besides, there's no one in their right mind who would *want* to email her.

I'm not sure how much more of this I can take.

I think longingly of other days, days of blissful freedom – London, my fabulous career, my penthouse in the Docklands, exotic holidays – all alone. There were times when it was difficult, but I was never lonely. I'm good at being alone with myself – they say that's a good sign, it's healthy. I was never the needy, clinging type. I'd still be there, you know – head of corporate finance – if I hadn't been framed. It was a set-up. They were jealous of me, all those ambitious young turks (men, of course), all after my job. They just couldn't hack taking orders from a woman, let alone an Irish woman. But I caught them out. They thought they could make a fool of me, make me look like a complete and utter idiot before the board with the figures for the company report. *As if.*

I was working flat out, like I always did, and luckily for me, I checked and rechecked everything inside out. I'm a perfectionist. I can't help it, it's just the way I am. I don't set standards for anyone else that I'm not prepared to live up to myself. So late that night, I went over everything Oliver, my assistant, had prepared, supposedly on my instructions. And I thought I was seeing things. The figures began to swim before my eyes. They were wrong – blatantly wrong. So the next morning I called him in, bawled him out, asked him what the hell he thought he was doing. And unwittingly, of course, I had walked straight into their trap. He went straight to Human Resources, said I had been impossible to work with and demanded a full investigation. They tried to make out that it was all my fault, that I had been overdoing it, showing signs of stress. Me? I laughed out loud when I heard that. But no one else seemed to find it amusing. And then I was called in to the chief executive's office. I was ready to let him have it, I can tell you, but when I went in, Tony, my CEO, wasn't looking his usual affable self. He was also accompanied by two members of the board.

'Caroline,' he indicated a chair, 'sit down, will you?'

So I did, and regarded them all levelly. 'Can we make this brief, please, gentlemen? I have a shareholders' report to finish, in case it had slipped your minds.'

'Ahem.' It was Tony, looking guarded, I noticed. 'I'm glad you mentioned that, Caroline. There's something we need to have a word with you about.'

'What?' I was irritated. 'Can't it wait?'

'No it can't,' Peter, the financial controller, interrupted. 'There's no point in beating about the bush – the figures are a mess.'

'I know that. It's that stupid assistant of mine, Oliver. Ever since you insisted I hire him, he's been nothing but trouble. I'm completely fed up with having to rehash all his mistakes. How he calls himself an accountant, I do not know – he'd add two and two and come up with twenty-two. Why, only last week I had to delete three whole pages—'

'Caroline,' Tony said gently. 'Look, I don't quite know how to put this, but Oliver is not the problem. We've been going through the accounts for the past few days, everything is just as it should be. It, well, it appears that your accounting . . .' He looked helplessly at the other two.

'Caroline.' It was Peter again, looking at me directly (he was loving this, I knew it). 'There's no other way to say this. It has been brought to our attention by more than one person that your behaviour of late has been becoming increasingly erratic.'

'Is this some sort of joke?' I laughed. There followed an embarrassed silence.

'Caroline, please.' It was Tony again, looking profoundly uncomfortable – the wimp. 'It's true, there have been complaints from the staff. Your PA had to have a word with Human Resources. It appears you must be under a great deal of stress. We really think it would be a good idea if you took some time out – you know, take a rest. You really haven't been yourself lately.'

The other two nodded in agreement. 'It might be a good idea to talk to someone,' Stuart from HR interjected. 'We all need to, you know, every now and then. Stress is an epidemic problem in the workplace, but there are techniques that one can learn to, er, manage these things.'

Noting the expression on my face – I was rendered momentarily speechless – Tony motioned for the other two to leave the room. 'Give us a minute, would you?'

When they'd gone, he started again. 'Look, Caroline, I know this must be hard for you, really, but Stuart is right – take some time out, as long as you like. Your office will be here waiting for you. Is there anyone we can call? Anyone who can take you home? I really don't think you should be on your own right now.'

I remember thinking then that no, there was no one I could call, actually. No one I could possibly even begin to contemplate telling about this. I decided to ignore him instead.

'Look, Tony, I don't know what's going on here, what kind of corporate game you're cooking up, but there's a shareholders' meeting on Friday and I have work to do.' I got up.

'I'm afraid that's out of the question, Caroline.' His voice was hard now, and cold. 'You can't possibly attend. If you won't avail of our advice and get yourself some help, then, well . . .' He let the unspoken threat hang in the air.

'Very well,' I said crisply and left the room, then went straight back to my office and locked the door. Whatever was going on, they weren't going to get rid of me that easily. There were legal implications, apart from anything else. I had rights.

In the end, my lawyer persuaded me to go quietly and to accept the pathetic pay-off they described as a 'token of appreciation' for all my efforts to date on the company's behalf. That's what it's like at the top – vicious, cut throat, and all the better if that throat belongs to a woman. Of course I was finished then – no financial firm in London would touch me with a bargepole. I remember being frightened, very frightened. My career was all I had. I had always been on my own, but now I understood the true meaning of it. There was no one who could help me. No one except one person, although it killed me to even think of it. But I had no choice.

So I picked up the phone and called Charlie. Although it had been over twenty years since I'd spoken to him (I had rung him to wish him well on his engagement, once I realised he was going through with it), he sounded exactly the same, and as we spoke, the years fell away.

'Caroline,' he said, sounding warm and genuinely pleased to hear from me, 'what a surprise. How are you?' And before I knew it, I had started to cry, me, Caroline O'Donnell, corporate whizz kid, who they used to joke made Mrs Thatcher look like a Cabbage Patch Doll.

He was wonderful, Charlie, really wonderful, couldn't have been better. Once I'd calmed down and he'd made me tell him exactly what had happened, he sorted everything out for me. 'Look,' he said, 'can you just sit tight until next week, Caro? I'm in London on Tuesday and we can meet up.'

I can't tell you how amazing those words were to me. So I did. I sat tight. And Charlie did come over, and we did meet up. And he did sort everything out. Charlie never let me down – not when I needed him. It wasn't long after that I came back to Dublin, something I'd sworn never to do, not on a long-term basis anyway. But the proposition Charlie put to me was impossible to refuse. I could work independently, he said, as a financial consultant – and he would be my first client. His company, Celtic Crest Investments, could use someone with my experience. In fact, he said I'd be invaluable to them. Those were his very words. When I hesitated, he said I could have one of his apartments in a spanking new development in an area I've always loved, see how things went, have a trial period on both sides – if I didn't like it, living in Dublin, I was free to go, no strings attached.

So I came back. I took him up on his offer and at the height of the Celtic Tiger. I set up my own consultancy, with Celtic Crest Investments as my number-one client. As things turned out, they were a full-time job all on their own. Even if I'd had other clients, I wouldn't have had time for them. Pretty soon I was working around the clock again – and loving it. There was just one problem. I had fallen in love again with Charlie, and he with me. I don't believe we had ever fallen out of it. But now there was a wife – Shelley – and children. No amount of corporate training and wrangling prepares you for having to deal with that. But like I said before, I'm a fighter. I don't give up easily, and I wasn't going to give Charlie up – not this time. And I don't believe he wanted me to. So what if there was another woman? She couldn't possibly be important to him. Charlie and I had something really special, something that had survived him marrying and having a family with someone else. Even if he did have another child, a son with this South African woman, whoever she was, I didn't care. It was probably an indiscretion, some girl got her claws into him one night when he was pissed, and bingo, hit pay dirt. It wasn't as if those emails were exactly intimate, were they? Not what you would call lovers' correspondence. Now that I thought about it, it all made sense. I wasn't going to give up on Charlie, not this time. This was our chance, a chance to get things right, set the record straight. I knew exactly what I had to do. But first I needed to go shopping.

Mac

I'm on the computer, updating my Facebook page. We're all in the kitchen – me, Mum, Emma and Gran, sitting at the table. Mum is going on about her trip to London and Em keeps asking her stupid questions about it. Even Gran is really interested. I pretend not to be listening, but I can do Facebook and listen at the same time. They're having wine (Em's allowed an occasional glass), except Gran, so they're talking quite loudly, which is irritating, and Em's face is getting red.

'So what was the plane like – exactly?'

'The main cabin was about the size of a long narrow room, sort of like a boardroom. And the walls were covered in suede.'

'No kidding.'

'Mm-hmm, and there was a table for people to sit around and work, and then about eight big squishy armchair seats that swivelled any way you wanted.'

'Cool.'

'Then at the back there was a bedroom if you wanted to sleep on long journeys, and a bathroom, of course.'

'And he flew the plane himself, Lukaz?'

'He certainly did, with a co-pilot of course.'

'Imagine that!' Gran shook her head.

'What about food – what did you get to eat?'

'Well, I think you could probably have anything you wanted, but it was really early, remember, so we just had some, um, orange juice.'

'And the hotel?'

Mum is smiling now. I don't look up, but I can hear it in her voice. 'I had a lovely big suite.'

'Wow.'

'I know, it was such a waste, we could have all fit into it. It even had its own dining room – a little one.' I bet she's making that up, but Em would believe anything. This Lukaz guy must be really rich, but I don't like the sound of him. Stupid name too.

'The auction must have been so thrilling – we read about it here, of course, it was in all the papers.'

I tune out for a bit now 'cos Gran is talking about paintings and boring stuff. Besides, Rocky Smith has set up this Facebook page called 'Do you think you might have been abused by a priest?' and it's *really* funny. He'll get into savage trouble if the priests or teachers at our school find out, but Rocky's brilliant at rugby, like all his older brothers, so he gets away with loads of stuff that nobody else would. Rocky's really funny. This week we had a priest come in to our class to talk about the missions, and Rocky and his mates at the back started whispering 'sex, sex, sex,' really loudly, and then the whole class started laughing. I tried really hard to keep it in, but I couldn't.

Our form master went ballistic, but then I felt sorry for the mission priest 'cos he looked as if he was going to cry. I told Dad about it, and I knew even though he didn't say that he thought it was funny too. But he wrote back and said it was important to remember that most priests were very good people and that all this stuff is really horrible for them and it's only a very small number that are weird like that.

I think sex is weird. I don't say that, of course, but I do. Obviously I haven't done it, but some of the lads at school had magazines of girls and stuff and say their brothers said it's brilliant. I didn't like the girls in those magazines, they looked kind of mean and had loads of make-up on. One of them looked a bit like Olivia, I thought. Em pretends she knows all about sex, but she doesn't 'cos she's never had a boyfriend. Anyway, Dad says all that stuff is different when you meet the right person, that you fall in love and that's special. But if I ever fell in love with someone I would never tell them to go away.

I shut down the Facebook page 'cos Mum is talking to me now.

'Mac,' she says, 'have you thought any more about what you'd like for your birthday, love?' I shrug 'cos I don't know, really. I don't care about this birthday, not without Dad here. And then I look at her and she has this soppy kind of smile on her face, and for a moment I think that maybe Dad is coming back for my birthday as a surprise. That's the kind of thing he'd do and no one would tell me.

'I dunno.'

'Well . . .' she says, drawing it out like she's got a really good secret to spring. 'How would you like to see Chelsea play this Saturday?'

Shit. I'd got my hopes up. I can watch Chelsea play anytime. But then she says something really wicked.

'How would you like to bring a couple of friends to see Chelsea play West Ham at Stamford Bridge?'

'For real?'

'For real. Really real.' She's grinning now.

'Like go over to London and see them play at home?'

'Yes. And you can fly over on Lukaz's private jet, how about that?'

'*Yes!*' I jump up and run up and down the kitchen and all around the table. Gran is laughing and so is Mum and Em is rolling her eyes. 'I can bring how many friends?'

'Two.'

'Would you like to come, Gran?' I'm out of breath now.

'That's lovely of you to think of me, Mac, and wonderful an invitation though it is, I think it would be much more fun if you invited your school chums, don't you? I'm a bit old for football matches.'

She's right, but still, I would have quite liked her to come. But I can just see the look on everyone's face when I tell them at school.

'Now off to bed, I'll be up to say goodnight in a few minutes,' says Mum, 'and I hope you've done your homework.'

I grab my laptop and say goodnight and kiss Gran.

Upstairs I get into bed quickly. I'll wait till Mum has said goodnight to me and then I'll email Dad – he won't believe this! And then I think maybe I won't tell him – not just yet anyway. It feels like it would be kind of mean telling him when he can't be there too. I wish he could be, though, that'd be magic. Dad and me both think Ashley Cole is the best midfielder in the world. He also married the prettiest girl in the world. I wish I could be a famous soccer player or rugby player when I grow up, but I don't think I'm good enough. Rocky Smith probably will be, though. Hope we're still mates then . . .

Elsie

To do list

Walk dog

Buy flowers

Look for nice summer blazer in BTs

I just couldn't face walking the dog today, although I was meant to, so instead I decided to treat myself to a morning in town. I hadn't been in to Grafton Street in ages and I needed to buy a nice summer blazer. Larry and I were off for a week to our timeshare shortly, in Gran Canaria, and I was looking forward to it immensely. I was just browsing through some nice casual wear when I heard a voice that had a familiar ring to it.

'Elsie? Is that you?'

I turned around, and standing there before me was Caroline, 'Charlie's Caroline' as I used to call her, although nowadays she was a poster girl for the Irish businesswoman success story. I had read about her being back in the country, of course, and indeed working with Charlie, and I had wondered about that . . .

'Caroline!' I said as she leaned in to embrace me. 'How lovely to see you, and you look so – so wonderful.' She did, too. She had always been a good-looking girl, striking and darkly dramatic.

'You haven't changed a day yourself,' she countered. 'Are you busy or do you have time for a coffee?'

I didn't, really, but how could I refuse? And to be honest, I was curious. Caroline might know something. It was worth a coffee at any rate.

I soon found out I was on a hiding to nothing, as they say.

'You haven't heard anything from Charlie by any chance, have you, Elsie?' They were the first words out of her mouth. And she looked worried sick, poor child. Charlie and she had been an item way back. To be honest, I'd been surprised when they had broken up, they had seemed so close, so united, but Charlie had been very definite about it. He was sorry, to be sure, but quite, quite resolute about the whole thing. And then, after a bit of a sowing his wild oats stage, he had met Shelley – and the rest was history. Unravelling history, it now appeared.

I hesitated for a split second and said, 'No, Caroline, I haven't heard a thing.'

She looked at me then, penetratingly. 'Are you sure?'

'Well of course I'm sure,' I said, my voice rising with indignation. Really, I mean I might have been telling a white lie, but the accusation in her voice, her body language, was most annoying. After all, it was Charlie my loyalties lay with – let's be clear about that much. 'Have you?' I countered. This seemed to take the wind out of her sales a bit.

'No. Not a word. I'm awfully worried about him, though – and Shelley, of course.'

It was only later I thought about that reference to Shelley, as if it was a sort of afterthought on her part.

'So am I, naturally. It's so out of character, all of this, don't you think?'

'Perhaps not,' she said matter-of-factly.

'What do you mean by that?' I asked, and she immediately looked evasive.

'Oh, nothing, just that, well, people can change, you know.'

'If by change you mean running out on your wife and

children and leaving an almighty big mess behind you, then no, Caroline, I don't know. All of this, every *bit* of it, is in total contrast to the man I knew and worked with. Charlie would never, *ever* do something like this without some sort of terrible provocation. I just know it as sure as I'm sitting here.'

'Perhaps he had another woman.'

I spluttered, almost choking on my coffee. 'Don't be ridiculous.'

'What's so ridiculous about that?' She regarded me speculatively.

'Well, it just is. Charlie is a one-woman man. God knows, I saw enough of them throwing themselves at him over the years and he never looked sideways at any of them.'

'Yes,' she said reflectively. 'You're right, of course.'

'Charlie must be absolutely lost without his family, they were everything to him. He's the most loyal person I know.'

'Yes, he is – he is loyal,' she said, looking into the distance.

'He must be climbing walls wherever he is, whatever trouble he's got himself into. I just can't work it out. If only . . .' I stopped, short of words.

'If only he had the right woman to turn to,' Caroline echoed my thoughts. 'Someone he could really confide in.'

'Yes,' I agreed wholeheartedly. 'If only Shelley could reach him, talk to him. All that man needs is the right woman beside him. Why, when I think of my Larry, he'd forget his own head if I didn't screw it on for him. What Charlie needs is his soul mate by his side. Just a few hours on their own and I know everything would be—'

'You know,' Caroline cut across me, her eyes shining, 'that's *exactly* what I was thinking. Great minds think alike, Elsie, and you know him almost as well as I do. And I'm going to do something about this right away.'

'You are?' She was already getting up from her chair and throwing a twenty euro note on the table without even letting me try to pay. 'Caroline, wait a moment, are you going to talk to Shelley?' I was concerned. 'Please – please don't say anything that might upset her, will you?' But it was too late. Caroline was already waving goodbye at me and giving me the thumbs up sign. I had no idea what she was on about. Perhaps she knew something I didn't. At any rate, there was little or nothing I could do about anything.

Feeling rather let down, I went back to half-heartedly searching for my summer blazer. A few days in the sun was just what I needed, I reflected. I had been getting far too caught up in all this carry-on. Charlie was a grown man, after all. Really, he was going to have to face the music one way or another – and neither I nor anyone else could do it for him.

Caroline

I'm not much of a clothes shopper, really – unlike most women. I usually find all that trawling through racks and rails mind-bendingly boring, and as for overly eager salespeople trying to flog you stuff you don't want, well, it's downright irritating. That's why I was so pleased when the concept of personal shopping was introduced to big stores, especially when I lived London, because it meant someone else got to take all the pain out of it for you. But today, for a change, I was really looking forward to it. Not just because it was a chance to get out of the house and avoid my mother, but because I had the best reason in the world there *is* to shop – selecting a drop-dead gorgeous capsule wardrobe of summer clothes, swimwear and lingerie, with the sole intention of making a man drool with lust and succumb to my carefully honed seduction skills. And since that man was Charlie Fitzgibbon, it would make the endeavour even more enjoyable, not to mention successful.

I didn't mention any of this to Elsie, naturally, when I had the good fortune to bump into her in Brown Thomas. I hadn't seen Elsie for years and years, not since Charlie and I had broken up. But I knew she was his closest confidante – she had been more like a mother to him than a PA. I knew if anyone knew anything about Charlie or his whereabouts, it would be Elsie. I asked her, of course, but she said no, that she hadn't heard from him at all. I'm not sure I believed her, but it didn't matter, because what she said during the course of our conversation over coffee made up my mind.

It was a sign. I'd been getting them all week. Everywhere
I looked, South Africa seemed to be flashing up at me. A
feature in the Sunday paper, a holiday brochure put in my
letterbox, even a bus side sailed past me this morning with
the delights of Cape Town plastered all over it. Then Elsie
saying what I had also been thinking of – that Charlie needed
his soul mate by his side. She couldn't have put it more
bluntly, could she? I mean, she was practically *telling* me to
go. Elsie must have known about Charlie and me – she might
not have been able to come right out and say it – but I knew
she thought Charlie and I were meant to be together. Like I
said, it was the final sign I had been waiting for.

Charlie was in Cape Town, as I had suspected. It hadn't
been too difficult to work that one out. I had kept copies of
the emails and had the address of the South African woman,
Annika Kellers. I had planned to email her, and then, on a
whim, decided to phone her instead. Early in the morning
(they're two hours ahead of us), when I knew I would have
a good chance of catching her, and held my breath as the
slightly old-fashioned ring tone burred. It was answered on
the third ring by a breathless voice, which by the sound of
it belonged to a young girl. 'Hello?' she said.

'Could I speak with your mum, please, if she's there?' I
asked.

'Sure,' she said, and then without asking who I was, I heard
her yell, 'Mum! Phone!'

'Hello?' said a well-spoken, modulated voice.

'Is that Annika Kellers?'

'Yes, it is. Who am I speaking to?'

I paused imperceptibly. 'This is Shelley Fitzgibbon –
Charlie's wife.'

I smiled at the recollection. The phone call had the desired
effect; a mixture of shock and acute embarrassment registered at the other end of the line. I wondered why I hadn't

thought of doing it earlier. It's amazing what you can find out if you catch people on the hop.

I pulled into Brown Thomas car park now and easily found a place. My mother would go mental when she had discovered I had taken her car (my company car had long gone), but I couldn't tell her because she would have wanted to come with me and she would have insisted on driving, both of which would have not only driven *me* gaga, but would have defeated the whole object of the expedition. Not unnaturally, I wasn't going to let my mother in on this latest turn-up in events. She would find out what she needed to know all in good time – when it was too late for her to interfere. Right now, there was too much she wouldn't understand about what I had to do, too many objections she would raise, all of them selfish – about her, not me.

In the beginning, I was angry with Charlie. That was only natural. The whole thing had come as such a shock. Not the financial mess – that was everywhere – but him disappearing like he did. I couldn't understand why he hadn't taken me with him. I would have stood by him, understood everything, if he had only explained things to me. That's what really hurt, that he couldn't confide in me, his lover, his oldest friend and ally. So of course I was angry. I felt angry and betrayed – twice over. First Shelley, now this Annika person – and then there was Jack, *the son*. I was beside myself after all the terrible upheaval of having to move out of the apartment and back into my own house, now complete with Mother as a permanent fixture. It was all a bit much, I can tell you. And the constant questions and haranguing from reporters and journalists I had been besieged by until interest in Charlie's disappearance had been replaced by the increasing fall-out from our property bubble bursting and the ensuing bank scandals.

But as time went on, I began to think – really think. I

applied logic to the situation, just like a man would. That was what had got me to the top of the game in my career, so why not my personal life? So I sat down and I thought. I guessed things couldn't have been good between Charlie and Shelley, whatever he may have implied, if he had gone away like this. Yes, yes, I know he'd lost the business and his house, and presumably Shelley wouldn't have been exactly thrilled about those emails, but I know Charlie, and he would never have left his wife and family like this unless there was something else. I mean, he hadn't even left for me.

Before Charlie left, I didn't know how much, if anything, Shelley knew about me or the South African woman. Whatever about me, I guessed she didn't know about her – after all, I had only found out myself. And Shelley wasn't the brightest, not the type to join the dots up even if they were staring her in the face. I never did see what Charlie saw in her. Oh, she was pretty I suppose, if you like the girl-next-door look – but not smart or sophisticated, not what I expected at all when I met her first – and not at all what Charlie needed. Charlie needed someone who could play the game, understand the rules, match him move for move, someone like . . . well, we were made for each other. Charlie always said that, right from the start. So when I found those emails, I knew I had to move quickly, tell Shelley in case – or before – Charlie did. Judging by what I heard the next day, that Charlie had gone, I knew it had been the right move to make. But even I didn't think he'd go underground like this. A couple of days, maybe a week of lying low, but to vanish and not a word, not even a phone call – well, that hurt.

But I got over that, and once my anger at him had worn off, I began to see things for what they were. You see, Charlie had a lot of *issues* with women. He was bound to, wasn't he, after what had happened to him? I mean, that whole business with his mother – it must have affected him hugely. No question about that. I'll never forget that day when we were just students, the pair of us, and she walked in on us in bed together – in his parents' bedroom. The whole thing was horrific. And even after all that, when I met Charlie later that evening, he could barely refer to it. I remember it well, that lovely summer's day that had been ruined. The shame, followed by the cold fear I had felt. We sat there in that small pub, in a corner table, just the two of us, while everyone else in their right minds was outside, enjoying the balmy evening. And I knew, the way you do, that something had changed irrevocably, that things could never be the same for us again. A nasty visitation of adulthood had intruded that day, and neither of us knew what to do about it. I was nervous, panicked, not just because of what had happened, but at the person I saw before me. He was grim, tight-lipped and remote. The Charlie I knew and loved had retreated somewhere I couldn't reach – he seemed to have aged before my eyes.

'Are you sure?' I asked him, probably for the umpteenth time. 'I mean, are you absolutely sure, Charlie?' I couldn't believe what he was telling me.

'Of course I'm bloody sure, Caroline,' he practically spat at me. 'I know what I saw.'

'But you were, what? Only seven or eight, Charlie, maybe—'

'I was eight years old.' His eyes bored into me, his mouth a thin line. 'And I know enough to know it wasn't my father she was in bed with.'

I didn't know what to say to that so I said nothing, just chewed my nail while Charlie pulled on a fag, something he rarely did.

'Anyway, you saw how she reacted – she wasn't exactly protesting her innocence. She's a good actress, my mother, but the mask slipped – she couldn't take the truth.'

'But why didn't you say something sooner? Didn't you tell
Patrick? Anyone?'

'No,' he said shortly, 'I just wanted to forget it. And I'd
like if you would too,' he added curtly.

'I just can't believe it,' I said numbly. And I couldn't, not of
Vera – anyone but Vera – I just couldn't imagine it. We were
at that age anyhow, Charlie and I, when the idea of anyone's
parents having sex is hideous, but adulterous sex . . .

He moved out of home the next day. At first, he shared
with a mate of his who was renting, and from that day on,
he never referred to it, not once. He got his finals that year,
and later a job, and eventually moved into his own place.
The rest, as they say, is history. Not a lot of people know
Charlie's history. In fact, I'd bet I'm the only one outside the
family who does. So I can understand his problems with
women, his lack of trust, his fear of betrayal. I've done quite
a bit of therapy myself, and I know enough to understand
that Charlie is following a pattern, subconsciously testing me,
us – the women in his life. Seeing who, if anyone, will stand
by him through thick and thin. Back then I didn't get it, but
now I understood and I wasn't going to let him down. It was
a cry for help – and only a woman who truly loved and was
worthy of Charlie would understand.

So I made that phone call to Annika in Cape Town. At the
most, I was hoping for a contact number for Charlie, maybe
even an address, any clue, however seemingly insignificant.
But what I found out was infinitely better – more than I
could have ever expected. Taking the initiative had paid off.
I was ahead of the posse once again, and this time I was
going to make sure they never caught up.

Annika

We met on an early summer's day in November, one of those perfect days when the wind doctor was absent, before the temperatures became uncomfortably hot. So we set off, me, you and Marge, for Glen Bay, a smaller beach than our local one at Camps Bay, but better surfing. And although you were only three, you were already obsessed by it. '*Surpers*, Mummy!' you would shriek, 'Look, *look*, surpers!' And Marge would pick you up and hurtle into that ice-cold Atlantic water (she always was thick skinned) and whoosh you around in the air as you swooped and splashed in your own little surfer's paradise. Occasionally some of the kids would play with you, let you sit on their boards and paddle with you at the water's edge, and the look on your little face was sheer bliss. You were a water baby right from the get-go.

It was a little while later, after I had unpacked, set up the umbrellas and beach chairs, made sure the icebox with our drinks and lunch was in the shade and lay down to watch you and laugh at your antics in the water with Marge, that I noticed him. It would have been hard not to. He was tall, blond and tanned and had an incredible body. He was with his two little girls who looked about the same age as you and he was having a hard time with one of them, who was crying and hiccupping in that enraged way that only small children seem to have down to a fine and practised art. The other little girl (identical, I reckoned they were twins) sat placidly on the sand, looking at her sister with mild curiosity, while her dad had that helpless look that dads get when no amount of lifting, swinging, cajoling or producing candies can restore calm or sanity to the implacable child. I became quite intrigued to see how he would resolve the situation, sneaking surreptitious looks at them from behind the pages of my book. His solution, whether born of desperation or genius, worked admirably. He took them both, one on each hip, complete with inflatable floater jackets, straight into the water. I can still see the look on Charlene's four-year-old face today as she hit that ice cold water – a mix of shock, horror and then, along with her sister Rosie, gasps and squeals of delight, the momentary tragic offence instantly forgotten as Dad splashed around with them both, looking a lot more uncomfortable. That image still makes me laugh to this day, and I remember thinking even then how great he was with his kids, and also thinking how lucky their mum must be, wherever she was.

It's not that we weren't perfect as we were, you and me, of course we were, for the moment. I adored you, always did and will do, but it's not always easy being a single mum. Most of the time we coped just fine. Marge was as good as any surrogate parent could be – better, maybe – but she was just your godmother, and my best friend. I had lots of other friends as well, guys and girls, and everyone loved you, wanted to spend time with you and brought you a ridiculous number of presents – that wasn't the problem. But you didn't have the one thing you needed and would continue to need. You didn't have a dad in your life, and I worried desperately how that must be and would go on affecting you. Most of the time I tried not to think about it, but even then, especially as you had just learned to talk and jabber away, collecting new words like prize trophies, trying them out over and over with delighted excitement and authority – even though you were only three years old, you had already mentioned him. *Your dad.*

'Do you know who that is?' Marge whispered loudly to me when she hauled you out of the water and I wrapped you in towels to rub you dry as you squirmed and yelled, 'Back in the water, Mummy, back in the water *now*!'

'Who *who* is?' I retorted, not at all convincingly, busying myself trying to get you to stand still for just a second.

'Earth to Annika,' Marge said witheringly, 'I'm referring to Mr Adonis in the water, he of the godlike stature with two cherubic little girls in his wonderfully bulked-up arms. But of course you haven't been watching him, have you?' She looked at me archly.

'Well who is he then?'

'That,' she said knowingly, 'is Greg Hanson.'

When I looked blank (I was interested, of course, but the name meant nothing, not at first, anyway), she rolled her eyes at me and said, 'Greg Hanson, as in former Springbok player on the 1995 winning World Cup team. The Greg Hanson who set up the winning drop goal in the final minute of extra time. The only man to have been tackled by Jonah Lomu and still left standing . . . *that* Greg Hanson?'

'Oh,' I said, 'I did think he looked familiar, now that you mention it.'

'As in godlike, drop-dead, gorgeously *sexy* kind of familiar, or just regular familiar?'

I laughed. Marge certainly didn't beat about the bush, and yes, I admitted, he was gorgeous. More importantly, I added a little wistfully, he seemed to be really great with his little girls.

'He's available.'

'What?' I was wrestling you into fresh swimming shorts and a T-shirt, with a fleece for extra heat until you warmed up again. Your little body felt blue with cold, even though you were tanned golden.

'I said, he's available.' Marge was unpacking lunch and opening a bottle of beer.

'How d'you know?'

'Hah, I thought that would get your attention, Ms Disinterested.'

'Okay, so I'm interested. So how do you know, for sure I mean, that he's available?'

'Because it's the kind of thing us women who are interested in available men make it our business to know.'

'Divorced?' I asked, tucking into the sushi we had brought.

'Nope, widower – it's quite a sad story, really.'

Now she really did have my attention. 'What happened?'

'He married Ruthie Simons, you remember her? Not quite Charleze, but a good enough actress.'

'Oh no,' I said, vague memories of the tragedy beginning to register.

'Yep – they got married in '98 or maybe it was '99, remember? The wedding was a big affair, full of movie types and Springboks, of course. They had twin girls, as you can see, and she died six months later from a brain haemorrhage.'

'That's so awful.'

'Yeah, it was sad all right. He's dated a few girls since, but nobody's made the grade – apparently he's fiercely protective of his daughters, probably doesn't think anyone's a good enough potential mother.'

'Well,' I said, letting out a long breath, 'I can relate to that. I can't say I blame him. You can't be too careful. It's not just about you, your child has to come first – that's the deal.'

'Not such a great one for the kids, though, maybe.'

'What do you mean?' I asked a little sharply.

'Well, I can't imagine having a lonely, frustrated single parent as the best deal in the world, can you?'

'I am not lonely or frustrated!'

'Maybe not now, but give it time. Don't get me wrong, Anni, Jack's adorable, but he's been the only man in your life since he got here – and you weren't known for your relationship staying power prior to that. You might want to think about, well, giving it another try before it's too late – for both of you.'

That stung, I can tell you, but Marge was nothing if not outspoken, and I knew she meant well. I just didn't need to hear it. Sometimes the truth can hurt, and this did.

'I just want to do the best I can for Jack,' I said defensively.

'I know you do, and you're doing a fabulous job – I'd just like to see you doing it with someone else to help. Jack's a boy, a gorgeous, adorable little boy, but he needs a masculine role model. Besides, for as long as I've known you, you were always complaining about being an only child yourself.'

That was true too. My parents divorced when I was a kid, and I remember all too well the loneliness of living alone with my own mum, a bitter and resentful woman devoted to hating all men, especially the one she had been married to. For a moment I was lost in memories, and encroaching guilt, until I heard Marge call out. 'Hey, those are two gorgeous little girls you've got there. You're Greg Hanson, aren't you?' She was already on her feet and strolling over to meet him as he waded out of the water with his girls.

'That's me,' I heard him say. 'I'd shake hands with you, but as you can see I've got them full!'

'Why don't you come on over and join our little picnic here? We could use some male company, especially little Jack here.' To my horror she pointed to me and Jack, who I just noticed was busy filling his banana and peanut butter sandwich with sand. 'He's kind of outnumbered.'

'Well,' said Greg, 'that's very kind of you. Let me just grab our stuff here and I'll bring it over.' And he began to do just that.

'What do you think you're doing?' I hissed at Marge when

she plonked herself down beside us again, wearing her 'result' expression all over her face.

'Just being a good godmother,' she said smugly. 'Make that fairy godmother.'

Although I didn't know it then, she was right. Not that she ever lets me forget it.

But that day, seven years ago now, we ate and we swam, we played and we laughed, you kids were quiet for about fifteen minutes until curiosity overcame clingy shyness and then you all bawled your heads off when we adults reluctantly decided it was time to go home.

It was while we were packing up that Greg said casually, 'I'm having a *braai* (that's pronounced bry, as in eye, and it's short for *braaivleis*, the word we use for a barbecue, Afrikaans for 'roasted meat') at my place tomorrow, just a few friends. You guys are more than welcome if you'd like to come.'

'We'd love to,' said Marge. 'Where do we show up?'

He gave his address, which Marge instantly copied to her mobile phone, making sure to get his number – 'just in case'.

'Anytime after seven,' he called as he set off with the girls. 'And if you can't get a babysitter, bring Jack too.'

'Oh, we'll get a sitter,' muttered Marge to his departing back.

'Oh we will, will we?' I looked at her. 'I'm not even remotely sure I want to go to this thing.'

'Well I do – and you're coming with me. It'll be good for you, Anni, you don't get out enough, and Betty will stay over with Jack. You know he loves her almost as much as he loves me.'

'Betty!' you crowed in delight, and Marge laughed. 'See? Even Jack needs a break from you.'

Betty did come and sit for you, and Marge and I did go to the *braai*, which was great fun in Greg's beautiful house tucked away in one of the narrow, twisty slopes of the mountain overlooking Camps Bay. And later, when the crowd was beginning to thin out and I was about to say we really must go, I realised that Marge had already gone, without me.

'You don't have to leave just yet, do you?' Greg asked. 'You have a sitter, don't you? Marge said.'

So I stayed for a while, and Greg and I talked a lot and eventually I asked him to call for a cab to take me home and he asked if he could accompany me. 'I just want to make sure you get home safely. I'm not sure I could face Marge's wrath if I didn't deliver you right to your front door.'

'Oh, she's made an impression on you, I can see.'

'Not as much as you have,' he said, getting in to the cab with me.

We didn't have far to go, and as the cab pulled up outside our apartment building, Greg got out and saw me to the door. 'How about you and Jack coming to the beach tomorrow with me and the girls?' he suggested.

'We'd love to.'

'Great. I'll pick you up at ten, if that's okay?'

'Perfect. Oh, and thank you for having us to the party, and for seeing me home. That was kind of you.'

'My pleasure,' he said before bending to kiss me lightly on the cheek. 'My pleasure entirely.' He waited until I had let myself in before getting back into the cab which pulled away.

I was humming a silly tune as I got into the lift. It was almost one o'clock as I quietly opened the door to our apartment to see Betty with her feet up, engrossed in an old movie. 'Hey, someone must have had a good time. Jack went out like a light.' She heaved herself off the sofa.

'Betty, I hope I didn't keep you up too late.' I immediately felt guilty.

'Are you crazy? You know I'm an insomniac. I was hoping you'd stay out all night,' she grinned wickedly. 'Well, maybe not on a first date.'

'It wasn't a date.'

'From the look on your face, darling, I'll bet you're seeing him again.'

'You've been talking to Marge, haven't you?' I sat down and took off my sandals before checking on you. 'You ought to know by now not to believe a word she says.'

'So when are you seeing him again?'

'Tomorrow, but it isn't a date – we're just going to the beach, me and Jack and Greg and his girls.'

'No Marge?'

'No Marge.'

'Now I like the sound of that,' she said. 'Whatever you want to call it.'

'Goodnight, Betty, and thank you.'

'Goodnight, darling, and enjoy yourself tomorrow.'

I went in to you then, quietly, and you were out for the count, flat on your back with both arms thrown out in abandon, your face flushed in sleep and your beloved teddy bear, Brian, beside you. I looked at you then and wondered if maybe Marge was right. Was it time to let someone into our lives? Or would it just open up a whole Pandora's box of troubles in our safe, cosy little world?

As things turned out, we did go to the beach the next day with Greg and his girls – and a lot of other days that summer too. And right from the start it seemed like we were a regular little family. Charlene and Rosie were almost a year older than you, the perfect age to play with, and as girls do, even at that age, they were delighted to have a new buddy to instruct and issue demands to, which you happily concurred with. Rosie in particular became quite proprietorial about you, referring to you as 'my Jack'.

And then it happened. It was inevitable, really, but I just wasn't prepared for it. I don't think any of us were. I had fallen in love with Greg by then – it would have been impossible not to. But what I didn't realise was that you had too. But no one had broached the situation, nothing had been said, although I was pretty sure Greg felt the same way about us – and he was terrific with you.

We were playing in the water, and Greg and I were taking turns throwing you and the girls up in the air and dangling you back in the water. 'Again, Daddy! Again!' shrieked Rosie as Greg whooshed her up. I was holding you and Charlene on your little surfboard, and as we went to swap over, Greg turned to you, saying, 'C'mon, mate, c'mon Jack, your turn now.' As he reached for you, you shrieked just as loudly, holding out your little arms to him, 'Me, Daddy! Me, me, *me*, Daddy!'

I wanted to die, I wanted the water to swallow me up I was so mortified, but Greg just looked at me and grinned and went on as if nothing had happened. But it *had* happened, and once you started, you couldn't, or wouldn't, stop. All day long it was Daddy this, Daddy that, Daddy, Daddy, Daddy, until I picked you up and said, desperately, 'Jack, stop, honey. Greg is n—'

But I didn't get any further because Greg reached over and pulled us to him and said quietly to me, looking at me meaningfully, 'Don't say it, Anni. Don't do it to the little guy, it's not important.'

'But it is, it's incredibly important,' I blurted. 'I can't let him think—'

'We need to talk,' he said. 'Can I come over to your place this evening?'

'Sure,' I said miserably. I was torn between anguish and guilt and a whole lot of other emotions I had been doing my best to ignore. I couldn't believe I had allowed this to happen, to play with your fledgling emotions so dangerously, never mind my own. But worse was the thought of our newfound happiness deserting us. I was suddenly very, very scared, so scared that I didn't even tell Marge. I couldn't take any advice or talking to, however wise or well meaning. So I asked Betty if she would take you for a couple of hours so that Greg and I could talk.

He came around at seven. I didn't want to eat, I was too wound up, but he brought a bottle of wine and we sat down, me awkwardly, Greg as relaxed as ever. He got straight to the point, which is one of the qualities I love about him. 'You never talk about Jack's father,' he said. 'It's none of my business, I know—'

'Of course it's your business,' I said wearily. 'You've been so good to us, and Jack adores you.' The words hung in the air and for some reason I couldn't quite bring myself to say *And so do I*. I felt as if it would be fishing, sounding needy.

'What about you, Anni? How do you feel?'

That took me aback. 'Well,' I tried to stall, 'the past couple of months have been so great, and – and—'

'Anni,' he said gently, but firmly. 'I really need to know.'

God, I was squirming now. I had never been good at expressing my feelings vocally, and whatever I said I felt a sword was hanging over my head. 'I – I love you.'

'You sure about that?'

'Well, can't you tell?' I was getting annoyed now, and beginning to feel really stupid.

'I don't like to be presumptuous but, yes, I kinda got that idea. And that's really good – because I love you too, you and Jack.'

A huge wave of relief rolled over me. Then we kissed, quite a lot, and then he pulled away and said, 'So tell me about Jack's father.'

This was the bit I hadn't been looking forward to. 'There's not a lot to tell, actually. It wasn't one of the highlights of my life, not something I'm proud of, but I'm terribly proud of the result.'

Greg smiled. 'So you should be. Go on.'

'Well, I was a lot different back then. I was still modelling, obviously, but I was messed up – spent too much time partying and not enough time figuring out who I was or where I was going. I couldn't seem to go the distance in relationships either. I was either too needy or too remote, there was no happy medium. I had just broken up with someone, someone I quite liked, actually, and as usual I was just blotting everything out, hitting the party circuit, one of which was a beach party. There was this Irish guy, quite a bit older than me, but he was really nice, good-looking, and there was something about him. He was warm and kind, and more importantly, seemed as keen to party as I was. He was here on some boys' rugby trip, I think, it was their last night, they were going home the next day. Anyway, him and his friends were the life and soul of the party.' I took a deep breath. 'We got out of our heads, I went back to his hotel room . . . and you know the rest.'

'Does he know about Jack?'

I shook my head. 'I didn't discover I was pregnant until about two months later, and by then, I didn't even have an address. I think we exchanged cards, the way you do, but we both knew it was just a one-night stand thing. By the time I knew I was pregnant, what was the point? I didn't even know the guy.'

'But Jack will want to. And this guy, whoever he is, has a right to know he has a son, don't you think?'

I nodded miserably. 'I know, I know. Don't think I haven't agonised about it, but I have no idea where he is or how to contact him – I just stuck my head in the sand about it. And Jack and me, well, we've been so happy, everything's worked out just fine. I can't bear to . . . I just don't want to go there.'

'That's understandable.'

'Is it?'

'Sure it is, but one day you're going to have to find him – for Jack's sake.'

'I know.'

And we left it at that. Greg went home and I went across the hall and took you back from Betty's and put you to bed. I should have felt relieved, but I didn't. My stomach was churning and I couldn't sleep. What happens now? Where did we go from here? And more terrifyingly, what lay ahead for us, you and me? Were you going to hate me one day for doing this to you?

The next time we were meeting Greg and the girls, which was a few days later, I tried to explain to you. 'You know we're going to see Greg and Charlene and Rosie today?'

'Daddy!' you crowed.

'Jack, sweetie, Greg is Rosie and Charlene's daddy, he's not your daddy. He . . . he's our very best friend, but you just call him Greg, okay, sweetie?

'Why?'

'Because that's his name, Jack. Like your name is Jack.'

'Daddy,' you said resolutely, and that's what you insisted on calling him. There was nothing I could do.

'Don't worry about it, hon,' Greg said later at his place. 'Let him call me what he likes.'

Then, while you guys were watching a DVD and me and Greg were having a glass of wine watching the sun sink down into Camps Bay, he called out to Rosie, 'Rosie, darling, can you bring Daddy that piece of paper I gave you?'

Rosie scrambled down from the sofa and came over and shyly handed me a folded piece of paper. 'We'd like you to read this,' she said, coyly.

I opened it, and inside it read, *Rosie, Charlene and I would really love if you and Jack would marry us. Please say yes.*

And before I could say a word, I began to cry. I couldn't help it. I was completely overwhelmed. Which must have alarmed Rosie, poor little girl, who immediately started to cry too, and then Charlene ran over, not wanting to be excluded, and the three of us were at it.

'Hey, hey!' Greg said, laughing and picking up his girls. 'That's not quite the reaction I was hoping for! C'mon, Anni, put us out of our misery!'

'Yes,' I gulped, trying to pull myself together. 'Of course Jack and I would love to marry you – we'd adore to!'

'What about you, Jack?' Greg went over to you, where you were still sitting on the sofa, resolutely ignoring the drama. 'How about it?' Greg got down on one knee and deposited the twins beside him. 'Would you like us to be a proper family? Would you like me to be your dad? Would you like Rosie and Charlene to be your sisters?'

You looked at him and solemnly nodded your head, then you reached over and hugged him and said one word: 'Daddy.' It was the sweetest thing I'd ever seen. Then you went straight back to watching your DVD.

'Well,' said Greg, sounding relieved, 'I think that's a collective yes – just as well I have some champagne chilling.'

And that was the beginning of the fairy tale.

Our wedding was a quiet affair, just close friends and immediate family and a small lunch afterwards at Camps Bay Hotel. Jack and I moved into Greg's house, which he had built and moved to after Ruthie had died. He had renovated and expanded the site of what had previously been a small holiday cottage into the present gleaming white, ultramodern house with a terrace overlooking Camps Bay and the best sunsets in the world. The original cottage had been included, and now housed Winnie and Des, Greg's parents' long-time housekeeper and her husband, a wonderful black couple who refused to retire and were coerced into accepting the cottage only on the understanding that Greg allowed them continue to work for him as housekeeper, babysitter and driver/odd job man. They were part of the family, and Greg's parents had paid for their children, now a doctor and lawyer, respectively, to go to college. Winnie and Des loved Greg and his family fiercely and protectively and had been a far harder task for me in the approval-winning stakes than either of Greg's parents, who were lovely people. But I must have passed muster eventually, because Winnie had given her seal of approval, which was to bake me her famous chicken curry potjie on our third dinner together at the house. I suspect she had also fallen under your spell and adored you just as she did Rosie and Charlene.

They were so happy, those first years, full of fun and carefree times. You all went to school at the Camps Bay School, which it has to be said is probably the best-located school in the world. At the weekends we played tennis and cricket in the club, right behind the Bay Hotel. Greg's competitive nature was rubbing off on you, and you and the twins were becoming scarily competitive, but it was surfing that was always your passion, and I suspect always will be.

And then, just two years ago, reality intruded with sudden and cruel severity.

It seemed such a silly thing at the time. Your hands had swollen up and you had been tired and complaining of a sick tummy. I thought it was an allergy, something you had picked up in the pool or perhaps an irritant in the sun block, combined with too much sun. But a few days later the swelling hadn't gone down, and your feet were puffy as well. We went to the doctor, who did blood and urine tests and prescribed some medication. There was blood in your urine, and when he spoke to me alone, he referred us to a nephrologist.

'Why?' I asked, alarmed.

'I'd feel happier if he saw a specialist. It could be something minor, but better to get it checked out,' he smiled reassuringly as he gave me the name of a consultant.

Two weeks later, we knew it wasn't something minor at

all. Greg had come with us to the hospital, where the consultant sat us down to talk it through. You were unlucky, he said. You had a severe form of IgA nephropathy. We listened, numbly, as he explained that renal failure is a silent killer and children often have no symptoms at all until the disease is advanced, presenting, as you did now, with tiredness, nausea, poor appetite and swelling of the hands and feet. The tests had revealed blood in the urine, proteinuria, and your blood pressure was elevated. You were already heading for renal failure. In the absence of a donor kidney, immediate dialysis was imperative.

The next few days and weeks passed in a blur as we tried to digest the news and get our heads around your dialysis. Although you were only eight, you were wonderful about it. You listened as we tried to explain that you were sick, that your kidneys were failing and that you would need to hooked up to a machine that would clean your blood out for you so you could be well again.

'So that's okay then? I'll be better then?' you said.

I couldn't answer that one; I was trying not to cry. So Greg simply said, 'You'll have to take it easy for a while, mate. We're just going to have to see how this thing works out, but yes, you are going to get better.'

'I can still surf, can't I?' The panic that entered your voice broke my heart.

'Sure, mate, but not for a while, eh?'

And that's when you began to suspect, I think, that this thing was bigger than anyone was telling you just then.

We decided on peritoneal dialysis because it could be done at home, and although Red Cross Hospital was wonderful, you didn't want to be going there three times a week for three to five hours at a time. But any kind of dialysis is a major lifestyle change, especially for an eight-year-old kid who lived to be in the water.

Once Greg and I had a chance to take it all in, we discussed our options. A transplant was the obvious goal, and although we could have waited for a cadaver kidney, we were keen to explore the living donor option. It all seemed easy to me – I would donate one of my kidneys to you, and hey presto! Everything would be back to normal. But in one of life's great ironic twists, when I went for the initial hospital tests, it was discovered I had been previously undiagnosed with a single kidney – don't ask me how, but apparently it happens; you can live a perfectly normal, healthy life with just one. In other words, I only had one kidney myself, and although I would have gladly given it you, it wasn't an option. Still, we were upbeat; how hard could it be? Someone was bound to be a suitable donor, and so the search for a live kidney was on.

Everyone was marvellous. The people who came forward and offered to help so generously overwhelmed me. Greg, of course, and even the girls wanted to help, but they were far too young. They busied themselves instead by entertaining you while you were hooked up to your 'exchanges' for four to six hours at a time. Greg's parents offered and Marge, of course, who said cheerfully, 'Darling, I'd gladly give him either of mine if they're acceptable after all the abuse I've heaped on them.' Even Winnie, bless her, although I wouldn't hear of her even trying to go for tests, and quite a few of our close friends. People who I never even considered offered to give you a kidney – time and time again I was amazed at the sheer courage, generosity and bravery that people were capable of, but sadly, no one was a good prospective donor. The crucial thing you needed was a compatible blood group. After that came HLA matching, but that wasn't quite as important. And here again, we ran into a serious setback. You were AB negative one of the most difficult blood groups to match. That's when I knew we were in trouble. Up until then I had been hopeful, desperately telling myself that we would find you a kidney, but now even the specialist was circumspect about your options. Suddenly things looked bleak again and I plunged into despair. You must have sensed it too because despite all our efforts at cheerfulness around you, you became silent and withdrawn even with your sisters, which frightened me more than anything.

One evening, after a particularly bad day when you were frustrated and crying, Greg sat me down. 'You know what we have to do, Anni, don't you?' he said gently. 'You have to get a hold of Jack's dad, whatever it takes.'

'But I have no idea where he is, how to find him.'

'We'll find him, Anni. It can't be that hard to track him down. We'll hire someone to find him – it's not impossible.'

This was the hard part for me. Of course I was willing to do it – I'd have done anything – but all I had to go on was a name and a nationality – that was it.

I met Marge for lunch to talk to her about the whole thing. She was the only one who had been there through it all, right from the very start.

'It was always going to come to this, Anni, one way or another.'

'I know, I know, it's just that I know absolutely nothing about the guy.'

'Didn't you get his card? I'm sure I remember you saying you had a card or an address or something?'

'Yes, but that was ten years ago, Marge.'

'Well look again, just to be sure. Turn the whole house upside down if you have to. I'll help.'

'Thanks.'

Then she brightened. 'I know – we'll get St Anthony on the case.'

'Who?'

'St Anthony, the patron saint of lost things. He can find

anything, but you have to promise him money. We'll get him to find Jack's father.'

'Marge, please, I'm in no mood for crazy stunts. This is Jack's life we're talking about here.'

'Precisely. All the more reason to get the heavy hitters on board.'

'You never struck me as the religious sort,' I said dryly.

'I'm not, I'm the best lapsed Catholic I know, but St Anthony works for everyone, trust me.'

I didn't pay much attention to her at the time, but we did go back to the house and go through every piece of clothing, handbags, boxes, cases – everything I still possessed – all to no avail. In the meantime, Greg was finding out about reputable security firms and private investigators.

And then, right out of the blue, a week or so later, I was having a clearout, going through a box of old photographs, silly ones mostly, from way back, and I picked one up of Marge and me in our heyday sitting outside at a table on the waterfront. As I looked at it, smiling, I felt something sticking to the back of it. I turned it around, and there it was, stuck to the back of the photograph– a torn business card. I could hardly believe my eyes. It was just as if it had been given to me. I realised I was holding in my hands the name and contact details of your father.

Emma

You know my weird family? Well, things just got weirder. Way weirder. First off, Olivia's started being really nice to me. Not that she was ever that horrible to me or anything – well, no more than usual – but now she's being *really* nice, and I just don't get it. In fact, I'd go so far as to say I'm suspicious.

Sophie says I'm just being paranoid. She's probably right, but who could blame me?

It all started when I told her I was going to my first Crescent disco that most of my friends go to. You've probably seen the queues on a Friday or Saturday night if you've been in the vicinity. Anyway, if I'm honest, I'm a bit anxious about it. I'm going with Sophie, of course, and a few of the other girls in our year and we're getting ready at Sophie's house and then Jackie is giving us a lift there, then Sophie's dad will be picking us up. There have been long, involved consultations and phone calls between Mum and Jackie about the 'suitability' of allowing us to go, but apparently conditions have been met. I've been wanting to go for years, but now that I actually am, I'm kinda scared. I've never had a boyfriend and I don't even have an older brother, so I'm not sure what you're supposed to do or how you're supposed to act around boys. And for all the talking the girls in our year do, the closest most of them have got to a relationship is heavily stalking some poor guy on Facebook. Anyway, I was saying all this to Olivia, which was when she decided she was going to take me shopping and 'style' me.

First we went for lunch, where she proceeded to lecture me.

'I think you should wear jeans,' she said. 'That'll let them know you're not a slag.'

'Liv!'

'I know what goes on in those places, believe me, and if you think I'm going to let my little sister get a name from some bunch of spotty geeks, you've got another thing coming.' She was referring to the rumoured trend where girls who wore underwear were considered 'prudes'. I'm not kidding either. Short skirts were the uniform and underwear was allegedly often removed by said short-skirted girls and worn around their wrists for the remainder of the evening. No wonder I was scared. The other kind of girls wore jeans and presumably danced among ourselves for the night.

'And no leaving the hall either and sloping off to do unmentionable things in the park with some fumbling hormonal jerk. I'll hear, you know, they all talk, and everyone in Dublin's related. You won't meet anyone there you like anyway – you never do.'

'Well thanks a lot, Liv. You're worse than Mum.'

'Of course I am, I'm your older sister, I know more. Anyway, I'm only looking out for you. Trust me, "look but don't touch" is the only look you need to work on Saturday.'

After that we went into A-Wear, which is one of the shops my friends go to quite a bit and not too expensive. I try and avoid shopping expeditions into Grafton Street 'cos I'm not a good shopper and money's tight and I don't want to ask Mum. But before I knew it, Liv had me trying on the whole shop, and although there was quite a bit of stuff I liked, by the end of it I was so tired and pissed off I told her I didn't want any of it. I just wanted to go home. She said I was an ungrateful girl and I told her I didn't want to profit from her ill-gotten gains anyhow.

'How dare you!' she said. 'I happen to have a job now, I'll have you know.'

'Are you pregnant, Liv?'

'What?'

'Are you pregnant?' I'd been wondering about that since the comment from 'littlewhitedove' on my ill-fated blog. 'You know, up the duff? Is that why you moved out and went to live with Guy? You can tell me, you know. I won't tell Mum, I swear.'

'Jesus,' she said and shook her head at me. 'I really don't know what to think about you sometimes, Emma.'

We went home our separate ways after that.

Then I felt bad, 'cos really, Liv had only been trying to help. And now I *really* had nothing to wear. That's when the other really weird thing happened, just a couple of days later.

I came home from school to find Olivia sitting in the kitchen with Gran. This in itself would have been unusual, but what was really weird was that Gran appeared to have been crying. I mean, like, really crying. Her eyes were all swollen and red and she was blowing her nose a lot. Oh, and Liv had made her a pot of tea. I know because Gran said that when I came in.

'Sorry, Emma, I'm afraid I'm a bit upset. I didn't want anyone to see me like this, but Olivia came in to leave you a present and she found me here making a bit of a fool of myself and very kindly made me a cup of tea' she sniffed. 'I was having a bit of a blub.'

I looked at Olivia, who was shaking her head at me and widening her eyes subtly as if to say, *It's a madhouse here, but say nothing*. But I couldn't – say nothing, that is. I mean, Gran never cried. It must have been something really bad, so I had to ask.

'What happened?' I said, sitting down opposite her while Olivia rolled her eyes at me and topped up Gran's cup.

'I – I had some very bad news today,' she said shakily. 'I know it won't sound anything much to you girls because you're both young and healthy, thank God, but I just had word that a . . . a very dear friend of mine died last week.'

'Oh, I'm sorry, Gran. Was it one of your friends from the shop?' I asked. I was relieved, really, because I couldn't imagine what would upset her so much. I thought something might have happened to Mum.

'No, not one of my friends from the shop. Thank you, dear,' she said to Olivia, who was adding sugar and stirring Gran's tea for her.

'Tea with sugar is good for when you've had a shock,' Olivia said knowledgeably. Olivia as paramedic was a new one to me. 'It was unexpected, then?' Liv went on. 'This friend of yours, um, dying? She wasn't sick or anything?' Liv was clearly in the dark as much as I was.

'It was a he, actually,' said Gran, 'and yes, it appears that he had been very sick for some time. I just didn't know anything about it until today.' She paused and took a deep breath. 'He was a great love of mine, once, if you must know.' She blew her nose again. 'I know I'm old, but I was young once too.'

Olivia patted her hand and nodded sympathetically, and Gran didn't even seem to mind. She was talking like they do in movies, when there's a sort of narrator talking about the past.

'Anyway, I think I'll go up and have a little lie down. Thank you for the tea, Olivia. I hope I didn't alarm you sitting here being maudlin like this.'

'Of course not,' said Liv.

I didn't know what 'maudlin' meant for sure, but I got the gist of it. 'Are you sure you're all right, Gran?'

'I'll be fine, I'd just like a bit of time alone to – to take it all in. It's brought back a lot of memories, this news, and at my age that can be upsetting.' She said, and smiled apologetically. She went to pick up the letter that was sitting on the table and paused. Then she said something odd. 'Have a read of it yourselves, girls. Maybe someone will write you a letter like this one day, although I hope under happier circumstances. And then she went upstairs.

We both pounced on it.

There were two sheets, the first one read like this:

Dear Mrs Fitzgibbon,

I have been asked to contact you on behalf of my late father, who just passed away yesterday, having been ill with cancer for the past two years. I am his eldest son and we were very close.

Some time ago, when he realised he did not have much time left, he asked me to post a letter he had written, after he had passed away, to your address, in the hope that you would receive it. I have enclosed this letter, as he asked, for your attention alone, also marked personal. I hope that God willing, whatever he wanted to say in his final days, it finds its way to you.

With best wishes,

Sincerely,

Felipe san de Segovia Suarez

But it was the next one that gobsmacked us. As they say on *Xposé*, take a look.

My beloved Vera,

It has been how long now since we parted? Forty-three years, I think, if my memory serves me correctly, during which time not a day has gone by that I have not thought of you.

I have not much time left now, cancer has me in its

final grip, but I cannot complain, I have had a rich and rewarding life and have been blessed with a loving family.

My only regret is how I had to leave you that final day in Dublin, a day which I have tried many times without success to forget. How it tears at my heart, even still.

Vera, mi amor, I want you to know you were the love of my life. The one and only. I am hoping you are still alive, still in Dublin, that charming little city which holds so many precious memories for me, and that you have had the happy and consoling life you so deserved. If so, I pray this letter will have found its way to you. Read it sometimes and think of me – fondly, I hope. The world we lived in was so very different then, was it not? I have so often wished that life could have turned out differently for us. Leaving you was the most difficult thing I have ever had to do.

So once again, my darling Vera, another goodbye, but if God is good to me, I will be waiting, impatiently, my love, until the day when we must surely meet again.

Until then, I hold you as I have always done, from the first moment I set eyes on you, my beloved – in my heart and in my soul. You have been in every breath I ever took, and always will be, up until the last.

Felipe

'Wow,' said Olivia, sounding impressed. 'That's some letter. Imagine someone being in love with Gran like that. I wonder who he was?'

'He was obviously Spanish, whoever he was. A waiter, maybe? A holiday romance?' I suggested.

'Yeah, maybe.' Olivia put the letters back into the envelope carefully. 'She didn't want to talk about him. It must have been back in the day, all right. No one writes letters like that any more.'

'Not even Guy?' I risked.

'He can barely send a text,' she said darkly, and then we both laughed. 'Better give this back to Gran,' she said handing me the letter. 'And don't say anything to Mum about it either.'

'Why not?'

'Cos love letters from absent boyfriends, however elderly, will only remind her of Dad, won't they?' She gave me a look. 'He hasn't exactly been in close contact, has he? Anyway, I have to go now.'

'Why don't you stay for dinner? Mum would love to see you.' I ignored the previous remark.

'Can't. I've got to meet some people and I'm working later. Oh, I almost forgot, I left something for you, it's on your bed. Let me know how you get on on Saturday. And text me if you need to.'

'Thanks, Liv,' I said as I closed the door behind her.

When I went upstairs, Gran's door was closed, so I gently pushed her letter under it. I went into my room. and there on the bed, all laid out, was my favourite outfit I had tried on in A-Wear. Liv must have gone back and bought it for me. She had also got a really cool belt and matching satchel bag in really soft butter-coloured leather to go with it as well. Wow! What had I done to deserve this? And it wasn't even my birthday!

Later that evening, we all sat down for dinner as usual. I told Mum about Olivia dropping in and buying me the outfit for Saturday. I said she really would have liked to stay for dinner but she had to work. Mum looked pleased and said, 'What a pity I missed her.' And when Gran smiled and said how well Olivia was looking, Mum commented, 'Vera, are you coming down with something? You look a bit peaky.'

Gran just said, 'Conjunctivitis – I've always been a martyr to it. Other than that I'm absolutely fine.' And she winked at me.

I said nothing, just like Olivia had warned me to.

Like I said, my family's weird – but not in such a bad way, I'm beginning to think.

Charlie

Right along the shores of Table Bay, at the Atlantic Beach Golf Club, I hit a particularly good drive straight down the fairway.

'Nice one,' said John, my neighbour, who was playing eighteen holes with me on this perfect autumnal Cape Town day. It was April and there was a fairly healthy breeze getting up, but the glorious setting, in the shade of Table Mountain with the ocean rolling beside us, made it about as idyllic as it gets. I was playing well today, for no apparent reason – except, perhaps, the fact that I didn't know when or how long it would be before I would be able to play a game of golf again. Once things had fallen into place, everything began to happen very quickly.

First of all, I met with Annika, naturally, and her husband Greg. Once the initial introductions and first awkward ten or fifteen minutes were behind us, it had been a pleasant if serious evening. Annika had suggested dinner at The Grand, one of Camp Bay's most popular restaurants, which was easy for all of us. We met upstairs in the bar first, for a drink, and despite the bevy of beautiful people eagerly thronging along the bar, I recognised her immediately. She was still an incredible-looking woman, and there were a lot of them in the room, believe me – tall, blonde, with striking features, but it was something in her expression, an earnestness, a sort of desperate hopefulness that singled her out. Her husband, Greg, was equally good-looking. An ex-Springbok, he had the powerful build of an athlete and clearly kept in shape. They made a ridiculously handsome couple. I immediately felt every one of my stressed out forty-eight years. Greg, I learned, now ran a sports marketing business and clearly they were well off, although I had gathered that from our earlier correspondence. He hovered protectively by her side, glancing at her continually, as if he was afraid she would falter or come to some unseen harm. It was obvious how in love they were. Envious, admiring glances covertly followed them from around the room. I was struck then, suddenly, by loneliness, a swift, powerful longing for Shelley and the way things used to be between us. How had this happened? How did a couple so thoroughly in love as we had once been end up so far apart we couldn't even talk without vicious accusations being hurled? Where had we gone so wrong?

I remembered the first time I had met Shelley, at a party in Dublin. I had broken up with Caroline, who had gone off to do her masters in Harvard, and secretly, part of me had been relieved she'd turned me down. I had loved Caroline at the time, no doubt about it – she had been my first love and a guy doesn't forget that kind of thing easily. She was brilliant, Caroline, had the finest mind of anyone I knew, and she was ambitious, sometimes terrifyingly so. Proposing to her seemed like the natural thing to do at the time, but afterwards, when I met Shelley, I realised what a lucky escape it had been for me that Caroline turned me down then. Despite her brilliance and her magnetic personality, there was something always hovering beneath the surface with Caroline, something brittle, fragile even, but I don't mean that in the classical feminine way. It was more like an uneven surface, a fault line that could rupture and break at any given moment. She could fly off the handle at the slightest thing and be moody and low for days afterwards, and then, just as suddenly, return to her sunny, dynamic, good nature, the cracks in our

volatile relationship mutually and quickly papered over until
we had our next explosive row. We weren't good for each
other. Now, of course, I know that poor old Caroline isn't
good for herself, either, and she certainly wouldn't have made
a good mother, not then – at least not the kind of mother I
wanted for any children I might have. She wouldn't have had
the patience, the temperament for parenting. Making her
mark on the world and her career was everything to Caroline,
but I don't think children, any more than marriage, ever
figured in her plans. Although maybe they would have been
the best thing that could have happened to her – who knows?

Anyway, that night that I met Shelley, I was drawn to her
straight away. It wasn't a kind of blinding attraction, a *coup
de foudre*, as the French say, but there was something incredibly alluring about her. She was with a pal of hers, a striking,
flashy-looking bird who had been trying to chat me up, but
it was Shelley, with her big green eyes, her warm smile and
gentle manner that got my attention. I thought she was
gorgeous. So I asked for her number, and later that week I
called her up and asked her out to a movie and dinner. My
first impressions didn't let me down either. She was so easy
to be with, not loud or raucous, although when she laughed,
which was quite a lot (I love that about her), it was the most
infectious sound I'd ever heard. She had a wicked sense of
humour too, once she got over her natural reserve. Quite
simply, Shelley was everything I'd ever looked for in a woman
– gorgeous, natural, sexy, fun and kind – that's a quality that's
very underestimated these days, but it's one of the most important. The only trouble with Shelley was that she couldn't or
wouldn't think of herself as others did. She was pretty insecure – make that *very* insecure – I have no idea why. She
had always been popular, never had a shortage of boyfriends,
and everywhere we went I could see men looking at her,
drawn to her, probably in the very same way I was – but she

just didn't get it. It was part of her charm, I guess, and most of the time it didn't bother me, unless it got out of control, and that didn't become apparent until we were married. For some reason I could never fathom, she became really bothered by 'other women'. Oh, I know it isn't easy to be married to a guy like me, I'm a complete extrovert, always have been, and I love women – but that's as far as it goes. I realise, too, that it can be tough for a stay-at-home wife, alone with only the kids all day for company, but being a wife and mother was all Shelley ever wanted to be – she said so herself, repeatedly. But when my business took off and I had to be away more often, work longer and longer days or we had to entertain or be entertained constantly, she just seemed to grow more and more insecure. I did my best to constantly reassure her, but nothing I said or did seemed to make any difference. I had never looked at another woman since I met Shelley, nor did I want to, not *that* way.

And then one day Caroline called me up, about two years ago, right out of the blue. She was in trouble. She'd been let go (well, they had given her the option of resigning with a decent redundancy package) from her job in London and she was in an awful state when she rang me. But that was the least of her problems, as it turned out. It wasn't until I had talked to her mother at length that I realised quite what had happened, or the implications thereof. I had to help her. She was my best and oldest friend, my first love, and she had never married. That's the trouble with careers – no matter how well you do, when something goes wrong, they won't take care of you when you're sick or in trouble. Caroline's mother was at her wits' end about it all. So of course I wanted to help – what else would I do? Between us we got her the help she needed, and then, when she had recovered, I organised for her to work on a consultancy basis for my company, Celtic Crest Investments. I even gave her the use of an apartment until she got back on her feet again. I knew she'd get better, and she did, and she was so grateful to me it was pitiful.

But I never would have guessed, not in a million years, how Shelley would react when she heard Caroline was back in the country and working with me. She completely flipped, saying Caroline was still in love with me and had designs on me, and well, you know, the usual stuff women go on with when they feel threatened by another woman. I couldn't tell her the truth, Caroline had a right to privacy. Mental illness of any kind is difficult enough without broadcasting it to the world in general, especially in a town as small as Dublin – especially when you worked in the financial sector. Caroline was the best I knew at what she did. She'd had a tough break and deserved all the help and support she could get, and I wasn't going to let her down on that front. But Caroline being back in town and working with me, well, Shelley didn't like it, she didn't like it at all, and it was from that point, really, that our marriage began to deteriorate.

But that evening, when I first met Annika and Greg together, and listened to them as they spoke about their life and their little family, well, it brought back a lot of stuff for me, stuff that I really didn't want to think about right then, so I concentrated on the most important matter to hand – Jack's sickness and his need for a suitable kidney. Of course I volunteered to be screened immediately, that was the main reason for going to Cape Town, apart from the fact that I needed space to do some serious thinking. It was the least I could do in the circumstances, although the look of joy and gratitude on Annika's face when I told her would have melted the hardest of hearts. What I really wanted to do, more than anything, was to meet Jack, but we all decided that would be best left until later. Annika didn't want to say anything to him that might get his hopes up unnecessarily. Instead, the very next day, I headed out to Groote Schuur Hospital to begin the tests that would take about a month in total, all going well.

Annika

The private investigator Greg hired, Mike O'Reilly, was a nice guy from a reputable firm, younger looking than I expected, but then, I didn't have any dealings with detectives on a regular basis, so who was I to have an opinion? He called around to the house, listened carefully to everything we said, took the relevant details and promised to get back to us as soon as possible. He reckoned it would take about a week or two, explaining that with the internet and other various high-tech tracking systems, it was a lot easier to trace someone these days unless they particularly wanted to disappear. I assured him I didn't think that would be the case here, but asked him to be as discreet as possible. For all I knew, there could be, and more than likely was, a wife and family involved on your dad's side – one who presumably would not welcome this unexpected intrusion into their lives.

'Don't worry, Mrs Hanson,' he said as he was leaving, 'as situations go, this one is pretty straightforward, and I can assure you discretion will be guaranteed.'

'Well, good luck then,' said Greg and we closed the door.

The days following that were difficult. I had no idea what to expect. What if he couldn't find your dad? What if, when he did, he thought this was a scam? Or refused to co-operate? I couldn't eat, sleep or sit still. And all the while, it was painfully obvious you were going downhill.

So when two days later my phone rang and Mike O'Reilly's number showed up, I was both surprised and pretty scared.

'Mrs Hanson?'

'Yes?'

'I made progress more quickly than I anticipated.'

'You've found him?'

'Well, yes, in a manner of speaking.' He paused, 'I think it's better if I call around and discuss this in person. Is your husband there now?'

'No, not right now, but he can be here in about half an hour, maybe twenty minutes. Can't you tell me whatever it is on the phone?'

'I'd prefer to talk to you both, if that's possible. Can we meet at your place in half an hour? I'm in the vicinity anyway.'

'Of course.' I quickly rang Greg and asked him to come home.

'He has news already?' he asked me, sounding upbeat.

'Sounds like it, but he was cagey, Greg, and he wouldn't tell me over the phone.'

'Don't worry, hon, we'll find out soon enough.'

Half an hour later, we were sitting with Mike over coffee, and I felt as every nerve end I had was screaming.

'Well?' said Greg, putting his arm around me. 'What's this news you have about Jack's dad?'

'We found him all right, that didn't take long,' said Mike. 'That's not the problem.'

'There's a problem?' I could feel Greg tensing.

'What is it?' I asked, holding my breath.

'Patrick Fitzgibbon is dead. He was killed in a car wreck almost ten years ago,' Mike said matter-of-factly. 'In fact, judging by the death certificate, he was dead before your Jack was even born. I'm very sorry, Mrs Hanson.'

'Oh no,' I heard myself murmur.

'You're sure about that?' Greg pressed.

'Absolutely, I have all the details and records here. It happened outside Toronto.'

'Well that's it then,' I said, feeling hopelessness envelop me.

'Actually, that's what I wanted to talk to you about. It may not be the end of the road, not quite.'

'What do you mean?' Greg asked.

'Patrick, the *late* Patrick Fitzgibbon, has a younger brother, Charlie Fitzgibbon. He lives in Dublin and he's married, with three children. With your permission, I could approach him about this. It might be worth a shot.'

'You have a contact address for him?'

'Yes I do, Mr Hanson, his company address and email.'

'Oh my God,' I said, desperate to clutch at any straw. 'That's wonderful. Of course we should contact him, but I'll do it myself, if that's okay.'

'Whatever you like, but I have to warn you, Mrs Hanson, he won't know anything about Jack – or you, more likely than not. People can react in different ways, sometimes aggressively, to being approached about this sort of thing. It might not be easy, is what I'm trying to say, so if you need me to confirm anything for you, I'm just at the end of a phone.'

'Anni,' Greg was serious, 'do you really think this is the right thing to do? It might be better to let Mike approach this, in a professional capacity. I don't want you getting hurt.'

'I'm sure it's the right thing to do – it's the only thing to do. We're running out of time. This guy, this Charlie Fitzgibbon, needs to know that I – that we're – genuine. I think it's better if I approach him myself, maybe he'll agree to talk to me. Then I can convince him and we'll take it from there.'

So that's what we did. Charlie was cautious at first, and understandably suspicious, but it only took a few emails and a phone conversation to convince him I wasn't some scam artist. And there was something I liked about the guy right away, something in his voice, although he almost always sounded incredibly weary when we spoke. At any rate, he agreed to come out to Cape Town and see what he could do to help. Then we didn't hear anything at all for a while, and then suddenly, the phone call saying, 'I'm here, I'm in town, when can we meet?'

Charlie

So here I am in South Africa.

I came for many reasons, not just to investigate and see for myself this new person who had presented herself in my life, this Annika and her son, my late brother's son, if she was to be believed.

I came here, as you now know, to get away – from my collectively collapsed business, marriage, life and, if at all possible, from myself. Cowardly, yes, for sure – I admit that. But you know that saying 'between a rock and a hard place'?

So I holed up in this house in Camps Bay that a mate of mine in England let me stay in. It was decent of him – he doesn't know how decent – because if I hadn't been able to go AWOL for a while, I don't know what I'd have done. I had enough cash to live on for a while, and after that – well, I couldn't really think about more than one day at a time. But once I had settled into a fairly mindless routine and my mind had stopped racing, I did a lot of thinking. And then, right before I decided on anything, I went to see Jack.

I went to *see* him, I said, not to meet him – that would come later. It was easy. I had Annika's address by then, although at the time I'm referring to, she didn't know I was out here. So I waited in the hired car I was driving until I saw a woman who had to be Annika, bundling three kids into her car and driving the short distance to the beach. I followed at a discreet distance. After she'd parked the car, I waited for a while, and then, with my shades on and baseball cap pulled well down, I strolled down the beach with my gear and set up shop behind them all, far away enough not to be noticed behind my newspaper but close enough to watch, and what I saw effected me more than I thought possible. Looking at the three kids, two girls and the boy, quite a bit smaller looking than his ten years would suggest, looking at that boy who was Jack, could *only* be Jack, was like looking at a younger, blonder clone of my own son, Mac – the resemblance was quite extraordinary. Except he wasn't demonstrating that mad exuberance that Mac, or indeed any ten- or eleven-year-old boy, usually did at the beach. On the contrary, Jack seemed quiet and withdrawn, hovering at the water's edge kicking sand while his sisters swam and splashed each other. After a bit he went back to his mum and there seemed to be a lot of fiddling with something that was attached to his tummy – I learned later it was a peritoneal catheter. Then there was a conversation and his mum taking him by the shoulders, looking into his eyes earnestly, and then some angry tears from Jack. The look of despair on his mother's face really got to me, but not as much as Jack wiping his tears away minutes later, apologising to his mum and sitting down to read a book, trying not to look at his sisters and failing hopelessly to disguise how miserable he was not to go in the water that day. After that, I didn't have to think or wonder any more – I just had to act.

So I met with Annika and Greg, said I was more than willing to volunteer as a donor, and I went to have all the necessary tests. The blood group was the crucial one, and fortunately I was a match. Apparently that was a big break-through, and even better, Jack and I matched for HLA antigens. And that day, when I was playing golf? I was waiting for the last test of the lot, a final CT scan of my kidneys to check for normal renal vasculature and anatomy. That came back clear too, so it was all stations go. I had a meeting with a social worker at Groote Schuur, Annika and I signed the necessary consent forms and then it was all scheduled for the following week. But first, I had to meet Jack.

Caroline

'Caroline, what are you doing?'

Christ, it was *her* again. She was all over me like a rash these past few days.

'What does it look like I'm doing?' I replied tersely, folding a particularly nice white silk top I had bought carefully into the case.

'Well, you appear to be packing. Are you going somewhere?'

'Yes, Mother, I am,' I sighed.

'And where, exactly, are you going if you don't mind my asking?' She was hovering at the door with that inquisitive look on her face.

'Actually, I do. It's none of your business.' I was way beyond pleasantries. My adrenaline was pumping and I couldn't wait to get out of there and head for the airport.

'Isn't this a bit . . . sudden?'

'I move where the spirit takes me, as you well know, strike while the iron's hot and all that.' I surveyed the array of swimwear carefully laid out on the bed.

'What iron would that be?'

I looked up at her. 'Excuse me?'

'I think I have a right to know what you're doing and where you are going, Caroline. I *am* your mother.'

'Actually, you don't have any right. You're living in *my* house, remember?'

'And you know perfectly well *why* I'm living in your house.'

'Oh just shut up, will you? You're driving me mad!' I shook my head, trying to clear it, to concentrate on the task in hand. I would ignore her – she would go away.

'Caroline, just calm down for a moment.'

'I'm perfectly calm, thank you. If you would just leave me alone in my own room – I have a right to *some* privacy, surely?'

'These clothes, Caroline, you've been shopping again.'

'My, but you're perceptive today.'

'But you don't even like shopping, Caroline. The last time . . .'

'The last time was a mistake. They made a mistake.'

'That's not how the store detective saw it.'

'I have paid for every one of these items.'

'How?'

'My company credit card hasn't been maxed out yet.'

'Oh dear.' She was sitting on the bed now, looking nervous. 'Caroline, just tell me, sweetheart – where do you think you're off to?'

What am I, a kid? 'I'm off to Cape Town.'

'Why Cape Town?'

'Because that's where Charlie, is.'

'Charlie? Charlie Fitzgibbon?'

'No, Charlie Chaplin.' What was she, stupid?

'Caroline, pet, listen to me.'

'No, you listen to *me*. Charlie is out there, and I'm flying out to join him and we're getting married there – that's all there is to it – and you're not invited.'

'Oh, dear God.'

'And don't think you can stop me. Anyway, why the face, Mother? You should be happy, this is what you've always wanted – me and Charlie, Charlie and me.'

'Caroline.' She was speaking very slowly now, annunciating every syllable as if I might not understand her. 'What makes you think that Charlie Fitzgibbon is in Cape Town?'

'I found the emails. I phoned the number on them and the woman confirmed he was indeed in Cape Town.'

'What emails? What woman?'

'The woman he had a child with, the woman who deliberately got herself pregnant – *that* woman. I saw it all in the emails, hidden in his office – the emails I gave to Shelley.'

'Oh, mother of God!'

'Yes, I don't think she was very happy about them, but Shelley doesn't understand Charlie the way I do. That's why he left her. That's why I have to go out there and show him that I *do* understand him. I'm the only person in the world who ever understood him. We're meant to be together – we've always been meant for each other.' I paused for breath.

'Caroline . . . ?'

'What?'

'You haven't been taking your medication, have you, pet?'

She was trying to be nice to me now, trying to trick me, but I wasn't going to fall for it – not this time.'

'I don't know what you're talking about,' I said crossly. 'And if you don't mind, I have a suitcase to pack and a plane to catch.'

'Caroline, answer me. When was the last time you took your medication?'

I wasn't going to listen to this. I put my hands over my ears and began to sing, 'la-la-la I can't hear you, la-la-la I'm leaving on a jet pla-a-n-e, don't know when I'll be—'

'Stop it, Caroline!' she cried. 'Stop it, you have to listen to me!' She was in front of me now, pulling my hands away from my ears.

'Leave me alone!' I screamed. 'I have to pack, Charlie is waiting for me!' I took her by the shoulders and shook her. I wanted to shake her until her teeth rattled. And then she hit me – whacked me right across the face.

'Oh, Caroline.' She was backing away from me now, white faced.

For a moment I was so shocked I just stood there, my hand to my burning face.

'Caroline, I'm sorry, pet,' she was gibbering, 'please forgive me, but I have to do this, you're not well, pet, *you're not well.* You must know that you're not.'

And I watched her, curiously, as she got smaller and smaller, as she backed out of my room, but not before she'd whipped the key out of the lock and closed the door behind her. I realised too late what she was doing and hurled myself after her, towards the door, but I tripped and fell over some really nice platform sandals I had bought for our wedding on the beach. As I got to my feet, I heard the lock turn. I banged on the door to no avail. 'Let me out! Let me out, you *bitch!*' I yelled. But all I could hear were her retreating footsteps hastening down the stairs.

Charlie

It strikes me that the only operation I've ever had, if you could even call it that, was having my wisdom teeth removed more years ago than I care to remember. Other than that, the only time I've been in hospitals is when Shelley was having the kids or I was visiting somebody. Hospitals don't bother me, they're just one of many random topics running through my head as I wait to be wheeled down to theatre.

It's a small room I'm lying in, like any other hospital room. The nurse comes in to administer pre-op.

'Hey, Charlie,' she says, 'here we go. Sure you don't want to change your mind?' she jokes. We've become mates, Letitia and I, although I was only admitted yesterday morning. She is big and black, with kind eyes and a wicked sense of humour. She moves with surprising speed for her size. 'This'll make you feel a bit sleepy,' she says. We'll be taking you down in about an hour – any last requests?'

'A stiff gin and tonic?' I say.

'I'll have it on drip when you come around,' she grins. 'Charlie?' She pauses at the end of the bed. 'This is a really brave thing you're doing, and generous – about as generous as it gets.'

'Don't go getting emotional on me, Letitia,' I say. 'I'm counting on you to get me through this. Did I mention I have a fear of scalpels?'

'You won't even see it coming.'

It is eight in the morning and I've been awake since five.

I wasn't prepared for how busy a hospital would be. Efficiency by rota – *Take this pill to go to sleep. Wake up! Time for your morning cup of tea*. Squeaking of professional soles on squeaky-clean floors, clanking trolleys of tea, biscuits, newspapers and medical equipment. Brusque, alpha male surgeons, quiet, hushed conferrals – all part of the collective noise. My surgeon is not an alpha male – at least I don't think so. I've never quite understood that term anyway, but Shelley uses it a lot. She used to say we were impossible to live with but that women loved us anyway. *We. Us.* Just words.

Doctor Williams is small and softly spoken, with quick, piercing eyes and an unusually wrinkled forehead. I liked him immediately. A man of few words, he doesn't beat about the bush. Letitia has informed me that he's brilliant in his field.

Eight thirty-five a.m.

I look at the date on my watch, sitting on the bedside locker beside me. It's April 11 – something about that date rings a bell – I should know – but I'm yawning now and I can't remember.

Eight forty a.m.

Letitia is back. 'One last check,' she says.

'For my vital organs?'

'Nope, we need those. What we don't need is your watch, *check*. Any dental plates, bridge work, you gotta lose those – *check*.' She pretends to peer into my mouth.

'Please, Letitia, do I look like a denture wearer?'

'You got nice teeth, honey, nice smile too.'

'Thank you.'

'Nail polish?' She checks my toes.

'Not last time I looked.'

'Good, can't be too careful. We gotta keep an eye on your tootsies in theatre in case they turn blue.'

'Thank you for sharing that.'

'My pleasure.' She exits.

Eight forty-five a.m.

I think of Jack.

We finally meet at Greg and Annika's house, Jack's home. I arrive with a Chelsea team shirt – Mac's team. He's their number-one supporter. I'm nervous, and I wonder why.

'Hello,' says Jack. 'You didn't have to bring anything for me, but thanks anyway.' He opens the shirt and puts it on. 'Excellent,' he says with a wide grin, although the shirt is much too big for him. 'I'm small for my age – it's part of my kidney thing, y'know? But I'll grow into it.' He seems wise beyond his years, serious, and I think of Mac, constantly giddy and laughing, and wonder if he has become serious too, now that he's had to grow up so quickly these past few months.

'Nice to finally meet you, Jack,' I say.

'Nice to meet you too, Uncle Charlie,' he grins. 'You're my birth father's brother, right?'

'Yes, Jack, that's right.'

'It's sad that he was killed in a car crash. Do you miss him?'

The question takes me aback. 'Yes, I do miss him, but he lived in Canada for a long time, so I got used to him being away.'

'Still, a brother's a brother, right?'

'Right.'

'I have two sisters. I wish I had a brother.'

'My son Mac is only a year older than you. I think you'd get along very well,' I say, 'although he's only a cousin.'

'Is he on Facebook?'

'I'm pretty sure he is.'

'Cool. I really appreciate this, Uncle Charlie,' he says suddenly, and without prompting. 'What you're doing for me, giving me your kidney, it's really nice of you.' He is solemn again, and I feel tears threaten.

'My pleasure,' I say. 'You are more than welcome to it. I hope it works well for you.'

'Yeah,' he grins again. 'That'd be cool. Dialysis is gross.'

'It's kept you alive and healthy, Jack,' says Annika, reprovingly.

'Only just.' He turns to me. 'I really hate not being able to go straight in the water whenever I want to without worrying about exit sites and catheters. I want to be a professional surfer,' he explains.

'Sounds good to me,' I say. And at that moment, looking into his eager, determined little face, I wish my brother was here to see him, this great little boy – *his son*.

'Your dad would be really proud of you – your birth dad, I mean,' I hurriedly correct myself.

'Greg's my real dad, though,' he smiles as Annika and Greg share a hug.

'We're a team, mate,' says Greg. 'You and me against the girls, yeah?'

And with a swift stab of loneliness, I realise that is exactly what I always say to Mac.

Eight fifty a.m.

Letitia re-enters my room, accompanied by a hospital porter. They unhook my bed and begin to wheel me out. I think of Shelley, my children, and I wish Shelley could be there when I come around.

'Good to go, Charlie?' It's Letitia, marching by my side.

'Can't wait,' I quip. 'Can't this thing go any faster?'

A lift, another corridor, a bend and then the double doors of the theatre loom. The gowned up team are waiting. Doctor William's voice comes through his surgical mask. 'Morning, Charlie. Word on the street is you've a spare kidney going?' His eyes are twinkling and I hear a smile in his voice.

'It's all yours, Doc,' I say.

'Good man.' He nods at the anaesthetist. 'Let's go, Jules.

Hope you like Bowie, Charlie. He's our current favourite in theatre.' Suddenly, the strains of David Bowie's 'We Can be Heroes' fills the room.

'You'll just feel a tiny prick,' says Jules as the needle enters my vein.

It's the soundtrack that does it. This was Patrick's favourite song – he used to play Bowie constantly. And that's when I remember – today, April 11, was his birthday. I think maybe, I am doing something for my brother he would be very pleased about – I hope so, anyway. That's my last thought as the coldness hits my arm and I go under.

Annika

Charlie is being operated on at nine a.m. Greg and I wanted to go see him yesterday in Groote Shuur, but he said not to bother, that he was fine, that in fact he'd prefer to just go ahead with as little fuss as possible. I can kind of understand that. All the same, I'm worried about Charlie. He's a long way from home, from his family. He doesn't say much about his life in Ireland. He says he came out here because he lost his business and he was having marital problems, and of course to meet you and ultimately (I still can't believe this) give you a kidney. The whole thing is kind of surreal for us. He showed us a photo of his wife, Shelley and his three children, Olivia, Emma and Mac, and they seemed such a lovely, happy bunch – but photographs can be misleading. You don't get the full three-dimensional story. I wanted to ask him about them, probe a bit, but Greg told me not to. He said it wasn't any of our business, that it wouldn't be fair. Maybe he's right, but I just wanted to help. After all, we're family now, in a way even more so after this operation.

We're sitting here, with you, here in the hospital and you are perversely excited. I had expected nerves, perhaps even tears – for all your bravado, hospitals can be scary places for kids. But no, you are worse than a kid on Christmas Eve waiting for Santa Claus. It's not that I'm not excited too – I am, of course I am – it's just that I know the risks, the chance that the kidney might not work or perhaps fail at a later date, and I cannot even contemplate it. I feel sick.

You have taken your oral immunosuppression medication and are frantically texting on your mobile, no doubt to your sisters, who wanted to come in too, but Greg and I persuaded them to wait until they could see you after the operation.

It is eleven a.m. now, and I wonder how Charlie is doing.

The nurse comes in to administer pre-op. 'This'll make you feel a little sleepy, Jack,' she says, smiling.

'I don't want to feel sleepy,' you say, 'I want to be wide awake right till the last minute. Does this mean I'm going to theatre soon?'

'Maybe,' grins the nurse, then she comes over to Greg and I and murmurs, 'I thought you might like to know, they've just harvested the donor kidney. All going well, it should be with us in about half an hour – we've just got the call from Groote Schuur.' She squeezes my arm.

'Oh thank you, that's great news.'

'Good luck,' she says.

I try to imagine it, and can't. My brain is racing too much. It's about a twenty-minute journey from Groote Schuur Hospital to here, the Red Cross Children's Hospital. Charlie's kidney would be packed up in ice and driven down through Mowbray, usually choc-a-bloc with taxis, then down onto the highway for about 700 metres before turning off for Red Cross next to Rondebosch Common. It would be rushed to theatre here, washed out with special transplant solution, and then . . . I can't think further than that right now.

'Okay, young man?' It was Nurse Brophy back again. Almost an hour had passed but it felt like minutes. 'There's a kidney with your name on it waiting in theatre for you – ready to go?'

'*Yes!*' you say, giving Greg a high five. 'Let's go!'

We say goodbye to the other kids on the nephrology ward who wish you luck. Two of them are in for post-transplant infetions and rejection complications – but I push this from my mind. We walk with you as you are wheeled the short distance to the theatre two floors down and I have to leave you. I had wanted to go right in with you to theatre until you were put asleep but you didn't want me to. You said, 'I'm not a little kid, Mum.' But that's exactly what you are – my boy, my precious little boy. So Greg and I agreed earlier to leave you and say goodbye outside.

'How are you feeling Jack? Ready to go?' It was our surgeon, Doctor Vourse.

'You bet.'

'Right, we're ready to rock here,' he smiles at us. I'm struggling to hold back tears. 'Don't worry, Mum,' he says to me, 'we'll take good care of him.'

'See you guys.' You can't wait to be rid of us. I can't speak, so luckily Greg does it for me. 'We'll be right here when you wake up, mate.'

'Cool,' you say. 'I'll be the kid with the new kidney.'

And then the theatre doors close, and I burst into tears.

Vera

.

It is April the eleventh – my late son Patrick's birthday. He would have been fifty today, had he lived. Middle aged, *heading up the ladder*, as Arthur used to say laughingly about both of us as we grew older. And yet I can remember the day Patrick was born as if it were yesterday. That's a mother's lot. No forgetting. Today I do what I always do on my children's birthdays – start the day with seven thirty Mass at our local Poor Clare convent. It's a small chapel, intimate, and has a dedicated band of regulars. It's not that I'm particularly religious – I'm not – but I've always been fond of the Poor Clares. They live what so many others merely preach about, in total poverty, withdrawn from the world to pray for all of us lot. And if you really want something? Something important? Well, I have a tip for you, whatever religious persuasion you're of or whatever you believe or don't believe. Go along to your local Poor Clare or Carmelite convent, give them a little money, whatever you can afford, and ask them to pray for your intention. Then sit back and fasten your seat belt. You might think I'm mad, but it really works. They have a hotline to heaven.

Anyway, as I was saying, I'm not particularly religious, but I do go to Mass occasionally, and especially on my boys' birthdays. Just to give thanks for them, and of course for my recovery. They were difficult years, those black years, and I couldn't be the kind of mother I wanted or needed to be to my sons, which still fills me with sorrow and guilt. And now they're gone. Patrick's dead, and Charlie? Well, it would appear I'm dead to him whatever way I look at it.

I worry about him, though, constantly. Where is he? Why has he run away like this? Is he in some sort of terrible trouble we don't know about? Perhaps I will never know. At least I have his family in my life now, even if I don't have my son. That was a blessing I certainly hadn't been expecting.

I have the house to myself this morning, and it's one of the days I'm not working, so Maura and Tom and I have arranged to meet for lunch. I'm looking forward to it. Maura was sorely missed in the shop during her bout of swine flu, and she had to take it easy for quite a bit afterwards. She's been back for a few weeks now, but we haven't had a chance to catch up properly. And Tom is always good, if acerbic, company. We are meeting in a little Italian restaurant in a village convenient for all of us, and on the Dart line, although I will probably take the car.

There's been a lot going on lately. Mac had his twelfth birthday, which brought him the astonishing opportunity to fulfil his lifelong wish to see Chelsea play at home at Stamford Bridge, all courtesy of this Russian billionaire who seems to have taken such an interest in Shelley. The whole thing was a resounding success and Mac hasn't stopped talking about it – and who could blame him? But it's Shelley I'm worried about. She still never talks about Charlie, and somehow I have a feeling she's hiding something, or perhaps not acknowledging something to herself. I'm probably miles off the mark here, but it's just a feeling I have. Still, who am I to question her behaviour? We're all healthy and reasonably happy, or at least functioning. And it's none of my business, even if I would very much like it to be.

After a bit of vigorous housework (good for building an appetite), lunchtime comes around and I drive to the restaurant. Maura and Tom are there before me, both with a glass of red beside them. I'm greeted heartily.

'I hope I'm not late.'

'No,' says Tom, tapping his watch, 'bang on time, we just pipped you to the post.'

'Oh, good.' I settle myself and order some water and glance at the menu, although we almost always order the same things, creatures of habit that we are.

We chat about the usual things, the weather, the shop, and I mention that it is (or would have been) Patrick's birthday today. I could say anything to Tom and Maura, they are my closest friends these days, and I love them both dearly.

Maura pats my arm. 'You poor dear.'

'How's the rest of the family getting on?' asks Tom.

'They're all well, as much as they can be, I suppose, under the circumstances.'

And then Tom asks the crucial question. 'Any word on Charlie?'

I shake my head. 'Not that I know of.' I pause, fork in midair. 'I just don't understand it, any of it, this running away business. I can't claim to have been close to my son, but even so, it just seems completely out of character. And so, well, cowardly.' There – I had said it.

'Don't be too sure about that, Vera.' It was Tom again, looking thoughtful. 'Who knows what he's going through?'

'What about what he's putting his family through?' I was angry today and I didn't know why.

'I remember reading something about people who disappeared, deliberately went missing,' Maura chips in, 'and it was likened to the same mindset of a person attempting suicide, a sort of cry for help.'

'A desire for oblivion, to walk away from your life. Yes,' says Tom, mulling it over, 'I can relate to that.'

'You?' Maura picks up her glass and puts it down again.

'Yes, me.' He continues mildly. 'There was a time in my

life when I seriously considered ending it all. Thankfully, I didn't. I was married then, and living in London – the swinging sixties,' he adds by way of explanation.

'You were married? I never knew that!'

'Very few people do, and most of them are dead now. But yes, I was married – I just never had any . . . how shall I put this delicately . . . carnal inclinations.'

Now Maura and I look at him incredulously.

'And it's not what you're thinking – I'm not gay, either, just . . . disinterested, really. Although my wife was a gorgeous girl, I was terribly in love with her, but the physical side of things, well, it was a bit of a disaster, as you can imagine. I thought she could change me, but, well . . .' he sighs. 'Anyway, she deserved better, much better. The marriage only lasted briefly. She remarried not long afterwards, happily, I might add, and had a lovely family of her own. In fact, I'm god-father to her eldest daughter.'

'Oh, Tom, I'm so sorry.' Maura looks dismayed. 'How sad.'

'But I'm not sad, not *now*, that's the point I'm trying to make. But I was terribly sad when I was trying to pretend I was someone I couldn't be. The pressure nearly killed me. So you see, what I'm trying to say is you never really know what's going on in other people's lives, even if they seem happy and picture perfect on the outside.'

'And you're sure you're not gay?' Maura was riveted.

'Positive. I adore women. As I said, I'm just not interested in that side of things. I'm happy living on my own with my books and my music.'

'But you're so attractive.' The words are out before I can stop them, and Tom grinned, quite wolfishly.

'Thank you, Vera darling, and I'm vain enough to say I've always taken pride in my appearance, but that made it all the more complicated. It gave off the wrong signals to women. I must have been a terrible let down to them.'

'You should have been a priest,' says Maura, practical as always.

'The uniform would have bored me to death, you know what a clotheshorse I am,' he grins. 'And spirituality has never been my strong suit either, if you'll excuse the pun. All I'm saying is you shouldn't judge your Charlie, not until you've heard his side of the story at any rate.'

'Not much chance of that as things stand,' I say miserably.

'At least you know he's alive,' says Tom firmly.

'We don't – not really, not for sure. I don't know anything about his whereabouts, except for silly rumours.'

'Have you involved the police?'

'Not as regards tracing him, no. I think that's for Shelley, his wife, to decide, and she, well, she doesn't want to seem to talk about it.'

'Who could blame her?' says Maura, shooting Tom a warning look that I pick up on immediately.

'What?' I ask, looking at them both inquisitively while Maura blushes, then blows her nose to try to disguise the fact.

'Ahem.' That was Tom, looking sternly at Maura. 'Since honesty seems to be the theme of our little get together today, you should tell her, Maura.'

'Tell me what?' I demand. They were hiding something from me.

'Oh Tom, it's nobody's business, and certainly none of ours,' Maura says sharply.

'There's been talk – in the shop,' Tom announces.

'Talk?' I repeat disbelievingly, 'in the shop?'

Maura looks simultaneously angry with Tom and flustered. 'I told you not to say anything!' She looks at me apologetically. 'It's only silly talk, Vera, nothing definite, concrete.'

'About what?'

'Go on, tell her,' Tom instructs.

'Well, you know Barbara was away on holidays . . .'

'Yes, vaguely. I remember someone mentioning she was away, the place has been blessedly calm without her.'

'Well, she was in South Africa.'

'Cape Town,' Tom confirms.

'And when she came back, well,' Maura takes a deep breath, 'she insisted she'd seen your Charlie in a café there, or restaurant or something.'

'In the company of a beautiful blonde woman,' Tom adds meaningfully.

'But you know what Barbara's like, such a busybody.'

'Yes, I do.'

'It's probably a lot of nonsense. Her imagination getting the better of her. You know how she dramatises everything.'

'On the other hand . . .' Tom lets the words hang in the air.

'Oh dear,' I say, suddenly losing my appetite.

'I told you not to say anything. Now look what you've done.'

'No, no, not at all, Maura. I'd much rather hear it, not be kept in the dark.'

'Precisely,' nods Tom, 'so would I.'

'Besides, she doesn't know your Charlie, does she? Never set eyes on him.'

'But there was an awful lot of press about it at the time,' I remind her, 'when the business went – and pictures of him.'

'Speaking of which,' It was Tom again, and this time Maura shoots him a look that would have reduced lesser mortals to squirming misery.

'Tom, no.'

'Let's have it,' I say.

'Barbara took the liberty of photographing the event – on her mobile phone.'

'Oh no,' I whisper.

'Don't worry,' says Tom. 'We warned her on no account

to show it to anyone, and I do think we got through to her, but I did get her to print out a copy. I thought you had a right to see it, Vera.' He reaches inside his breast pocket and pulls out a small photographic print and hands it to me.

As I look at it carefully, that shot of a couple looking intently at each other across a small table, two things immediately become apparent to me. Firstly, unless he has a doppelganger, the man was indeed Charlie. And secondly, the woman he was with was an exceedingly beautiful blonde. I'm not sure which realisation threw me the most.

Later that evening, at home watching television, I catch part of a documentary about a woman who had donated her kidney to her nephew. For some reason, I find the whole thing very moving. They seem such a loving, united group as they all talk about the whole thing, and I find myself wondering for the umpteenth time how some people manage to be part of such loyal and supportive families.

Seeing that photograph had shocked me more than I'd let on. I can't get it out of my head. But what should I do? For all I know, Shelley may very well be aware of where Charlie is and who he is consorting with. I resolve not to say anything about it. No good could come of it, and it might not even be Charlie in the photograph – although I know that's prob-ably wishful thinking on my part.

Instead, I pull myself together and focus on something positive. I have an adorable twelve-year-old grandson who is willing to take the time to teach his old grandmother how to use the computer. If that isn't family love in action, what is?

Shelley

I was trying to behave as if everything is normal when my surreal life has taken a turn for the insane. *If I keep showing up*, I thought, *if I keep going about my duties in the gallery, typing invoices, dusting sculpture, making tea for Ernie, I can pretend everything is normal, ticking over.* I almost succeeded. Ernie was being tactful for a change, saying very little, but he had taken to whistling a cheery tune as he pottered about, which was driving me mad. When it happened, when the phone call came, I just thanked God I was alone.

'Ernie's Eclectic Art,' I said automatically as I picked up the call.

'Shelley?' a woman's voice on the other end of the line asked brightly.

'Yes, this is Shelley,' I replied, wondering if I should recognise it.

'Shelley Fitzgibbon?'

'Yes, can I help you?'

'Yes,' she continued, 'you certainly can. Would you like to tell me what it's like dating a Russian billionaire?'

I gasped.

'Our readers would be very interested to know, Shelley. Would you confirm rumours that you have been seen in Lukaz Mihailov's company both in restaurants and, indeed, boarding his private plane – with your son?'

'I – I have no comment to make,' I managed to gibber.

And then, just before I put down the phone, I heard her

clearly continue, 'Does your husband, Charlie, know about this friendship with Lukaz? Have you heard from him recently? Is it true that—'

I banged down the phone. My hands were trembling. It rang again immediately. I tried to ignore it, but after half an hour of solid ringing I wanted to scream, both out of frustration and terror. So I took it off the hook. I sat there, numbly white faced and shaking, and that was how Ernie found me when he came in at ten o'clock.

'Melly, dear, whatever is the matter?'

So I told him, the words tripping over themselves, and he listened and tut-tutted, making soothing noises.

'You leave this to me, Melly,' he said firmly. 'Go and make us both a stiff cup of tea, and then I think you should go home. Take the rest of the day off.'

The phone rang again and he picked it up. 'No, this is Ernie Huggard, and no, Melly is not available for comment, but I can confirm that I represent Lukaz Mihailov in the capacity of art consultant, and— Oh,' he said, sounding disappointed, 'she hung up on me. How *rude*. No manners, these people, no manners at all.'

I brought him his tea but couldn't stomach any myself. I was too upset.

'I don't want you worrying about all this, Melly, just leave it all to me. I'll get rid of them. Really, what a nerve they have.' He took a sip of his tea and I noticed that he was looking pleased, delighted even, although he was trying hard to be disapproving. Of course Ernie would love this – it was good for business apart from anything else, and he was quite a gossip himself at the best of times. I even found myself wondering if he was responsible for this, if he had leaked something to the press, and then felt immediately guilty. I owed Ernie a lot. I wouldn't have been able to get through the past couple of months without this job.

'You're sure you can manage without me today?' I said as I grabbed my coat.

'What? Yes, yes, of course, Melly.' He waved me off. 'Don't worry your little head about this. I know how to handle the media, I can tell you. If they think they can tangle with me or my employees and clients, they are sadly mistaken.'

'Well,' I said doubtfully, 'if you're sure.'

'Go on with you!'

I ducked out the door, furtively looking left and right as if I were about to be set upon. I hurried to the nearest taxi rank – sod the expense, I had to get home, away from that ringing phone. At least the media wouldn't have Vera's number. I would go home, and then I would think about all of this.

When I got in, there was no one home, thank God. Vera was out, but it wasn't one of her days in the shop, so she could come in at any moment. I threw my coat off, made a cup of tea and sat down to try to collect my thoughts.

How had this happened? When had I appeared to lose all control of my life, not to mention a husband and daughter. And more to the point, how was I now being spoken of in the same conversation as a Russian billionaire? *Dating* a Russian billionaire? Because I wasn't – was I?

It had all started with that trip to Christie's, when Lukaz flew us to London. Up until then it had been strictly business – still weird, but these things happen, I suppose, except usually not in my world. But until then there had only been the odd lunch or three, and Ernie often accompanied us. Sure, I would have been seen out and about with Lukaz, but then he was an unknown, just another (very rich) art collector. But of course it was only a matter of time before people got hold of the fact that he was an oligarch. We hadn't had our share of them in Dublin, at least not to my knowledge anyway. But Ernie was beside himself with delight at having nabbed him, in a professional capacity. He had already made enough through his dealings with Lukaz to retire all over again, very, very comfortably.

But that night in London, when Lukaz took me out to dinner in Nobu and told me that he knew Charlie – I'll never forget it. I felt as if I was losing my mind, going through the whole dreadful scenario again of Charlie leaving, and wondering if everyone around me knew more about my own husband than I did. I really thought I was going to fall apart then. It was just a step too far. But then Lukaz had been so kind, so understanding, so open about his own life, that I found myself talking to him, really talking, opening up to him in a way I couldn't or wouldn't with anyone for as long as I could remember – and it was such a relief. Despite being in one of the poshest restaurants in London, in a private dining room, we could have been sitting across a kitchen table from one another. Despite all his vast wealth, Lukaz was actually a very simple man, forthright, and I found that enormously reassuring. Simple was good. I could do simple – it was 'complex' and 'intriguing' I wanted to run screaming from. Only my husband, who was both, had apparently run, screaming or otherwise, from me.

And then there had been the incredible trip Lukaz had organised for Mac that I was able to give him as a birthday present. I still couldn't believe it. It had been sheer magic to see his face light up when he heard. I felt as if I had got my little boy back at last. And the trip itself had been amazing. We had flown over with Lukaz – me, Mac and two of his chums, and the crew had served Big Macs to the boys. I think that impressed them more than the Gulfstream. Then we went straight to Fulham Road, into Stamford Bridge Stadium, and I thought the boys were going to self-combust with excitement. I'm not a huge soccer fan, but even I got caught up in it, you couldn't not have.

We were in the west stand, and while Lukaz and I enjoyed

our VIP lunch in the Directors' Dining Room, the boys had burgers and chips. Then it was into one of the Millennium Suites. Ours was the Harris Suite, named after Ron Harris, and we settled down to watch Chelsea play West Ham. The whole thing was unforgettable. By the end of it the boys were completely hoarse from screaming, and as luck would have it, Chelsea won. Then it was back to City Airport and the flight home, and that evening, even though I was already exhausted, I took Mac, Vera, Emma and Olivia, who had deigned to join us on account of it being Mac's birthday, to Eddie Rockets. I've never known a boy to eat so many burgers in one day, but it was worth it all, just to see Mac electrified with excitement. He could hardly eat he was so busy telling Vera and the girls about it all, although Olivia was trying to appear unimpressed. But she had bought Mac a lovely present of an Xbox game and some iTunes vouchers, and although she was cool and distant with me, the evening was another great success.

By the time we got home, Mac was practically asleep on his feet. But there was one surprise waiting – Vera's next-door neighbour had dropped in a gift handed to her by a woman walking a dog, she said, and it was addressed to Mac. It was an iPhone, and there was a note with it that Mac wouldn't let anyone see. It was from his dad, he said. 'I knew he wouldn't forget my birthday,' he said triumphantly. And that, apparently, was the best birthday present of all. Ever since then, he's been a different boy. I feel I've got my son back – and I have Lukaz to thank for that in no small way.

Since then, well, we've been spending more time with each other, Lukaz and I. I've had dinner with him several times, and on each occasion he always behaves impeccably, nothing at all inappropriate. It's just like having a lovely – all right, sexy and extremely rich – new friend in my life who is beginning to feel like an old one. Lukaz makes me laugh, and it's fun to look at the world through his eyes – he's had such an extraordinary life. It does feel strange, though, having dinner with another man, even if it's entirely innocent. And Vera never says anything, except things like, 'Have a lovely time, Shelley dear,' which makes me feel incredibly guilty. She never asks me anything about where I'm going or what exactly is going on, which is just as well, because I'm not sure I know myself. Emma hasn't said anything either, although I've caught her throwing the odd speculative glance my way. I feel as if I'm on some sort of trial and that everyone's watching me, waiting for me to trip up or do something awful, and then all hell will break loose. But I can't think about that any more than I can think about Charlie or what *he's* doing. I'm having fun for the first time in what feels like centuries, and guilty conscience or not, I'm enjoying it.

And that's the thing that frightens me most of all – that I could go along like this thinking nothing would happen, that no one would notice that I was spending time with a Russian billionaire – I mean, how stupid can you get? But that's exactly how stupid I was, because all I could think about, even after that awful reporter's phone call at the office, was our last lovely dinner together, and how, this coming weekend, Lukaz had asked me to spend the weekend at his country estate, just an hour or so outside Dublin.

'Of course you will have your own room, a suite of rooms, Shelley – that goes without question,' he said to me that night. 'But I would love to show you the place. I have done quite a bit of work to it, and we could go to the races on Saturday afternoon, have a quiet day on Sunday and I will have you back home early on Sunday evening. What about it?'

When I hemmed and hawed, he continued, 'Don't you think it would do you good to get out of Dublin for a couple of days, away from your mother-in-law? I know how fond of her you have become, but it can't be easy for you being there *all* the time.'

He was right, of course. I was dying to accept his invitation, absolutely dying to, but I was terrified too – not of Lukaz, but of what I would say. What would I tell my children, Vera? *Well everyone, I'm off for the weekend with my good friend Lukaz, see you Sunday, cheerio!* I just couldn't even begin to imagine it. But then a sneaky little voice would remind me that Emma was going to Brussels on a school trip that weekend (Vera had insisted on chipping in and giving it to her as an advance birthday gift) and Mac could easily stay with one of his pals if he wanted to, or even with Vera – although Lukaz had suggested I bring the kids along too if that was a problem.

The more I thought about it, the more appealing some time on my own with just adult company was becoming. Then I would squirm with apprehension at the thought of bringing up the subject with Vera. *You don't have to tell her*, the little voice reasoned, *you could say you were staying with a girlfriend.* And even though I knew she would never probe for any details, the thought of lying to her after all she had done for us was even more awful. It was ironic, I thought. I was forty-five years old and equally afraid of my children and my mother-in-law's opinion of me – or was it that I was simply afraid of myself and my own selfish desires? Spending time with Lukaz was reminding me again that I was a woman – something that had slipped my mind over the past few months in favour of other, more practical issues. And suddenly, out of nowhere, I found myself wanting to respond to that feeling of desirability. I was so tired of being the abandoned wife with a marriage in limbo, tired of being a single parent to the kids even if they were being wonderful (well, Emma and Mac at any rate). I wanted to escape from my life for a couple of days, to just be a woman in the company of an extremely attractive man who was making me feel a flicker of something I had long ago buried inside me. I didn't

want to think about Charlie. I was sick of thinking about
Charlie, sick of his hovering ghost wherever I was, whoever
I was with. If Charlie could go AWOL indefinitely, what was
wrong with me taking a couple of days off? There wasn't
anything wrong with it, I reasoned, it's just that whatever way
I looked at it, I felt this crushing guilt.

After a lot more agonising, I decided to be brave and to
bite the bullet. I was a grown woman, for heaven's sake, not
a teenager. So later that evening, when Emma was in the
bath and Mac was in the kitchen on his computer, I broached
the subject tentatively with Vera, who was watching television with me.

'Um,' I began, 'I was just wondering . . .'

Vera looked at me, interested. 'Hmm?'

'I – well, that is, you know my friend Lukaz, who, um . . .'

'Of course I know Lukaz, your Russian friend who brought
Mac on that wonderful trip.'

'Yes, well, he's invited me down to see his country estate
in Kildare at the weekend. There's a race meeting at the
Curragh, and I was wondering, well, what you thought about
that.'

'What *I* thought about that?'

'Well, yes, if you'd, um mind.'

'Why on earth would I mind, Shelley? What a thing to
think!'

'But it would be for the weekend, you know, Friday till
Sunday evening.'

'I do know what a weekend is, Shelley,' she looked at me
archly. 'I think that sounds like a lovely invitation, if you want
my opinion. Where is it, this estate of his? I'm sure you've
mentioned it, but I can't recall.'

'It's just outside Celbridge.'

'Of course, I'm sure I read something about it. I love that
part of the country, Arthur and I used to spend lots of

weekends with friends in the country around Kildare. Arthur was very keen on the horses, he loved going to the races, just didn't often have the time to do it. It'll be lovely to get out of town, and with the new motorway I'm sure it takes half the time it used to in my day.'

'It's just that . . .' I struggled to find the right words. 'Well, I'm worried what the children might think.'

Vera looked at me keenly. 'They'll think whatever you tell them to think. Shelley, dear, it's absolutely none of my business, and I don't know, nor do I want to pry, about what happened or didn't happen between you and Charlie, but you might want to think about yourself a bit more – about, well, taking the reins up in your own life again. You're an attractive young woman with the rest of your life ahead of you. You have a right to a life of your own.'

'Thank you, Vera, but I'm hardly a spring chicken.' I could hardly believe what I was hearing. Was my own mother-in-law encouraging me to get out there again?

'Take it from me, forty-five is young,' she went on, 'and you've been dealt a tough hand over the past year, a very tough hand, and for what it's worth, I think you've handled things remarkably well in the circumstances. I think, as the Americans say, you need to cut yourself some slack. It's your life too, you know, and it goes by terribly quickly. As I said, it's none of my business, but this Lukaz man seems like a nice chap. You certainly seem to be in better spirits these past few weeks, and I don't think there is anything wrong with spending a few lovely days in the country with him. As for the children, you can't live your whole life according to their opinions. Emma's away this weekend, isn't she?'

I nodded.

'And Mac, well, I'm not sure he's come down from whatever planet he's been on since that trip, but he's welcome to have a friend stay here if he likes, or I'm sure he'll be happy to go and stay with one of his many soccer-mad pals. Forgive me if I sound brusque about it, but they'll probably hardly notice you're away. And I would tell them the exact truth – that you're spending the weekend with your friend Lukaz at his country place. If anyone has any views on the subject, we can deal with it then.'

'I suppose you're right,' I said. This certainly wasn't the reaction I'd expected from Vera. But there was something else, something in her expression I couldn't quite read. It was terribly reassuring to hear she was on my side, but it was almost as if she knew something, something that was making her encourage me – and then I reproved myself. I was becoming completely paranoid of late. It must have been that phone call from the journalist that did it. Vera was just being her usual sensible, non-judgemental self. She really was an incredible woman. I was almost going to tell her about the phone call at the office and then thought the better of it. What was the point in worrying her?

The weekend came, and late Friday morning found me with a heavily packed bag but a considerably lighter heart. Vera had been right, as usual. Emma had set off early that morning with her school chums and barely registered me mentioning that I was spending the weekend at Lukaz's stud farm.

'Can I borrow your hair straighteners, Mum?' she asked distractedly the day before. 'Now that Olivia's gone I've no one to nick stuff from.'

Even though I had planned on taking them with me, I gladly gave them to her.

'Brilliant,' she said, 'have a great time.' And that was the end of that.

Mac was equally dismissive. 'Oh good, 'cos I've been asked to go to Rocky's house tomorrow. Some of the lads are staying over, so does that mean I can too?'

'Only if you leave Gran the number and I can ring to check with Rocky's mother beforehand,' I said firmly. I may have been flustered, but I wasn't stupid.

'Mum!' he protested. I'm twelve years old, I'm not a kid.'

'Fine, then you can stay here with Gran and have a friend over if you'd prefer.'

He glowered at me and mumbled something reproachful.

'It's a phone call, Mac, it's what parents do – vigilant parents, at any rate,' I reasoned.

'Dad wouldn't give me this hassle.'

That pulled me up in my tracks. It was the first time Mac had used the situation against me, and I was stung. 'Dad isn't here,' I said crisply. 'If he was, I can assure you he would agree with me.'

'Your mother's right,' said Vera, intervening quickly. 'It's only for your own good, Mac.'

'Fine, whatever.'

'Good,' I said, refusing to feel guilty. 'Then get Rocky to give me his mother's number and I'll give her a ring.'

'When?'

'No time like the present.'

'She'll be at work,' he said defiantly.

Rocky Smith's parents were both high-powered medics. The father was a neurosurgeon and the mother a plastic surgeon, and while I admired and respected them enormously, they seemed to work around the clock and spend remarkably little time at home. Rocky was the class character, and like his three older brothers, a sports star, but the thought of what might very well turn out to be an unsupervised gathering of like-minded twelve-year-olds . . . well, those of you with teenage sons will know what I mean.

'So I'll leave a message,' I said, 'and she can ring me back.'

After a phone call and much incoherent mumbling, Mac returned from the hall and gave me a mobile number. I duly rang it and left a message for Mrs Smith, asking her to ring me and confirm that there had indeed been an invitation extended to my son Mac, because like all twelve-year-olds, he tended to be confused about such details sometimes.

Around lunchtime on Friday, Mrs Smith did ring me back. She sounded like a nice woman, if brusque. 'Hello, Shelley, is it? Wendy Smith here. Yes, your Mac's more than welcome to come around tonight, Rocky's having a few of the pals over, they probably want to watch lots of unsuitable movies and so forth, but don't worry, my husband will be there. I'm at a conference this weekend, but Harry will make sure there's no nonsense. Can you have him picked up on Saturday? Can't stand having them hanging around all day, my four are bad enough. What? No, no trouble at all. Mac's very sought after these days since his trip to Stamford Bridge, sounded amazing. I can tell you it's raised the bar for the rest of us,' she laughed heartily. 'Mac and the other boys can come anytime from after school today – Rocky's brother, Philip, will give them a lift. Must dash, I'm due in theatre now, cheerio!'

Feeling considerably better about the prospect, and being the bearer of good news to Mac, who was naturally elated, although studiously pretending not to be, I left the relevant numbers with Vera and had made sure Wendy, Rocky's mother, had Vera's number, just in case.

Which meant that once I had packed Mac's overnight bag for him, when two o'clock came around and I was picked up by Lukaz's driver, I was able to set off with a happy sense of expectation. I said goodbye to Vera, who was on her way out herself shortly, and thanked her.

'You're sure you'll be all right with everything Vera?' I suddenly felt guilty leaving her all alone.

'Perfect. I shall enjoy myself, Shelley, and you make sure you do too. I'm looking forward to hearing all about this wonderful estate. Oh,' she said, suddenly fishing in her purse, 'that reminds me. If you think of it, would you put a tenner on number five in the two thirty tomorrow – only if you're going to the Curragh,' she added anxiously, handing me the ten euro note. 'Otherwise I can go to the local bookie – I got a hot tip from Tom at the shop,' she explained. 'He says it's a sure thing, which probably means the poor horse will trail in last, but I enjoy an occasional flutter.'

'Of course I will, I'll be glad to, but keep your money, I'd be delighted to stand you this.'

'No, I insist. I've always been a stickler for standing over my own bets – put your money where your mouth is and all that.'

Suddenly I hugged her, and although she was a little surprised, I think she was pleased. 'Thank you, Vera. I don't know what I would have done without you these past few months, really I don't. I don't know what would have become of us. You've been so good, so generous.'

'Nonsense,' she said, going a little pink, 'but I'm glad to have been able to help a little. Have a lovely weekend, Shelley dear, and don't worry about a thing.'

So I didn't. I sat back in the Maybach, leafed through a magazine absentmindedly and gazed out at the canal sparkling in the late morning sunlight, admiring the swans that glided serenely along. Then it was on to the motorway and we picked up speed.

I must have dozed off then for a bit, because when I woke up we were turning off a small country road. I checked my watch and it was ten past three. I rubbed my eyes as the car turned slowly through a set of huge wrought iron gates, and then looming up ahead of me was the most beautiful house I had ever seen. Rossborough Demesne was like a mini Versailles. A perfectly proportioned Palladian villa, it waited, bathed in mid-afternoon sunlight, at the end of a mile long driveway, on either side of which sat immaculately manicured lawns complete with fountains.

A man in traditional butler's uniform opened the door, and then Lukaz appeared from a room to the left of the vast tiled hall. 'Shelley,' he said, kissing me on the cheek, 'welcome to Rossborough Demesne. Igor, 'he instructed the driver, 'take Mrs Fitzgibbon's bag to the Hawthorn suite. How about a glass of champagne, Shelley? I have some chilling in the library. Come in, sit down and tell me about your week.'

'It's beautiful, Lukaz, so impressive,' I said as I followed him into the library. 'I had imagined something lovely, of course, but—' I was about to say words failed me, because they did.

'What? You imagine some over-the-top Russian monstrosity?' he grinned.

'No, of course not, but this is, well, just exquisite.'

'I'm glad it meets with your approval. I will show you around later, and tomorrow morning we can see the stables. I need to meet with my trainer for an hour or so in the morning. You are welcome to join me, or you could have a rest. It's up to you entirely.'

I sank down gratefully into one of the enormous sofas on either side of the fireplace, in which a perfect log fire was burning, and we chatted. As I sipped the champagne and listened to Bach playing softly in the background, I began to feel the week wash off me. Lukaz had been down here for ten days already and was looking the better for it, definitely more relaxed, although something told me he was never, ever off guard. Afterwards, I went to settle into my room, which I fell in love with instantly. It was painted a beautiful Wedgewood blue with high ceilings and almost floor length multi-paned windows. At the far end, was an Adam style fire-place and the delicate furniture was perfectly in period with a magnificent Chippendale cabinet sitting between the wondows and a pair of darling Hepplewhite chairs against the wall. The bed, which was enormous, was invitingly feminine and decorated in glazed blue and white sprigged cotton. I felt as if I had walked straight on to a film set of *Pride and Prejudice*. Then Lukaz showed me around, quietly proud of his beautiful home, as he had every right to be.

That evening we had dinner at home, served in the library at a beautiful George III round table set in a small alcove off the main room. Afterwards we had coffee by the fire and I found myself suddenly dog tired. At about ten thirty I could hardly keep my eyes open.

'Dinner was lovely, Lukaz, thank you. I really enjoyed it, but would you mind if I went to bed now? I'm suddenly exhausted.'

'Of course not, you must go upstairs immediately. If there's anything you need, just dial zero and my housekeeper will take care of it.' He stood up and walked with me into the hall, and taking my arm, gently kissed my cheek. 'Goodnight, Shelley,' he said, 'I hope you sleep well. I usually have breakfast here in the library, but I will be going to meet my trainer at ten thirty. If I don't see you, I will assume you are having a well-deserved rest and breakfast in bed. I should be back by about twelve.'

'The breakfast in bed bit sounds very appealing,' I said, heading for the stairs. 'Goodnight, Lukaz.'

As I undressed and cleansed my face and crawled into the huge bed, I wondered if I should ring Vera to make sure everything was all right, but then my head hit the feather-soft pillow and before I knew it, I was fast asleep.

When I woke up, sun was streaming through the gap in the curtains, and checking my watch, I was stunned to see it was already ten o'clock. I had slept like a baby for the first time in months. I had a leisurely bath (the luxury of it!), pulled on my jeans and a top and went downstairs and headed in to the library. As if on cue, the butler, whose name I didn't know, appeared silently and enquired gravely if I might be requiring breakfast. 'Oh, thank you,' I said. 'Um, just some tea and toast would be lovely, thanks.'

'Very good, madam.' He disappeared. I noticed all the morning papers were laid out on the table and had a quick flick through the *Irish Times*. The tea and toast – and croissants and muffins and a selection of equally delicious-looking pastries – materialised minutes later. When I had finished and was wondering what to do with myself, I heard the front door open and Lukaz's voice in the hall. As his footsteps approached, I suddenly felt a little shiver of excitement.

'Good morning, Shelley,' he said, coming in. 'Did you sleep well?'

'Like a log.'

'That's good?' He looked perplexed.

'Very good,' I explained. 'I haven't slept so well in ages.'

'Good, must be the fresh air.'

'I haven't really had any, though.'

'Let's do that now, then. Would you like to look at the stables? We have a few beautiful mares and foals at the moment.' He checked his watch. 'And then we need to leave for the Curragh, yes?'

'Lovely,' I said.

I had a guided tour of the yard and the stables, and admired the adorable foals shyly staying close to their mothers.

Then it was time for me to go and get changed for the races. I'd brought a chocolate brown suit and my favourite camel coat which was last season's Max Mara and covered a multitude, as they say. But I knew the Curragh of old and how cold it could be if a wind whipped up, which judging by the forecast was very probable, rain too. There was already a good crowd there when we arrived and we made out way through to the lifts and then up to Lukaz's private box. He had invited a few other guests too – a local vet and his wife, some business people and, of course, his trainer, who popped in and out throughout the afternoon. The rest of us just enjoyed the delicious buffet lunch being served washed down with liberal amounts of champagne. I had a really lovely time and I even managed not to forget to put Vera's bet on for the two thirty, which turned out to an excruciatingly close finish, although her horse won by a nose. I was delighted and texted her immediately. *Yes!* came the reply. *Very exciting, watching it here on the telly. Have a glass of champagne on me! V.*

That evening, Lukaz took to me to dinner in a well-known local country house restaurant, and as I looked at the menu, I couldn't help thinking how relaxed I felt in his company, and how nice it was to just be me for a while, not think about work or responsibilities or, well, anything. It would all come flooding back tomorrow but, for tonight, I just wanted to enjoy the weekend as much as I could.

The food was excellent, straightforward and unpretentious. I had a delicious fillet steak and Lukaz a sirloin. We shared a bottle of red. Afterwards, when we were ordering dessert, although I didn't feel as if I could eat another thing, I discovered I was perfectly able to polish off a sublime apple and blackberry crumble with lashings of cream. Seems the fresh air had given me an appetite. Then I made a remarkable discovery – Lukaz had never had an Irish coffee.

'I don't believe you!' I said. 'You've dined in the most exclusive restaurants all over the world and you've never had an Irish coffee?'

'Is that an offence?'

'One that we shall have to rectify immediately.' So we both had one, and Lukaz remained unconvinced, so we had to have another. By the third he was a convert. In the Maybach back I felt warm and woozy, and as Lukaz casually put his arm around me, I snuggled into him, my head on his shoulder.

Back at the house, there was coffee waiting and a roaring fire in the grate. The silent butler hovered by the door.

'I think we need another Irish coffee, don't you?' Lukaz prodded the fire.

'Definitely.' I collapsed into a sofa.

'Two Irish coffees, thank you, Gavin, and then that will be all for tonight,' Lukaz said to his butler, who now had a name, I realised.

'Immediately, sir.' He coughed discreetly, and I saw a look of approval on his face for the first time. 'They happen to be a speciality of mine.'

'Imagine that,' I whispered when he had glided out the door.

'Hmm,' said Lukaz, 'Gavin is full of surprises. I don't think he approves of me – I am not enough of the English gentleman for him.'

'But this is Ireland,' I pointed out, and for some reason we found this particularly amusing.

About halfway through our Irish coffee, Lukaz flicked a remote control and the sound of Nina Simone flooded the room, crooning 'My Baby Just Cares for Me'. He got up then and gently pulled me to my feet.

'Dance with me, Shelley?' Something in the way he looked at me made it seem like another very good idea. It was so effortless to slip into his arms, to move slowly to the music, Lukaz laughing softly, holding me close, and it was only then I realised how much I wanted, no, *needed* to be held by a man, especially a strong man, a man who could kill with his bare hands, one of which now moved expertly along my spine and found the knot of tension exactly around my third vertebra that had plagued me for months and kneaded it intuitively, magically relieving it.

'Oh – oh, that feels so good,' I heard myself murmur.

'How about this?' He was kissing that spot at the crook of my neck and collarbone that I had forgotten existed, but now every nerve ending had suddenly come to life. Then he tilted my face to his and kissed me, slowly, thoroughly, and I found myself responding eagerly, melting against him as if my body had turned to liquid. We kissed like that for quite a while, and then Lukaz broke away and said, 'Come to bed with me, Shelley.'

And I wanted to – I really did. Every cell in my body was shouting yes, but there was something nudging at the back of my mind, as insistent as my desire to be swept away to Lukaz's bed. I tried to shut it out. *I need this, I deserve this,* I thought as Nina launched into summertime and living being easy, and then I shook my head and pulled away.

'What is it, Shelley?' Lukaz looked concerned.

'I'm sorry, Lukaz, I just can't do this.' I remembered, not that I could ever forget, dancing with someone else a long time ago to that song. Someone I was madly in love with then. 'Summertime' was our song. Mine and Charlie's.

'I'm so sorry, Lukaz, I just—'

'You are still in love with him, aren't you?' He smiled ruefully at me.

'I – I don't know. I hate him. I don't know anything any more.' And whether it was the confusion, the guilt or too many Irish coffees, I began to cry.

'Hey, hey.' Lukaz pulled me close again. 'It's okay, shh, it's okay. You are not ready, and I understand that.'

'Do you?' I felt horrible, as if I had been leading him on. Well, I had – there was no two ways about that. But it was wishful thinking, bravado. Suddenly, what had felt so delicious minutes ago felt – I wasn't sure what it felt. I was just horribly confused.

'We will go to bed, Shelley – our own beds, much as I would like you to accompany me to mine. I have never had to persuade a woman to do something she has not wanted to, and I certainly don't want to start now,' Lukaz, sighed. 'Forgive me if I have taken things too quickly, but you are an extremely attractive woman, and I am only a man.'

'I'm so s—'

'Shh, no more apologies. After a good night's sleep it will all seem better in the morning. We will laugh about it, yes?'

I wasn't so sure about that, but I managed a weak smile.

'Shelley, there is no rush. I can be a very patient man. Come.' He led me by the hand and I followed him upstairs, where he kissed me briefly outside my room and murmured, 'Sweet dreams.'

I didn't have any, needless to say – sweet dreams, that is. I had the presence of mind to drink lots of water and knock back the Alka-Seltzer that had thoughtfully been placed on the bedside table, and then I must have passed out. But I woke up at four a.m. and tossed and turned, panic surging through my veins at the thought of what had almost happened – and the possible consequences if it had. What had I been thinking? Was I mad? Coming here had been an awful, stupid mistake. The thought of facing Lukaz in the morning was almost more than I could bear. I slept on and off fitfully, my semi-consciousness interspersed with dreams of Charlie walking along a beautiful beach, hand in hand with a gorgeous blonde whose face then morphed disconcertingly into Caroline's – and there was a little boy whose face I couldn't see, swimming in the sea, and a great white shark was slicing through the water in his direction. I wanted to scream and couldn't, and woke up again bathed in a cold sweat. By seven I couldn't stand it any longer. I got up, had a bath, tried to bring my face back to life a bit and headed downstairs with the idea of going for an early morning walk to clear my head. But as soon as I got downstairs, I heard Lukaz call me, his voice coming from the library. 'Shelley? Is that you?'

I went in and saw him sitting on the sofa, immaculately dressed, looking as fresh as a daisy. He'd probably already done his two-hour workout for the day – the man was unbelievable. I was prepared to feel sheepish, incredibly awkward, but something in his expression took me aback. He seemed concerned, preoccupied, angry, even.

'Shelley.' He stood up and walked over to me, and I knew there was something wrong.

'What?' I asked, suddenly afraid. 'What is it?'

'Have some breakfast, Shelley, then we can talk.'

'Talk? About what?'

'I had hoped this would not happen, at least not yet, but unfortunately . . .' He gestured towards the footstool, where a number of Sunday papers lay opened, and then he picked one up and handed it to me. 'I had hoped you would not be subjected to this sort of thing, but I'm afraid it eventually follows me wherever I go. I have become used to it, but it is not easy for other people. I wanted to protect you from it – but it's better that you see it.'

I looked at the double-page spread in the reasonably respectable tabloid newspaper, one favoured by Vera, and gasped as I sank onto the sofa, hardly believing what I saw. The first thing that struck me were the shots – one of me and Charlie, taken at a function about two years ago, another smaller one of Charlie at a business meeting, looking stern, and various grainy shots of me and Lukaz, obviously taken from a distance or by mobile phone, emerging from a well-known restaurant and one of me going up the steps to his Gulfstream. They had managed to lose Ernie from that one, although he would have been two steps behind me. The headline read 'Cheeky Charlie Fitzgibbon loses out to the Russians'. It went on to say that 'Shelley Fitzgibbon, abandoned wife of ruined businessman Charlie Fitzgibbon, is taking comfort, it would appear, from her close friendship with Russian oligarch, Lukaz Mihailov. The couple have been seen out and about recently in various restaurants in the city and even taking a trip abroad in the oligarch's jet . . .'

The other paper, a broadsheet with the biggest circulation in the country, was equally explicit. 'Why lose sleep over losing a millionaire when you can pick up a billionaire?' asked the article, written by a woman who, under the guise of supporting divorced, newly single women made me sound like a menacingly predatory gold-digger. 'In a turnaround for abandoned women everywhere, Shelley Fitzgibbon has struck a fantastic blow for wives who've been traded in for a younger, racier model by trading up herself to a newer, not to mention considerably richer and indeed powerful man – none other than the elusively single Lukaz Mihailov . . .'

I didn't bother reading any further, the words were already swimming before my eyes, because here, in this paper, there was another shot of Charlie on a beach in Cape Town, and beside him was the same beautiful blonde, applying sun lotion to a little boy, and that was when I felt my heart twist. The little boy was looking straight into the camera, as if he was looking directly at me. And it could have been Mac, right down to the gap-toothed grin and the lock of hair that fell straight into his eyes. He was smaller and skinnier, and the hair was blonder, but that was all. Suddenly I couldn't speak. I couldn't do anything, I just sat there, frozen.

'Shelley, I know this is difficult for you, but please, come, have something to eat, some breakfast, and we can talk about this.'

'No, no, you don't understand,' I was gibbering. 'I – I have to go home now, *now* Lukaz, this minute.' A million thoughts were racing through my mind, all of them vying for blood-curdling awfulness. Vera – my children, oh God, what would they think, what could I do? I had to get home – I *had* to.

'Of course, Shelley, I understand. I have the car waiting outside, but you must eat something before you go – really, it will only take a few moments.'

He was right, I knew, but my stomach was churning almost as much as my head. I had never wanted to get out of anywhere as much in my life. My hangover had been banished, replaced by a sickening dread that was far more menacing.

I sat down gingerly at the table while Lukaz poured me tea and I managed to make a half-hearted attempt to eat a piece of toast. All the while he encouraged me, gently, as if talking to a small child.

'Tea is good, toast too, it is important to regulate your blood sugar, very bad travelling on an empty stomach, no?'

I wanted to scream at him to shut up. Didn't he realise what was left of my pathetic life was crumbling around me as I sat there, trapped in this house of horrors? I knew I was being unfair about it. It wasn't Lukaz's fault, it was mine – I had stuck my head in the sand, thought of nothing but my own selfish escape and enjoyment, and for the second time this year had shown a blinding contempt for my family, my . . . I couldn't even bring myself to say the word marriage, not even to myself. I just wanted to crawl under a stone and never come out – but I wanted to do it at home. Or rather, Vera's home. Vera – oh God, what time was it? Seven thirty . . . maybe I could make it back in time before she got the papers. What time did she go out to get them? I couldn't remember . . .

'Shelley, please, talk to me.' Lukaz's voice intruded on my mental litany of potential disasters.

'What do you want me to say?' My voice was flat. 'What a hoot, my children will get such a kick out of this, their mother, the abandoned wife turned gold-digging, third-rate celebrity. Have you any idea what it's going to be like for them going into school with this crap? And my mother-in-law, Vera, oh God.' I put my face in my hands. The shame. What would I say? Worse, what would *she* say? Vera, the most respectable woman in Dublin . . .

'I know all this is horrible for you now.' Lukaz was talking again and I wished he would stop. 'But you have done nothing wrong, Shelley. I will have my people on this immediately, but there is only so much I can control. The media, well, you know what it's like.'

'I do now,' I said bitterly.

'I will drive you home myself, and—'

'No!' I almost shouted. Then, 'I'm sorry, Lukaz, I know this isn't your fault, but I need to go home alone, I need to think what to say.'

'Very well,' he sighed. 'I understand. Igor will take you – as I said, the car is outside.' He sounded weary now and I almost felt sorry for him, but was still churning with fear, with rage, against myself, but I hated him too, for his stupid money, his obscene wealth that had brought this mayhem into my life. *And whose fault is that?* said the little voice. *You didn't exactly discourage him, did you? Shelley, the abandoned wife. Wasn't there a certain amount of satisfaction that this enigmatic man was clearly finding you so attractive? You didn't mind that at all, did you?*

'I need to get my things,' I said, standing up and brushing crumbs from my jeans. Then I left the room, and ran upstairs.

Lukaz

Shelley has run upstairs. She is very upset, naturally. But so, too, am I. I walk slowly around this room, full of beautiful things – art, antique furniture, first edition books even, and like the rest of this house and my other homes, it is empty to me without the right woman. And that woman, I am more convinced than ever, is Shelley.

I am lonely. And I have been lonely for quite some time – I realise that now. I want a family around me again, a woman who loves me for what I am, not for how much I am worth. And here is the irony. Shelley is the first woman I have ever met since I have become rich who doesn't want my money. But much more serious, she doesn't seem to want me either. This is a very unusual situation I find myself in. I must think carefully, logically. But then I remind myself, when has love ever been about logic? I am a trained and skilled soldier, ex-Spetsnaz. I know how to invade and storm any building, but the fortress of a woman's heart remains a mystery, even to a man like me.

I did not sleep last night. My instincts would not allow me to. Instead I remain awake, alert, as if I am waiting, watching for the enemy. And in this case the enemy is an absent man. How ridiculous is that? An enemy I cannot fight. Shelley is still in love with her husband. If she doesn't know it, then I do. I have never been afraid to face up to a challenge. But Shelley is a woman who cannot be bought. I must handle her like a frightened colt, timid, unsure, about to bolt at any moment. I cannot fence her in. But I can try to win her. There is still a chance. I must believe that. These papers make me very angry. Everywhere I go, I am followed by this media machine. Most women love it – but Shelley, of course, is not most women. I understand why she would shun publicity. She fears for her family, her children. Also, she has class. This too I recognise and admire. This makes me want her even more. I hear her coming down the stairs now, and I go to say goodbye to her. I will not let her see how worried I am. How I fear this may have damaged me in her eyes. I will not wear the mantle of defeat that is so unattractive to the human spirit, man or woman.

I will remember my Irish great-grandfather, how he struggled, how he was renowned for his bravery. I will not dwell on the other reason he left Ireland all those years ago that my mother tell me when I was a child. The reason he was such a fearless soldier and fighter, the reason he died alone in a strange country. He came to Russia not just because of his part in Irish revolution, but because the woman he loved left him for another man. He ended up a prisoner in Stalin's gulag. I am thinking I am in a prison too, of my own making – a different kind of prison, but a prison nonetheless. I am a hostage to my fortune – all 4.6 billion euro of it.

Vera

I like Sundays, always have done. There's something rather restful about them. Even nowadays, when all the shops are open and everything, you still get the feeling that for the most part, the city is taking it easy, a last breath before the onslaught of the week to come. I'm a creature of habit these days. It happens, you know, sneaks up on you before you know it. Then you find yourself embracing habits and sayings of your own parents that you abhorred when you were young and vowed never, ever to repeat – but you will.

I get up early. I just can't manage to sleep on past my usual waking time – another disadvantage of advancing years – so I might as well get up. I go to six o'clock Mass on Saturday evening, which means I don't have to go on Sunday any more (what a welcome change it was when they brought that in!). Once I'm up, I walk to the local shop, pick up the Sunday papers and occasionally some croissants if I'm in the mood, then settle down at the kitchen table with a nice pot of tea and a light breakfast to read. It's a very pleasant little ritual. No one else is awake yet and I have the kitchen to myself for a couple of hours. But this morning Shelley and Emma are away, not due back until later, and Mac is sound asleep, so the house seems even more quiet than usual.

I turn on the radio to Lyric FM for some soothing background music and start with the smallest paper, the only tabloid I favour, the *Sunday Chronicle*. It's a good little paper, aimed at women readers, well written and put together, and

usually tells me all I need to know. I skim through the first
couple of pages, nothing of particular interest, and then I
turn overleaf and the page in my hand stops in mid-turn as
I gasp at the spread on the following pages. It's the photo of
Charlie and Shelley that I notice first, and then, with sickening realisation, I take in the other shots, the lurid headline
shouting the general theme and tone of the article. Something
makes me check the other papers before I can bring myself
to read the offending article, and I hurry through them,
flicking pages. Nothing in *The Sunday Times*, but the *Sunday
Herald*, the Irish broadsheet with the biggest readership in
the country, is not to be outdone. It too has a feature on
Shelley, Charlie and this Russian billionaire. But that's not
the worst of it. The shots in the *Herald* are far more upsetting. Not only are Shelley and this Lukaz chap featured, but
there, clear as day, is my son, Charlie, on a beach in Cape
Town, according to the caption, and with him a beautiful
blonde woman who must be the same girl I saw in the photograph Tom showed me only last week. And strangest of all
is the little boy in the photograph with her – her son, presumably – because looking at it, for a moment I'm convinced it's
Mac.

I pour myself another cup of tea, give my glasses a good
wipe, and with a heavy heart, I begin to read.

Olivia

Sundays used to be the best. Long, lazy, mornings in bed, sex and, well, more sex. Then Guy would pop out to get the papers, we'd have coffee and croissants in the kitchen and read the papers together – *Sunday Chronicle* for me, *Sunday Times* and loads of other business papers for Guy, although I must admit I really like the mag with the *ST*. Then we'd go somewhere trendy for a late brunch, like the Expresso Bar, and maybe go for a walk on Killiney Hill or somewhere and then chill out at home. Like I said, they used to be the best. How was I to know everything would change?

The first month was brilliant, like a sort of long honeymoon. Okay, so we weren't travelling or on holiday or anything, but it *felt* like a long holiday. I didn't have a job yet, but looking after Guy was turning out to be hard work. It all started when his wife went mental. It was one thing apparently when he was 'seeing' me, as Guy put it – she could handle that – but when we moved in together, well, she had a complete meltdown, or so she said (I wouldn't mind, but they were separated, you know, it wasn't as if he had moved out *because* of me). First her hair started falling out, then she started having panic attacks and finally she developed a mystery illness for which there were endless symptoms but no diagnosis. His friends froze him out and his two spoiled brats of twin daughters wouldn't speak to him either. They were only twelve (that's, like, Mac's age), but they could have passed for twenty-five. I got a good look at them one day when Guy brought me to pick them up from a tennis match, and they didn't say a word to me the whole way home in the car. Well, what would you expect? They had been coached by their mother.

Funnily enough, every time I saw the wife, Lauren, which was quite a lot if you followed the social pages, and I do, she looked bloody great. She'd lost weight and was all dolled up to the nines, and she was always being mentioned in the social columns as 'newly single Lauren' who was embracing her newfound freedom (like she had a choice?), taking up painting again and calling herself a 'recovering artist'. I mean, have you ever? And worse, Guy seemed to be following her progress with interest. If he saw a picture of her he'd murmur something really annoying like, 'Yes, I remember Lauren was a very talented painter, she was always sketching my profile on honeymoon.' And if I tried to tell him to wise up, that it was all a big act she was putting on to try to get his attention, he got this pathetic, sort of pained, smug look on his face and said, 'Lauren is trying to be strong, Liv. She's really lost without me, you know.' Well, you can imagine how *that* made me want to puke.

Then the callouts started, as I referred to them – you know, phone calls on a Sunday morning, usually, funnily enough – *The boiler's acting up again, Guy; The girls are having their photos taken professionally, they really want you to be in one with them; The roof's fallen in, Guy, and aliens have landed in the house* – you get the drift. Which is why, this Sunday, I'm lying here in bed on my own. We had a blazing row after she called him yesterday evening, just as we were going out, and he bloody ran as soon as she clicked her fingers. Said she was sobbing on the phone and that someone had 'followed' her home (at seven p.m.? She should be so lucky). I told him if he wasn't going to stand up to her and cut out this running back and forth, then he could stay with her, 'cos he certainly wasn't going to be welcome back here. Of course I didn't really mean it – I thought he would come back and apologise and after a suitable amount of grovelling I would let him make it up to me. But he didn't, the bastard. He didn't come back.

Instead I got a text at midnight – *midnight!* – saying, *I need some space, Olivia. Your selfish, immature behaviour is becoming very stressful for me. All this fighting is very unhealthy for both of us. I would like you move out of the apartment over the weekend. Guy.* I couldn't believe it! I still can't. I mean, the nerve of him! What did he think I was? Well, whatever he thought, he thought wrong. What a weak, pathetic, cowardly old man he is. I texted him that, of course, along with a few other relevant comments. And I'm not upset, in case you're thinking that. I'm angry. No, anger is much too small a word for what I'm feeling.

I get up, pull on my jeans and go out to get a coffee and the papers, 'cos the Nespresso machine isn't working and I can't be bothered to make instant. I'll pack up my stuff later. In fact, I'll leave most of it. Send all the clothes he bought for me round to his house. Lingerie too. See how he and Mrs Recovering Artist like that. No bloody man is going to just walk out on me like that, especially one old enough to be my father. I stop for a moment and gasp at the sudden realisation. Now I know how Mum must have felt. And as if that wasn't bad enough, I'd gone and found my own version of Dad to walk out on me all over again. I took a deep breath. *Liv, honey,* I said to myself, *get your act together. As Dr Phil would say, you need to drop that habit like a hot potato.*

So I went to the shops, came back and had a quick flick through the papers, just to check if there were any pictures of *her,* Lauren, and that's when I saw it – them. My own mother. A double-page spread in not one, but two Sunday papers. Shit – double shit. I quickly scanned the articles, simultaneously riveted and horrified. I couldn't believe it. I mean, this was – this was – the end. I would be a laughing-stock. My own mother had a love life that commanded more interest than mine – with a Russian billionaire. Wait till my friends got a load of that. And as for the photo of Dad and that blonde one, well, I'd had enough. I was going back right now to demand to know what the hell was going on. No need to mention my falling out with Guy. I could now claim to be moving back out of sheer daughterly concern. Which is partly true. Parents, jeez – and they lecture us!

Suddenly I couldn't wait to leave. I rang a taxi (Guy had an account) and began to fling my stuff into a case. I left a note for Guy telling him never to even think of contacting me again. He would, of course; the minute he saw that article, he'd want the lowdown, but he wasn't getting it from me. With a glow of triumphant self-righteousness, I slammed the door behind me. In the taxi, I tried calling Emma, but there was a foreign ring tone when I dialled (who could blame her if she'd left the country?). I left a message and told her to ring me immediately. Just as we were almost at Gran's house, my phone rang – it was Guy's number flashing on screen. I pressed 'reject'. He wouldn't like that. Nobody ever does.

Emma

Our school trip to Brussels was brilliant. We came over on Friday lunchtime and now it's Sunday and we're at Charleroi airport to get the two o'clock Ryanair flight back to Dublin. We saw the European Parliament of course and the Grande Palace where we ate our own weight in ice-cream and chocolates. And then we had to go and see the Manneken Pis. This is apparently, like, the landmark in Brussels and wait for it – it's a small bronze fountain sculpture of a little kid urinating. Sometimes they dress him up – go figure – in fact he has a wardrobe of more than 600 costumes our guide told us – all kept at the City Museum. We also went to see the site of the Battle of Waterloo between Wellington and Napoleon Bonaparte in 1815 and of course everyone started singing the Abba song the minute we got off the bus, which we thought was hilarious but made our teachers quite pissed off.

I've decided I'd like to be a diplomat, or maybe an MEP, and come and work here. It wouldn't be easy, I think you have to do loads of exams and stuff, but living and dealing with my family must make me almost halfway qualified already. I mean, apart from learning a couple of languages, how hard can it be?

The flight home is uneventful, except for our French teacher, Eloise, and our history teacher, Mr Carbury, sitting together, who we are convinced are having an affair. Mr Carbury is married but, as Sophie points out, since when has that ever made a difference? Eloise is Parisian and looks a bit like a cross between Linda Evangelista and Jennifer Anniston. Her features are all slightly crooked and edgy but somehow just all combine to work perfectly. She's short sighted too, so when she looks at you she kind of leans in and narrows her eyes, which are an electric blue-green (coloured contacts, Sophie says). It makes her look really sexy, and she's always tossing her glossy but tousled black waves while she's looking at you. She's doing it now to Mr Carbury, and he's going a bit red and loosening his collar. Farther up the aisle, Lisa and Mary, who are sitting behind them, are making vomiting-inducing gestures and drawing hearts in the air.

The plane lands and we go straight through customs. We were only allowed carry-on bags (we had to wear our school uniforms all weekend, can you believe it?), so we don't have to hang around baggage reclaim, which is good. One by one everyone's phones start beeping as they are turned on again and messages come through. There's one on mine from Olivia telling me to ring her. I put my phone back in my pocket. I can ring her when I get back to Gran's. We go through the doors into arrivals, and Sophie's dad is there to pick us up. He's hiding behind a newspaper because he's quite well known and doesn't like people coming up to him and asking his opinion on the 'current economic situation', which apparently they do quite a lot. When he sees Sophie, his face breaks into a huge smile. Sophie is the only girl in her family and is the 'apple of her dad's eye', as Jackie is always telling everyone. He hurriedly puts away the paper and says, 'Welcome home, girls. Did you leave Brussels still standing?'

'Hey, Dad!' says Sophie, hugging him while I hang back, feeling awkward.

'Hi, Mr O'Neill,' I say.

'Hello, Emma,' he says. He has long given up telling me

to call him Liam. Mr O'Neill is just one of those dads who will always be 'Mr' in my mind.

I smile and thank him for giving me a lift, while Sophie chatters away ten to the dozen. 'Mum said to say thank you too,' I add.

'Oh, um, right. No trouble at all, no trouble at all, my pleasure.' And for some reason, he gets a bit of a coughing fit.

We are just headed for the main exit doors when a group of girls who were huddled around the class bitch, Iris O'Donnell, look over at us and burst into sniggers. Then Iris calls out, 'Hey Emma, is it true your mum is shagging a Russian?' They all double up in mirth as someone else shrieks, '*Ohmigod*, Iris, I don't believe you just said that!'

For a moment, I'm rooted to the spot. Then Sophie gives me a shove and hisses, 'Don't mind them, Em. Iris O'Donnell's a stupid cow,' while Mr O'Neill coughs some more and starts talking very loudly about the weather.

Shelley

The drive home is interminable. Although there's no traffic and the Maybach speeds along with Igor silent at the wheel, the minutes feel like hours. Finally we pull up outside Vera's house, its semi-detached exterior as well groomed and welcoming as the woman herself. But once I go inside that door, once all this media display is on the table for Vera, my children – make that the whole country – to see . . . what then?

Suddenly, as I drag my bag to the front door, I feel weary and beaten. Who am I? What sort of a woman loses her head as I have? What sort of a woman puts her own selfish enjoyment before her the well-being of her children? No wonder Olivia left home. No wonder Mac won't talk to me (at least he won't be reading the papers, but what about school?). And Vera, and her unstinting support for me, for us. Even Emma – oh God, what horror will this latest mess of mine throw at us? With a heavy heart I turn my key in the door, put my bag under the hall table and close the door softly.

'Shelley?' Vera's voice comes from the kitchen. I take a deep breath. 'Is that you?' She pokes her head around into the hall. 'Oh, it *is* you. Come in and have a cup of tea, I've just made a pot. Did you have a lovely time?'

'Vera,' I begin as I follow her into the tiny kitchen, and then I see them, the Sunday papers, neatly folded on the table. I try to speak, but no words seem appropriate. 'Vera, I need to talk to you, to tell you something.' I feel sick.

She looks at me, topping up the pot of tea with hot water, and pours two cups. 'It's all right, Shelley, I've seen it, that nonsense in the papers, if that's what you mean. Sit down and let's have a chat. You don't look like you've had much sleep.' She smiles ruefully.

I look at her face, the kindness in her bright, questioning eyes, the enquiring but never inquisitive expression, the gentle, encouraging smile, and suddenly it all gets to me – the hopelessness, the loneliness, the non-stop roller coaster my family and I have been on for the past four months – and it's all my fault. I sit down, put my head in my hands and sob. I cry and I hiccup and I keep on crying. There is nowhere left to hide and I don't care who sees me or how I seem. I'm vaguely aware of Vera going over to shut the kitchen door, and then she sits beside me and puts her arms around me, which makes me worse. 'Shhh,' she is saying, over and over, rubbing my back. 'There, there, you poor dear. You've been so brave.'

'No,' I gulp. I have to make her understand. 'You don't understand, I've been awful, Vera, really terrible. I've been stupid and selfish and I'm a terrible mother and I was a worse wife.' I take a couple of shuddering breaths. 'It's all my fault that Charlie left. I – I told him to go.'

'We all say silly things, Shelley, things we don't mean.'

'But I *did* mean it, I meant every word of it. And I wouldn't listen to him, give him a chance to explain. I just told him to get out of our lives.' I leave out the *South African hoor* bit before taking the tissue Vera hands me and blowing my nose loudly.

'And then,' I continue, still hiccupping, 'when he went and all this awful nightmare started, with the business gone and, and the house . . .'

'Yes, yes, I know, it must have been so dreadful for you.' Vera is sitting back now, patting my hand on the table and making clucking noises.

'I was so angry, so scared and angry, that I didn't care what he did. I didn't even care if he was dead. I wanted to kill him anyway. I wanted to be the one who could run away, and then I almost end up in bed with the first man that pays me the slightest bit of attention.' That brings a fresh fit of sobbing on. 'And I *wanted* to go to bed with him, Vera, I really did.'

There is no stopping me now – a full confession is spilling out whether or not Vera wants to hear the gory details.

'Well, I can understand that.'

'And he was having an affair, you see—' I stop short. 'What did you say?'

'I said I can understand you wanting to go to bed with this man. Lukaz, isn't it?'

'But – but how?' I must sound demented. 'I mean, why? How can you understand that? I'm your daughter-in-law,' I sniff again. 'I'm married to Charlie – at least I think I am.'

'Oh Shelley, dear, I understand a lot more than you think I can. I had an affair myself, many years ago now. I'm not proud of what I did, and I paid a very high price for my behaviour. I don't believe anyone gets away scot free from these . . . unforeseen episodes in life.' She suddenly looks immeasurably sad. 'So nobody knows better than I do about playing with fire, about playing fast and loose with the hearts of those you love and who love you. I'm afraid I know all about being a bad wife, and I certainly wasn't the kind of mother my boys, or indeed any children, needed, not back then, and by the time I had learned some serious lessons, the damage was already done. You, on the other hand, have been and continue to be a wonderful mother. I won't have you saying anything to the contrary. If Charlie was having an affair, which I'm truly sorry to hear, well, I don't know anything about that. But I do know that he had a less than desirable role model in his mother, one that has no doubt left him scarred emotionally in ways I can only speculate upon.'

I stare at her, open mouthed, as Vera goes on. 'Oh, I know I'm an old woman now, and this must sound like utter madness to you, but perhaps it's time I told you about Charlie and me. It might help you understand him, possibly shed some light on things for you, perhaps your marriage even. Although it was always obvious to me, even from a distance, that he adored you. Perhaps he just wasn't very good at showing it. Many men aren't.'

And then she begins to talk. We sit there for the best part of an hour while I listen, agog, to the most extraordinary account. Looking at her, listening to her talk, I'm riveted, my own troubles suddenly forgotten as the past comes alive with her telling. Vera is seventy-nine, but her former beauty is still evident in her fabulous bone structure and a still slim and shapely figure. I've always thought she has a strong look of Honor Blackman, the actress who played Pussy Galore in the Bond movie, and *she's* into her eighties. But listening to Vera now as her voice catches occasionally, and seeing the pain that is evident in her eyes, etched on her face, for the first time I see the accumulation of the years and how heavily sometimes they must weigh on her.

Vera

I told her everything. I didn't leave anything out, much as some of it pained me to reveal to her. Shelley had a right to know. After all, Charlie was my son. Whatever kind of a man or husband he had turned out to be, I was partly responsible. I wasn't going to run away from that admission. So I talked and Shelley listened, looking at first shocked, and then, as the story unfolded, by turns distressed and fascinated. But when I came to the bit about Caroline, that awful day I found Charlie and her in a, shall we say, compromising position, well, I couldn't tell Shelley about that. It would have been too hurtful and altogether unnecessary (*too much information*, as Emma would say), so I just skimmed over that bit and said instead that when Charlie and I were having a row about something stupid, like tidying up his room or something, that he had lost his temper and finally let me know what he had seen that day as a little boy. Even in that version, I could see in Shelley's face the realisation, the horror of how awful it must have been for Charlie, how damaging for him to have kept it to himself for all those years. But she never said a word in judgement against me, not throughout the whole thing, except to say at the end, 'Oh Vera, I can't believe it. How awful it must have been for you. The whole thing's just so bloody sad, I can hardly take it in.'

And then she became thoughtful and said, after some deliberation, I could tell, 'Caroline's the one he's been having an affair with.' Before I could comment, she went on. 'But there was another woman involved as well, a South African woman, apparently.'

Now it was my turn to express dismay. I had imagined rows, of course, and perhaps some minor indiscretion, but as I said, even though I had failed miserably in my own marriage vows, I was somehow sure that Charlie would never let Shelley down, despite of – or rather because of – the awful way *I* had let him down. I always felt that Charlie's loathing of me, his palpable recoiling from me when he had a go at me – well, I always sort of assumed that he would go out of his way to make sure his own marriage was different. But then, the road to hell and all that . . . Who knows what patterns, destructive or otherwise, are being played out in our subconscious despite out best intentions?

When Shelley told me about Caroline calling around to her house that day and the awful scene that ensued, I could hardly believe it. Then, when she reiterated the story of the South African woman and the emails Caroline threw at her to back it up, and with tears running down her face mentioned a little boy called Jack – that's when my heart slowed down and almost stopped. 'You saw it, Vera, you must have, in the paper this morning.' I nodded, remembering the photo Tom had showed me as well, but of course I didn't mention that. 'It was like looking at Mac,' she whispered.

'Oh, Shelley.' I really didn't know what to say, so I kept my mouth shut and took her hand. Sometimes there just are no words.

'So it's all my fault, you see, that he's gone to her. That's what I yelled at him, the day he left, the day we had that awful row. I told him to get out of our lives and F-off to his South African woman . . . or words to that effect. I just never thought he'd go, not like that. It was only afterwards I found out that everything was gone, that that's what he'd been trying to tell me, along with the other stuff, I suppose. But I miss him, Vera. I miss him so much it hurts.'

'I was afraid to ask you that, if you still felt anything for him.'

'I'd give everything in the world to have him back. Everything.'

'Have you tried to contact him?'

Shelley shook her head. 'I almost did, lots of times, but I just lose my nerve.'

'Well, maybe it's time we did something about that.'

'But he's got another life now, hasn't he? Out there with her. I couldn't bear it if I asked him to come back and he said no. I couldn't blame him either, not after what I said to him.'

'Sometimes you have to go out on a limb and risk everything, Shelley. It's the only way you'll ever know.' It was easy for me to say, I know, but looking at her strained face and sunken eyes, I knew that if Charlie didn't come back, well, I don't know what would happen with her or the children. I could understand her avoiding the issue, of course I could – I had been that woman myself. But sooner or later, life moves on whether or not you're ready to move with it, and I worried what that might do to Shelley. But things couldn't go on like this, they just couldn't. Something would have to give.

Emma

I didn't go straight home. Sophie suggested coming back to her place for a while and getting a lift back later. After what happened at the airport, that suddenly sounded like a very good idea. So I rang Mum and said I'd be back later, if that was okay, and she said yes, of course, that she was dying to see me and had I had a good time? I said yes, and that I would tell her all about it later when I got home, around six. She sounded tired, I thought, kind of weary. I thought about the stuff in the papers and felt sick. I had seen it after a friend had rung Sophie and asked if it was true. Mr O'Neill had left the Sunday papers on the back seat of the car, a whole pile of them, so I was able to leaf through them casually, although Sophie and I planned to study them at length upstairs in her room once we got home to her house. I needed time to digest this. I also wanted to avail of Sophie's fabulous en suite bathroom. Nothing ever seems quite as bad after a long, hot bubble bath. That's what I told myself, anyway.

After my bath, swathed in hotel-worthy fluffy white towels, we lay on Sophie's bed and read the offending articles. 'They're not *that* bad, not really,' Sophie reasoned. 'I mean, it makes your mum sound pretty hot, doesn't it? How many people get fancied by a Russian oligarch? Hasn't happened to me yet. My mum will be dead jealous.' I knew she was trying to make me feel better, put a positive spin on it. That's what Soph was great for. She was the best kind of best friend, no bullshit – but no pity either. Even she couldn't stop herself

looking caught out and embarrassed at the shot of my dad
and the blonde woman, and weirder still, the little kid who
looked like Mac. She nearly said it out loud, before stopping
herself. She looked at it and said, 'Is that—?' And then, quickly,
turning the page, 'Is that the place in Cape Town Wendy's
family used to go to on holiday?' But Sophie didn't fool me,
even if she was quick to avert an upsetting observation.
Anyway, I'd seen enough.

'I'd better go, Sophie,' I said, getting back into my school
uniform for the journey home. 'Thanks for letting me use
your bathroom. I'd almost forgotten what a power shower
looked like. You don't know how lucky you are,' I added enviously. I didn't just mean that Sophie's family still had money.
I meant that they still were a *family* – Sophie, and her two
older brothers, and parents who still loved each other. Even
when Jackie was giving out about Mr O'Neill, which she did
quite a lot, you could tell by the way they looked at each
other when they thought no one was looking. It was the kind
of thing I noticed all the time now, wherever I was – those
sorts of looks between couples. I suppose Mum and Dad
must have looked at each other like that too once, but I wasn't
watching, not back then. Now I'd give anything to see it. How
weird is that?

I get a lift to Gran's house with Sophie's brother Edward,
who has just got his driving licence and is offering to drive
everyone everywhere. He's good looking, I think, sneaking a look
at him while his eyes are fixed firmly on the road ahead, but
the thought of going out with your best friend's brother just,
well, weird. Not that I'm likely to be attracting anyone while I'm
in my school uniform. Sophie said school uniforms turn some
men on, but they have to be mental or weird old pervs.

Edward drops me off and I say thanks and lug my wheelie
bag to the door. I open it and stop in astonishment. There
are four big suitcases blocking the hall. For a mad moment

I wonder if Dad is back, but then I hear the unmistakable tones of Olivia's voice, raised, as usual, coming from the kitchen. She's back. Obviously. I might have known.

Olivia

It was easier than I thought it would be. For starters, Emma wasn't back yet from her school trip and Mac was upstairs in his attic room, so there was just Mum and Gran to face. Actually, I was a bit worried about Gran – I don't think I was what she considered a model daughter or granddaughter should be. Not that she ever said anything, but I could tell. I'm not stupid, you know; that role was reserved for Emma. But like I said before, being the eldest is never easy. You have to push the boundaries. It's your job.

All the same, I was wary of Gran. I reckon she could be a hard nut if you crossed her, and there must have been some really bad reason for Dad not speaking to her for all these years. Which brought me back to the purpose of my home-coming – I wanted to know what the hell was going on in my family, if you could call us that any more, and I was going to demand an explanation. I was ready with my opening line and all: 'What the hell is going on?' I wanted to barge in and say, taking them by surprise.

Well, I did that for sure – take them by surprise – but before I could say anything, Mum had got up from the kitchen table, come out into the hall and looked at me as if I had sprouted wings and grown a halo and said, 'Oh, Liv, honey, you've come home, you've come home,' over and over, and smothered me in a bear hug, which threw me off my guard. Then she dragged me into the kitchen and said to Gran, who looked first surprised and then pleased, 'Look, Vera, my Liv has come home – you have, haven't you, sweetheart? I mean, those cases must mean you're staying. Please tell me they do.'

'I hope so,' said Gran, smiling, but there was something else in her tone that I detected but couldn't quite make out, 'because we certainly don't have any space here in case she's thinking in terms of temporary storage facilities.'

'Oh, she's not,' said Mum, looking all misty eyed, 'are you, Liv? Tell me you're back. Emma and Mac will be so thrilled.'

That kind of threw me off tack, so I said yes, for the foreseeable future, looking at Gran then and adding, 'Um, if that's all right with everyone?' which was the only phrase that sprang to mind.

Then Gran said, 'That's splendid. You're just in time for dinner and Emma should be back any minute.'

Mum hugged me again and said, 'Oh Liv, you don't know how much this means to me, really you don't.' And when I looked at her, properly, I could see she'd been crying, probably for hours. Her eyes were all puffy, even though she was wearing eye make-up to try to hide it. And although I tried to feel angry, I just couldn't. Also, I was very hungry and the roast chicken I could smell was making my stomach grumble. What with all the carry-on with Guy over the past day or two, I had practically forgotten to eat. That, and the newspaper crap. I was starving. Men. They were all a pain in the arse, really.

So that was all fine, and I was sitting at the kitchen table being treated like the Prodigal Daughter, when Emma arrives in, still in her school uniform, and says, 'Oh. You're back,' then goes over and kisses Mum and Gran respectively.

Then Mac is called down for dinner and Mum says, 'Look, Mac, Liv is back. Your sister's home, isn't that great?'

Mac said, 'Yeah, brilliant – *not*,' under his breath and Emma giggled, then when Mum turned her back he stuck his tongue out at me. God, I'd forgotten how ridiculous twelve-year-old boys could be. Ridiculous – but sly. I wasn't going to forget the trouble he got me into blowing my cover with Guy that time. Not that I'd have to worry about things of that nature for the moment. But still.

So we have dinner and everyone is listening to Emma's totally boring account of her school trip to Brussels. But no one is saying what's really on our minds – well, on everyone's mind except Mac's, presumably – which is the newspaper spread about Mum and that Lukaz guy. I haven't met him, but Guy wasn't impressed by him, or at least he had tried very hard to pretend not to be – not that he had met him either. Anyway, he was probably just jealous 'cos Lukaz was way richer than him. It annoyed me at first, that, but now I'm glad. Guy could be a real muppet sometimes, as Emma would say. Not that I was going to tell anyone that. But when I told him that Lukaz had taken Mac and his school pals to see Chelsea play at home, he just shrugged and said, 'Anyone could do that if they wanted to.'

So I said, 'Well, you never have.' He was irritating me even then.

'I never took you for a footie fan,' he said and got all huffy. As if that was the point. Anyway, I digress. I was feeling more relaxed about everything now and I felt it was my duty to probe a little.

'Well, Mum,' I begin, 'are you going to tell us what's going on?' I see Emma's eyes dart nervously and Gran quickly take a sip of water.

'What do you mean, what's going on?' Mum looks worried.

'Oh come on, all that stuff in the papers about you and dad. Don't you think it's time you told us what's going on? I mean, we're your children – we have a right to know.'

'What stuff in the paper?' Mac asks.

'There were pictures of Mum with your football-loving friend Lukaz in the papers,' I tell him.

'He's not *my* friend,' says Mac sulkily.

'And pictures of Dad with another woman, in Cape Town. On a beach.'

'Liv, can we talk about this later, please, after dinner?' says Mum, sounding tired.

'I think that would be a very good idea,' adds Gran, looking at me meaningfully – make that threateningly. But I don't care. I'm sick of this charade. Like I said, we have a right to know.

'We might as well talk about it now, while we're all here around the table. That's the trouble with this family. Nobody talks about anything – not until it's too late, anyway.'

Suddenly Emma looks as if she's going to cry and Mac looks mutinous.

'So what's going on?' I ask again. 'Are Dad and you getting a divorce? Are you dating this Lukaz guy? And is Dad—'

'He was having an affair, all right?' Mum suddenly blurts. 'Your dad was having an affair.' She flings down her knife and fork and puts her hands to her face. She takes a couple of deep breaths and I watch as Gran reaches over and pats Mum's shoulder, making sympathetic noises, but she's looking worried. This seems even more surreal than what I'm hearing.

'I don't believe you.' Emma looks at Mum accusingly.

'I'm sorry, darling, I didn't want to say anything, but Olivia is right, we have to talk about this.'

'I don't believe Dad would have an affair with *anyone* and I can't believe *you'd* believe that of him. He wouldn't do that to you – to us.' Her voice is like ice but is cracking.

Suddenly I feel sorry for Em. She worships Dad. She's going to be the worst casualty in this mess, I can see that now. I thought it would be Mac, but it won't – it'll be Emma. Tears start rolling down her face and she wipes them angrily away. 'I wish he was here,' she sobs. 'I just want Dad to come back. Why won't he come back?'

Gran's hand flies to her mouth as she tries to stifle a gasp.

Mum looks stricken. 'Oh Emma, darling, I didn't mean to upset you, I just—'

'Wanted to go on sticking your head in the sand?' I demand angrily. 'Keeping us all in the dark?' And I *am* angry, much angrier than I realised, watching Emma sob, and looking at Mac, who is chewing his lip, his face white as chalk, and he's getting those two red spots on his cheeks that he does when he's upset or in trouble. *They're only kids,* I think to myself. But Mum – she should know better. Dad too. They should have talked to us.

'He's not coming back, though, is he?' I go on. I know it's harsh, but I'm determined to get the truth. 'Not now. I mean, the bloody newspapers seem to know more about our own family than we do! Why can't you just *tell* us what's going on, for God's sake!'

'Because I don't know. I don't know what's happening.' It's almost a whisper from Mum.

But then Mac jumps up from his chair and shouts, 'Just shut up, Olivia. Shut up! Dad is coming back – he is.' And then *he* begins to cry.

'Then why is he out there and not here?' I yell back at him. I know it's mean of me, but I can't stand any more of this denial. It's too cruel, too damaging. 'Dad's not coming back and we need to get our heads around that.'

'He is *so* coming back. You don't know anything, Olivia. Dad *is* coming back. He *is* – he promised me he was coming back and Dad never breaks his promises.'

A hush descends around the table as we look at Mac, shouting, distraught, desperately trying to believe what he is pretending to himself. It's heartbreaking. I wonder if he's losing it, having a sort of mini-meltdown.

Mum looks frightened, as well she might. 'Mac, darling,' she tries, gently. 'Sit down, sweetie, please. Listen to me.'

'Why should I listen to you?' Mac yells at her. 'It's your fault he went away, it's all your fault.' He is pointing at her now. 'She told him to go – I heard her.' He looks at us now, me, Gran and Emma, all of us open mouthed. He is fighting for breath. 'I heard her, I heard both of them shouting, that day Dad left. I was outside the door. I heard you – I heard Mum yell at Dad, "Why don't you just fuck off out of our lives and off to your South African sewer!" That's what you said and don't try to deny it!' He's looking wildly from Mum to us. 'So he did go, he went, and I don't blame him. I'd have gone too if I could. I wish I had – I wish Dad had taken me with him. I hate you, and I hate it here without him.' And with that, he flees from the room and upstairs.

For a moment there is a stunned silence, then Emma gets up and runs from the table, after Mac, and the rest of us just sit there, Mum with her hand over her mouth and mascara tracks running down her cheeks. 'Oh no,' she says over and over. 'I don't believe this.'

'Is it true?' I ask finally.

'In a manner of speaking, yes.' Mum's voice sounds as if it's coming from very far away, as if she's not here.

'What exactly are you on about?' I'm trying to keep my head. 'I'm losing the plot here, between South Africa and sewers and—'

'I meant his girlfriend, his – his whatever woman he was having a relationship with. I was yelling at him, I was out of control, but I had no idea Mac was in the house, he was supposed to be at soccer practice. What I yelled at your father was "why don't you f-off out of our lives and off to your South African hoor", not sewer,' she says flatly.

'Oh dear,' says Gran.

I shake my head disbelievingly at both of them. Clearly I have come back not a moment to soon. *The Jeremy Kyle Show* has nothing on this lot.

'I think I'll just make some tea and coffee,' says Gran. 'Don't move, Shelley dear, I'll be back in a mo.' She looks back at Mum as if she might suddenly shatter into tiny pieces, but Mum just sits there with her head in her hands.

I wonder whose side Gran is on. This is all very strange.

Mac

I try to pull up the folding stairs and close the trapdoor, but Emma is too quick for me. Suddenly she's standing in front of me, huffing and puffing and all red in the face, looking like a sergeant major or something.

'What was that about?' she says.

'Nothing.' I'm sitting on my camp bed thingy with my laptop on my knees. I wipe my nose with my sleeve.

'Don't give me that crap,' she spits. 'I'm not Mum. What the fuck is going on with you? What was all that stuff you were talking about down there?'

I try to think of something to say and can't.

'Mac! Look at me – what the hell were you talking about, Dad promising you he was coming back. Are you making that up?' She's leaning over me now, and looking scary.

We're a team, Mac, you and me – us against the girls. I try to think what Dad would say, but my head is buzzing now and Emma is roaring.

'Mac!'

Women will run rings around you if you let them . . . we have to stick together, you and me..

'*Mac!*'

I think Emma might be going to hit me, so I talk. 'He *is* coming back. He told me so. It says it right here!' And I turn around my laptop and point to the email.

Emma snatches it from me, sits down on the bed and reads it – all of them – all the emails Dad ever sent me, scrolling back down through all of them. I don't care. I know I'll get into savage trouble, but I don't care any more. I hate it here in this house full of women.

'Jesus!' Emma is muttering as she reads. '*Jesus!*' She looks up at me and I swallow. I have never seen Emma this angry. 'He told you to tell us!' She is jabbing at the first email on the screen and her finger is trembling. 'It says it right here, you little bastard – *tell Emma and Olivia I love them and can't wait to hear from them.*' She looks like something out of a horror movie. Her face is all twisted and she's making funny gasping sounds.

She gets up, throws my laptop on the bed and lunges for me – but this time I'm ready. I dive through the trapdoor and hurtle down the ladder. I make a break for the front door – I'm so nearly there – but Emma yells, '*Stop him!*' and Olivia dashes out of the dining room and tackles me by the collar, nearly choking me.

Game's up. It's all over now.

Charlie

It had been two weeks since the operation. I'd lost a kidney and gained one very happy (and I hope healthy) young nephew. The transplant had been a complete success, thank God. The kidney 'plumbed in' right away, as they say, which means, without going into too much gory detail, that it began producing urine before Jack was even off the table. It's what they call a best-case scenario. The post-operative ultrasound confirmed good blood flow, and the following day the mag3 scan showed healthy perfusion. Now we just had to hope that all would continue to go well and that Jack and his new kidney would have a long and happy relationship. The odds were good, if he didn't reject. A cadaver kidney transplant has a lifespan on average of eight to ten years, but one from a living relative has better prospects, from ten to fifteen years, and some have even gone on for twenty. Things can go wrong, of course, there's no guarantee, but for the moment, things were looking good – and the moment was all any of us wanted, especially Jack, who was giving a whole new meaning to 'living in the now', according to Annika, his main goal being to stay in the water for as long and often as possible, preferably attached to a surfboard.

I was having dinner with them tonight, Annika, Greg, Charlie and the girls, just to say goodbye really, and I was sorry to be leaving them. They were such a happy little family unit. Even when Jack had been in the grip of his sickness, their love and humour in the face of such difficulty had been heart-warming to witness. And I knew then that coming out here, even if it had felt like a form of running away at the time, had really been a very necessary detour on a journey I definitely needed to make. A journey that would ultimately lead me back to myself, and more importantly, back to the people I loved, back to what mattered.

It was Jack who said what I needed to hear, in the end. 'What are you going to do now, Uncle Charlie?' he asked. 'Are you going home?'

There was an embarrassed silence for a second, then Annika told the girls to bring in their dishes. I had never talked about what had happened between Shelley and I, and neither Annika nor Greg had probed for details. I think they'd probably deduced we were having marital difficulties.

'Because if you are,' continued Jack, 'I'd like you to give this to Mac.' He produced a Springbok rugby shirt. 'I wanted to friend him on Facebook, but Mum said to I had to wait and ask you if I could..'

'Jack,' Annika said, looking apologetically at me. 'Take your plate in, sweetheart. I want to talk to Uncle Charlie for a minute.'

'Charlie,' she began while Greg made a great show of going to look for a book he had promised to lend me, 'I didn't want to mention this while you were in hospital, but I got a phone call here one day, from a woman.'

'A woman?'

'Yes, she said her name was Shelley, your, um, wife.'

'Shelley? Shelley phoned here?' Oh God, Shelley had phoned and I hadn't even known.

'Well, that's just it.' Annika looked uncomfortable. 'She sounded kind of peculiar, this woman, strung out, wanted to know exactly where you were living, and who with, and some other stuff. I hung up as soon as I decently could, I didn't want to say anything out of turn. But then, the next day, I got another phone call, from a woman who was very distressed. Her name was Carmel O'Donnell – she said it was vitally important that you speak with her, and that I was to tell you, that you would know, that she was Caroline's mother and that it had been Caroline who rang me that day previously, *pretending* to be Shelley.' Annika looked bewildered. 'It was confusing, to say the least. She said to tell you that Caroline wasn't well, that she hadn't been taking her medication and had become delusional again, and that she, Carmel, was afraid Caroline had been making trouble with your wife, Shelley, and would you ring her as soon as possible?' Annika let out a breath. 'I hope I've done the right thing Charlie.' She looked worried. 'It just all sounded like a kind of soap opera, but does this make any kind of sense to you?'

I nodded wearily. 'Yes, Annika, I'm afraid to say it does.' My mind was beginning to spin, but there were a few telling sentences from what I had just heard that had the ominous ring of truth about them.

'She left this number.' Annika handed me a piece of paper. 'Charlie, forgive me for prying, but is everything all right with you? I mean, you're family now. If there's anything Greg and I can do to help, you know we're here for you, don't you?'

It was that one word, *family*, and the kindness and concern in her eyes that brought me back to my senses.

'You've done so much for us, for little Jack. We can never repay you, but if there was anything, anything at all we could do to help . . .'

'You already have, Annika. You, Greg, Jack and the girls – you've helped more than you can ever know.'

'So . . . what *are* you going to do?' she asked as Greg came back and joined us.

'I'm going to go home, back to Dublin. I'll get the overnight flight to Heathrow tomorrow.'

'You'll stay in touch, won't you?' she asked anxiously. 'I mean, after all this, after finding you, and for Jack . . .' She looked close to tears.

'Of course I will.' I hugged her and shook Greg's hand. 'All going well, there should be a lot of contact happening between Cape Town and Dublin from here on out – I'd bet on it.'

'If you need anything, Charlie, anything at all – if anyone wants to ring us here, or confirm anything . . .' She let the words hang in the air.

'Anything, anytime, mate,' Greg nodded emphatically. 'We're here for you.'

'Come back soon,' said Annika. 'Come and stay with us, bring the family.' Then she called Jack and the girls to say goodbye.

'You take care of yourself, young man,' I said bending down to Jack, who hugged me surprisingly tightly.

'I will, Uncle Charlie, and I'll take even better care of your kidney. I promise,' he said, solemnly.

Then I had to get out of there, because I suddenly felt close to tears and I knew that if they started, they would never stop.

'So long, guys,' I managed.

'Call us and let us know you've arrived safely.'

'I will.' And then I turned and waved one last time at the little group who reminded me so acutely of my own beloved family, who were never out of my mind or heart for a single second.

Where would we go from here? I missed them all so terribly. Would Shelley have me back? Could we start over? Would my girls ever speak to me again? Only Mac seemed to be willing to talk to me – at least that was something. But I hadn't even heard from him in the past few days, come to think of it.

I would find out the answers soon enough, I reflected, when I boarded my British Airways flight to London Heathrow tomorrow evening, and then, the following morning, caught the connecting flight home to Dublin.

Vera

Well I can't *begin* to tell you what chaos ensued on Sunday evening when Olivia came home and started her interrogations and then Emma discovered that Mac had been in contact with his father all along. I really thought for a moment I was losing my mind, what little I have left of it. Emma, bless her, was so angry she was practically beyond speech. And when she managed to explain the situation, so were the rest of us. Then of course collective anger followed the dawning realisation, and for a moment I thought poor Mac was going to be set upon. Olivia had hauled him into the room by his shirt collar and the poor boy looked as if he was about to be hung, drawn and quartered. He broke into loud sobs and said that it wasn't *his* fault, he had only been protecting his dad from people who seemed to hate him. And that had a justifiably calming effect as we all took a moment for self-reflection. After that, Shelley had told the girls to leave her and Mac alone to talk, and I gather that he had calmed down somewhat then, once he realised he wasn't going to be eaten alive, and came clean about the whole dreadful mess.

Dear me, I'm not the better of it all myself. My nerves are in shreds. So I came into the shop as usual, although I'm really not any help to anyone at all – my mind is all over the place. But I know Shelley wanted some privacy to digest everything and that I would probably be driving her mad pottering about the house. Olivia's there, of course, but after instigating the intervention, she seems to have taken to her bed again. I can't say I blame her. So I thought I'd go to work and drive them mad in the shop instead.

At eleven o'clock, when my tea break came, I found the tearoom remarkably crowded. Barbara was there, taking up half the table, Zoe, looking elfin beside her, and Tom at the other end, browsing through an old *Vogue*. The minute I walked in, Barbara quickly closed the newspaper she had been poring over and fixed an insincere smile on her face. 'Did you have a nice weekend, Vera?' she asked innocently.

'Yes, thank you.' I popped a tea bag into a mug and turned on the just-boiled kettle.

'I'm sure it must have been upsetting for you all to read those dreadful newspaper articles yesterday.' She shook her head disapprovingly.

'What dreadful articles?' asked Tom mildly.

'Well, the *Sunday Herald*, and the *Chronicle*, of course, you couldn't miss them.' She sounded indignant. 'Dreadful stuff about Vera's son Charlie and her daughter-in-law and that Russian.'

'I never read those rags,' said Tom, looking surprised. 'Do you, Vera? I take the *Sunday Times* myself, if I bother at all.'

'I'm afraid I don't read any Sunday papers.' I was pleased to see Barbara's smile falter. 'My late husband Arthur used to say if you had read the daily papers properly, then you were only getting a rehash of the week's news, a total waste of money.'

'Couldn't agree more,' smiled Tom.

'I only like the mags,' said Zoe, obliviously, ''cos they're cheap.'

'But you *must* have seen them. I mean, even today's *Post* has a mention.' Barbara spluttered crumbs and rushed to open her tabloid again.

'You know what they say.' It was Maura now, coming in

to join us. 'Today's headlines wrap tomorrows fish 'n' chips. And I ought to know – my late father was an editor.'

'Really?' said Tom.

'Barbara?' Joan called as she popped her head around the door and tapped her watch. 'Hurry up, please, you're needed out on the floor, it's way past your tea break.'

And Barbara, looking very disgruntled, reluctantly got up from the table and took her newspaper with her.

'You all right, old girl?' asked Tom.

'To paraphrase my granddaughter, I'm hanging in there.' I poured a drop of milk into my tea and sat down.

'Jolly good,' said Tom.

'That's the spirit,' said Maura.

Zoe looked at us as if we were mad. 'Vera,' she suddenly said, 'I've been thinking of losing some of these piercings.' She pulled at a ring in her nose. 'And maybe even my tongue stud. What do you think?'

I could feel Tom and Maura holding their breath collectively.

'Well,' I said carefully, 'sometimes it's good to try a new, um, look.'

'Yeah,' she considered. 'Yeah, I think I might. These are a bit *yesterday*. I want to go for something more groomed. Like the stuff you guys wear, kind of a *Mad Men* vibe.'

Maura and I looked bewildered.

'It's a popular American television series,' Tom explained to us over his magazine. 'About advertising people, set in Madison Avenue in the early sixties. You know – *our* generation. The styles are enjoying a current vogue.'

'Oh, I see,' I said.

'Does that mean we're back in fashion?' enquired Maura.

'We were never out of it, my dear,' quipped Tom.

How I loved my little band of friends in the shop.

The rest of the morning was busy, if uneventful, and feeling a little more tired than usual, I knocked off early. It was

Shelley's day to do dinner, but with all the drama, I wanted to make sure I was home in plenty of time if she wasn't feeling up to it, and I wouldn't mind doing a grocery run while I was at it, so at about two o'clock, I got the Dart back.

When I got home, all was quiet. 'Shelley?' I called, but there was no sign of her. Then I found a note saying *Gone for a blow-dry, back in time to do dinner!* Bless her. I had forgotten her friend Sally had given her a present of a voucher for a hairdressers. It would do her good. So no need to worry about dinner then. And perhaps I would leave the grocery run until tomorrow. Mac and Emma were at school, and Olivia – well, who knew? I thought I'd have a cup of tea and then maybe do a bit of dusting and hoovering. All those suitcases Olivia had dragged in with her had left quite a bit of dirt behind them, especially on the stairs.

I had just hung my coat up when the doorbell went. Probably one of the children, or maybe Shelley had forgotten her key. I walked into the hall and opened it cautiously. I was on my guard for reporters and so forth, but standing on the doorstep was someone altogether more unexpected.

'Hello, Mum,' said Charlie quietly. 'May I come in?'

Shelley

I got out of the hairdressers at four after a trim and blow-dry and I hadn't been for *ages*, but then I ran into an old neighbour of ours who was determined to corner me and grill me. She wasn't the worst – at least she asked outright. It was the smirking and insinuations of other so-called friends that got to me. But I didn't see any of those people any more, and I didn't miss them. So as soon as I could extract myself, which I did with indecent haste, I popped across to our local Tesco and picked up the things I needed for dinner. It was shepherd's pie night, always a favourite. And since Liv would be joining us, I bought a bottle of Merlot in her honour. I looked at my phone. There were about ten missed calls, but I didn't bother checking them. I knew they'd be from Lukaz, who had been hounding me since the media incident, but I couldn't bring myself to talk to him – or Ernie, for that matter, who was also hounding me (at Lukaz's behest, I'd bet). I had texted Lukaz to say I needed some time alone with my family and would be in touch. But he had been bombarding me with calls and texts ever since and was really beginning to irritate me. I knew he meant well, but still.

When I got home, Vera's car wasn't there, which was strange. She was usually back by now, but it was always nice to have the house to myself for however short a time, especially pottering about in the kitchen. I don't think you can ever be quite at ease cooking in someone else's kitchen, can you? It's sort of sacrosanct. Years of ingrained rituals, traditions, recipes and conversations inhabit a woman's kitchen just as obviously as its appliances. I always feel as if I'm trespassing, there more than anywhere. I open the front door, pick up the grocery bags and kick the door shut behind me.

'Vera?' I call out, just to make sure she's not in, but there is no reply. No one home. But then, as I dump the bags and take off my coat and rifle half-heartedly through the post on the hall table, I hear another voice. A voice that makes my heart stop – and then turn over, slowly. A voice that has always been able to make every nerve ending in my body quiver in delighted anticipation. Or in this case, perhaps dread. 'Shelley.' It says.

I look around and hardly hear my own voice, which is barely more than a breath. 'Charlie,' I whisper.

For an eternity, or maybe a second, we look at each other, scanning, searching. I see in that instant our whole lives, intertwined – flashes of joy, laughter, pain and sorrow, love and loss. I see he is tanned, but there is a pallor beneath it, more lines fanning out from his eyes, around his mouth. He is thinner, definitely, than I remember, and he doesn't need to be. He seems sad, and worn, and yet more handsome than ever, and there is something hopeful in his face when he says again, softly, 'Shelley?'

And that is all I need. We reach for one another, across a narrow hallway, across a lifetime, and I cling to him. I cling to him as if I will never let go.

Later, we are sitting in the kitchen, after we've had a chance to talk, just a bit, and Charlie has showered and changed. We have opened the wine and are sitting at the kitchen table, and I cannot take my eyes off him. I follow his every move, his every gesture, hang on his every word. I feel as if I'm in a movie, but it's one I never want to end. My phone beeps. It's a message from Vera (of course all the missed calls had been from her, trying to alert me). She will be staying with her friend Maura from the shop, she informs me, who looks after an elderly brother, and Vera is 'helping her out' for a few days. She hopes everything is all right? I text her back and say everything is better than I could ever had imagined. She texts back, *I'm SO pleased. We'll catch up soon. God bless.*

I haven't said anything to the children, who are due back any time. Emma has extra computer studies and Mac is 'studying' at his friend Rocky's house. They're all due back for dinner, even Olivia, who has been uncharacteristically subdued since the last family drama. I'm worried about her.

Emma and Mac show up first, together, as luck would have it. We hear them bickering in the hall and the door slams, schoolbags drop with a thud, and I watch as my husband's face lights up, but there is apprehension there too. I take his hand. I have a little idea of the welcome he's going to get – even though he does not, or perhaps cannot yet, believe it.

'Mum,' says Emma, looking distracted as she comes through the door, 'have you seen—' She stops dead, and across her face flit shock, disbelief and indescribable joy. 'Dad!' she screams. 'Dad!' She hurls herself at him and Charlie laughs and hugs her tightly, very tightly.

Then Mac hurtles through the door, his eyes wide, and yells too and punches the air, then sort of jumps on Charlie like a monkey, and I think they're going to fall over, but Charlie has the counter behind him to steady himself on.

Amidst the noise, the laughter, the shouting, I somehow manage to remember the shepherd's pie and retrieve it from the oven before it's burnt to a crisp. I put on the peas to boil and dart inside to lay the table in the dining room, quickly flinging knives and forks and napkins at each place, but taking extra care with the one I never expected to fill. When I go back into the kitchen and watch the peas, listening to the thrilling sound of my children laughing and talking at once,

Charlie's voice resonant with emotion, I wonder if I'm dreaming.

And then the front door opens again, for the last time, and Olivia walks into the kitchen. There's a sudden hush. For a moment, I feel everything slow down again, and the happy, joyous frame freezes, like a scene from a TV show. I am watching my studiously nonchalant, disapproving, eldest daughter look at her father as if she's seeing a ghost, and then, quite unable to stop them, tears pour down her face and she runs to him, pushes Mac out of the way, throws her arms around Charlie and cries her heart out. This sets Emma and me off too, of course, but for once Mac doesn't seem to mind. He is running around the kitchen and out into the hall, whooping and yelling, 'I told them, I told them, *I told them*, but they wouldn't believe me!'

Finally we manage to sit down to dinner. Although the rest of us can hardly eat, Charlie seems ravenous. 'Shepherd's pie,' he says as I dish up. 'Mmm, my favourite.'

'No it's not,' says Mac indignantly. 'It's roast chicken.'

'How did you know that?' asks Charlie.

'Gran told us.'

'Well,' says Charlie carefully, 'Gran's quite right. Roast chicken is my favourite, but shepherd's pie is a close runner-up.'

'Does this mean you and Gran are speaking again?' Mac wants to know. 'Have you made up whatever fight it was you had?'

Charlie catches my eye and smiles at Mac. 'Yes, I'm pretty sure we have. It's all water under the bridge now.'

'Well that's good,' says Mac, ''Cos we all really like Gran, don't we?' He looks around the table for confirmation.

'We certainly do,' I say.

'What I *really* want to know,' says Charlie, a wicked grin spreading across his face, 'is how you all managed with just one bathroom? Especially you, Piggy.' He looks at Olivia, speculatively. 'I didn't think you'd be able to stick it for even a week!'

Olivia's eyes dart nervously in my direction. 'Um, well, you know,' she says and toys with her fork.

'Olivia's been wonderful, Charlie,' I say. 'They all have. You can be very proud of our children – I know I am.'

I am rewarded with a smile from Olivia that lights up the room and giggles from Emma and Mac. And as I meet my husband's eyes across the table, and hold that gaze so full of love, it almost seems as if he had never been away.

One month later

Mac

I told you he'd come back – and he did. I got into savage trouble that day, though, when Emma found out I'd been emailing Dad and hadn't told anyone. But Dad explained everything anyway and now he's back so it's all okay. I even heard him and Mum laughing the other evening when they were in the sitting room. The door was shut but I could hear them. It's shut quite a lot now, which is annoying, 'cos there's only one television in this house and that's where it is. But Mum says she and Dad have a lot of catching up to do. I nearly went in that evening, when I heard them laughing, but I didn't. It was nice to hear, though. I'd forgotten what it was like. When I'm older I'm never going to forget to laugh.

It's really cool I've got a new cousin none of us ever knew about, not even Mum and Dad. His name's Jack and Dad gave him one of his kidneys, which was one of the reasons he was away so long. I'm not sure what the others were. Jack's eleven, so he's a year younger than me, but we're Facebook friends now and that's cool. He also sent me a Springbok shirt, which was really decent of him.

I looked up transplants on the internet and when you get a new kidney some of them only last ten or twelve years, but Dad said if you get one from a living relative they can last for fifteen, even twenty years. So I said Jack could have one of my kidneys if Dad's didn't work, and then Emma and Olivia and Gran could give him one (well, maybe not Gran) and he'd never run out of kidneys and he'd outlive the lot of us – and that made everyone laugh.

We're going over next Christmas for a holiday to stay with Jack and his family in Cape Town (he has two older sisters, like me). I can't wait. Gotta go now – I've got an essay to do on global warming. Rocky just texted me about it and he says he's going to say that his house gets global warming every time his brother plays Shakira's new video. But Rocky'll get away with that. There's no way I would, and I've been in enough trouble lately. Don't need to push my luck.

Emma

I don't have to share a room with Olivia any more, yay! And no, unfortunately, she hasn't moved out again. It happened like this – when Dad came back (still can't believe it), a lot of things happened really quickly. Gran told Mum and Dad she and Granddad had bought a small apartment, like years ago, for their retirement. But until now, she had never seen any reason to move out of her house, so the apartment was rented. But with the recession and all, it hadn't been rented since the last tenant moved out, which was, like, a year ago. So to make a long story short, Gran has given her house to Mum and Dad and moved into the apartment, which has two bedrooms, so we can come and stay if we like, or she can have a friend over. Anyway, she says she really likes it and wishes she'd moved into it years ago. It's quite near here too, and she comes to us every Sunday for lunch, and us kids drop in a lot and Mac is still giving her computer lessons. So that meant Mum and Dad were able to move into Gran's old room, Olivia got Mum's old room (which used to be Dad's when he was a kid) and I get to stay (alone!) in the room I used to have to share with Olivia. There was a lot of fuss from Mum and Dad when Gran said she was giving them the house, but she said she wouldn't hear any of it, that Dad would get it anyway when she was dead and why not give with a warm hand? That's what I love about Gran, she never bullshits.

So now that Dad isn't working – I think he's trying to set

something up again, but it's not easy – he's able to do a lot of work around the house and we're redecorating it ourselves. Stripping off wallpaper and painting and stuff. We're even getting new kitchen cupboards, which are not expensive, apparently, if you keep the carcasses and just change the doors. We're stuck with one bathroom for the foreseeable future, though, but I don't care. It's worth anything to have Dad back. Like I said, I still can't believe it. Neither can Mum, I think, or Dad even.

Remember those looks I talked about, that I used to see other couples giving to each other? Well, I catch Mum and Dad looking like that at each other all the time now. I've even seen them kissing, which was quite gross really. Liv saw it too. We walked in on them unannounced, so to speak, and Liv made a face and said, 'Jeez, get a room, will you?' and rolled her eyes, and Dad said, 'We would if we could but we can't afford one.'

So things are finally back to normal, as much as they can be. Sophie and I talk about it for hours in her bedroom. She said her mum is fascinated by what went on – make that the whole of Dublin – and keeps telling her to try to find out stuff from me. I just grin and say, 'What can I say, Soph? I have unconventional parents. It's a bummer.'

Vera

What an extraordinary time we have all been through. I feel quite exhausted by it all, which is hardly surprising at my age. I'm almost eighty now, you know. They say history repeats itself, and in many ways it has, especially in my family, sometimes not always in a good way. But this latest development is more of a new beginning, I hope – for all of us. Charlie is back, alive and healthy, and we have had a long, long talk and put the ghosts of the past to rest. And in what came as a truly *wonderful* surprise, I have discovered I have a new grandson. How bittersweet that was, to discover him now, when his father, my son Patrick, died without even knowing about him. But there is still that money Patrick left to me and Arthur that I never touched. It never seemed right, and now I know why. There's a reason for everything, even if we don't see it at the time. So I was able to make the money over to little Jack, to be held in trust until he comes of age. His parents are well off, I believe, and he won't need the money, but still, it will be nice for him to have something from his father, even if he never knew him.

Life can be hideously hard sometimes, but it can also be indescribably sweet and uplifting. You just never know which is going to happen when. So when people ask me for advice, which they often do at my advanced age, I always tell them to enjoy the good times when they come along, grab them and hold on to them with every fibre of your being. And when the awful times come – and they will – I think it was

Winston Churchill who said you just have to keep buggering on. Good advice, if you ask me.

And now, I'm afraid I really must dash. My son Charlie is taking me out to dinner, just the two of us, and we have an awful lot of catching up to do.

By now, I'm guessing you'll understand how very much that means to me.

Lukaz

I am very unhappy. So unhappy that I fly to St Petersburg to stay with my grandmother. I need to evaluate things, be with my own people. My grandmother is very old, very wise. I seek her opinions.

'What is it, Lukaz, my child?' she ask. 'What troubles you like this?'

'It is a woman, Grandmother.'

She shakes her head. 'You have too much money, Lukaz. That is the problem. Too much money brings too many bad women.'

'You don't understand, Grandmother,' I say. 'I have found a good woman – the best.'

'Hah!' she laughs. 'That is what you say to me every time. The last good woman you found divorced you and took all your money.'

That is not exactly true, but my grandmother is very loyal to me. Very protective.

'This woman does not want my money. She doesn't want me. She won't even return my calls.'

'It is an act,' says my grandmother. 'That is what the clever ones do. Have nothing to do with her. Are you sleeping with her?'

'No, she won't even sleep with me. She is still in love with her husband who has left her.'

'An abandoned wife! Lukaz! What is the matter with you?

You want another man's discarded woman? Have you been drinking?'

'No, Grandmother,' I say wearily. 'But I would like some vodka, now that you mention it.'

She brings two glasses and a bottle of vodka. She shakes her head as she fills the glasses. 'You need a young woman, Lukaz. One who will give you sons. That is what your parents would want, Lord rest their souls – what your great-grandfather would want. I think Ireland is not good for you. If he left it all those years ago, why go there now? Leave the past with the past, Lukaz – and that is where that woman belongs.'

I check my phone, hopefully. Maybe Shelley has returned one of my messages – but there is nothing. Only twenty-nine missed calls from Natascha.

Shelley

He came back. I still can't believe it. And although sometimes it feels as if he's never been away, in other ways,
our whole life has changed irrevocably. For the better, I have
to say. Sure, Charlie lost the business and we've lost all our
so-called wealth, our fancy house, some, though not all, of
our old friends, but what we've gained is so much more
important. We've found each other again, and we've talked,
really talked, and vowed to keep on talking. No more assump-
tions, no more avoidance, no more secrets. And of course,
we've found Vera. I'm not sure that Charlie and she will ever
have a completely comfortable relationship with each other;
that's sort of a work in progress. But she's been so good to
us, so incredibly generous, and I know Charlie is trying hard
to put the past behind him. One day at a time, as they say.
It's all any of us have. The kids are thrilled, of course, and
that's the best thing of all, really, for both Charlie and me.

There *was* one pretty difficult thing I had to do, though,
but when I actually got around to it, which was a couple of
weeks ago, I was very glad I did do it. I went to visit Caroline,
in hospital. I didn't want to, not because I was angry with
her, with what she had done – how could I be, once I understood about her illness? – but I hate hospitals of any kind,
and even though this one was lovely and normal and cheerful
and not at all like, well, a psychiatric hospital (which is what
it was), I don't mind telling you I was dreading it. But her
mother had spoken to Charlie and begged him to ask me if

I could find it in my heart, that it would mean the world to Caroline and help her recovery immensely if she could talk to me. Apparently Caroline was riddled with guilt and remorse about the whole thing. So of course I said I'd go and see her. Before I went, though, I made sure to read up a bit about her illness. She was bipolar, and on top of that suffered from delusional disorder, which can exist on its own or, in Caroline's case, alongside another mental illness. In her case, it manifested mostly in erotomania – sounds glamorous, but basically it means the sufferer becomes utterly convinced the subject of their fixation is completely and utterly in love with them.

So I drove up that day and asked for her in reception, as I had been told to do. I had brought some perfume for her, and a scented candle. The woman at reception told me I would find her in the coffee shop, which was located towards the back of the ground floor. I have to say I was pleasantly surprised. The whole place resembled a rather upmarket hotel, not a straightjacket or needle wielder in sight (sorry, but I have a very vivid imagination). Caroline was there all right, just as they had said, sitting at a table for two beside a window which looked out onto a well-kept lawn. She waved to me as I approached, then stood up to greet me, taking my hands in hers.

'Shelley,' she said, 'thank you so much for coming. You have no idea how much this means to me.' And then she began to talk, and I listened, and marvelled at her candour, her frankness, her bravery. She was still very thin, painfully so; even the expensive cashmere jumper and matching wrap failed to disguise the protruding collarbones, and her cheekbones jutted out sharply in a face that appeared younger and surprisingly vulnerable. How had I ever found this woman intimidating? Her hands, as she held her coffee cup, trembled occasionally, and she explained it was a temporary effect of the medication she was on. By the time she had told her story, I had trouble fighting back tears. How awful for her, having to carry this burden, and all alone. After almost an hour, I said I'd better be going, and she walked with me to the door. Her mother was due in shortly to visit.

'Do you know when you'll be . . . ?' I asked tentatively.

'When they'll let me escape, you mean?' She grinned. 'Oh, not too much longer, a couple of weeks at most, my doctor says, just as soon as they get the meds right. Then the trick is to keep taking them.' She smiled ruefully. 'Shelley?' she said as I was about to leave.

'Yes?'

'I just wanted to say – it wasn't all madness on my part, you know, loving Charlie. In my opinion, you'd have to be mad *not* to love him.' And with that, she smiled and walked back through the lobby.

I've never forgotten that, what Caroline said, and I never will – because she's right, of course.

I'm one of the lucky ones. I've been given a second chance with the person I love most in all the world – and it's a chance I'm going to be grateful for as long as I live.

Epilogue

The Scene with Harry Fegan

Dublin is abuzz with comings and goings this month. Just last week we welcomed the new French ambassador, His Excellency Pierre De La Fontaine, and his soignée and elegant wife Fleur, rumoured to be very close friends with a certain diminutive President's wife. Apparently they modelled together.

On a more poignant note, le tout Dublin is *desole* at news of Russian billionaire Lukaz Mihailov's rumoured forthcoming defection to London. Ireland's favourite (well, only) oligarch had extensively remodelled Rossborough Demesne, his magnificent stud farm in Celbridge, and was a regular and popular fixture at all the major race meetings. Lukaz, regulars of this column will remember, was recently allegedly romantically linked with the lovely Shelley Fitzgibbon, wife of Dublin's favourite absconded millionaire, Charlie Fitzgibbon, rumoured to be sunning himself on foreign shores in the company of a beautiful blonde. This snippet of third-rate reporting was dished up by our rival papers *The Post on Sunday* and the *Sunday Herald*, who as usual were way off the mark. My most reliable source on the Dublin scene informs me that the Fitzgibbons were seen walking on Sandymount Strand just this Sunday *en famille*, and that Charlie and his beautiful wife Shelley looked relaxed and very much in love.

The Scene says welcome back, Charlie. Home is obviously where the heart is.

Acknowledgments

A huge thank you is due to the following people who helped make *Without Him* an infinitely better book:

As always, the wonderful team at Hachette Books Ireland: In particular my endlessly talented, patient, and encouraging editor, Ciara Doorley, fortunately always at her best when I am at my worst! And the rest of the Dublin gang who make it all happen so seamlessly – Breda Purdue, Peter, Ruth, and Margaret Daly.

Huge thanks too, to the London Squad, led by the inspirational Sue Fletcher of Hodder & Stoughton, who I have lunch with far too infrequently.

Grateful thanks also to my wonderful agent, Vivienne Schuster (every needy author's dream) whose guidance, support and encouragement go far beyond the call of duty. You are appreciated more than you know. And to her co-star, Felicity Blunt, who in Viv's absence, props me up valiantly when I'm feeling wobbly (which reminds me, we must be due a lunch?).

Without Him began with a relatively simple idea, and, as books will, turned into quite a different and intriguing journey. Happily help and information were provided generously at every twist and turn, particularly by nephrologist Dr Peter Nourse, of Red Cross Children's Hospital in Cape Town, who took the time from his demanding schedule to provide invaluable insight into renal disease and transplants. Also to Cynthia Lake, who supplied current information and details for Cape Town and cheery support on FB when I was flagging. Any mistakes in this area are entirely my own.

My nieces, Jennifer and Stephanie O'Brien, were of great help too, advising me on where a fifteen-year-old girl might shop these days.

Being completely unfamiliar with the music tastes and computer game preferences of twelve-year-old boys – I was enlightened by dear friends Catriona O'Neill and Dickie Jeffares respectively.

As always, unstinting support comes from *Those Who Know*: Patricia Scanlan for stalwart kindness and the pink crystal which is beside my computer as I write. My darling friend the multitalented Kate Thompson, always at the end of the phone and whose counsel and own books I escape to when the going gets tough. It was Kate who, generously as ever, was responsible for coming up with the title of *Without Him*.

This book is dedicated to another treasured friend – Cathy Kelly, whose kindness, help, and support are legendary – but on a personal level will never be forgotten.

Much as I might like to think so – I do not do this on my own. Without unflagging prayers from both the Carmelite sisters in St Joseph's Monastery, Kilmacud, and my dear friends the Poor Clare's on Simmonscourt Road, I am convinced there would be no book. When I am lost for words (or indeed anything) I bribe St Anthony. And, of course, most important of all, is the source of *all* creativity – the Holy Spirit, who I pester daily for inspiration – and who has never yet, miraculously, let me down. I can only urge you to try them all!

To my beloved family and friends (you know who you are) who feed, entertain, regale and inspire me and remind me there is life beyond the word count – 'thank you' sounds hopelessly inadequate – so lunch is on me.

Finally, grateful thanks to you, dear reader, I truly hope you enjoy the journey as much as I did.

Let's do it all again soon.

Fiona

If you like happy endings . . .

You have just come to the end of a book.

Before you put it aside, please take a moment to reflect on the 37 million people who are blind in the developing world.

Ninety per cent of this blindness is TOTALLY PREVENTABLE.

In our world, blindness is a disability – in the developing world, it's a death sentence.

Every minute, one child goes blind – needlessly.

That's about the time it will take you to read this.

It's also about the time it will take you to log on to www.righttosight.com and help this wonderful organisation achieve its goal of totally eradicating preventable global blindness.

Now that would be a happy ending.

And it will only take a minute.

Fiona O'Brien supports the right to sight and would love it if you would too.